Explore . . .

The mega corps may rule the world, but the struggle for freedom lives on—in a garden of hope amid the ruins of what used to be China.

He's an ex-cop turned artist. She's a mathematical genius who could save the world . . . or destroy it. It all depends on how much they're willing to risk.

What's in a name? For on_____ the answer lies in the mirror and in the hidden world behind it—a world of unlimited possibility and danger.

Behold . . .

Deep in space, in a world of deception, treachery and brutality, one soldier vows never to surrender . . . his honor.

A mythic creature rises from the ashes . . . with an ingenious plan to cheat death.

The Inquisitor has come to a forsaken planet to destroy a man-made abomination. But what if there is God in the machine?

Discover . . .

Sweet love, sweet revenge, sweet dreams—they're all for sale. If you're willing to pay the price.

What became of the lost souls of Hiroshima? Can their voices be heard in the void? Have the children of the bomb paid a price? The Shadow Man knows.

She races for charity, and the competition is fierce—sabotage, assassination, win at any cost. When you run for your life, there are no limits to how far you'll go.

Journey . . .

The road from illusion to beauty, from the art of deception to the ultimate truth . . . leads across the Dizzy Bridge.

For one fourteen-year-old girl, an interstellar colonist thirty light-years from home, coming of age is a real monster.

A real man, an Artificial woman, together they've been to the stars and back. Now they're about to discover how far they'll go—to stay together.

"It all started when I won the Writers of the Future Contest. They were my first publication. My foot in the door. Without them, I can honestly say I would not be where I am today."

—Patrick Rothfuss, Author
Writers of the Future Contest winner

"The Contests are amazing competitions because really, you've nothing to lose and it provides good positive encouragement to anyone who wins. Judging the entries is always a lot of fun and inspiring. I wish I had something like this when I was getting started—very positive and cool."

—Bob Eggleton, Artist
Illustrators of the Future Contest judge

"A very generous legacy from L. Ron Hubbard—a fine, fine fiction writer—for the writers of the future."

—Anne McCaffrey, Author
Writers of the Future Contest judge

"Some of the best SF of the future comes from Writers of the Future and you can find it in this book."

—David Hartwell, Editor

"Winning the Contest was my first validation that I would have a career. I entered five times before winning and it gave me something I could reach and attain."

—K. D. Wentworth, Author
Writers of the Future Contest winner
and Coordinating Judge

"The first-rate stories show incredible variety."

—Robert J. Sawyer, Author
Writers of the Future Contest judge

"The aspect I personally value most highly about the program is that of working with my fellow professionals, both artists *and* writers, to accomplish a worthwhile goal of giving tomorrow's artists and writers recognition and advancement in the highly competitive field of imaginative endeavor—the only existing program that does this."

—Stephen Hickman, Artist
Illustrators of the Future Contest judge

"L. Ron Hubbard's Writers of the Future anthologies are a road map—they show the future of science fiction by showcasing tomorrow's writers today."

—Jay Lake, Author
Writers of the Future Contest winner

"Here's skill and storytelling fervor aplenty—these writers of the future have already arrived."

—Robert Silverberg, Author
Writers of the Future Contest judge

"The L. Ron Hubbard Writers of the Future Contest has carried out the noble mission of nurturing new science fiction and fantasy writers . . . with resounding success."

—Eric Kotani, Author
Writers of the Future Contest judge

"Looking back now it is easy to see that winning the Writers of the Future was a watershed moment in my career."

—Steven Savile, Author
Writers of the Future Contest winner

"This Contest has changed the face of science fiction."

—Dean Wesley Smith, Author
Writers of the Future Contest winner

"The Illustrators of the Future Contest is one of the best opportunities a young artist will ever get. You have nothing to lose and a lot to win."

—Frank Frazetta, Artist
Illustrators of the Future Contest judge

"I only wish that there had been an Illustrators of the Future competition forty-five years ago. What a blessing it would have been to a young artist with a little bit of talent, a Dutch name and heart full of desire."

—H. R. Van Dongen, Artist
Illustrators of the Future Contest judge

"These Contests provide a wonderful safety net of professionals for young artists and writers. And it's due to the fact that L. Ron Hubbard was willing to lend a hand."

—Judith Miller, Artist
Illustrators of the Future Contest judge

"A first-rate collection of stories and illustrations."

—*Booklist*

L. Ron Hubbard PRESENTS
Writers of the Future

VOLUME XXV

L. Ron Hubbard PRESENTS

Writers of the Future

VOLUME XXV

The year's twelve best tales from

the Writers of the Future

international writers' program

Illustrated by winners in

the Illustrators of the Future

international illustrators' program

With essays on writing & illustration by

L. Ron Hubbard / Robert Silverberg / Ron Lindahn

Edited by K. D. Wentworth

GALAXY PRESS, LLC

Garden of Tian Zi: © 2009 Emery Huang
The Shadow Man: © 2009 Donald Mead
Life in Steam: © 2009 Grá Linnaea
On Writing and Science Fiction: © 1983, 2009 L. Ron Hubbard Library
The Assignment of Runner ETI: © 2009 Fiona Lehn
The Candy Store: © 2009 Heather McDougal
Risqueman: © 2009 Mike Wood
Gray Queen Homecoming: © 2009 Schon M. Zwakman
The Dizzy Bridge: © 2009 Krista Hoeppner Leahy
Gone Black: © 2009 Matthew S. Rotundo
The Reflection of Memory: © 2009 C. L. Holland
After the Final Sunset, Again: © 2009 Jordan Lapp
The Farthest Born: © 2009 Gary Kloster

Illustration on page 31: © 2009 Douglas Bosley
Illustration on page 71: © 2009 Brianne Hills
Illustration on page 97: © 2009 Ryan Behrens
Illustration on page 131: © 2009 A. R. Stone
Illustration on page 199: © 2009 Jamie Luhn
Illustration on page 256: © 2009 Evan Jensen
Illustration on page 283: © 2009 Tobias A. Fruge
Illustration on page 331: © 2009 Aaron Anderson
Illustration on page 375: © 2009 Luke Eidenschink
Illustration on page 454: © 2009 Oleksandra Barysheva
Illustration on page 484: © 2009 Joshua J. Stewart
Illustration on page 529: © 2009 Mark Payton

Cover Artwork: Homecoming © 2009 Stephan Martiniere

Interior Design: Jerry Kelly

ISBN-10 1-59212-436-4
ISBN-13 978-1-59212-436-7
Library of Congress Control Number: 2009907540
First Edition Paperback
Printed in the United States of America

CONTENTS

Introduction

BY K. D. WENTWORTH

K. D. Wentworth has sold more than eighty pieces of short fiction to such markets as F&SF, Alfred Hitchcock's Mystery Magazine, Realms of Fantasy, Weird Tales, Witch Way to the Mall *and* Return to the Twilight Zone. *Four of her stories have been finalists for the Nebula Award for Short Fiction. Currently, she has seven novels in print, the most recent being* The Course of Empire, *written with Eric Flint and published by Baen. She has served as Coordinating Judge for the Writers of the Future Contest, has now taken on the additional responsibility as Editor for the Writers of the Future anthology and lives in Tulsa with her husband and a combined total of one hundred and sixty pounds of dog (Akita + Siberian "Hussy") and is working on another new novel with Flint.*

Introduction

Only another writer can know how very hard it is to persuade oneself to set out on that long winding road to publication with all its back alleys and notorious dead-end streets. You not only have to convince the publishing world that your work is worthy of seeing print, you have to defeat your own self-doubt which is at least as hard, if not even harder.

After a long and illustrious career in producing fiction, best-selling author L. Ron Hubbard understood how difficult the lives of would-be writers were. He had a genius for creating compelling characters, swashbuckling plots and colorful settings, but, equally as rare, he had a firm grasp on communicating how one might accomplish these elements in one's own fiction. Though he had published a number of well-received "how to" articles in various creative writing magazines and spoken to numerous audiences on the subject, he wanted to do more to encourage and mentor new voices in the field.

So, in 1983, he created and endowed the Writers of the Future Contest for up-and-coming science fiction and fantasy writers just on the edge of breaking out. Designed, with its substantial cash prizes (and no entry fee!), acclaimed annual anthology to showcase new writing and yearly workshop with seasoned professionals, to rapidly advance novice writers in their budding careers, the L. Ron Hubbard Writers of the Future Contest has by now, in its twenty-fifth year, sought out, instructed and promoted three hundred winners.

Have they all gone on to stardom? No, but an impressive percentage have achieved sterling careers that delight their audiences. Some of the names, such as Dave Wolverton, Jo Beverley, Nina Kiriki Hoffman, Karen Joy Fowler, Robert Reed, Dean Wesley Smith, Bruce Holland Rogers, James Alan Gardner, Sean Williams, Steve Baxter, Patrick Rothfuss, Nancy Farmer, Eric Flint, Steven Savile and Jeff Carlson, are ones that you will already recognize. Others are just now making their mark and you'll be hearing about them soon in the years to come.

Of course, sometimes winning in the Contest is as far as a writer ever gets. That is because what Mr. Hubbard has generously provided here for us is a chance to jump-start your career and what you make of that opportunity after going home from the workshop is up to the individual. L. Ron Hubbard, with his gift for getting to the heart of what makes a story work, has laid down a guide map for newcomers. We still have to put his lessons to work and remain committed to a difficult journey.

I know this program is effective, though, because it worked for me. In 1987, soon after I began writing seriously, I bought a copy of the L. Ron Hubbard Writers of the Future anthology in a bookstore and started entering the Contest. The only signs I'd ever had up to that point that I wasn't wasting my time writing were occasional scribbled lines of criticism on form rejections. Then in the last quarter of 1988, I won Third Place. It was the headiest moment in my life up to that date.

When Algis Budrys, the Coordinating Judge, called me to see if I would be able to attend the week-long Workshop, I told him that winning was the best thing that had ever happened to me. He gruffly answered that he most sincerely hoped it was not, but in many ways, it was. That phone call telling me I had won was the first time in my life that it seemed possible I would achieve my long-cherished dream of having a career as a writer.

And, for three more people, quarter after quarter now for twenty-five glorious years, a similar phone call has been that moment for them, too, when it all comes into focus and they can see the dreamed-of future becoming real. It is for that magical moment that L. Ron Hubbard created that Contest and so many well known and distinguished writers in the field have been willing to serve as our judges and Workshop instructors.

Today, the Contest is widely known and respected. It has become the standard by which all striving science fiction and fantasy writers can measure their work and we receive entries each quarter from not just all over the United States, but all over the world. Perusing the table of contents of previously published volumes is akin to reading a list of who's hot and new in the speculative fiction field.

Publishers Weekly recognized the Writers of the Future Contest as "the most enduring forum to showcase new talent in the genre." Once a writer can mention "winner (or even finalist) in the Writers of the Future Contest" in their cover letter, many doors which were previously closed are now suddenly open. Editors pay attention. Agents are willing to take a look at an unknown's work.

In 2005, *Library Journal* presented the Contest its Award of Excellence "in recognition of XXI years of discovering, fostering and nurturing writers and illustrators of speculative fiction and successfully infusing new talent into the fields of literary and visual arts." It's no secret that the science fiction and fantasy genre enjoys the most vibrant and successful short story market in America today. It's still flourishing while other professionally paying short story venues become ever more scarce. As *Library Journal* noted, the Writers of the Future Contest has been a hugely positive influence in keeping the speculative fiction short story market alive by encouraging so much new talent.

Winners have gone on to have major careers, publishing more than five hundred books and three thousand short stories. They have won Nebula and Hugo Awards, created fictional series enjoyed by countless readers, become bestsellers, then gone on to teach workshops and mentor other new writers themselves, and it all began for each of them with that phone call. Our field has always had a tradition of "pay it forward." What Mr. Hubbard very generously gave us, we now do our best to honor by helping the next generation of talented writers to find their way. In serving as Coordinating Judge of the Contest, it is my very great pleasure and privilege to give back to the field at least some small measure of what that spine-tingling phone call once gave to me.

In 1988, the scope of the Contest was widened to include budding artists with the creation of the Illustrators of the Future Contest which also provides substantial cash prizes and a showplace for their artistic efforts. At the end of the Contest year, the artist winners from each quarter are assigned one of the Writers of the Future stories to illustrate and then transported to an invaluable workshop taught by Ron Lindahn and Val Lakey Lindahn on how to develop and manage a career as a professional artist. You will find the fruits of the new artists' extraordinary talents accompanying each story in this anthology. Again, the goal is to jump-start their professional lives and help them avoid many of the pitfalls emerging artists can face. Over the years, our artist winners have gone home and subsequently sold thousands of professional illustrations to a wide array of markets, matching the writers with their success.

Why are the Contests important? Their scope extends far beyond the impact they have upon the actual winners themselves. They are invaluable to everyone who enters. So much of the publishing world is a closed door to the beginner. When we start out, we send in story after story only to receive form rejections which give us no clue what we're doing wrong. This is because we are competing with seasoned professionals like Tim Powers, Robert Sawyer, Orson Scott Card, Nina Kiriki Hoffman, Sean Williams or Robert Silverberg (all Writers of the Future judges, by the way) whose work is professionally polished and whose name on the cover of a publication will help sell copies.

But the single most crucial thing that will make you a better writer or artist is to practice your craft and keep producing new work. If you get discouraged and quit, you will certainly never make it. The two Contests are only open to new writers and artists so that entrants are competing with their peers. Winning is a goal that is conceivably within their grasp while publishing a book with Tor or Del Rey, a story in *Fantasy and Science Fiction,* or illustrating a cover for Baen may not be at that point in their budding career. *The Contests keep us working when we might otherwise give up* and for many that industriousness will get us there eventually. I entered the Contest five times and each of those five stories, including the one which won, would not have been written if I had not had the Contest as my goal.

As for those who are not aspiring writers and artists, the Contests are important to them too. L. Ron Hubbard said, *"A culture is as rich and capable of surviving as it has imaginative artists . . . It was with this in mind that I initiated a means for new and budding writers to have a chance for their creative efforts to be seen and acknowledged."* As he told us, we need these new talented voices and eyes to help us dream our dreams and shape the future. Thanks to L. Ron Hubbard's foresight, we have the opportunity each year to read a new set of remarkably talented fictional voices and see through the eyes of another new group of amazing artists.

This book contains twelve edgy, inspiring and thought-provoking stories judged by top professionals in the field to be the best we received in the past Contest year. They have each been illustrated by one of our twelve equally talented Illustrators of the Future. Note the names and keep an eye out. You're going to be seeing a lot from them in the years to come.

In the meantime, may the Contests continue another twenty-five years, enriching the lives of writers, artists and readers everywhere!

Garden of Tian Zi

written by

Emery Huang

illustrated by

DOUGLAS BOSLEY

ABOUT THE AUTHOR

Emery Huang was born in Fairfax, Virginia, but moved down to Orlando, Florida, at age five and hasn't left. As a young boy, Emery was "self-directed" in his learning, having little understanding of the difference between fiction and nonfiction. Books like My Teacher Is an Alien made him squint funny at his schoolteachers, while James and the Giant Peach made him clutch tightly to fruit in fear that his lunch might fly away. Though the passage of time has disabused his mind of such fanciful notions, his heart still believes. To keep his heart happy, he feeds it a steady diet of fantasy, science fiction, anime and comics.

As a writer, Emery's dream is to finish a series that places China's rich dynastic background firmly on the map of American fantasy literature. He also wants to regale the literary world with tales of mystery and wonder about frogs and/or jellyfish. Until these lofty goals have been accomplished, Emery will be in his room reading and writing. This is his first published story. Last thing: he's a Pisces, something Emery says only a Pisces would care to mention.

ABOUT THE ILLUSTRATOR

Born and raised in the upper Mojave Desert of Southern California, Douglas Bosley and family eventually found themselves in rainy Washington state by 1997. The split of climates parallels Douglas' own split of academic interests: In 2001, he began at Edmonds Community College with an interest in visual arts and was soon introduced to more esoteric studies in social sciences and critical theory.

Earning his Associate Arts degree, Douglas transferred to Western Washington University, where he studied oil painting while continuing his theoretical explorations into post/human philosophy and cybernetics. He graduated in 2007 with a bachelor's degree in fine arts, and now considers painting and printmaking to be his primary artistic media. After a stint as an instructional assistant in drawing and painting classes, Douglas says he developed a passion for teaching. He's currently pursuing graduate work to propel careers as a professional artist and fine arts academician, with his philosophical leanings close behind.

Garden of Tian Zi

The Movement dropped me off on the outskirts of Urumqi city, deep in Xinjiang province. They sent me there to get lost in the wilderness of what used to be western China, to stay hidden in one of the few places left on Earth that hadn't been claimed by the mega corps. It was a dry, windy day, the dust kicking up and the truck's old diesel engine coughing dirty fumes in my face.

Not much was said. It was just another job. They handed me a bottle of water purification tablets, a thick stack of bills denominated in yuan and a terrarium of frogs.

The frogs were my golden geese, genetically engineered to secrete a protein-antibody mix that was the key ingredient in manufacturing peptide computer processors. My instructions were "take care of the frogs, set up shop, don't get caught and we'll be in touch."

I approached one of the landlords. He was a withered man, browned by the sun and missing a few teeth, probably heir to one of the old tribal

11

leaders. They claimed a lot of the land out here when the People's Republic of China dissolved.

I told him my name was Tian Zi and I was interested in renting something a little ways out of the city. It was a good way to avoid attention. In the desert, nobody goes sightseeing without a destination in mind.

He took me around and showed me a few options. I told him they all looked like deathtraps. Then he showed me an old Buddhist temple. It was weather-beaten and a lot of the walls had been scoured of their red and gold paint, but it had a stone foundation and stone lasts. I peeled off a few bills, gummed with him for a bit, peeled off a few more and it was mine.

The temple had three rooms, one on each of the east, west, and north sides. On the south side was the gate. It had both doors left, but the hinges would need replacing.

First thing I did to fix up the place was clear the well. It was a narrow one, set in the middle of the courtyard, and ran deep underground. Inside were branches, dirt, some dead animals and discarded beer cans. The cans probably came from some city kids sneaking into the temple for a night of drinking and telling ghost stories.

There was still a rope and bucket intact, so I used them to clean the well out, then shook in about a quarter of the water tablets. A few days and the aquifer would wash it all clean. For everything else, I had to go to town. I tucked the frogs' terrarium away in the northern room, threw a cloth around the tank walls and headed out.

Now, Urumqi is my kind of city. I'd been through Vienna, Budapest and Cologne lately. I was tired of seeing endless trees and mountains covered in yet more trees. Urumqi had that nakedness to it, bare rock and scrub grasses exposed to the wind. The wind alternated between baking hot and bitter cold, but always had that dry taste of powdered rock and earth salt. The salt made me hungry.

I stepped out onto one of the main streets, a reddish-brown haze of dust in the air and the sun beating down on the back of my neck. Then the beggar swarm found me. Only the old cities ever seem to have them. It takes a while for civilization to rot.

They were the typical bunch, dirt smeared on their faces, loosely sewn clothes and that shuffle walk that says they just never had the self-esteem to learn how to walk upright. I waved them back to get some room, yelling at them in a pidgin of Turkic and Mandarin.

I'm Han Chinese and born in Shanghai, so the Mandarin was no problem. It only took a week of training to get the Urumqi accent down. I even threw on old clothes to help blend in, gray pants that cut off at the ankles, cheap sandals with plastic straps and a white T-shirt. The beggar kids pegged me as a foreigner the minute they saw me.

I didn't bother with the cover after that. I asked where I could find a good place to eat, and they started pushing and shoving each other, fighting for who got to be my guide. I got tired of waiting and grabbed one by random.

She had those big green eyes that Xinjiang girls

13

are known for, and her black hair was tied up in a braid. It's a distinct look, the product of thousands of years of Turkish and Mongol nomads mixing with the Chinese traders that did business along the old Silk Road.

I didn't know what her age was, but she was in that gawky phase of maturity, thin and long-limbed with none of the curves that make a girl worth talking to. Not that I'm sexist. I could care less what someone's packing between their legs. I just know the difference. Kids are annoying, girls are fun and women are trouble.

She told me her name was Khulan, which I later learned meant "wild horse" in Mongolian. I followed behind her as she trotted along, walking zigzag up and down the street. I was taller than her then, but she ate up distance fast enough to make me stretch to keep pace.

"Where are you taking me, Khulan?"

"Royal Gold Noodle Shop," she said over her shoulder. Chinese people have a habit of making everything sound like it belongs in the palace at Versailles, and I guess it transferred over to the Uyghurs out west. Usually, the fancier the name was, the crappier the place. But there was a corollary rule to that: the crappier the place, the better the food. Think about it. Who in their right mind would keep paying at a place if it looked terrible and the food sucked?

Royal Gold stayed true to the rules. The walls looked like used toilet paper, and the door was so warped the only way it'd stay shut is if they nailed it closed.

"Nice place," I said.

"Sure. Money now?" She cupped her hands in front of her, like I was a Merry Buddha and she was offering prayers. I took a bill out of my pocket and held it in front of her.

"Make change for me," I said.

She gave me a hard look.

"Come on. I'm not paying twenty yuan for a walk."

"You want to go somewhere else after you eat?" *Good. The girl knew how to think.*

"Tell you what. You get some stuff for me, meet me back here with it and I'll give you a hundred yuan."

She nodded in agreement.

"You got anything I can write on?"

She tore one of the flyers off the restaurant's wall and handed it to me. I scribbled what I needed on it and handed it back to her. She looked at it for a moment, talking under her breath, counting on her fingers rapidly.

"I can't buy this much with twenty yuan," she said. I handed her a hundred yuan note. She winked at me and ran off. I didn't know if she'd just run off with the money, but I figured what the hell. Make a friend, right?

I stepped into the noodle shop and there was a fat bald chef, sweating all over and pushing noodles around on a flat-top grill. I dropped down onto a stool and asked for a beer, a dark lager that came in a chilled green bottle.

Behind the chef, a long string was nailed to the wall with a dozen or so wooden placards swinging

15

from it. I'm guessing they didn't have the money to print individual menus. I ordered a bowl of noodle soup with *ququ* dumplings. It was spicy, filling and cheap, exactly how I like it. I talked some trash with the chef, took note of a few of the faces, stared for awhile at the muted TV in the corner, paid my tab and walked outside.

Khulan was crouched outside the door, smoking a cigarette with a cloth bundle tied over her back. I gave the bundle a shake.

"This mine?"

"Yeah." She flicked the cigarette on the ground, not bothering to stamp it out.

I put it out for her and then reached for the bag.

"Great. Can I have it?"

"Where's my hundred yuan?"

"Where's my change?"

She patted the bundle behind her. "You asked for a lot of stuff and it's a hot day. I bought a tea."

I tossed a hundred on the ground in front of her. She unhooked the bundle with one hand and dangled it in front of me. I took it from her and she disappeared almost as fast as I can. Not bad.

The next few weeks were spent setting up. Khulan turned out to be quite an asset, shuttling materials from the city to the temple and taking care of business that would get a foreigner noticed. I took a liking to her. She was smart, fast and didn't ask dumb questions. I told her she could stay at the temple and she chose to bunk in the western room. I slept in the eastern one.

"What's with the frogs?"

"Hobby of mine." I went back to putting screws into the steel frame. I was building a greenhouse for the frogs. They'd start reproducing soon and I needed something bigger than a twenty-gallon terrarium.

"You don't seem like that type."

"What type?"

"Dunno. The sit around and look at animals type."

"Looking at you now, aren't I?"

She gave a snort and scooted off, hands in her pockets, whistling some old Mongolian tune.

A week later, the greenhouse was done. I dug up most of the stone paving in the northern room, so the enclosure had a nice reddish-brown soil bottom. The walls were made of glass panes in steel frames. I also dug out a very shallow pool. Khulan knew a good potter, so she had him shape and fire a clay frame for the pool. I poured some well water in it and used another water tablet for safe measure.

The frogs the Movement gave me were Chinese gliding tree frogs. They weren't the swimming type, so a deep pool would drown them. But they needed it for midnight soaks and later on they'd be laying eggs in it.

"You came all the way to Urumqi to grow frogs in a temple? You some kind of exiled monk or something?" Khulan asked.

"Don't worry about it."

"What'd you do, Tian Zi? Get a nun pregnant? Kill someone?"

"Both."

Khulan's eyes widened at that. "Wow, really? A killer, huh?"

"Cold-blooded."

"I bet." She nodded happily. She wasn't at all bothered, even though I was just saying things to entertain her.

"So, what's your story?" I asked. "Why the orphan routine?"

I was sitting down with my back to the wall, watching the frogs hop around the dirt and clamber up the glass. She squatted down next to me, inspecting her fingernails before speaking.

"Not a routine."

"No? What happened? You get dumped off at an orphanage?"

"Got killed in a motorcycle accident."

"Tough."

She shrugged. "Sure."

Something about the way she said that got to me. Maybe it reminded me of my younger sister from back in the day. Maybe I didn't think it would be a big deal if some orphan girl knew what the Movement was. It's not like the mega corps didn't already know about us.

"The Movement's an organization that helps people."

"What kind of people?" she asked.

"Underdogs. Small corporations. Brain trusts. Research initiatives."

"What do you mean?"

"Have you ever been out of Urumqi, Khulan?"

"An old boyfriend took me to ride horses in Karamay once."

I laughed so hard it hurt my ribs. "What are you doing running off with boyfriends? How old were you?"

"I don't know. Eleven, twelve."

"How old are you now?"

"Sixteen. Get on with it."

I started grinning at her. "Sixteen, huh? I don't believe it."

"Get to the point."

"Well, okay. What's your citizenship?"

"Don't have one. Why? What's yours?"

"Zhao-Xi Combine."

Her eyebrows rose in surprise. "I've seen their stuff. Their cargo planes fly over Urumqi every now and then. You must be rich."

"I was a board director's son, but not anymore."

Khulan whistled in appreciation. "So what happened? Your dad kick you out?"

I shook my head at the memory. "No. I ran away. I wasn't cut out for it. Too many restrictions, too many expectations and way too much corruption."

Khulan gave me a blank face.

"It's all a scam. When the nations broke apart, everything divided along economic lines, right?"

She continued to give me a blank face.

"Have you gone to school?"

She shook her head.

"Okay. Well, think of it this way. You know what a crocodile is?"

She nodded.

19

"Imagine a crocodile sitting in a lake. It's just a mean old bastard, swimming around, eating everything it can find, getting bigger and bigger by the year."

"Sounds good to me."

"Only if you're the crocodile. That's the problem. There can only ever be a few of these monsters. Everything else gets eaten, even other crocodiles. If they're smaller, they die. We call that a monopoly. The mega corps, the ones sitting on the dense population centers, the ones who hit the ground running with scientific and industrial infrastructure when the national governments started to dissolve, they're too big. They're choking off the rest of the world because they keep eating everything and they don't share."

Khulan shrugged. "They earned it, right?"

"No. It's not supposed to be that way. There's supposed to be regulation. In nature, even the big ones get sick or injured, and then they eventually die. But, in our world, without governments, nobody has the power to stop it. That's where the Movement comes in. We steal from the big ones and then we sell to the little ones, give them a chance to grow up."

"Why not just give it to them?"

"Fighting a war with the big dogs doesn't come cheap. We need the money and the tech."

She seemed to take that as good enough of an answer. Later on that night, I sat in bed and thought about our conversation. It was the most I'd ever said to her about my real job, and to be honest, it felt good. I was always on one mission or the other; sometimes it was nice to kick back and actually remind myself of what and why I was doing it.

I started harvesting protein a few days later. I used a fine-threaded cloth and strained it through the frog pool to gather the shed skins floating on the surface. It looked primitive, but it worked. The protein from the skins, after some centrifuging, and filtered into an aqueous solution, sold for more than a hundred thousand times their weight in gold. More even.

The solution contained a unique type of protein and monoclonal antibody that was pivotal in the fabrication of peptide computers. The technology was similar to how silicon chips produced binary data, but instead of using logic gates, the processors read the interactions between protein and antibody. That meant instead of only two states of being, it had twenty.

At the time, most of the world was working with a fusion of DNA and silicon. Only a few of the most powerful companies had developed peptide computing. The Movement had gotten wind of it, put together a raid operation, and got what we needed to fabricate our own.

It was the new X-factor. Combined with research software using genetic algorithms to make breakthroughs, companies were getting about ten, fifteen times the amount of research done with the same amount of resources as a company using DNA computing.

I was one of a few dozen production and distribution centers orchestrated by the Movement. We were all single cells, one-man operations that did everything from raw materials to point of sale.

After everything was up and running, I made a call to the number they gave me and an olive-colored jeep rolled around the next day. An agent from the Movement jumped out and we shook hands. He was a skinny guy, short hair, twitchy eyes, and had a real fast walk. But when he talked, he had a voice that made people listen, low and crystal clear.

"Let's see what you got," he said.

I showed him inside. I'd made sure to send Khulan to town to buy some stuff, so she wouldn't complicate things needlessly. "Population should triple within the year."

He ran his hands along the glass and gave the frame a few stiff pokes. I watched his eyes mostly. They were counting how many frogs.

"You're going to be able to move a lot. Maybe fifteen grams a month." I agreed with him. "I'll set it up then."

I nodded. "Just send me the contact info ahead of time. I'll make it happen."

I reached out to shake his hand when both of us heard the sound of someone breathing. The corners of his eyes tightened, and I finished the handshake, keeping my face expressionless.

He didn't say anything, but we knew we weren't alone. The fact I hadn't reacted meant it was someone I thought was safe. He wasn't happy about it, but he gave me the benefit of the doubt.

I walked him out the door and he got back in his jeep and took off.

A minute later, Khulan tiptoed in.

I turned to look at her. "I told you to go buy me some papayas."

"Sorry. I forgot to bring money with me."

"Don't give me that shit. When I tell you to go, you go."

"Whatever." She rolled her eyes at me. She dodged fast, but I was a lot faster. I kicked her and she went tumbling across the doorway. She scraped her elbows on the stone floor and started coughing violently as she tried to stand up.

I stood looking down at her. "I'm not your buddy."

She took a moment to recover, sucking air on all fours as she shook her head. "That hurt."

"It'd hurt a lot more if you got a bullet through the head. He knew you were here. I knew you were here. You're just lucky I'm an old-timer."

She gave up trying to stand and sat back on her haunches, holding her sides and wincing. "I don't even know what you're talking about."

"Hope you never do. Now come on. We'll go into town together."

She ignored me, sitting on the floor and pouting, while she shuffled her feet to turn her back to me.

"I'll buy you some red bean cakes."

She jumped up and followed me out the gate.

To do business, I needed a cover. It wouldn't make sense if a foreigner showed up in Urumqi and started talking to lots of suits. And I had to create the cover on my own—part of the Movement's policy. We create our own and we maintain them on our own. If I couldn't do at least that much, I didn't belong.

I pretended to be a fruit vendor. For a few months I sold the ordinary stuff, bananas, peaches, papayas, kiwis. Most of the suits came dressed as tourists, pretending to want to eat some honest farmer's fare on their trip in the vast wilderness of western China. Nobody paid me much attention. I'd mumble stuff under my straw hat, and the suits would pretend to have difficulty understanding.

Khulan put the word out to the other street kids not to mess with me and not to hang around when I was talking to tourists. When the tourists weren't around, I'd toss them a fruit or two, sometimes a five-yuan note.

After a while, I started selling more exotic fruits. It wasn't necessary, but I was bored. We tore up a lot of the hard-packed dirt behind the temple and planted a garden. The soil wasn't too bad to work with, a lot of clay so the acidity was low, but we took care of that with some fertilizers. I had to teach Khulan most everything. She was a city girl and didn't know much about how to make plants grow. But the garden made her happy, and after awhile, it made me smile too.

I imported a variety of fruits over the Internet, collecting saplings, plant grafts and pouches of seeds from the tiny strip of pavement that was Urumqi's airport. The first crop we grew were milk oranges imported from Wenzhou.

The fun part of eating a milk orange is the peeling. I remember the first time I handed Khulan one, and she started grinding away at it with a thumb. She didn't see what the big deal was until she gave it a good tug and a cloud of mist swirled into the air. She gave a short surprised laugh and started peeling more of it, spraying citrus juice everywhere. See, milk oranges are juicier than regular ones, and the juice doesn't run clear. It's a cloudy white color, so when you peel it, it starts billowing a sweet-smelling vapor that looks like what comes out of a bucket of dry ice.

After the milk oranges, I started bringing in exotics at a rapid pace. It was almost like a game. I kept trying to think of new ways to entertain Khulan, and I think she was happy to have someone take an interest in her education.

We planted chocolate berries, paw-paws, kiwano melons, lemon meringue fruits, custard apples, eta fruit, almost everything I could get my hands on. We ended up expanding the garden twice, and our hard work caused quite a stir at the marketplace.

At first, I was worried we might draw too much attention, but then I thought maybe it was best to hide out in the open. It's easier to do business when everyone expects you to talk to lots of people.

It was a peaceful life. I felt a part of myself let go for a while, relax and unwind from the constant tension of moving from one mission to the next. It got to the point that I could swear I was putting down roots.

Meanwhile, Khulan looked healthier and happier than I'd ever imagined. Although, one time, she came home bruised with her clothes torn.

I asked her what happened.

25

She said, "I fell down."

"What do you mean 'fell down'?"

"Sorry. I was clumsy." She hung her head and a thick silence fell between the two of us.

I let it go and she didn't say another word. She just went to her room, slammed the door and didn't come out until dinner time. She had a black eye for three days. I swear I've never seen someone look so aggressive while so beat up at the same time.

Later on, I found out the sons of some of the other fruit vendors had tried to beat on her. They called her the fruiter's whore, and said she was still nothing but a street rat, and that if I ever left, they'd kill her.

They didn't get away with it. The other street kids had poured into the alley within minutes, and the vendors' sons were the ones who got mobbed and beaten. Khulan had a roof over her head now, but she would always be one of them. Or at least that's how the street kids explained it to me. I gave them a couple hundred yuan for their trouble and they were happy.

A week later, I talked to Khulan about teaching her how to fight.

"I know how to fight," she said. I heard she had managed to kick one of the older boys' teeth in, but I thought it would make me feel better to see what level she was at.

I put my hands up in a ready position. "Show me."

She paused for a moment, thinking about it. "I'm not going to fight you."

"You'll be all right. Just come at me."

"Nope." She shook her head.

I put my hands back down and gave her a look of disappointment. That's when she tried to kick me in the groin. I blocked it with a knee. She started laughing and ran off.

Later that night, while we were sitting down for dinner, she started asking questions.

"How'd you learn to move so fast?" she asked.

"What do you mean?"

"That time you kicked me. I've never seen anyone move that fast."

There was a voice in the back of my head that said I'd regret telling her about myself, but there was another voice that wanted someone to talk to.

"I've been trained by the Movement."

She popped a grape in her mouth and then a slice of breadfruit. We had so many fruits growing it had given her a decadent palate. One fruit wasn't enough anymore. She had started inventing cocktails on the fly.

"Training doesn't make anyone move *that* fast," Khulan said.

Usually I never beat around the bush, but I had trouble figuring out how to explain nanomuscles to a street orphan.

"My muscles have been modified. They're stronger than the normal human." She frowned, which kind of irritated me. "Okay, imagine my arm is a rope."

"Okay," she said, while dangling a cluster of grapes in front of her face.

I held my forearm out to show her. "Now a

27

normal human's muscles, they're like a rope made of cotton. But mine . . ." I reached out and flicked one of the grapes, making it explode in a shower of juice. "Mine are like spider silk."

The demonstration was a little flashy, but it was the best I could come up with. What my muscles actually had were a much denser and efficient layer of artificial myofibrils that attached to my ligaments, tendons and skeletal muscles to enhance their performance. On the surface, I was no bulkier than the average fit male, but beneath the skin, I out-performed even the most gifted natural athletes.

Khulan wasn't happy with my demonstration. She yelled at me for being a jerk and ran off to find a towel to clean her face. A minute later she was back to asking questions.

"I don't get it. If you can do that, why are you here in some run-down old place, wearing beat-up clothes and pretending to be some poor fruit grocer?"

I thought about how to explain it to her for a second. Telling her it was my cover was too simplistic and she wasn't stupid. She was asking something deeper. I told her what one of my mentors had told me.

"The world's got two types. Predators and prey."

She nodded. "Rich and poor."

"Similar, yeah. Well, what do you notice about the two?"

"One eats the other."

"Right. But other than that?"

"I don't know." She thought about it for a second.

"One is fat and defenseless and the other one has teeth and claws and stuff?"

"Getting there. Okay, let me give you an example. You have a tiger, right? What's a tiger?"

"A predator."

"What's a rooster?"

"Food."

"Exactly. Now look at the behaviors of the two. A rooster does what? He gets up in the morning, yells a lot, struts around all day puffing his chest out."

She bobbed her head like a chicken and started laughing.

"Now a tiger. A tiger doesn't do any of that. What do tiger stripes do?"

"They make it blend in."

"With what?"

"With grass."

"Grass. You see that? A predator tries to look like grass. That's how you know the difference between the two. A predator always tries to blend in, always tries to stay hidden. A predator doesn't want to be seen. They can't eat if people know they're there. All the prey will run away. But prey? Prey spends all day trying to look like a predator."

"So that's why you dress like a farmer."

I tipped my beer at her before taking a long draw.

Things were going great. The fruit gardens out back were growing nearly out of control, the frogs were bright green, plump and shedding skins every week and Khulan had a way of making me laugh over little things like I hadn't in a long time.

29

Then the Germans came, two tall men, blond-haired, blue-eyed and clean-shaven with square jaws. They weren't twins, but they had that factory-made look.

"Kiwi?" I asked.

"Plums," they both answered.

"I've got apples. Do those work?"

"I think we'll stick with kiwis."

The code changed every week. It was pretty damn unlikely that some random customer would come by and guess the sequence.

"Here's the deal. Five grams. More juice than a couple thousand of the best DNA computers could do you."

"That sounds good," they both said in flawless English.

"You know the price?"

They tilted their heads at me.

"Every blueprint of H&K's first-generation products. Prototypes too."

That started a discussion between them. "That's a lot to ask," the one on the right eventually said.

"Standard market price. What you guys got, I can go buy at a trade show. What I got? Only the Movement has."

"Not true," said the one on the right. "Zhao-Xi Combine, Yokomitsu Industries, LM-Boer."

I laughed. "And they're selling, right?"

The two exchanged looks.

"Didn't think so."

"How do we know it's the real thing?"

I dead-panned. I wasn't in the mood for bullshit. They both stood there for a few moments, shuffling their loafers.

DOUGLAS BOSLEY

"Okay, give us some time to think about it. We'll talk to the board. Get back to you soon."

I nodded back at them. They took off. An hour or so later, I packed my stall and headed home too. Khulan joined me once I turned down one of the small side roads.

"You're being followed."

I had noticed it a while ago, but was waiting two more turns to be sure. "Thanks for the heads-up," I said.

"What are you going to do about it?"

"Don't know. You better go though."

She kept following me silently. We took another turn. They were still there. I counted three in my peripheral vision, but I wasn't sure how good they were at hiding. Could be a lot more.

"Beat it, Khulan. Get lost."

"I can get backup."

"I don't need backup. I need you to not get hurt."

She gave me a look. I knew the kind of look, and it was way too messy to deal with right now. "Khulan. Just take off. You stay any longer and they'll think you're with me. I can't watch both our backs at once. I'll meet you at the house."

Her eyes were shiny when she looked at me, but she took off and that's all that mattered.

I took another turn and ditched the fruit cart. I started walking faster. They'd know I was on to them, but that's what I wanted. If they were thinking now or never, they'd flush into the open. The buildings started flashing by, cloth awnings casting long shadows and old ladies gossiping in crooked chairs. I counted three, four, five. I think there were five after me.

I ducked into a shop, bowed at the owner and pretended to look at some of the pottery he had for sale. Poor guy. I did a fast count to twenty in my head and then stepped to the side of the door. Almost on cue, the door swung open, two large European men stepping inside. I moved behind the first one and rabbit-punched him in the neck. He dropped to the floor, and I kicked him in the temple. He stayed down.

The other one was drawing his pistol, but human reflexes just couldn't compete with my nano-enhanced ones. I was next to him before he could react, pushing his elbow back down, pointing the gun in toward his chest and pulling the trigger for him three times. I stripped both their guns and waited for the next move.

The shopkeeper was yelling at me to get out, wringing his shirt in his hands and threatening to call the police. I doubted he even had a phone and I doubted even more highly that the local cops would respond.

"Quiet down, unless you want me to shoot you." I pointed one of the guns at him for emphasis. His mouth widened into an O, and he scooted back behind the store counter. "Stay down, and don't get up until it's over." He lay on the ground as best he could. He had a potbelly though, so he had to curl over on his side.

I looked out of one of the windows to see what they were doing. Nothing was in sight. They were going to try waiting me out, maybe call in more people. I needed to move. "Stay down!" I shouted one more time at the storekeeper. No need to get innocents killed for being stupid. It'd draw attention and I'd probably have to get out of town.

There was an exit out back. One of them would definitely be waiting there. Another would be watching the entrance. That left only the third, the wild card. It was a fifty-fifty chance. Either they thought I'd try to sneak out the back or they'd figure I knew the back exit was cliché and I'd go out the front. The logic went on ad infinitum. I figured what the hell and went out the back.

I heard his breathing before I saw him, but I ducked his first shot and got hit in the leg with his second. It didn't slow me much. I bowled him over, and I think, more than anything, it was his surprise at my mobility that let it happen. I shoved both guns into his ribs and let it rip. His partner probably figured he was a goner, because the next second I got shot in the back. I felt it pierce clean through me, leaving a decent-sized hole in my side.

I rolled off the dead guy and blind-fired upward. Only a few angles someone can shoot a person from when they're lying down. I heard a scream and knew I'd guessed right. A woman with an assault rifle crumpled against the opposite building, a bullet hole in her neck pouring blood.

I took off running as fast as I could, trailing blood and hoping the nanomeds in my bloodstream could handle it. A few minutes later, the wounds had scabbed over, but I could tell the damage was very much present underneath.

Khulan was waiting for me when I got back. She

helped me into bed, cut up some bandages and gave me a cup of water. I lay down, breathing heavily, hoping whichever mega corp they worked for had dispatched a small team.

The next day, I was walking on crutches. The nanomeds in my body had done a lot of work while I was asleep, but I knew I'd need more for a full recovery.

Nanomeds were a technology in its infancy stage, but the Movement gave field operatives the best they had. They were molecular structures designed to mimic the capabilities of pluripotent stem cells, the only difference being they could transform into specialized cells at a much faster rate. Instead of weeks to become a lung or kidney cell, it took hours.

The nanomeds were specifically tailored to my DNA back at one of the labs, using a skin graft to culture cells, and then reverse engineering them to create stem cells. While actually in my body, they stored themselves in my lymphatic system, taking cues from my body's immune responses to pinpoint actual locations for repair. The only catch was the nanomeds couldn't change back once they transformed into a specialized cell.

While I recovered, Khulan helped me around the place, sweeping away leaves, straining the frog pool and taking buckets of water to the garden. I think the sight of me limping around really got to her because next thing I knew she started making it an issue.

"I want to join up."

"No way."

"Why not?"

"You're too young."

"I can do small stuff. I work for you all the time. Isn't that like being a part of the team already?"

"You don't want to be part of this team."

"Why not? You guys are the good guys."

"No such thing."

That managed to piss her off and she stalked out of the room. It took me a few minutes to track her down, but she was just taking care of the daily chores. The frogs needed to eat, and they only ate live food. I had been buying crickets off one of the local farmers, but the large amounts I ordered had him asking questions I didn't want to answer.

Instead, Khulan had thought of another way to get the frogs food. She sliced up some fruit, left it out in the open and waited for the insects to come. It was the desert. Food was scarce, but insects were everywhere. It'd take a while for them to notice, but once they did, the fruits would get swarmed.

We sat outside, me with my shirt off, sipping hot tea and waiting for the flies to come. Khulan looked at me, making me self-conscious for a second, but I was in shape and she was a kid. We sat this way for about half an hour with her stone-faced, waiting for me to talk while I enjoyed my tea.

"You heal a lot faster than normal," she said, smoking a cigarette. She told me she'd cut back on it, but I'd catch her lighting one every now and then. I couldn't stand the stuff myself.

"Perk of the trade."

"Pretty good perk."

"Only if you get shot a lot."

She showed me one of her scarred elbows. "Or get kicked," she said in an angry tone.

I laughed and put my arm around her shoulder, giving her a hard squeeze.

She snorted and leaned away from me. "So what happens now?"

The question sobered me pretty fast. "I expect we'll get a visit from the Movement."

Sure enough, a few hours later, some people from the Movement made contact. I heard the rumble of an old jeep pulling up to the gate, its tires growling over the rough sand. Using automobiles kept us below the radar. Nobody important traveled by road anymore, or at least that's how the thought went.

I recognized one of the agents that climbed out. His name was Donovan, and he was a big Irish guy. He had a mop of brown hair, an easy smile and broad ham hands. I did a lot of wet work with him down in Panama a couple years back. I hadn't seen him since, but he was reliable.

The rest of them were new to me, which was standard. An old military maxim is "cut off the head and the rest of the snake will die." The Movement was more like an earthworm. Cut an earthworm in half and you get two, much better than snakes. So, it was unusual to have more than two or three of us together other than for big operations.

"What's going on, Donovan?" I shook his hand.

He clapped me on the shoulder with the other hand. "Heard you ran into some trouble."

"Those H&K people. Can't work with them no more."

"Hegel and Kritz? They were bought out last week."

"I was shot up by people claiming to be from H&K."

The other agents exchanged glances. Donovan was frowning. "That doesn't sound good."

I shook my head. "Nope." I knew what answer was coming. I felt my guts twist and I looked for a hole in his logic, but there just wasn't anything to say.

"Pack up time," he said.

I nodded. It was one of the few times I hated having to agree with common sense. I'd gotten way too attached to the place, to the temple outside Urumqi.

Donovan handed me a syringe of nanomeds. "I'm guessing you're running low."

I took it from him and shot it into my left forearm. It would take about an hour or so to kick in, but I was expecting I'd be fighting fit by the next day. "You guys want to take the frogs now?"

"Why not? We got a biokit in the jeep. Shouldn't be a problem."

I led them back to the house. Khulan didn't bother hiding. She watched them with a troubled expression, and her face contorted like she wanted to say something when they started taking the frogs away. I put a finger to my lips and shook my head to let her know now was not the time.

They cleared all the frogs out and cleaned the greenhouse, using chemicals and scanners to make sure no trace of the proteins was left. I gave them the peptide solution I had on hand, about thirty grams, and that was it. I talked to Donovan for a minute before they took off.

"I bet she reminds you of your sister, doesn't she?"

I wasn't comfortable talking about my past, but Donovan and I had been through some hairy experiences together in Panama. It makes people close, no matter how you look at it.

"Yeah. She does."

"Dangerous."

"I'm a big boy."

"Take a few days. Say your goodbyes. Then we can ship you out someplace else."

"Might settle down for a bit."

Donovan got a look on his face, and I knew that look.

"Don't even, Donovan. I can still put you on your ass before you even blink."

He raised his hands in mock surrender. "Hey, I didn't say anything."

I couldn't help laughing. "It's not like that."

"Of course not. Never is." He put an arm around my shoulder and leaned in close. "You know you can leave any time. We'll set you up somewhere quiet. But I don't know if we can take the girl."

"She knows my operation."

"No big deal. We're shutting this down anyway. We've done our job. Market for peptides is pretty much mainstream by now. We forced their hand. They've started selling the manufacturing process. The smaller companies have to pay royalties on it for a while, but they'll all get the tech within the year."

"She wants to join." I could hear the desperation in my voice. I think it surprised me more than it did Donovan.

"We'll see how it goes. A lot of people owe you favors. May take some time though. It looks real raw trying to bring her in so fast."

I nodded. There was nothing else to say. We shook hands again, he got in the jeep and they drove off.

Khulan took the news hard. It was painful for both of us, but her reaction made it worse. At first, she begged me to take her along. Then she cried for hours. In the end, she drifted around the temple, ghostlike, smiling to herself sometimes, shoving and kicking at things other times. I tried explaining to her what was going on, but she wasn't in any mood to listen. I didn't want to tell her she might be able to join the Movement. She'd just be crushed if it didn't come through.

She moped around like this for two days straight and I should have been long gone, but it didn't feel right leaving her like that.

On the third day, I woke early and went to town. I thought it would be a nice gesture, buy some groceries, cook some food, throw Khulan a nice party before I left.

But on the long walk back to the temple, I started to feel a little silly, and a whole lot of helpless. How are steamed carp, fried pork and a tray of sweet egg custards going to make up for the life we'd made together? It felt almost insulting to put a nice face on it, like I was lying to Khulan and disrespecting her intelligence. Maybe I was. But I wasn't the type who did nothing when he didn't know the right thing to do.

The first indication I had of something wrong was the distant sound of crackling fire. I gripped my bags and walked faster. Then came the scream, long, loud and anguished. Khulan. I dropped everything and ran.

The temple's gate had been knocked down, the two columns supporting it, a splintered wreck. There were three guards outside, and I took a shot in the shoulder on the approach. The force of it knocked me back on my heels, but I recovered my balance and leapt as hard as I could into the air, kicking one of them in the chest. I felt more than heard his ribs snap, and I stomped his throat before grabbing his machine gun.

I knew some people from the Movement were in the area because the two other guards got hit by sniper fire and dropped to the floor around the time I kicked the first one. Six of them shimmered into view, their light-refraction suits flickering as they tried to compensate for movement.

"Donovan," I said.

He saluted me. "Tian Zi."

"Give me a report."

"Six hostiles inside, four in the north room, one in both the east and west rooms. Hostage is being held in the north room."

I felt a lump form in my throat, but I kept it icy.

"What's her status?"

"We've had the temple on sat-surveillance, but we bugged it on that last visit. She should be all right.

41

They haven't done any major work on her. Don't think they know who she is, and they might be holding back in case they can use her for leverage."

"Cake walk," I said. One of them laughed. I gave him a look and he grew a brain. "Fast and clean. Let's get it done."

They scattered. The fight didn't last long. I made sure to kill the torturer myself, and I used his tools to do it. It was fast, but I got to hear him scream plenty before I was done.

When I came back out of the temple, they had Khulan pumped full of painkillers and were carrying her by stretcher to the jeep. I walked over and took a look for myself. She was in worse condition than Donovan had let on, but I think he did that to spare me the worry. It's always easier when I see it up close. I can get a grip on it, understand the exact parameters. It's the imagination that screws with my head.

"You okay, kid?"

Khulan looked up at me, the pain swimming in her eyes. She was unconscious when we rescued her, but she had come around a few minutes after they got her into the stretcher.

"Tian Zi?"

I squeezed her hand, careful not to touch the tips, where the fingernails were splintered. "I'm here."

"I kept quiet." She smiled at me, her hair in disarray, but her eyes burning with that wild light she always had.

"I'm proud of you. You did good, Khulan. I couldn't have asked for better."

I didn't know what else to say. It's not that I wasn't used to seeing people get hurt out in the field, but I think saying sorry would have pissed her off more than anything.

Her eyes teared up and she rested her head back on the stretcher. The other agents took that as their signal and started walking toward the jeep again. I think everyone was uncomfortable with standing around while I talked to her swinging from a stretcher.

"She'll be fine, TZ." Donovan approached and offered me a cigarette.

I waved it away. "Yeah. I know." I wasn't in the mood to talk to anyone. It was irrational, but I held it against them that they stood by while Khulan had been tortured.

"Word came in. They'll let her on the team. We sent a field report on her conduct. She could have talked. She could have said a lot. Even though they already had the intelligence, there's no way she would have known. She could have talked for an hour, but she didn't."

"Thanks, Donovan." I started walking away before I said something I'd regret. I knew the rules. The Movement only helped their own. Bystanders were off limits. It was hard enough keeping ahead of the mega corps, no need to add to the burden.

He grabbed me by the bicep. "Hear me out, man. You want to hear this."

"I want to go see if my garden's all right."

"Get it together, TZ. It's gone. First thing they did was run through it and try to see if anything was there."

I felt a hot surge rush through my body. I wanted to go back inside and stab the torturer a few more times. "Fine. Finish what you have to say."

"She did a good job. You taught her well. When they were cutting her up, she screamed and cried, and carried on. I swear, even we thought for a second she didn't know anything. She's a natural. We could have gone in earlier, but we knew you wanted her on the team. We gave her a chance to prove herself, and she did."

It was a bittersweet feeling. At least she had taken my words to heart: be a tiger, act like grass.

"She'll get fixed up and then go in for training. I don't know when you guys will see each other again, but it'll happen."

"I'll count on it," I said.

Donovan left me alone so I could see what my garden had become. Everything was a mess. Trees cut down, roots torn up, fruit smashed to pulp and flowers shredded all over the dirt. I sat down in the middle of it all and I cried like I hadn't since I was a boy. They gave me space. We shared the same struggle. They knew how lonely it could get.

I cried until my eyes flowed like rain. But there was a delicious aroma floating up around me. All that smashed fruit, the insects buzzing around, the smell of tree sap and crushed flowers in the air. I felt like I was sitting in the placenta of Creation, and I drew strength from it. This was what we were fighting for. This was the Movement.

We had grown a garden here, and now it was gone, but watching all those insects come crawling out to feed and looking at those seeds dot the soil, I knew I could leave, and my garden would still be here. It wouldn't look as pretty, and soon enough those plants would start fighting amongst themselves for who would have the run of the place, but life would go on. The struggle would continue.

The Shadow Man

written by

Donald Mead

illustrated by

BRIANNE HILLS

ABOUT THE AUTHOR

Unlike most writers, Donald Mead hated reading when he was growing up . . . at least until the fifth grade. That's when he came upon Tolkien's The Hobbit *and his world changed unalterably. Not only did he gain a love of fantasy novels, his grades steadily improved, ultimately leading to academic success in both undergraduate and graduate school.*

Don credits his first professional sale to the Writers of the Future Contest. His first entry three years ago didn't make the final cut, but was critiqued by Writers of the Future winner and judge K. D. Wentworth. He made several improvements based on her comments, then sold "iKlawa" to the magazine of Fantasy and Science Fiction. *His most recent story, "A Thing Forbidden," was also published in* F&SF *and was chosen for* The Year's Best Fantasy and Horror *anthology.*

Don works in the payroll department for a college in Bloomington, Illinois. He's part of a local writers' group, appears at cons throughout the Midwest, and is a member of the online writers' community Codex. Don holds a third-degree black belt in iaido (traditional Japanese swordsmanship) and a first-degree black belt in Japanese kendo (bamboo sword fighting).

ABOUT THE ILLUSTRATOR

By the time Brianne Hills entered college, she had won multiple local and national awards as a high-school student. These included the Silver Key award from the long-running Boston Globe Scholastic Art Awards, as well as Massachusetts and national honors for the 2004 Federal Junior Duck Stamp Conservation and Design Program promoting wetland and wildlife conservation.

After graduating from Brigham Young University with a Bachelor of Fine Arts in illustration, Brianne took up freelancing and now works as an illustrator for a children's gaming company, where she computer illustrates characters, clothing, settings and all manner of devices. Brianne enjoys any kind of art, ranging from J. W. Waterhouse to Mary GrandPré. She also loves writing (and illustrating) her own fiction, short stories and, recently, poetry. Her aspirations include publishing her own works, illustrating for a publishing house and someday working as a concept artist for animated films or TV.

The Shadow Man

"Are you the Shadow Man?"

Jiro Ota bowed. "An unfortunate title. Not one of my choosing. Please call me 'Jiro.'"

The man returned a brief bow, not bothering to take the cigarette from his mouth. "Jiro-*san*. I've been waiting. I'm Haro Fujii."

Jiro squinted at Hiroshima's naked sun. He guessed Fujii-*san,* the site foreman according to the stitched title on his sweat-drenched gray shirt, had been at the building demolition for most of the morning. Even now, sweat leaked from under the man's helmet, the cloth *hachimaki* wrapped around his head unable to soak up any more.

The foreman pointed at the handful of scraggly men resting in the shade of the dilapidated building's wall. "If we could hurry this up—I'm on a schedule, and the boys would stay there all day if I let them."

"Of course. When did you find the shadow?"

"An hour ago. One of the boys was knocking out a plaster wall to get at the brick. He came running when he saw what it was. I pulled the rest off the project until I could figure out what to do."

The foreman led the way through the roofless one-story building, dodging brick piles, twisted copper tubing and broken roof tile. They stopped before the wall of an interior room. Much of the plaster had been ripped away, exposing an area of brick measuring roughly three meters high and six meters wide. A dark shadow lay on its dusty red surface. Up close from the workman's perspective, it wouldn't have been identifiable. But three meters back where Jiro and the foreman stood, it was clearly the shape of a man. The head and broad shoulders were quite discernible, along with a hand emerging from a wide cuff. The shadow was bell-shaped where the legs should've been. A *kimono,* Jiro thought. Or *yukata,* given the August heat of thirteen years ago.

Jiro thought the foreman to be a pretty tough customer, but he stamped out his cigarette and stood reverently.

"A shadow in no need of sun," the foreman said.

Jiro nodded and pulled a folded sheet of paper from the breast pocket of his work overalls. "I need to show you this. The city's permission—"

The foreman raised his hand. "Unnecessary. I know who you are. I heard about it on the radio. I called city hall to get your number."

Jiro put the paper away. "Do you think it's macabre, my collection of shadows?"

The foreman drew a cigarette and lighter. "No. It's all part of remembrance." He waved his cigarette at the demolition. "All this, for example. It's going to be an expansion to Peace Park."

"Oh, yes," said Jiro, finding a reason to smile. "I want my collection to be part of the exhibition. The city council has been receptive to my proposal."

The foreman turned to the shadow. "What's next? Should my boys knock it out and then you reassemble it at your museum?"

"Not that way," Jiro said. "It has to stay intact. Always intact or . . . it's not the same. Can they knock out the surrounding brick? I've devised a bracket that will fit around wall sections. I can lower it onto a sleigh and winch it into my truck. I've got a couple of men who'll help me unload it. But I'll have to back my truck in here somehow."

"We can do all of that," said the foreman. He lit his cigarette and took a puff. "Knock out the surrounding brick and clear away this crap so you can get in."

Jiro regarded the foreman. "You've been very helpful. Mind if I ask you a personal question?"

The foreman raised his eyebrows.

Jiro continued. "You're a pretty rough fellow, anyone can tell."

"What's your point?"

"You could've knocked down the wall and hauled it away. Nobody would've been the wiser. But you didn't."

The foreman sighed and took another drag. "My father must have been within a couple of hundred meters of the hypocenter. Vaporized while walking to work." He glanced at the blazing sun. "And these shadows. What if one of them is him?"

"Yes," Jiro said. "The rays of the bomb did strange things. Why don't you come to the opening of the museum? It might give you some peace."

"Oh, no. Thank you. I'd break down and cry like a baby. I couldn't do that in public."

"At least think about it."

The foreman nodded.

"Let me ask you another question."

"Sure."

"Have there been any strange occurrences at the worksite? Unexplained voices? Equipment being moved overnight?"

The foreman dropped his cigarette. "How did you know?"

Ota."

The voice behind Jiro belonged to "Four Fingers" Yamata, a foot soldier for the local syndicate.

He kept walking.

In the early morning bustle of Hiroshima's Otemachi district—the crowded sidewalk, honking cars, clattering streetcars—an inability to hear could be justified. Perhaps Four Fingers might even figure out that if he added a proper *"san"* to Jiro's name, he'd get a more polite response. But one played a delicate game when teaching politeness to the *yakuza*.

He came to the museum door and fumbled with his keys. Maybe if he was fast. . . .

"Ota!"

Jiro sighed and turned. He couldn't justify ignoring his bellowed name. So much for lessons.

Four Fingers stopped before Jiro and looked him up and down, a scowl on his face. His scarred bald head and knocked-out front tooth lent to his reputation as a street tough. The missing pinky on his right hand left no doubt as to his affiliation. "Wax in your ears, Ota?"

Jiro wrestled back a number of biting responses, any one of which would've resulted in a broken nose. "I guess I didn't hear you."

Four Fingers barked a short humorless laugh. "I guess you're full of shit." He held out a piece of paper.

Jiro stared. "What's this?"

Four Fingers' scowl deepened.

Jiro took the paper.

"Smart move," said Four Fingers. "It's the address for the Fukuya Department Store. They stopped paying dues so the Rice King says you've got to send over a spook."

"Maybe the Rice King forgot to tell you—"

"The Rice King doesn't forget anything."

"—that our business arrangement was concluded last month."

"Nothing's concluded until the Rice King says so!"

Jiro unlocked the museum door. "Listen. The opening's today. Why don't you come up and we'll talk about it?"

"Nothing to talk about."

Jiro pushed the door open. A dark narrow staircase led up to the second floor where the exhibits were displayed. He turned to Four Fingers. "Come on. This early in the morning you still might hear them talk."

Four Fingers looked up the staircase. His eyes narrowed and he shrank back a few paces. "I'm not going anywhere."

Jiro suppressed a smile. "I've got an idea. Why don't you take one of the shadows? You can use my truck. Just bring it back when you're done."

"Now you're just screwing with me," said Four Fingers. "I won't have anything to do with those things. None of the Family will; talk about bad luck. The boss wants a spook delivered, and you're going to do it."

"Send my regrets to the Rice King. He's not getting any more shadows. Our relationship is over."

Four Fingers grinned. "I'll tell the boss. You know, it's going to be a pleasure breaking your arm."

"I think you're bluffing," said Jiro.

"Then you're dumber than I thought."

Jiro pocketed his keys and entered the museum. "I'll call the police."

"Now who's bluffing?" Four Fingers called after him.

The creaking stairs led to a vacuous room with a new wooden floor. Widely spaced pillars sported fresh white paint. There were lights, but Jiro rarely used them due to the natural light coming from the floor-to-ceiling windows along the east and north walls.

Soft voices rose on Hiroshima's thick air as Jiro walked among the shadows. He stopped before the newest acquisition, the man in the *kimono,* now mounted on the wall.

My brother's getting married.

"Congratulations," said Jiro. "What's his name? Maybe I know him."

There was no answer. There never was.

He moved on.

Another exhibit was a woman with her hair bound high and a child in hand.

Where are we, Mama? came a child's voice.

Don't worry. The streetcar will be here any minute, the woman answered.

"Can I give you directions?"

Silence now, but Jiro liked the game. Maybe someday they'd answer. He wondered about their lives as shadows. He wondered if they knew about his mother.

A free-standing display was nothing more than the stone steps of a bank. Jiro sat next to a dark half circle.

Where should I have lunch today? a woman's voice asked. It was barely audible now that the sun was creeping into the room.

"Someone moved my tools last night. Getting curious about your new home, aren't you?"

The shadow made no confession.

Jiro stood, took off his jacket and hung it on a wall peg. Four Fingers was right about one thing: he couldn't go to the police. The Rice King's money had funded the entire museum. If the city counsel found out, they'd take everything away. His life's work lost.

He'd have to dodge Four Fingers until the Rice King found more worthy game.

He crouched in front of another floor exhibit before the sun silenced them all. It was nothing more than a 24-centimeter piece of iron bridge railing with a hand imprinted on it.

I was cheated, said a man. *I want justice!*

"That's what you say every day. And what would you do if you had your chance?"

I'd have my revenge.

Jiro stood and stepped away, unsure if the imprint had found a new phrase or if it had actually answered him. He gulped and crouched again, touching the hand. "What would you do?"

I would kill!

Look at me, not the camera," said the newsman.

Jiro nodded and smoothed down his hair. He had made an effort to look his best in a traditional maroon *kimono* with ginkgo leaf stitching, but he felt self-conscious next to the newsman in a pressed dark suit, neat haircut and make-up.

People milled about the exhibits: businessmen in suits, mothers with children, older people in *kimonos*. A class from a middle school was scheduled later in the day.

The cameraman switched on two floodlights extended on tripods.

"Let's begin," said the newsman. "Just like we discussed over the phone."

He plugged a microphone into an instrument box and raised it between them. His voice became clear, deep and confident. "We're speaking with Jiro Ota, the curator of a most unusual museum in Otemachi district. Ota-*san,* please describe your collection."

Jiro cleared his throat. "Well. It's the shadows of citizens created by the atomic bomb blast. People going about their daily lives, and then one morning, they were instantly transformed—integrated into surrounding stone, steel and masonry. Captured for eternity."

"Why this subject?" the newsman asked. "What's your motivation?"

"We all have a history with the bomb. The public history we share with others. It's our collective horror. And then there are the private sufferings we keep in our hearts. Dark pain that changed us. By displaying these shadows in public, people can gather to confront these horrors. Perhaps by realizing we're united in our grief we'll find a way of easing our private horrors."

"And your own history, may I ask?"

"Not nearly as traumatic as most," said Jiro. "I was riding a streetcar to meet my mother at Hiroshima Bank and was knocked unconscious by the blast. My first recollection was walking along the stone embankment of the Motoyasu River. The people were bloated by burns—only dark slits for eyes and a mouth. They cried for water, but you're not supposed to give water to burn victims; I remembered that much from air-raid training. I did what I could, but many fell silent that night. We waited for someone to tell us what to do, where to go. The radiation sickness started a week or two later."

"And you?"

"Ah. No injuries," said Jiro. "But the rays of the bomb had other odd effects."

"Oh?"

"Yes. For example, I don't dream anymore when I sleep."

"Really?"

"Yes. Strange, isn't it?"

"Very," said the newsman. "Tokyo will host the 1960 Olympics. I understand you have an idea for promoting your collection to foreign visitors."

"Absolutely. But not just my collection—all of Peace Park. With eighteen months to prepare, there's plenty of time to consult with hotels and airlines to arrange weekend visits from Tokyo. The whole world should see it."

A forlorn groan caused Jiro to glance over his shoulder. A visitor, a middle-aged man dressed in dark slacks and a collared white shirt, had slumped before the shadow of the woman with the child. He reached up and touched the image. "Sachi! Nami-*chan*!"

"Oh no," said the newsman, waving to the camera operator. "Don't film that."

"Does that embarrass you?" Jiro asked.

The newsman looked at the sobbing visitor. "Well, yes. I can't help but look away. I'm sure he'd like some privacy in his sorrow."

"I'm not so embarrassed," said Jiro. "That's what this exhibit is all about—Hiroshima's public suffering. Perhaps this man will have questions resolved today. Maybe part of his soul will find some peace. I might be so bold as to say the shadows themselves may find peace."

"And you?" the newsman asked. "Have you found your peace?"

"I think I have—or shortly will. I've given up hope of finding my mother, either her remains or her shadow, but my son has heard of my work. He disappeared after the bomb, and I found out later he was living with his uncle in Kyoto. My wife, his mother, had died of tuberculosis before the war."

Jiro paused to fight a swelling in his throat. "I was content to leave him in Kyoto. No need for him to be tainted by this stigma. I suppose he thought I was dead all these years. It was for his own good."

The newsman brightened. "Ah! What a happy ending."

"Yes. I hope so. He sent me a letter, and he's coming to visit. It will be a tearful reunion. He'd be twenty-two years old now."

They turned as the visitor moaned again and collapsed before the shadows. "Thank you."

Jiro raised his head from his folded arms to find himself seated at his desk in the museum. He smacked his lips and squinted at the orange ball pounding in light through the eastern windows.

Another dreamless night.

He fingered through the stacks of correspondence that had kept him from bed. Letters from people interested in a visit. From the Olympic Committee requesting details about his exhibit. Even from a Japanese university asking to borrow his collection for their own exhibit. But most precious was the letter from his son, Takeshi.

Jiro picked up the handwritten letter. It was strangely short, but emotional—promising reconciliation.

> Father, I learned about the exhibit on the radio. I heard your voice. Imagine my shock! I will come to visit you on May 18th. I won't be able to hold my tears. Together we will set everything right.

Takeshi ended with a haiku.

Kites rise in autumn
Their shadows dance in rice fields
A river shrine waits.

It seemed a sentimental happy haiku. They'd flown kites together when Takeshi was a boy, no doubt a happy memory for him. "Shadows dance" was another expression of joy, and "shadows" no doubt referred to Jiro's collection. "A river shrine" was a bit of a mystery. They once had a family shrine on the Temma River, but it was destroyed by the bomb. The ashes of his ancestors were gone forever.

They would discuss it when he arrived.

A woman's voice rose from behind him. *The Senda streetcar!*

Jiro wheeled about in his chair, heart pounding. The voice still echoed as though calling from a tunnel. This wasn't a shadow's faint voice. It was clear, resonant. Something about a streetcar.

He stood and stared at the empty hall, the shadows his only audience.

Mama! Will we see Papa! The child's voice was just as loud and real as the woman's. It came from somewhere in the western corner of the room. Jiro crept in that direction. "Who's there? Where are you?"

No, Nami-chan. We said goodbye to Papa. Remember!

It came from near the stone step exhibit. Jiro followed. "Can you hear me? I just want to talk a bit."

Will there be dragonflies when we get there?
"No. Please stay."

The child's voice was soft and distant. It had an odd metallic ring to it. The woman's voice answered, just as metallic and barely audible. *Yes, Nami-chan. I think it will be a wonderful place. Ah! Here's the streetcar.*

Jiro leapt at the fading words. "No! Please! I have so many questions!"

He came to a stop on the western wall again. There were no more voices. The bell of a streetcar clanged in the distance.

Jiro sank to his knees and put his hands to his eyes, unable and unwilling to fight tears. "I just want to know. I just want to know about my mother."

No sense in counting minutes when one cried, and Jiro didn't try. Once his sobbing eased, he noticed the sun's rays had fully wrapped his desk in gold light. A beckoning to work—a return to the living world.

He found his feet, only to be frozen into place. The exhibit that had once been the shadows of a mother and child was now an unblemished brick wall.

Jiro cursed at the knock at the staircase door. The museum wasn't scheduled to open for another two hours, and he had sent a dozen people away so far. A bigger sign giving the opening time was needed along with a trained monkey to point at it with a stick.

The knock came again, louder. "Coming!"

Jiro started down the staircase.

He chided himself for his lack of patience. He'd been plagued all day thinking about the now shadowless wall and the man who'd collapsed in front of it the day of the opening. His sobbing "thank-yous" suggested he had heard something. Perhaps the shadows' voices, but they had never spoken at midday before. That's why Jiro had opened at that time. No need to cause a panic with talking shadows. No need for an army of priests at his doorstep making demands.

He unlocked the door only to have it slammed against him, knocking him to the floor of the entryway.

Four Fingers closed and locked the door behind him. "Hello, Shadow Man. Forget your assignment?" The brute sported a smile that made Jiro shiver.

"Get out!"

He rolled to his stomach intending to stand, but Four Fingers kicked him in his ribs. He sprawled and gasped for breath.

Four Fingers grabbed Jiro by his shirt lapels and yanked him to his feet. He clasped his hand around Jiro's throat and squeezed. "I'm going to give you a choice, Ota. I can break your arm or your leg. Got a preference?"

Jiro tried to cry for help in the unlikely chance that a passerby might hear, but Four Fingers' grip cut off his breath. All he could manage was a hoarse squeal.

"Huh?" Four Fingers tilted his head as if listening. "Did you say 'arm' or 'leg'? Maybe you said 'neck.'"

He shoved Jiro into the stairs.

Jiro took a gulp of air. "Help!"

"No one's going to help you," said Four Fingers. "Come on. You're stalling. Arm or leg? Otherwise, I get to choose. Of course, you could just deliver the spook and we could forget this whole ugly mess."

Jiro steadied his breathing and regarded Four Fingers. "I'm not playing this game."

Four Fingers frowned. "How the hell does he know everything? The Rice King said you wouldn't go for physical threats, and I had you pegged for a sissy. Dammit if I couldn't prove him wrong just for once."

"So you're going to leave me alone?"

"Hell, no. I'm going to set your museum on fire."

Jiro gulped and pushed himself up to stand. "Wait. You can't!"

Four Fingers shrugged. "I've got to."

A fire would wipe it all out—a decade of work. If the heat didn't crack the masonry, the soot and carbon would destroy the shadows.

"Maybe just one more," said Jiro. "But after that, it's finished."

Four Fingers smirked. "The Rice King said you'd say that too." He turned and unlocked the door. "Tonight, Ota. This is your last chance."

He left, closing the door after him.

Jiro rubbed his throat, wishing Four Fingers had sacrificed a thumb instead of a pinky. "Tonight," he murmured.

Four Fingers flicked away a cigarette butt. The ember glowed orange in the twilight before disappearing off the end of the wharf. He reached into the breast pocket of his jacket for another.

Seagulls hovered over the churning waves looking for a final meal before dark. They were scavengers, beggars. They reminded him of the bomb. People begged then too. Food, clothes, a place to stay— and not many from the surrounding villages were generous. He'd been an orphaned seagull after the bomb. Then the Rice King found him and put him to work. A new Family to replace the dead.

Four Fingers turned at the sound of a slamming door coming from the warehouse.

The dark-suited figures of Chado and Sakaki approached.

"The Rice King's hungry," said Chado. "We're going to that Chinese place on Miyajima Street for some dumplings. You want anything?"

Four Fingers lit a cigarette and took a drag. "Yeah. Get me a bowl of noodles."

Chado nodded. "Noodles, right. I think you can get it with vegetables or fish—"

"None of that crap," said Four Fingers. "Just noodles. Maybe a little five-spice."

"Five-spice. Got it."

"Hey, Four Fingers," Sakaki said. "You think the Rice King's acting funny?"

"I don't think nothin'."

"Right," Sakaki said. He looked at Chado. "Let's go."

They turned toward a car parked at the end of the wharf. Sakaki looked back. "I think he's acting funny."

"Go get the damned food," said Four Fingers.

"And stop thinking so much. Your brain might explode."

Sakaki shrugged and turned.

Four Fingers watched as they drove the white four-door down the wharf's service road. Its puttering motor was swallowed up by the growl of trucks that dominated wharf traffic.

Yeah, the Rice King was acting funny. Ever since Four Fingers had told him the Shadow Man had agreed to deliver the spook. He still had the smug smile he got when one of his predictions hit dead-on, but this time the smile was accompanied by pacing, hand rubbing and constant questioning. "Did you hear that?" "Did anyone hear anything?" The boss's agitation reached a peak an hour ago when he ordered Four Fingers outside to keep a lookout.

So far, there was nothing to report other than the cry of seagulls, the chop of waves and the rumble of trucks.

But he wouldn't begrudge the boss a few quirks. Who the hell was he to judge anyone? He was an Enforcer for the Family, the Family that paid him, fed him and gave him a reason to get up and get dressed in the morning. And the Rice King asked for so little in return—as long as you didn't screw up.

Four Fingers absently touched the stub on his right hand.

She'll wear a blue and gold kimono.

Four Fingers whirled. "Who's there?"

The remaining sliver of sun revealed empty walkways along the wharf. The warehouse loading

65

bay was dark and an awning darkened its detail. It was the only place for someone to hide. Four Fingers took a few steps toward the bay, perhaps ten meters distant.

My daughter will meet me for lunch. I hope her pregnancy is going well.

It was a woman's voice, though barely loud enough to be heard over the distant traffic. Four Fingers couldn't tell the direction, but it had to have come from the loading bay. He reached into his pocket for a knife.

Not another air-raid siren!

This time it came from his left along with an icy presence, a hand, touching his arm. He yelped and slashed at the darkness.

Ghosts! Four Fingers thought. Damned ghosts. Right here on the wharf. As bad as the Shadow Man's museum. Hell, worse! He didn't have to deal with those ghosts.

Four Fingers tucked the knife back into his pocket and rubbed the sweat off his forehead. He wondered if he should tell the Rice King, but what would he say? "Hey boss, I heard a ghost." Not likely. The boss was a no-bullshit kind of guy.

Why is she so late? My feet are so tired.

"Screw your feet!"

His voice echoed off the brick wall of the warehouse.

A walk around the warehouse was what he needed. Just to keep a lookout like the Rice King asked. By the time he returned, the boys would be back with the food and the ghost would be gone.

Four Fingers turned and headed down the wharf. He turned right up the service road. Just one lap around the building, he thought. Just five minutes. What could happen?

Jiro pushed open the door to the warehouse office. It was a sizeable room, with space for an oblong conference table and a desk with a chair. It was painted a dingy yellow and well lighted with buzzing fluorescent lights. The stagnant odor of cigarette smoke made him wonder if the walls had been painted white originally. A curtain covered a three-by-three-meter section of the wall, and a percolator full of coffee sat on a small corner table.

The Rice King sat staring, placid, in a stuffed leather chair behind the wood-veneered desk. His gray hair was cut to a half-centimeter length around the sides of his head, and he was bald on top. He was clean-shaven, and there was a sag to his eyes and jowls. Jiro guessed he was about sixty years old. His white shirt showed staining under the armpits, and a black suit jacket hung on a coat rack near the desk.

"Ota-*san*. What a pleasure to meet you," he said without bowing. His voice was gravelly and deep.

Jiro bowed and took a step in, pulling the hem of his *kimono* after him. "Please call me 'Jiro.' You don't seem surprised to see me."

"Not at all. I knew you'd come tonight."

"Four Fingers mentioned you had a gift for precognition."

"And Four Fingers has a gift for exaggeration,"

67

said the Rice King. "I just know people—*some* people, that is. People who survived the bomb. Their outlooks and motivations change. If you spent time studying a survivor, you'd notice patterns too."

"Oh?"

"Sure. Take Four Fingers. I bet you scared him off with one of your ghosts."

Jiro nodded.

"Instead of coming to me like he should've, I knew he'd retreat. He's not really afraid of ghosts; he's afraid of looking foolish in my eyes. A kind of insecurity. It reminds him of the bomb and the day he lost everything." The Rice King shook his head. "Still, he abandoned his post, and there has to be punishment. I'm afraid he'll be known as 'Three Fingers' next time you see him."

"But that's why I'm here," said Jiro. "I don't want to see him again. Or you for that matter."

If the Rice King was insulted, he gave no reaction. "What do you predict I'll say?"

Jiro paused and spoke. "You will say 'no.'"

"You see? It's really quite easy. I'll threaten to kill you if you stop providing shadows, but you won't be intimidated. And then you'll threaten me. We're so much alike, we children of the bomb."

"I'm nothing like you," said Jiro. "You're greedy and cruel."

"But we are alike. We were both remade by the bomb. I became the 'Rice King' and you, obviously, the 'Shadow Man.' With our new titles we gained new strengths and weaknesses."

The Rice King stood. He bent behind his desk and, with a grunt, lifted a sledgehammer. He let it rest against his shoulder like a rifle, its iron head next to his cheek.

Jiro gasped and took a step back.

"Oh, this isn't for you, Jiro-*san*. But it necessitates the next step in our meeting. My prediction is that you're going to threaten me. Let's have it."

"I—" Jiro struggled to organize his thoughts, but he couldn't tear his eyes from the hammer. Despite the Rice King's claim, he imagined his skull being crushed by the weapon.

"If you . . . uh—"

"Come on, don't be shy. Not everyone gets a chance to threaten the *yakuza*."

Jiro took a deep breath. "If you don't leave me alone, I'll set a shadow on you and your family. Your real family. Your children. Mysterious voices will follow them. They'll be shunned for the rest of their lives by both legitimate society and *yakuza*."

The Rice King smiled. "Ah! An excellent threat. And one worth considering if circumstances were different."

Jiro felt a flush in his face. "Circumstances? What circumstances? We both see this situation for what it is! And I'm tired of your smiling superiority. I'd almost prefer you to act like the thug you are!"

Jiro stiffened. He might die tonight, but he didn't want to hasten the process.

"A fair response," said the Rice King. "The circumstance I spoke of involves pure luck." He took a few steps toward the curtained part of the wall. "No matter how predictable events are, luck changes everything. I knew our relationship would come to an end one day, until two months ago when luck smiled on me."

He yanked the curtain and it fell to the floor. A section of brick wall stood, propped up by wooden supports on either side. A shadow of a woman was burned on its surface with the flowing arms of a kimono and hair pinned up high upon the head.

Jiro. What took you so long? We meet with the bank manager in an hour.

"Mother?" Jiro felt himself sway.

"I knew it!" A vicious gleam grew in the Rice King's eyes. "Can you imagine my shock when the boys found this shadow? When I heard it mention your name? Pure glorious luck! Something I never could have predicted."

There was an air-raid siren an hour ago, Jiro, but nothing happened.

It was his mother—moments before the bomb. Jiro's vision clouded with tears. "Run, Mama. Run." But he knew she hadn't run. He was talking to her shadow, not a time machine. Nothing he said would change the outcome.

Don't be silly. Come on. We're late.

Jiro took a step forward but stopped as the Rice King tilted the hammer toward the wall. It landed on the brick near the shadow. A handful of red chips rained to the floor.

Jiro looked at him. "You bastard!"

"Now here's my threat, *Shadow Man.* I'm going to keep your mother, and you're going to provide me with all the ghosts I need to ensure my clients pay their dues. You'll still get your cut, but the day you cross me is the day I'll smash your mother to bits. Understand?"

"No. Please."

BRIANNE HILLS

"That's not the answer I predicted." The Rice King swung back the hammer with both hands.

"Yes! I mean yes! I'll do what you want!"

The Rice King held the hammer for a few seconds and then released it to the floor with a thump. His smile returned. "That's more like it."

Jiro let his shoulders slump forward and he stared at the floor. "I still don't understand."

"You don't understand what?"

Jiro looked up. "Why you think we're alike. I know how I was remade as the Shadow Man. But how were you remade? How did you become the Rice King?"

"Oh. Luck again, if you can call the bomb lucky. I was away in Mihara seeing to business when the bomb fell. In less than a second, I went from being a minor player to heading the Family. We were already raking it in from all of the shortages due to the war. When the bomb fell, we were able to jack up the price of rice ten times what I thought people would pay—easy to do when you have the trucking industry wrapped around your finger. That's how I got my name, though I'm sure people said it with distaste."

"You cheated people," said Jiro.

"They were willing to pay. Those who didn't, or wouldn't, starved."

"You evaded justice."

The Rice King hesitated and blinked. "Well, that's the definition of a successful criminal. I wouldn't look good in a prison uniform."

"You're right," said Jiro. "You can't predict luck."

"Very true. You see the hopelessness of your situation?"

Jiro dropped his hand into the sleeve of his kimono and drew out a 24-centimeter-long piece of bridge railing. He flung it to the floor, and it landed next to the desk. "Your luck just changed."

The Rice King reached into his pants pocket, for a weapon perhaps, but then stopped and gave the metal a confused stare.

On the metal's surface was the darkened image of a hand. In an instant it disappeared.

I was cheated! I want justice!

The Rice King grasped his throat and staggered to the corner of the room. He made a wet choking sound as his face reddened. For a few seconds he locked eyes with Jiro, glaring with malevolence. But as his face turned purple, the malevolence fled and panic took over. The Rice King reeled onto his desk, clawing at his neck for relief. After another minute, his thrashing ceased and he went limp.

Jiro found himself touching his own neck. He'd seen so much death, yet the Rice King's writhing end left him shaking.

He finally shook himself from the sight and approached the brick wall. "Mama?"

We have to go, Jiro. The bank . . .

"No, Mama, I have to stay. But you can move on now that I've found you."

You're being obstinate for a man your age. Her voice was growing more distant. It had a metallic ring.

"You're almost gone from me, Mama." Jiro felt

73

his eyes burn with tears. "Do you have anything to tell me?" He sobbed. "I love you."

Oh, Jiro. Her voice was barely a whisper. *Stop being stubborn.*

Jiro leapt out of his desk chair at the sound of the knock. He hustled past the exhibits and down the stairs. It wouldn't be Four Fingers this time.

He yanked open the door.

A young man on the other side jumped and stared wide-eyed at Jiro. He was thin at the waist, but a squareness in the shoulders hinted at athleticism. His hair was well groomed, a bit long for Jiro's taste, but that was the fashion nowadays. His chin was dimpled like his mother's, and movie-star cheekbones and long eyelashes made Jiro think he might be a ladies' man. He wore gray slacks and a plain blue shirt with an open collar.

"Father?"

"Takeshi!"

His son hesitated, but Jiro didn't wait for him to find his courage. Jiro seized his shoulders and pulled him to his chest. "Takeshi!"

"Father!"

Jiro felt Takeshi's arms around him, unsure at first, but then tighter. "It's true; it *is* you."

They parted, wiping their eyes.

"How have you been—all these years?" Jiro asked.

"Fine. Uncle Hiroshi treated me like a son. I never wanted for anything."

"Good. That's good."

"Oh, and I'm married now. Her name is Anzu."

"That's great! A nice girl?"

"Of course. We both teach at the same secondary school in Kyoto."

"You're a teacher. Oh, Takeshi, life has turned out so well for you. Come upstairs where we can talk."

"Yes, it's time," said Takeshi. "I want to see."

They climbed the stairs and entered the museum. Late morning light flooded the room.

Jiro looked at Takeshi and swept his arm before the exhibits. "Here it is. What you've heard about on the news. My life's work—my new life, that is. I want all of Japan to see it. The entire world. The dead who refused to die. Forever with us to testify about the horrors of the atomic bomb."

Takeshi walked among the exhibits, sometimes pausing, always wide-eyed. He returned to Jiro. "Atomic shadows," he whispered.

Jiro nodded. "Listen, Takeshi. I have to explain something. These past thirteen years, I couldn't see you. It's not that I didn't want to. I agonized about it constantly."

"You hardly had a choice, Father."

"Sure, I had a choice. But the bomb changed everything. I couldn't move away from Hiroshima. This new calling of mine, you know. I had to associate with bad people—only for money of course. It was better that you weren't here. It was better that you thought I was dead so you could carry on with your life."

Takeshi's gaze had wandered as Jiro was speaking. His wondrous expression had transformed to a smile.

"I'm so proud of you, Father. Has anyone said that to you yet? Has anyone given you credit for this achievement?"

"No, Takeshi. But hearing it from you is more precious to me than cheers of the entire city."

"What a gift you've left for Hiroshima, for me. What you've started here, I will finish. Anzu and I will move to Hiroshima—I don't fear the stigma anymore. I promise the world will know of your efforts."

"Well, I'm hardly dead yet," said Jiro. He touched his throat. His voice had a funny ring to it. Too much crying, no doubt.

"I estimated you were directly below the blast," said Takeshi. "The rays of the bomb did such strange things. In these cases, it left shadows. But your shadow had dimension, movement and sound. It's almost as if you're real."

Jiro snorted. "That's not even funny." But his voice sounded muffled as if his ears were clogged by a cold.

Takeshi turned to him. "I'm so happy I got to see you—to tell you that I love you. To say how proud I am."

"No!" Jiro reached for Takeshi, but his hands were little more than shadow, gray smoke hanging in the air.

"You've earned your rest, Father. Go, and join the shadows."

Life in Steam

written by

Grá Linnaea

illustrated by

RYAN BEHRENS

ABOUT THE AUTHOR

When Grá Linnea was a kid, he wanted to be motorcycle daredevil Evel Knievel. Now he lives in an intentional community in Eugene, Oregon. While he didn't become a stunt man, that's probably for the best. In his many working lives, he has been a recording engineer, a composer, a counselor and a guitarist in a touring heavy metal band.

He began writing fiction four years ago, and it has quickly become so important that he says the rest of his life has warped around its gravity, like a black hole. The same time he placed in this year's Contest, Grá graduated from the esteemed Clarion Writers' Workshop, won the Whidbey Writers Award and sold twelve short stories. He is now an associate editor for Shimmer magazine and facilitator for the Wordos writing workshop, whose members have consistently placed in this anthology.

Grá currently works as a gay-rights activist and open-source software advocate and teaches classes on how to be happy.

ABOUT THE ILLUSTRATOR

Ryan Behrens of Olympia, Washington, must have been waiting for a reason to make the Illustrators of the Future Contest his first art contest entry. That's because Ryan has been painting for about seven years and drawing for far longer than he can remember (and he can remember a lot). In 2002, at just 19, Ryan attended the Art Institute of Seattle, studying graphic design. Now, at 25, Ryan's ambition is to make a living with his art. In the meantime, he's been cashiering at a local grocery store for the last five years.

When not at work helping customers, Ryan is likely animating his own cartoon creations, creating a comic book series or in the middle of painting something. He says the Contest posed quite a challenge to stretch his mind farther into the science fiction world than he had been in the past. In fact, Ryan finds every new piece of artwork has its challenges (artist willing). Ryan's idea of success is to wake up every morning and be able to put his "God-given talent" to use. He's especially excited to have been selected and looks forward to having his artwork appear on the cover of a book.

Life in Steam

> *You ask proof of God's work? Look only to the vault of heaven. He created the sky as a solid firmament, that we might cross it. He gave us the knowledge to build machines that cling to that firmament and crawl the distance from our island of rock to many others. What other proof would you ask?*
>
> —*The Gospel of Arden Clock-Maker*

The *Ira Deus,* like all spider-ships in the Dominican Armada, had protectively small windows with thick plate glass that obscured vision. Mendel could still see the dark curve of God's firmament through the port window in his quarters. But after four months aboard, he missed seeing the full expanse of creation and missed, even more, standing on real ground in fresh air.

He looked old. At forty-two, half his hair was gray. He adjusted the miter on his head and wished he could look dignified, but young. He asked the Lord's forgiveness for his vanity.

It was about time for Adson to fetch him. He steeled himself but still flinched when the sharp knock came. The sliding door to his quarters opened before he could grant Adson permission to enter.

Mendel didn't turn from the window. He knew Adson would be standing at attention in the door frame. Adson was adept at looking disrespectful while maintaining a subservient pose.

Mendel still looked with wonder—and a little nervousness—on their ship's ability to cling, like a tick on a dog, to the inner surface of the great sphere of Heaven. A huge iron spider leg passed his window and hooked into the firmament, pulled the *Ira Deus* closer to the planet known locally as Wood.

Adson cleared his throat. He was a grim man, fifteen years younger than Mendel, but somehow he looked older, resigned. Church regulation called for at least two visible crucifixes on all clothing; Adson wore a ring of eight around his neck.

Outside, steam shot from the leg joint and dispersed to tiny wet diamonds. Mendel rubbed his temples. Each rumbling movement brought him closer to the artificial being on Wood—a being he had been sent to try, judge and destroy.

It was night, so the surface of the firmament reflected little light. In a few hours it would brighten to brilliant blue as the central ball of the sun reignited and illuminated the cosmos.

Mendel turned from the portal and adjusted his inquisitional robes, dyed deep purple to mark his rank as Inquisitor in the order of the Dominicans. The fibrous cotton was too stiff to lie evenly.

"It's nearly time." Adson often said the obvious.

The ship jerked hard and Mendel grabbed the bulkhead to steady himself. Adson simply shifted his weight with the ship. The noise of the steam engines was overshadowed by a cacophonous rumble of iron crunching into stone. The planet Wood, yet another rock island embedded in the firmament, rose into his view.

Ancient accounts described people who believed planets were balls of rock floating on air. He smiled at the idea. It was only after the development of spider-ships hundreds of years ago that people risked moving past the edges of their world.

A spider leg left the firmament and tore into the scree at the edge of the planet. What had once been solid rock had been broken up by the comings and goings of many ships.

Adson still stood at attention. The grim priest had been assigned to Mendel, supposedly as an assistant. Given Mendel's last two failures, he assumed Adson was present to spy on him for the Church. Mendel's job as Inquisitor was likely at an end if he didn't take care of this Babbage machine to the Church's satisfaction.

Adson shouted over the noise, "Inquisitor, we have nearly reached the city."

"I am well aware."

The racket was deafening. Mendel thanked God that the town center was close to the edge of this world.

Heat from steam engines warmed the internal metal walls and the door stuck as Mendel tried to close it. Together they walked the narrow hall.

81

The stiff robes rode Mendel's neck with each step toward the loading dock. His stomach lurched as the ship lowered its belly for his exit. Crew and soldiers stood ready around the portal.

With a furtive glance to the men at his side, Mendel adjusted his robe again. Adson signaled and the walkway lowered, revealing a rocky expanse past the legs. The walkway was already surrounded by an agitated crowd, perhaps the entire town.

Mendel was struck by the dusty emptiness of the surroundings. *Why name such a barren planet Wood?* A short distance away was a town of low stone buildings. Further still was a huge wooden complex set into a mountain. *Was the Babbage machine there?*

Adson and the crew stood aside. It was Church policy that Mendel first meet the people alone. A symbolic gesture, as if he, they, came unarmed. This was of course patently untrue. The *Ira Deus* and the other six well-armed spider-ships accompanying Mendel could reduce this town to so much rubble.

He took a few steps out into the air and loud angry voices. The situation was already out of control.

He adjusted his miter, a signal to his crew hidden behind slit windows above. *Possible violence.* He dropped his face into a kind but stern mask, hating himself for the act.

The crowd stepped back as he strode, deliberately slow, down the walkway. He stopped ten steps from a woman at the vanguard of the crowd. She wore thin metal plates over velvet breeches. Ceremonial armor, the symbol of her status as Prefect.

Mendel held her stare. To complete the planetary landing ritual, he said, "Permission to visit?"

The Prefect's voice was tight. "Granted."

She apparently would not be placated by trivial ritual.

Someone yelled, "Murderer!" A stone struck him painfully on the shoulder. The crowd noise rose. Mendel clutched his arm, but forced himself to raise a hand in signal to belay his men from firing.

The Prefect's voice cut through the din. "Stop!"

The noise ceased, followed by uncomfortable silence. Mendel wondered if this time he'd die, killed by this crowd with the dust of their forsaken planet in his nostrils.

The Prefect stepped forward. "Apologies, Inquisitor. The rabble-rouser will be dealt with."

Mendel couldn't tell if he heard fear or insincerity. He kept pain out of his own voice. "Of course."

He adjusted his miter again. With tensions this high already, avoiding violence felt all but impossible.

The Prefect sighed, pinched the bridge of her nose. "Please address me as Dorgo, if you will."

Mendel heard Adson and the soldiers march down the walkway, no doubt forming three ranks behind him.

He looked up at the gleaming bulk of the Dominican spider-ship. Its brass belly had been lowered, making the iron legs jut toward heaven, as if it were a real spider, feeding on a bug trapped beneath it. Between the nearby legs, a polished brass cannon was leveled at the town.

He looked back to the Prefect. "I am called Mendel, Prefect Dorgo."

He heard Adson make a noise. It was considered unconscionably vulnerable for an Inquisitor to give his name. While here, he was not a person, he was his station. All they needed to know was that he was here to judge.

Why had he told her his name? Adson would no doubt make note of it.

The Prefect turned. "I suppose we shall take you to quarters."

Mendel unpacked his small case in the bunk room, using the repetitive movement of folding clothes to calm himself. As always, Adson himself stood guard outside Mendel's room.

Mendel stepped onto the bed, using a hammer to pound an iron nail to mount a crucifix to the wall. Soon he would see the artificial being. His breath caught, his thoughts a confusing mix of guilt and excitement. It was true, he was eager to see it, giddy. But his mind drifted unbidden to his purpose on Wood. He gave up hanging the crucifix and let it drop to the bed.

The last two planets he had visited were home to interesting Babbage machines that used iron gears to run fantastic programs. He had forgotten his station a number of times in his excitement. He had been reprimanded later.

On one planet there was a difference engine the size of a cabin. One could type statements in through a set of keys. The machine would slowly letterpress a response onto parchment scrolls. It was programmed to respond as if it were listening, repeating part of the entered text back. A reasonable mockery of life, but not an abomination as defined by the Church.

Another planet had had a steam-driven ordinator. It communicated through punch cards translated through a sort of player piano. He had had many interesting "conversations" with it, like speaking through teletype with an intelligence on the level of a dog.

He had given the scientific staff recommendations, areas of investigation to avoid in case the Church returned to check their progress. They didn't exactly meet this offer with delight, but at least he had tried to help them.

Adson had been assigned to him shortly thereafter.

Then there was the Babbage Mind, the last true artificial being he had interviewed. His breath hitched and he picked up the crucifix, asked God to forgive him. He had been told many times that feeling guilt for doing God's work was an affront to Him.

The Prefect had suggested Mendel not leave his room till they came for him. The din of shouting mobs hadn't ceased since he'd arrived. He smoothed the sheet on his bed, repeating in his mind that he need not fear. It would take a single word to initiate a full attack on this planet. The same would happen if he was killed.

Adson rapped on the door. It was time.

The Prefect's office was whitewashed to gleaming. Unlike other structures Mendel had seen so far, it had real glass windows, similar to the *Ira Deus'* portals, but thinner and more wavy.

As he sat, Mendel noticed how sparse she kept her workplace. No pictures of family. No pictures at all. Just wood file cabinets, papers and her desk. He felt sad looking at this room.

Adson stood ramrod stiff by the unadorned door. The Prefect ignored Adson, but regarded Mendel with such intensity that Mendel felt the urge to rush out his thoughts, but he stayed silent.

Eventually she sighed and said, "I'm trying not to blame you personally."

Her bluntness shocked him. He spoke without thinking, "The politics of this are out of my control. I—" He stopped, knew his eyes must have flicked back to Adson. It took a moment to pull his composure tight again.

She looked disappointed. "We are a poor planet with little resources. You know this. We have logged and mined our planet bare. My people have put much of themselves into our Babbage machine."

Adson said, "The Church is aware."

Mendel raised a hand, hoping to keep Adson quiet. The Prefect opened a drawer in her desk. "I have a letter of protest from the navigational guild. They require our calculations to plot shipping routes."

Mendel said, "I have not yet made my evaluation, so there is nothing to protest."

Her cheeks flushed red. "The Church has overlooked Wood for decades. Now that the business district is pressuring them . . ." Her eyes flicked to Adson and she lapsed into silence.

Mendel looked away, embarrassed. She was

right; he was here because the Church had made a new political alliance. A hundred years of peace on Wood was to be thrown away for new financial bonds. He was here to eliminate competition, nothing more.

He wished he could speak so bluntly. *I know the navigation guild depends on your Babbage machine. I know the Church is being influenced by competing guilds.*

I know. I know. I know.

"Inquisitor, our Babbage machine is all we have."

I know. "Prefect Dorgo, I will be fair in my duties."

The Prefect put her hand to her hairline. When she brought it down, her eyes looked dead.

Mendel stood. "I'll need to see the Babbage machine now."

The conversational chamber was plain and smelled of wood oil. Slats of light came from long thin windows, forming lines that met over an inlaid brass sundial in the center of the wood floor.

Mendel was surprised to step into this tiny room. The structure outside was huge, easily the size of his ship. If the Babbage machine were even half the size of the building containing it, it would be remarkable indeed. He wanted to rush through the inner door, see the workings. An almost imperceptible rumble vibrated the room, like the room was alive. Mendel found it inexplicably calming.

Adson seemed to take in the room with a glance, then stood near the door. The Prefect moved to the other side of Mendel, as if to put him between her and Adson.

Similar to the floor, the walls were made of dark wood. The overall effect, he had to admit, was of a chapel, but darker and with no pews. On the far side of the room, where the altar might go, Mendel saw three frames. The center rectangle was a boxed grid, much like a wine rack, but with ebony dowels stacked within each square. On either side of the center box were two other rectangles, raised slightly with smooth tan surfaces. Tendrils of steam floated from a door beneath the leftmost box.

Mendel looked to Adson. "Please wait outside."

The priest looked as if he would argue. There were not many times Mendel could pull rank on Adson, but Mendel still had the right to do his duties uninterrupted. Adson looked at the Prefect, bowed and stepped out.

Mendel had never seen a Babbage machine of this sort. *The gears must be hidden behind these walls, but where was the input device?*

"Is this your difference engine?"

The Prefect hesitated, then said, "Just the speaking interface."

Speech? He suddenly felt shy, like a child. "How do I speak with it? Will it hear me?"

"He . . . it is already listening."

He. Mendel was about to comment when the noise rose dramatically. Steam fluted from hidden holes in the corners of the room. More flowed from beneath the door and between the dowels.

Dowels shot in and out from the center box, glistening with black oil. A low hum surrounded

Mendel and his eyes were drawn to the tan frames. They vibrated, visibly changing with the tone. Within the hum were other sounds, almost discernible as words.

The immediate noise stopped but the deep hum continued, lower, distant.

"How . . . how do I ask—"

With a great clacking sound, the dowels recessed in unison. Then the impression of a face formed, as if a giant pressed his face against the dowels from behind the wall. The face looked like a man, older than Mendel, somehow wiser. A deep wheeze vibrated the tan panels.

The voice surrounded him like a great pipe organ forming words. "Welcome, honored guest of the Dominican order."

The dowels changed to create the appearance that the lips moved, but the huge voice came from elsewhere, everywhere. Mendel could feel it as much as hear. His mind spun. Perhaps the tan squares were leather stretched over a frame, somehow vibrated to make sound. The room's acoustics made the voice sound close and loud as if the Babbage machine spoke at his ear.

Mendel tore his gaze away to the Prefect, forgot to feign detachment. He looked back to the wooden face. "Thank . . . Thank you, Babbage machine."

The face seemed to turn toward Mendel. *How could it see me?* Mendel waited through more clacking and wheezing. "The people call me Wood."

The Babbage machine was named for the planet? "Should I call you Wood?"

Clickclickclick. "If you don't mind."

Mendel again looked at the Prefect. She was avoiding his gaze. He regained his composure, remembered his station. His job was to prove or disprove the validity of this machine's intelligence. Everything he had experienced so far could be a theatrical ruse.

"I'll need to see its workings."

The Prefect spoke rapidly. "This display is merely a demonstration of our—"

Mendel cut her off with a hand. "Prefect Dorgo, it would be best if I spent some time with just the machine. Perhaps a technician could show me around."

Muscles worked in her jaw. "Of course."

She walked to the inner door and knocked. It opened and a cloud of steam spat out an old man, dressed in loose-fitting leathers. He was followed by more steam and noise. He quickly closed the door behind him.

The Prefect said, "Ah, engineer Benson."

Mendel tore his gaze from the wooden face and composed his features before walking to the engineer and shaking his hand. "You are the programmer?"

The old man had looked angry as Mendel approached, but now laughed. "Really more of a maintenance man."

He had a warm smile, covered in wrinkles. The smile unsettled Mendel. This was the most kindness he had received since he had arrived on Wood, or long before that. He had to work hard to maintain his formality.

The Prefect, with a nod to Mendel, took her leave. Benson led Mendel through the door into the steam and noise. The air smelled of mineral oil and hot water. Mendel couldn't see more than a few feet.

Ahead he heard Benson's voice. "Watch your step. Stairs ahead."

Steam cleared away from thin iron stairs. He was not in a room, but a huge chamber, a chasm.

Pipes ran everywhere, some venting steam. The center of the room was occupied with a whirling mass of metal and wood, axles and spinning disks. The rods themselves twirled and connected to other axles. Disks transferred from one rod to another.

Mendel marveled at patterns appearing and disappearing in the flashing intersection of rods, flowers and triangles, circles and spirals. Shapes held together for moments and moved along the surface, only to disperse into individual spinning brass disks on separate axles.

He squinted to look closer. The disks themselves spun and rotated in any number of directions, intersecting with each other. The mass changed shape, growing and shrinking, as if it were building and unbuilding itself over and over. With the ever-present steam, he couldn't see the edges of it.

Mendel yelled above the din. "This is the brain of your Babbage machine?"

Benson kept walking. "This is merely a fraction of Wood's consciousness."

Mendel was sorry to leave the amazing display, but followed Benson further into the chasm. As they distanced themselves from the pipes and steam, Mendel expected it to become cooler. The air became drier, but hotter.

Benson said, over his shoulder, "We're approaching

the foundry, just a few levels above the mines. The building on ground level is merely housing for miners and engineers. You can see Wood is much, much larger than the building above."

Mendel could see the stairs go farther down, beyond his sight. "The Babbage machine is entirely self contained?"

"Wood is much more than he appears."

Again, he.

They stepped off the stairway into a hallway carved in the stone. It ended at a chamber with low whitewashed ceilings and bright magnesium lighting. Workers sat at wooden tables laboring over metal discs.

Benson led Mendel to a near table. He picked up a brass disc from a slot at the edge of the workbench. "We call these neurons."

The disc was beautiful, cut with a mad filigree of holes, slots and round tabs—some fixed, some fitted to slide.

Benson spoke with joy. "The disks fit together, interact with one another in a variety of ways that even I don't understand."

Mendel had so many questions he could barely contain himself. He was confused with a mix of excitement and fear. "Who conceived of this? It's genius!"

"In a way, Wood himself is the creator."

Mendel felt pain skitter across his scalp. He had to know more about this marvelous machine, but dreaded the conclusion he was drawing.

Benson lifted a hand to forestall Mendel's questions. "I'll show you."

He led Mendel to a desk connected to the wall. Embedded in the desktop was another square of thin dowels set together in a grid. A worker placed a sheet of grid-marked paper onto the square. The dowels beneath raised and the worker rubbed the paper with charcoal, revealing a quarter circle with intricate markings on it.

"Four of these etchings give the basic template for a new neuron. Other stations give instructions as to refinements and insertion of moving parts."

Benson led Mendel to a station near a back door. Mendel followed, almost in a daze.

"Here the disks are polished and eventually fed into the system."

Benson picked up two disks. They gleamed like mirrors. "These two disks can interact with each other in hundreds of ways." He slotted two sharp edges of one disk into the holes of the other. "The genius was in training Wood to design his own neurons, over two hundred years ago. Since then, no human programmer has touched Wood."

He turned one disk until the two fit together like puzzle pieces. With another twist the disks came together like a clamshell. "The neurons act as number crunchers as well as a memory system."

Mendel couldn't breathe. His heart sank.

Benson looked Mendel in the eye. "Inquisitor, I am not going to let anything happen to Wood." Mendel noted that he was very alone and everyone in the room was looking at him.

Benson continued, "And yet, I am leveling with you. The Prefect would like me to trick you somehow. You are much kinder than I expected and I can see your love of machines, so instead I'm showing you how marvelous Wood is. It's hard to damn something so beautiful, isn't it?"

Mendel looked at the floor. This Babbage machine far exceeded the Church's edicts. It was an abomination.

"It's ingenious," he said.

The Prefect was pacing her office when Mendel and Adson entered. Mendel stood motionless until she noticed them.

"Inquisitor. Please join me at my desk."

Mendel lowered his eyes and walked over to the proffered chair. Adson stayed at the door.

The Prefect waited till Mendel was seated before circling her desk and sitting. "Do you intend to destroy our livelihood?"

Mendel didn't look up from the Prefect's desktop. "Wood is a very impressive piece of technology."

It took her a while to answer. "Yes."

He wished he could send Adson out of the room. "Your people think of it as 'him.' He has a name. The way Benson speaks, it's almost as if people worship Wood."

The Prefect spoke slowly, as if she was choosing her words carefully. Mendel noticed she was looking back and forth as she spoke, from him to Adson. "Wood is not alive, but merely a reasonable facsimile of life. We are dependent on the wisdom we can glean from . . . it."

He could parry with her all afternoon. But there was nothing he could do. He had his orders and knew the outcome the Church expected. Everything else was formality.

He felt numb. "Prefect Dorgo, by the order of the Dominican council, I must order the destruction of the abom—"

The Prefect slammed her chair against the wall behind her as she rose.

Mendel forced himself to continue. "The artificial being known as Wood."

Mendel didn't look back at Adson. "My order is destruction, by burning, at noon tomorrow."

Adson cleared his throat. "Church policy dictates disposal within a half-hour of your final decision."

Mendel looked back at the Church spy. "The Babbage machine will be burned *tomorrow*." He might lose his position in the Church, but it was the closest thing to mercy he could give these people, time to say goodbye.

The Prefect gripped the edge of her desk as if to restrain herself. "The people may not allow that to happen. I can't guarantee your safety."

The threat was clear. Mendel got up and turned his back to her. "Adson, prepare the ship and have the men ready."

He stood motionless until Adson left. He thought he might try to say something consoling, something human. When he couldn't stand to be with her any longer, he rushed to the door.

It was cold out in the night, and the rock Mendel lay on colder still. He shivered as he gazed into the vast starry firmament miles above him.

Tomorrow he would confirm his order to destroy the Babbage machine, if the people didn't kill him first. He almost wished to die, but then the Church might order the planet razed as an example.

He reached to the sky above, meditated on the clockwork precision of the firmament, the divine order of God's creation. His mind again drifted to the last time he had ordered an abomination destroyed. He pressed his palms against his eyes.

Praying failed to calm his swarming thoughts. *Why was artificial life an abomination?*

He wanted to scream into heaven, demand an answer. Just once, he'd like to hear directly from the Creator. He knew he should ask forgiveness for demanding anything of God, but a thought bounced around his head. *Forgiveness from who?*

He lay there, alone, waiting for his answer.

The conversational chamber was pleasantly warm and moist compared to the cold night outside. It was late; Mendel imagined Benson and the day-shift engineers were sleeping in the huge dormitory above, but the chamber was still loud with steam and distant machinations. He walked to the brass circle and gazed into the center frame. His body shivered with the outside cold held in by his robes.

The clatter intensified and the dowels sorted out into the familiar face. "Welcome, Mendel."

Mendel forced himself to smile. "Wood."

The wooden lips moved. "How are you?"

Mendel started to pace. When he looked up, the face was tracking him. "I am troubled."

RYAN BEHRENS

A clattering pause and Wood said, "I would like to help."

Mendel stopped pacing and spoke with his head bowed. "You shouldn't want to help me."

The wooden face frowned. "Why?"

"You know what the Church wishes me to do."

Clickclickclick. "You have sadness about that."

Mendel's chest constricted. He couldn't talk about his duty. Not yet. "The people worship you, don't they?"

Clickclickclick. "Some."

"What do you think of that?"

The face rearranged into a frown. "I am not a god to be worshiped."

Mendel looked up. "What are you then?"

"I am me."

Mendel rubbed his face. "Do you *feel* alive?"

Clickclickclick. "I am a reasonable facsimile of life." The face altered to smile.

Mendel couldn't help but smile himself. "That sounds familiar."

The face raised an eyebrow. "The Prefect has asked me to give certain answers. She impressed on me that my meetings with you were, in her words, crucial."

Mendel's eyes felt hot. "That may be true."

"Sadly, I am not very adept at lying."

Mendel's chest got tighter still and his sight blurry. He felt too short of breath to speak.

Wood spoke again, "Your duty. You have done it before?"

Mendel's knees let go and he hit the floor. His

tears fell onto his hands and his breath came out in violent puffs.

Finally his voice came to him. "It wasn't nearly as advanced as you." He had to pause to let breath come. "It was like a child."

When he looked up, he saw the face of Wood staring down at him. Maybe it showed sadness.

Mendel raised his hands to Wood. "It . . . it never understood what was happening to it. It wasn't smart enough to understand death."

He let his hands fall. "In the end, as it was burning, it asked me for help."

He ran the long path from the conversational chamber to the Prefect's building. His robe and rumpled miter were balled under one arm so as to not slow him. He wiped tears from his face as he formed the conversation he would have with the Prefect.

He would be blunt. He would tell her everything and together they would figure how to deceive the Church. They would have to pretend the Babbage machine was a fake or had been destroyed. Something.

He heard gun shots as he passed the first of the stone buildings on the edge of town. Then the sky reflected flames.

He rounded the corner and saw the *Ira Deus* burning. A mob, townspeople in dark clothes, burst from its loading dock, followed by Church forces. Other ships fired into the crowd with steam-powered repeating guns. The low rhythmic pop of the guns was followed by cracking earth and screaming men and women. The crowd scattered, forms leaping over bodies. Some ran at soldiers, others ran for cover behind stones and buildings.

Some, yelling, brandishing hammers and saws, ran toward Mendel. He ducked into the shadow, trying to be silent, listening to his own rushing heart. Somehow, he had to signal his men to stand down. But he'd never make it across this sudden battlefield to his ship.

He felt a hand clamp to his forehead and a knife press against his throat. Prefect Dorgo's voice spit in his ear. "Your work is nearly complete."

"No." He felt his sweat bead under her hand. "I came back to find you."

He could almost feel her bitter smile. "I'm sure you did."

With each intake of breath he could feel the knife bite into his neck. "I spoke to Wood."

"Wood is much more forgiving than I am, priest."

"Let me help."

She jerked him back a step. "The only reason you are still alive is that you may have value as a hostage."

Mendel looked up into the madness. People had taken guns from dead soldiers and gunshots snapped across the open plain between the town and the spider-ships. One of the Dominican ships was powering up. Soon it would overrun the city. "The Church won't bargain."

The Prefect hissed in his ear. "Then we'll take you with us."

"Will you listen?" Mendel craned his neck to make eye contact with the Prefect, wincing as the knife cut deeper. "Even if you defeat the Church's forces, they'll just send more."

She looked lost. Mendel reached up and grabbed her knife hand. The knife bit deeper but he didn't pull it away. "If I can speak with them, maybe I can make them stand down."

Mendel made his way along the outer edge of town, following the Prefect's suggested route. His belt sash was wrapped around his neck to staunch the bleeding. The Prefect had promised to do her best to get the townspeople to retreat. If Mendel could get his men to stand down, perhaps he could somehow frame this as a misunderstanding, that the Babbage machine was not an abomination.

He made his way through a muddy trench alongside a wrecked building. The battle had passed through here and there were bodies, many townspeople, a few soldiers. Mendel tried to think of a prayer for the dead, but the Lord's words felt flat and meaningless.

He thought he heard less shooting, maybe the Prefect was getting people to listen. He dropped down into some scrub when a band of townspeople passed, their faces and clothes blackened with coal dust.

The shooting had definitely lessened by the time he sidled along the wreckage of the *Ira Deus*. He had the foresight to worry that his men would not recognize him under the mud and blood on his clothes. He put on his miter and turned his robes inside out. The robes were wet, but at least the purple of his station showed again.

Looking through a structural hole in an iron spider leg, he saw an encampment of Church soldiers. He walked to them making the hand signal for "don't shoot."

Adson sat at a wooden table, incongruously set up amongst rubble and bodies. He was reading a paper tape, spit from an electrified teletype.

Mendel forced power he didn't feel into his voice. "Adson, I was mistaken. You are to have the men stand down."

Adson looked up, his face contorted with rage. He took a shaking breath. "Inquisitor Mendel, the Church fears you have been compromised. The situation has been remanded to me." He stood up. "Please let my men walk you to the *Logos Deus*."

Soldiers crowded Mendel, but none touched him. His status, although undermined, clearly still created awe in these men.

Adson didn't look awed. His words slipped through clamped teeth. "Perhaps God will forgive you."

Mendel rounded on Adson. "There is no God!" he screamed.

And he believed it. No God could let all this happen.

Soldiers gasped and took a step back. Before he could think to be afraid, Mendel walked through the wall of men, who parted for him. He dropped the purple robe of his station and ran.

Mendel worked his way through brush alongside of the structure containing the Babbage machine. As he approached the door, Benson slipped out with a gunpowder rifle. "You will not harm Wood."

The Prefect had clearly not gotten to the old engineer. Mendel raised his arms. "We have no time! My men will be here any moment."

Benson raised the rifle to his shoulder. Mendel sputtered, "They can't burn the Babbage machine with me inside." He hoped that was still true.

Behind Benson the clacking noise increased and Wood's voice boomed from inside. "Please let him in, Benson."

Benson froze, his finger tightened on the trigger of his rifle.

After a moment he lowered it and motioned Mendel inside.

Mendel looked up to Wood. "If I stay with you perhaps my men will stand down."

Wood smiled. "For how long? We are delaying the inevitable and people are dying. Unacceptable."

Mendel looked back at Benson who leaned against the door, fingering his rifle nervously. Wood said, "Let them burn me."

Benson snarled, "Like rot, they will."

The three of them waited in loud silence. Mendel wrung his hands. "I know there is a way. We have to trick them somehow."

He glanced at the door to the outside. "Adson didn't see your inner workings."

The wooden face smiled and looked to Benson. "I wonder if I might be merely a puppet. Something Benson makes talk?"

Mendel laughed. The Babbage machine was clever. He considered the wooden eyes. *Did God make this being in His own image?*

A slow grin grew on Benson's face. "Inquisitor,

maybe you found me in the works, pulling strings."

Mendel was about to speak when the door burst from its frame and Benson fell. Soldiers, followed by Adson, flooded in with swords, guns and torches.

Mendel shouted to Adson, "I found—"

Adson grabbed Mendel by the shirt. "Burn it, quickly. Before this gets any more out of hand."

Soldiers split and moved to the four walls, spraying them with oil. Torches bobbed in their hands.

Wood's voice filled the room, making them jump. "Please, let us—"

Benson's gun barked. A hole splintered above a torch holder. The soldier dropped his torch and the oil lit. Many rifles rang and Benson fell back into the doorway. The room lit with flame.

Adson let go of Mendel and Mendel was suddenly lost in smoke. He could just barely see soldiers running for the outer door. Flames roared up the walls and seemed to come back down from the ceiling.

He made his way to the inner door and burned his hands pulling at the brass knob. Before he stumbled in, he looked up and saw the burning face of Wood.

Wood said, "I forgive you."

It was the Prefect herself, covered in soot, who found Mendel days later in the inscribing room. She sent away the people with her and sat on the stone floor next to the priest.

Minutes passed as they sat listening to the sizzle of her torch.

The Prefect said, "They burned the conversational chamber and the entire dormitory to the ground. Adson said we were lucky they didn't raze the town. We've been burying the dead for days."

Mendel picked up a brass disk from the floor next to him.

The Prefect said, "You didn't tell them."

He rotated the disk in his hands. The sharp edges bit his burned fingers. "They destroyed what they thought was Wood."

The Prefect sighed. "For all it matters."

Mendel thought about God and Wood. Where in the disks and pipes was Wood's soul? "Most of what makes him Wood is still intact below ground. He can be rebuilt."

She set her torch on the stone floor. "Benson is dead."

They sat in silence for a bit.

Mendel waited till she looked up again. "I could be Benson. I would like to replace him."

She sat for a bit, then started to smile, sadly, and just a little. "That may be possible, if we can keep you from being lynched."

Mendel replaced his robes with thick overalls and a knit cap to cover the scars where his hair had burned.

The sundial was now scraps of twisted brass. The voice boxes were gone. The wooden face was still frozen as he saw it last, but smooth and featureless, a bare outline.

They would have to hide Wood. Perhaps at best

they could sell calculations on the black market. Mendel would teach them what the Inquisitors would look for.

Past where the inner door had been, the iron staircase remained. He rolled up his sleeves and walked down into the heart of the brass god.

On Writing and Science Fiction

BY L. RON HUBBARD

With over 250 published works of fiction totaling over four million words in every popular genre, L. Ron Hubbard was one of the most accomplished and prolific writers of the twentieth century. In 1980 and in celebration of fifty years as a professional writer, he penned the internationally-acclaimed New York Times *bestseller,* Battlefield Earth, *a 428,750 word science fiction epic written in just eight months. That he would return a year later to write the 1.2 million word, ten-volume* Mission Earth *epic in eight months—with each volume becoming a* New York Times *bestseller—bears testament to him as a master storyteller.*

Promoting the release of Battlefield Earth *which was partly set in and around Denver, Colorado, Mr. Hubbard conducted an interview with the* Rocky Mountain News *published February 20, 1983. The following article contains excerpts of this interview published for the first time since. In it, Mr. Hubbard provides invaluable insight into the art and craft of writing, the role of science fiction in society, how he viewed himself as a writer and, possibly the most important, offers some sound advice for aspiring writers everywhere.*

On Writing and Science Fiction

*An excerpted interview with L. Ron Hubbard
as printed in the* Rocky Mountain News,
February 20, 1983

Q: *What made you return to science fiction writing after all these years?*
A: There are some activities that are simply so much fun that one can't give them up. Writing is that for me. I love every opportunity to write.

Many young writers are told to write in order to learn how to write. That is good advice. I used to find any excuse to write because I loved to do it. If I didn't have a typewriter, I wrote in longhand.

So when my fiftieth anniversary as a professional writer came around, I decided to celebrate it by doing it. It was like a present to myself, so to speak.

I chose science fiction because there is great versatility in this genre. (A writer must pick his medium as carefully as a painter must pick his brush and colors.) Besides, science fiction is no longer the stepchild of literature. *Star Wars* created an entirely new following. . . .

Plus, look at the bestseller lists and you will see the pattern repeating. Science fiction and space travel are dominant.

Q: What direction do you see science fiction taking now? Is the trend toward epics and battle stories such as Star Wars?
A: You must remember that science fiction is simply a method or a means of telling the story. Regardless of the genre (science fiction, western, spy, romance), you will find that people like a story that is both real and has a purpose. It has to say something or achieve something.

There is always an element that promotes your valueless or no-hope society, but compare their success with stories like *Star Wars* or *E.T.* . . .

Science fiction points a direction because it does advocate a future. It is about Man and his Future.

Q: What role did science fiction writers and their readers have in the development of space technology and travel—and public acceptance of it and its funding—in the 1950s and 1960s? What role does it play today in future commitment to space exploration, colonization, exploitation?
A: If you will go back through those old, gaudy pulp magazines that were being ridiculed and confiscated by irate teachers, you will find a lot of articles on space technology scattered amongst the fiction. That was because there was no other outlet for such vision.

Some who wrote for the pulps were called "just science fiction writers." But history has proven that

109

they were the ones who brought about the future—
not the naysayers.

We knew then that Man would travel to the stars
and we know it still.

There are still those who cannot create a vision
for the future and they, as before, still click their
tongues to make a living and they will, again, be
forgotten simply because they cannot create—they
can only criticize.

*Q: How would you assess the broader audience science
fiction has today? Years ago, science fiction was considered
as something for children which was not "serious"
literature. Its popularity today knows no age boundaries.
Is this indicative of an escapist attitude by readers? Or a
look to the future and what we could be?*
A: The future is the only frontier without limit
and the frontier that we will all enter and cross no
matter what we do.

Science fiction is and always has been the
literature about the frontier. Science fiction appeals
to every age group because it is about the future
and the human potential.

*Q: How do you draw from your past track in creating
character and plot? Is this the place from which science
fiction comes in general, whether the writers know it
or not?*
A: Experience helps any writer or anyone who
wants to write.

I traveled through the Far East and sailed the
high seas and did a few loops in some bi-winged

planes and gliders in my day and drew upon these for stories. I also did a lot of research for other stories.

But what is more important is the ability to see what is in front of you. Plus you have to have the ability to assume the viewpoint of your reader.

For example, in *Battlefield Earth,* the reader looks through the eyes of the hero and through the eyes of the alien. This is done by describing how each person would describe the scene and objects. It gives the reader a feeling of what it would be like to assume that viewpoint. The reader at first does not recognize the object either but should be able to do so as the description continues. But, in the process, the reader can experience the same mystery as the character in the story.

That is the ability to see what is in front of you and the ability to assume another viewpoint.

It is a good exercise for writers.

So experience is helpful but you need much more.

Q: *What does science fiction writing do for L. Ron Hubbard personally?*
A: I can answer that better if you don't restrict it to just one genre.

Writing offers creation, expression and the ultimate ability to communicate, whether you write poetry or a novel.

Science fiction is just one means or method of doing that.

With writing, you must take an idea and turn

it into little black marks on a sheet of white paper so that someone will look at it and lift those little black marks off the page and form the idea of the author.

In short, it boils down to communication.

Q: How would L. Ron Hubbard describe himself as a writer?
A: I don't know if I can take it any further than that.

I've always had the ability to put an idea down on the page. I don't really outline. I just write.

I think if I wanted to be characterized in a certain way as a writer, I would ask that it be that I am a writer who loves to write.

That is not as axiomatic as it may sound. There are a lot of writers who don't like to write and some who even hate it but are still called "writers" because they make a living at it—the 9-to-5 type, so to speak.

But it has never been that way with me. I don't watch the clock when I write. In fact, I've gone days without sleep just because I was enjoying myself so much I plain forgot.

How could one forget to sleep?

Well, imagine doing something that is more exciting than anything you have ever done and see if you worry or think about a "coffee break," or what time it is.

That's what I mean by my being a writer who loves to write.

There's really no other way to say it.

Q: *How do you work? Do you dictate or pound your fiction out on your old typewriter? Do you keep any set schedule when doing a book? Do you work from detailed character sketches and plot outlines or do you wing it? Have your working methods changed over the years?*

A: My goodness, but that covers a lot!

What I write determines how I do it. Sometimes I type, sometimes I write longhand, and sometimes I dictate.

Battlefield Earth was typed on a manual typewriter. The length was about 3,000 pages.

Each day before I went to bed I would sketch out the plot that I would cover the next day. Plus I would list out anything else that I wanted to accomplish.

I do set and follow a schedule when I want to get certain things done in a day—like exercise, if only a walk.

So I generally lay out what I want to accomplish for the day, the week, the month and then I do it. I would say this is perhaps my primary development since those early days in getting organized. It has allowed me to get more accomplished: to lay out a schedule and then do it.

Q: *What do you think about writers who take years to write a single book?*

A: I really don't think many do. They might research something for years, but I can't figure out how somebody could keep a plot in his head that long.

Some people try to equate quality with slowness. If an athlete did that he would lose every game.

Q: What advice do you have for budding writers?
A: Write and write and write and write. And then when you finish, write some more.

It may not be original advice, but it is still quite true. You learn to write by writing.

Don't try to learn *how* to write in order to write. I've seen a lot of great writers killed off when they decided they wanted to learn how to write.

Just take an idea and go with it. You may find a story that pulls you along. The story takes off on its own. It sounds silly but it happens. You have this character walking down the street and you are all ready for him to get into a taxi but he walks right on and turns into a movie theatre. Whoa! What is this? Well, follow him and see what happens.

The main thing is to write and learn the business of writing—that tough market you have to live with.

The Assignment of Runner ETI

written by

Fiona Lehn

illustrated by

A . R . STONE

ABOUT THE AUTHOR

Child of a cellist and a travel agent, Fiona Lehn seemed destined to live a life of passion and drama in other worlds— or, at least, to write about them. Her own world began in Stockton, California where she read Nancy Drew mysteries, wrote poetry and dreamed of becoming a musical sensation just like Karen Carpenter. But it was science fiction that literally hit her: While working on a BA in creative writing at UC Santa Cruz, the Zoë Fairbairns' novel Benefits *fell from the shelves of a local bookstore and landed on her head. Soon the works of Gilman, Tiptree, Le Guin and Russ got inside her head as community and inspiration.*

Since then, Fiona has worked as a high-school teacher for at-risk youth, an audio editor for film and TV and a freelance editor. She didn't lose her musical dream either. Her record label Droidfingers has released several CDs of her original music for those who dream of other worlds.

Although Fiona has had short pieces published in local magazines and the UK's Litro, this novelette is her first entry to Writers of the Future and professional sale. Fiona now makes her home in Vancouver, British Columbia.

ABOUT THE ILLUSTRATOR

A. R. Stone's work first appeared in an art show at age four with a picture entitled "If the Hippo Bites the Balloons They Will Break." By age twelve, A. R. wanted to learn to illustrate books. By eighteen, A. R. left home for Hollywood to continue a career as a costume designer. Unable to get work, A. R. took up a job in a sweatshop and then in a bookstore. A. R. was accepted into college in Colorado and earned an undergraduate degree. After working many years as an accountant, A. R. got accepted into a high-end art gallery where A. R. ended up as manager, learning tips from working artists like Sandra Bierman and Robert Venosa.

Through it all, A. R. admits that books and graphic arts have always been a first love: "Something about paper and pencil speaks to me." Relocating to Oregon, A. R. joined the Wordos group in Eugene, which encouraged A. R. to enter the Illustrators of the Future Contest. The entry's success helped inspire A. R. to sell over 300 illustrations last year in over twenty publications. A. R. is currently working on an online series of graphic novels called The Tales of Anieth.

The Assignment of Runner ETI

[THE RACE/START FILE]

Day: 1. Kilom: 0. Runners: 8.

I scuffed my racing sole against the trail and stamped my feet in an attempt to ground. The gravel of East Cherzia scraped and shifted under my weight same as in the far north, but the land here stank like unwashed socks. I had run on worse, yet terrain was no longer my only opponent. Down below me, in the thinning darkness, my competitors prepared for The Race in their own ways.

"Runner—"

I spun at the sound of the low, compelling voice in my ear, but found no one beside me on the dike-top trail. I pressed my fingers to the graft point behind my left ear where ETI's surgeon had installed the Inter-Cerebral Communicator last night. I kept forgetting it. Too much to think about. Too much thinking, not enough moving.

"Guide, need a moment," I sent back at

thoughtspeed via the ICC. I flexed, relaxed and stamped again, longing for my body to take control.

"Return to the secured area," sent Guide.

"Not yet," I sent. "I can't just get up and run 500 kiloms after spending all night on a plane. Do you know anything about body knowledge?"

"Plenty." His tone sharpened. "Nevertheless, if someone assassinates you now, then you *can't* run 500 kiloms either."

"No one followed me," I sent, scanning my dim surroundings and the hushed camps of the other Runners on the dry marsh below. All quiet, except for a low buzz from the crowds at the police barrier half a kilom away. "And even if someone had," I sent, "I could handle them. My records don't lie."

"That's not the point."

"Runners run," I sent. "Guides cannot interfere—"

"Runners try to survive," Guide interrupted. "Few succeed. Runner, ETI approached you, over hundreds of others, for a reason. But if you disobey me, I will have you reassigned."

My quads twitched. I had no desire to face reassignment. Ever.

"Fine," I sent. Better to surrender to his lead now than to waste energy sparring. Trust could come, if at all, later. I trotted down the dike bank, across the spongy ground, back into the compound created by ETI's security team. Still stamping, I peered out from behind barriers draped in giant "End Terminal Illnesses" banners, watching the newscams weave amidst similar compounds scattered around the dry marsh. The white *ETI* on my green fullbod jersey began to shimmer in the growing light. Dawn, and Race start, had nearly arrived.

Schools/Arts Charity Conglomerate had set up nearest ETI. Their publicist spoke into a newscam while their Runner, deep into her ritual, writhed on the ground, uttering incantations. I didn't need that Runner's mum-jum. I had my oath, my tenets, my will.

"Runner," sent Guide, "are you listening?"

Before I could ask for clarification, he had begun sending audio via ICC.

"Listen to everything," he sent.

I set my memchip to "direct-input" and blipped through the media feed as the memchip stored it.

". . . That's correct. Without schools, our society's future generations will roam the streets like wild animals. Without arts, our children's souls will remain undeveloped, unconnected to humanity. Who nurtures our future? Schools/Arts Charity Conglomerate serves everyone, *Feeding the Souls and Minds of Our Future . . .*"

The sun peeked over the horizon then, transforming the thin darkness into vibrant fuchsia and gold. Never had I seen anything so alive, so free. I had melted, puddled and nearly evaporated by the time Coach's words burst from some memchip archive into my consciousness, "Emotion will outrun you. Lock it down. Lock it down!"

Resolutely, I turned away and repeated my oath until it resonated within my core. *I race for my life to give life to others, I race for my life . . .*

Across the dry marsh, in the pink Homeless Aid Charity Conglom compound, Runner HAID alternately paced and pranced before a newscam. At the marsh fringes, Blue Runner ANCA stretched in silence at the center of her own enclosure. They looked like beasts in a way—lanky, muscular, taller than the security teams that guarded them, and covered sole to scalp in the colors and enigmatic letters of their host Charity Congloms.

". . . Carcinogens in suburban areas have reached an alarming level. A good seventy percent of our population now is debilitated by this issue. Anti-Carcinogen Charity Conglomerate works for everyone. . . ."

Within moments, thick fog had obscured visibility beyond a quarter kilom and coated everything in mist. No more sunrise to tempt me into wayward emotion. The damp, sickly smell increased; I almost longed for the stale, dry air of the Training catacombs.

". . . we even have to ban the public from Race start for the Runners' protection. Until all humen are safe on the streets and in their homes, Women Safe Charity Conglomerate is needed. . . ."

The buzz from the crowds at the distant fences increased. I imagined the people there, hungry, cold, waiting in vain for a glimpse of the Runners. How many had sold their daughters off to the Training program, hoping to give their daughters a better life, or merely to rid themselves of another mouth to feed? Did they suspect that Training offered the greatest gift anyone could ever receive?

Surrender to your will and run any distance
Run beyond all limits
Run until you reach the whole you seek

Training had saved me from far more than starvation. And ETI now gave me the opportunity to reach my true goal.

". . . yes, ETI exists because of the insidious nature of terminal illnesses. They have one modus operandi—a simple one but deadly—to gain power and strength until they can grow no more . . . Yes, always at the expense of the host. When they reach the point of no further possible growth, they've killed their host. . . ."

A round man wearing a pale silk suit shuffled into a circle of newscams by WOSA's compound, turned on a dazzling smile and said, "Welcome to the 13th Annual Race for the Government Gift. I am Representative Cozveli. It's my pleasure to represent our beloved government Leader here today on this historic occasion. The Leader sends his regrets. The War in Squazi demands his utmost attention."

Representative Cozveli scanned the dry marsh. "I see we have eight Runners here, representing the eight Charity Conglomerates of Cherzia," he said. "I want to wish each Runner luck on this demanding 500-kilom course. For our viewers' edification, this is not a staged race. The clock doesn't stop until a Runner has successfully passed through all five checkpoints along the course and crossed the finish line." He wiped his brow and continued. "The Runners' abilities testify not only to their superb athleticism, but to our excellent government-funded Training program that welcomes girls from unfortunate circumstances and develops them into strong, disciplined young women."

I stamped my feet, wishing he would hurry.

Bowing his head with an air of solemnity, Rep Cozveli checked his watch. "In times like these, when the public cannot support health and welfare organizations as it should, the government is proud to award a gift of 5 million lukra to the winning Runner's host Charity Conglomerate. As you know, the government generously makes this gesture above and beyond our actual responsibilities."

"Runner," sent Guide, "good luck."

"Luck with you too, Guide."

Rep Cozveli turned his back to the newscams and shuffled over to the Starting Line, a thick red strip painted on the ground. "Now then," he said, "without further ado, Runners take your marks."

The words I had trained for all my life had at last been spoken. I trotted across the dry marsh to line up with the other Runners. Acting as official starter, Rep Cozveli pulled a small red flag from his pocket and held it high.

"Get ready," he said.

Frenetic energy buzzed around me. I didn't like the Runners so close. Pink Runner HAID jostled Runner PHE at the far end of the line, vying for the full attention of a newscam. Could Runner HAID truly serve such an ego, or was she bluffing? I'd know soon enough.

I stamped again and focused on Coach's final

words from Training: "When The Race begins, all is within your reach."

"Go!" Rep Cozveli dropped the flag, and we were off—no crowd, no cheers, little excitement—my first and only real race had begun. I formed a kernel of a new Runners' Tenet in my mind then: *Training stops when the flag drops.* Or perhaps: *Silk-suited Cozveli has an overfull belly.* Under my face cover, I half grinned. Making up tenets is not so difficult. The challenge lies in creating tenets of everlasting truth. Perhaps I am too young yet to define such truths, but my tenets give me something to gnaw on.

"Runner," Guide sent, "we now have the course maps. 145 kiloms today. Dike trails, all sea level. Keep with the field and keep alert; while planning I can't monitor the scanners. That said, have me scan all bridges before crossing. Oh," he added, "steep climbs tomorrow so don't pull anything. A few minutes gained isn't worth injury."

After 24 hours of travel, briefing and virtually no running, I welcomed 145 kiloms of flatlands. Sourcing body knowledge at last, I kicked leisurely, hung back and examined the intricacies of the field.

Yellow Runner SART exhibited a delicate gait, her head bobbing like a little bird's. Runners WOSA and PHE, in orange and red respectively, loped behind her like wolves. Pink Runner HAID, exuding leonine arrogance, took an early lead, while Birthing and Population Conglom's Runner, in gray, slunk like a fox low at HAID's heels.

I instantly recognized the gait of Purple Runner NOD from No Drugs Charity Conglom. We had trained together years ago in First Stage, before we each were sent to other Training complexes for Second Stage and beyond. She'd quite possibly know me too if she looked behind her. Even with my features altered and covered, I suddenly felt very exposed.

Kilom: 3.

Store this to memchip," Guide sent, "just in case:

"To C1, head E by old dike tops, 145 kiloms.

"To C2, take cliff trail 43 kiloms, note 2,500 meter ascent.

"To C3, head SE through Toppling Forest, 32 kiloms.

"To C4, head E on hilly paveways, 37 kiloms.

"To C5, head NE across Gantugar Flats, 194 kiloms.

"To Finish, head E through Trilpa to the Capital, 48 kiloms.

"I've included detailed maps and star charts too. Keep on course. Hit each checkpoint. And take care of yourself."

Kilom: 6.

My fullbod jersey's self-hydro system amazes me. I don't feel like I'm carrying extra weight, yet water is available when I need to drink. And unlike the mocks we used in Training, this one handles and recycles all nonsolid bodily waste.

Runner NOD murmurs incessantly. She establishes

no real pace, darting ahead and falling behind again repeatedly. Reminds me of a rabbit. Thing is, she's built like a sprinter, she has the attention span of a sprinter and this is not a sprinter's race.

Blue Runner ANCA could leave us all behind. Her form and gait glisten like pure royalty. She bears the marks of a jaguar—stamina, stealth, speed—but she tries to hide it. Or doesn't know it. Nipping at the heels of Runner HAID, ANCA appears content to mimic HAID's pace. For now, at least, ANCA is merely a copycat.

Guide says I'm a deer, with endurance, strong frame, excellent mechanics, and the will to outlast anybody on the course. I told him I'd rather be an antelope than a deer, but it doesn't really matter.

Kilom: 16.

Amidst a leafy bramble, dike-side, Guide's support team dropped me a bundle containing infrared goggles and a feather-light wristwatch with navigation and positioning capabilities. I threw on the IR goggles and nav-watch and caught up to the field as they dissolved into a mass of zero-viz fog. When I entered the dense mist, I heard a scuffle and a splash, then a Runner's curse. Activating the IR on the goggles, I scanned ahead. What I saw stopped me sharp.

All the Runners had *disappeared*. I blipped through my memchip for mass Runner abductions and came up empty.

"Guide," I sent.

A splash on the right dropped my focus to Runner SART climbing out of the slough below.

"Runner?" he sent.

WOSA sat at the edge of the water looking dazed, and Runner NOD crouched almost at my feet, examining her ankle.

"Never mind."

Following headings from my new nav-watch, I eased around a tight left-hand curve and spotted the rest of the field trotting up ahead. Without the gear, I'd have missed the turn and gone for a dip too, or worse. It makes me think, based on Guide's plans alone, we could win The Race ten times over. Of course, we are not alone.

Kilom: 145. C1 Camp. Runners: 7.

Runner PHE died today while crossing a sabotaged bridge. I trotted not 20 meters behind her. A low boom sounded, then dust and debris exploded all around. Guide had me scramble down the inner dike slope and swim, through fetid mud and razor-edged reeds, to the other side. I kept picturing Runner PHE smothered by a bloody cloud, and me with her. I trekked up the far dike, tripped on a squash vine and fell on my face. To be honest, I don't remember reaching Checkpoint 1.

I suppose I was in shock. Training taught us that death played a part in The Race, but that didn't make it easy to watch. I'd run behind PHE the whole day. She'd loped with stamina and discipline. But this wasn't Training anymore. PHE wouldn't return tomorrow in a different color jersey.

ETI med squad and security team had set up camp at C1. I checked out with just a bruise on my wrist, no cuts. The reed grass alone would have shredded me without my jersey fullbod, which I now guessed bore a life-protect rating of five-star. I gave my tent a five-star rating too—tall enough for me to stand in, three times my cot's width, with a climate controller in one corner and a shower compartment in another—it was huge compared to many Training quarters and had more comforts than any home I'd ever had.

The Government Gift Representative made a public statement regarding the death of Runner PHE and the subsequent elimination of her host Conglom. Guide relayed it to me via ICC while I stretched.

"It is with sadness that we accept the withdrawal of Physical and Emotional Diseases Charity Conglomerate from this year's Race for the Government Gift," said Rep Cozveli. "This Conglomerate, established to eliminate all nonfatal physical and emotional diseases through research and treatment, wants to remind you all that 'PHE Cares.' The search continues for the perpetrators of this horrible crime. Meanwhile, our hearts go out to the friends and family of this young Runner, who clearly gave all she had to The Race."

"In all the Race records I've seen," I sent, "I never noticed his insincerity."

"How so?" sent Guide.

"Runners have no friends or family. Training orphans us and competition keeps us friendless. Yet he says the Runner will be missed. Nobody misses nobody. Why lie?"

"She died in the field," sent Guide.

"And the field is dying," I sent, stretching a tight calf gently. "Did I tell you, he wears a silk suit? Cherzians are starving and—"

"He's a politician," sent Guide. "So are you, now. Decide what matters to you and focus on it. Just leave him to me. Runner PHE is gone. We'll have to deal with losses later. Let's get our minds back in The Race. Have you packed for tomorrow yet?"

C1 camp. Time: 0232. Direct input to memchip.

Guide—"

"Runner? Everything all right? The scanners show nothing unusual."

"I can't lock it down."

"Runner?"

"The explosion. PHE. I tried meditation and even blipped through my memchip for anything that would help, but I came up empty."

"What *did* they teach you in that Training program?"

"Need sleep. Help?"

"Okay, Runner. Tell me about the day. Can you do that?"

"The day, yah. All day, *outside*."

"Better than running in Training catacombs?"

"Yah, but no trance-running."

"Did you get overtired?"

"No, but I'd expected trance-running."

"What else, Runner? What went well?"

"The fog burned off around noon."

"Good, and?"

"That horrible smell went with it."

"Yes?"

"I hit a good pace, reaching out into the energy that is."

"You ran strong?"

"My feeling of belonging resonated strong."

"You made good time?"

"I glimpsed end-time, could run forever."

"Tell me more, Runner."

"Guide dropped bags with shoes, food, med supplies. My feet swelled little. Iron stomach stayed strong. . . ."

Day: 2. Kilom: 146.

I slept nearly four hours until awakened by Guide. The med squad had filled me with IVits and hydros; I felt better than new. I taped my feet, stretched, ate, defecated and trotted on course before dawn. How many times have I practiced this routine? I feel like I am at last living my life, not merely preparing for it.

Kilom: 165.

Question: Why train Runners to master trance-running?

Answer: So they can win The Race.

Question: If the Runners must constantly remain present to conquer difficult terrain and avoid attack, when would they have the opportunity to trance-run during The Race?

Answer: Never.

Question: Why train Runners to master trance-running?

Option 1: To keep young Runners sane while putting the mileage in.

Option 2: To build up the Runner's body confidence, so when the time comes, the Runner never worries about the actual *running* of The Race.

Option 3: Need more information.

Kilom: 178.

After five hours on this slimy, scree-riddled switchback, I've covered only 32 kiloms. The steep grinding ascent, cut to challenge the mountaineer, humbles the strongest Runner. The trail, little more than a narrow ledge, pushes me toward the inner face, away from the crumbling cliff edge. My pack repeatedly scuffs against the inner wall, dislodging rocks and dust to fall at my heels and down onto any Runners below. Likewise, scree and rocks rain down on me from above. Guide chimes "take cover" every few minutes. No opportunity for meditation, only a vague notion that patience would run with me. I try to focus on that.

Kilom: 180. Runners: 6.

Runner WOSA has been condemned to reassignment. Scree felled her two strides behind me on the cliff trail, then a large boulder tumbled down from above and bowled into her before bounding over the cliff edge. Her legs were crushed.

Without thinking, I had grabbed the nearest Runner, SART, and pulled her out of danger.

I can't explain it.

A. R. STONE

Have I lost my edge? If I'd left SART alone, I'd have lost two competitors in one blow. I run to win, but I keep thinking about what I should have done. Nothing comes clear. I almost feel bad for not saving WOSA. Am I a traitor to ETI? To myself? What will I do if SART lasts all the way to C5?

Coach used to talk about locking down regret. I blipped through my memchip to access the file. "You cannot control your instincts," she said. "You can only give in to their wisdom. They live without emotion, without past or future. A Runner must live in that same space if she wants to win The Race."

Kilom: 184.

Runner NOD sat back against the inner face, knees bent, blocking the trail. When I approached, her mumbling turned to song:

"Kick on, Kick on, I'm kicking on into the night."

I knew the song well because I used to sing it out loud when I first started Training.

"Lose your voice?" Runner NOD leapt to her feet. "Coach taught you to hide yourself while teaching the rest of us to notice you. So notice you, I did, *Singer*!" She tossed a fistful of scree at me and darted up the slope, laughing.

"Sprinter!" I yelled, charging after her, but I'd lost my focus and stumbled. *Emotion will outrun you.* (Such a small tenet, so hard to remember.)

"Runner?" sent Guide.

"Well, she is one."

"One what?"

"Sprinter. Loathsome to all distance Runners for her lack of depth. Guide, Runner NOD identified me from First Stage. Coach prohibited my singing for this very reason."

"Singing what?"

"A running song I made up."

"What for?"

"Before I learned the tenets and came to understand their power, I felt lost, lonely. The song kept me company." I began trotting up the trail once again, with focus this time.

"Let's hear it," he sent.

"Kick on, Kick on, I'm kicking on into the night."

"Not bad."

"Not bad," I sent, "but external. Like ego. Coach was right. It betrays a weakness. And NOD knows it too."

"Runner," Guide sent, "your strength lies within, song or no."

Focusing on running from within, I soon passed both Runners NOD and BIP. Only a competitive field could complete that climb and reach Checkpoint 2 before sundown. We all did it. All except WOSA, I mean.

Kilom: 188. C2 Camp.

ETI had set up camp inland from the cliffs, about 50 meters from the forest edge. A dry southeasterly drifted brown pine needles against the side of my tent. I ate, stretched and cared for my feet. Guide briefed me while I sorted through the gear for the next stage.

Media coverage of The Race has trickled in, Guide said. The government's war in Squazi continues to dominate the spotlight. Military spending has reached an unprecedented two billion lukra, with one fiscal quarter remaining. Many speculate that the amount of this year's government gift will be reduced due to the war effort's rising costs.

That news tripped me up, but what came next sent me sprawling.

"If only the public would fulfill their inherent obligations to the Congloms," I sent, "then—"

"The public never defaulted," sent Guide. "The Charity Congloms depend upon the gift because of the government."

"Who says?"

"Everyone," he sent. "Except the government. When they came into power, they seized everything and funneled all monies into the military. Charities had to scramble."

"But charities don't know how to manage money," I sent.

"Who says?"

"In Training, we learned all about it."

"Consider the source, Runner," he sent. "In desperation, charities held increasingly more public fundraising events and grew competitive with others who did the same. Eventually this led to intercharity violence and sabotage."

"Didn't they lose their charity status?"

"Sure," he sent. "So they formed Congloms. When the violence had escalated, bordering on a multifactioned civil war, the government decided to subsidize one Charity Conglom a year via a sanctioned competition, rather than referee disputes year round. And so The Race was born."

Guide's perspective seemed plausible, yet I lacked proof. It occurred to me then that Training had taught me to trust no one, yet I'd never applied that rule to the core of Training itself. So the government starved the people and started The Race and now wanted to starve The Race? If so, then how would the Congloms and the public respond? And when it came right down to it, what was I running for?

Puzzled, I extracted an unmarked blue canister from the gearbag. It had a button on one end, a spout on the other.

"Guide, need information."

"Push the button only once per swarm. The can contains fifty swarmbursts, total," he sent. "More than you'll need."

"Is there something I should know, beyond avoiding a few exposed roots while running a 32-kilom soft trail?"

"Runner, this trail bisects the Toppling Forest."

I scanned my memchip and came up with a file marked "B." My quads began to twitch. "Forests never were my strong point," I sent. "Too many *bugs*."

"Toppling Forest," he sent, "once the grandest Dougla-Ponda pine forest in the world, now terminally infested by the mysterious mites of DuSanto."

"Guide, I think we missed something in our pre-Race briefing. Have we discussed bugs?" I lightly pummeled my trembling thighs.

"They won't bite. They might swarm, though, seeking warmth."

"Blood is warm." I stamped my feet. "How about, you let me sleep an extra hour, and I'll run extra fast?"

"Runner, you could take the path *around* the forest at less risk, but that would double the distance."

"No. Thanks."

I massaged my quivering quads, packed the canister and went to sleep.

Day: 3. Kilom: 189. Runners: 6. Terrain: Buggy.

Virtually no sleep tonight. Hazy voices: "The Race is less about running than you think, and more about you than you can imagine."

Coach's voice morphed into Guide's lower timbre and woke me with two words, "Runner, go."

I went.

Dragging my pack with me, I crawled out of the tent and into a battle. While holding off about twenty rod- and rock-wielding attackers, the ETI security crew lobbed hundreds of shiny packets over and behind them. When the invaders retreated to collect the packets, I escaped.

A media copter circled low, swirling dust and pine needles up into the sky. Its blades chopped the clamor into stuttering howls. Its spotlights blazed through the dusty mess like the lights a Runner sees before she hits a mental wall. Adding another star to my tent's rating for soundproofing, I followed Guide's directions into the forest.

"Guide, who—?"

"Food raiders," he sent. "No surprise. One Rations Day a month has never been sufficient. I'd hoped we could beat them while you slept, but they can fight. They hit other camps too. Two Runners have entered the forest ahead of you. Another took the outskirt trail."

I stopped at a clearing to stretch and tape, aware of an incessant clicking, or chirping, surrounding me. I imagined millions of little mite jaws gnashing and a tremor shot down one leg. Far off in the distance there was a great crack followed by a low smothered boom, accelerated chirping and a rushing hiss. I ducked involuntarily, my hand sliding to the canister in the front of my pack.

Fear will outrun you, I reminded myself.

"Only 32 kiloms, right?" I sent. "I'll kick out of here in less than two hours, way before dawn."

"Don't push too hard," he sent. "You have 37 paved kiloms after the forest, all hills."

"Okay."

And I felt okay, a bit shaken but gaining focus. As I trotted off, into the tireless southeasterly, my body pulsed with confidence. I surrendered to its knowledge and hit stride within moments.

The moon emitted a ghastly light on the corpses of the shattered trees. Shadows sank deep and I relied heavily on my nav-watch for navigation. Near the heart of the forest, I took a wafer out of the pack, opened it and nibbled until it was gone. Then I ate the wrapper too.

That's when I heard the man's voice. "It must be done!" it cried. "Forgive me!" With a sharp crack, the tree on my right suddenly toppled across my path.

The hollow bark hit the ground with a brittle clack and shattered. Tiny white specks spewed forth. They combined into one giant swirling mass.

"Guide, tree down," I sent.

"Runner, grab the can."

I stumbled on the great tree's remains. Hissing surrounded me.

"Can't see," I sent.

"Use the spray, Runner," commanded Guide. "Hit the button."

My gloved hands fumbled with the can. My feet sought firm footing, finding only bark shards and pine cones. My fingers pressed the button—it jammed—spray spewed—"Forgive me!" pierced the enervating hiss—I lunged toward the source—spun on a pine cone—lost the can—flew back—light flashed—a loud boom sounded—the voice howled—I fell against a tree—it toppled—tremendous crash— swarming mites—

I think I lost consciousness.

At some point, I heard Guide's voice: "Runner! Runner!" I remember that when the mites dispersed, the moonlight returned, blazing with a warmth and light far stronger than the sun's. The light caught in my nose like, like smoke. Then everything came clear—the roar, the crackling, the heat, the suffocation, the toppling, the rumble—

"Guide, *fire!*" I coughed.

"I *know*! Damage report?"

I scanned, full body. "Undamaged."

"Then get out of there."

The southeasterly raged. I ran against it, ignoring the topplers falling behind me, the mites swarming and disappearing into the heat. I left that forest with a mighty kick and hit Checkpoint 3 on the heels of the two leaders, Runners HAID and ANCA.

C3 Camp. Kilom: 220. Runners: 5.

After a precautionary fumigation and minor singe treatment, I stored the preceding account to memchip and planned to rest in my tent until the other field leaders mobilized. In those few hours, we lost half the forest and another Runner. Schools/ Arts Charity Conglom reported that the fire had consumed Runner SART.

Guide relayed today's headlines to me: "The Race: Sabotage!" The attack on our camp by "over-zealous fans" served as the teaser. Turns out the voice I'd heard in the forest belonged to a saboteur who'd toppled the tree onto me and lit the fire. He hadn't expected my spray can to explode in his face. A newscam captured him fleeing the forest. He made a full confession to the media.

"The government gift belongs to Anti-Carcinogen Charity Conglomerate this year," he said. "They haven't won for over five years. There will be no environment left if they don't receive more funding now. My daughter's asthma worsens daily and will soon be untreatable. And the forest—look at it— wasteland! If the government won't do anything, then we must join together—"

News of the War in Squazi interrupted at that moment. Our troops had fallen into another ambush, and Squazi's leader still roamed free.

Guide cut the signal. "Kind of like watching a cancer progress," he sent.

"Sounds like something Rep Cozveli would say."

"I wasn't making a joke."

(Neither was I, but there was no point in arguing about it.)

Later, Guide relayed Rep Cozveli's latest public statement: "It is an appalling thing to risk and lose young, promising lives this way," he said. "A falling rock injured Runner WOSA yesterday. She will be reassigned. Thus, we announce the withdrawal of Women Safe Charity Conglomerate from The Race. Women Safe wishes to remind you that they *'Look to a Safer World for All Humen.'*"

My quads twitched at the thought of WOSA losing everything, reentering the world devoid of hope, with only immoveable things to push against, people who didn't understand, didn't care, didn't reach beyond or within. Dead people. Moving from one Rations Day to the next. Reassignment held no wholeness, no freedom. Only emptiness. Only death.

". . . Equally distressing," Rep Cozveli continued, "we mourn the untimely death of Runner SART in the forest fire today and the subsequent withdrawal of Schools/Arts Charity Conglomerate. Schools/Arts works to create and improve educational and artistic facilities and programs, *'Feeding the Souls and Minds of Our Future.'*

"Tragedies such as this should never have occurred. The government Leader has commissioned a tribunal to determine the merits of sponsoring such a dangerous competition at this time."

"I've never heard the Rep suggest canceling one of the Races before," I sent. "Do we keep running?"

"Yes, I feel certain they'll want you to continue."

"Then why did he say that?"

"Not him, Runner."

"Who, then?"

"ETI," he sent. "Among others."

Rep Cozveli's statement prompted a massive gathering in the government city of Trilpa. Thousands assembled at the Capitol, milling around the building grounds and blocking up the city center until the police arrived in force, at which time the crowd dispersed, leaving no trace but one: The military statue of the government Leader that guarded the Capitol steps now sported a new uniform, a black fullbod jersey like the Runners wore in The Race. The letters on the statue's jersey sleeve were crimson and spelled "WAR."

My cot cradled unrest too. Maybe because I'd inhaled so much smoke in the forest, or because sleep often eluded me at sunrise. Or because I'd saved SART, only for her to die a few hours later. Coach had never mentioned how helpless a Runner feels when another Runner dies. Or that the government could end it all at any moment if they chose to. Coach trained Runners to run, impervious to peer fatalities, assassination attempts, shifting government policy and bugs. So if I was already feeling the strain, did that make me a fraud? Where was my discipline? Had I ever truly committed to my oath?

The silence unhinged me. In a brief restless hour or two, I'd lost the certainty of my body. I rolled off my cot and lay on the tent floor beneath it, putting my ear to the ground. I could hear the world breathe that way. Matching my breathing to that rhythm, I regained the sense that I was a part of the world; I could feel it in every cell of my body. As I fell into the thick sleep I craved, my oath fluttered from my lips, "I race for my life to give life to others," and I whispered, "I swear."

First, the smell tickled my consciousness. I knew its name. *Acrid*. That wasn't it. Then I heard the fizzing, and there was a *pop* that reminded me of the tranq gun they used in Training when a Runner lost her edge. Half a second later, the cot shuddered above me. The fizzing increased. I forced clarity.

"Guide, attack—" I sent.

"Runner?"

"Pops, fizzing, on cot." A drip hit my hooded scalp and the vibration bore into my skull. Not acrid. Acid.

"Acid darts," I sent. "Guide—"

"Runner, get clear," came his command.

I ripped off my hood, rolled until I hit the far tent wall and sprang into a crouch. I scanned the darkness. No one. The cot suddenly collapsed in a mound of steaming metal and cloth. A shaft of sunlight from the wall nearest the cot pierced the dim mist.

"Guide, tent wall breach, cot side."

"We see them. Are you clear?"

"I think so."

With one eye on the punctured wall, I splashed water on my head and gathered my gear. Shapes collided outside.

"We got them," sent Guide. "Damage report?"

"Need out."

"Shower."

I tested my scalp where the drop of acid had landed and felt a blister the size of a grain of sand. I thought.

"Need a new hood," I sent.

"Runner?"

I climbed into the shower compartment.

"Shower, out, how?" I sent, blotting my scalp with a damp towel. Following Guide's instructions, I removed the lower wall panel and crawled out of the tent into a supply box cave. At my feet sat a green hood with a white "ETI" printed on it. I pulled it on, ignoring the burning sensation on my scalp, and scanned the ETI campgrounds.

To my left, the security squad jostled two humen in ETI medic uniforms, one of whom was attempting to swallow an acid dart. On my right, a flash of white darted toward me. I lurched away—the blow grazed my jaw—I dove right, knocking my attacker's legs out from under him and taking down one wall of the cave with our bodies.

"Runner!" Guide sent.

Boxes, med and food supplies, rained down on us. The assassin tried to fight but had no chance. I had rest, I had adrenalin and I had no desire to stop. Not until the assassin lay unconscious and

ETI's security squad stood around me, at a cautious distance.

"Damage report?" sent Guide.

I scanned the squad's faces, finding no aggression.

"Only three of them?" I sent.

I didn't wait to find out. I secured my shoes, strapped on my pack and started running.

Guide tried to apologize for the acid dart incident, but what was the point? He'd proven himself in countless other ways, so why would I have blamed him? His life hung in the balance as much as mine, but he seemed to feel a desperation beyond that. Or maybe I read too much into what he said. And didn't say.

I didn't care who hired those assassins; it made no difference. But while I crouched there, watching the acid eat through my sanctuary, an unfamiliar urgency took hold of me. Coach had once lectured on that point in The Race when the Runner becomes so hardened. I blipped through my memchip and accessed it.

"In every race," Coach said, "the Runner hits her stride. She can run on for an undetermined amount of time—infinitely, if uninhibited by outside factors. She has reached end-time, endless time, the place where a true Runner lives. In The Race, after enough exertion, both mental and physical, the Runner begins to view end-time as the only true reality. She comes to perceive everything else as chaos, dragging her down and away from her goal.

Wanting only to reach and live in end-time, she instinctively blocks everything else out. This can be a dangerous thing to do in The Race. It can also be your only salvation."

Kilom: 221. Runners: 5. Memchip set on "direct-input" (will edit later).

We run on old paveway, gentle peaks and dips. Guide says this road, once scenic and flanked by lush greenery, carried travelers between forest and lake. But now, with forest toppling and lake long dry, every barren hilltop reveals only the Gantugar Flats down below, a constant glare stretching beyond the far horizon. The sky above Gantugar is the whitest white I have ever seen. The air warms as we descend into the high desert fringes.

The field still looks strong, although we now betray the fact that we are hunted by running in a loose defensive cluster, each Runner wary of pulling ahead or falling behind too far.

"Hold back, stay with the pack," Runner NOD chants to herself like a mantra. I am convinced she's on synth-endures gone bad.

"Guide," I send, "can we get a drug test for NOD?"

"Gantugar will test her," he replies.

Runner HAID struts out front with Gray Runner BIP trotting at her heels, imperceptibly off form. I'd bet my memchip that BIP's knees are sore. Gantugar will test her too.

Blue ANCA remains a fearsome joy to behold. She glistens in the sun, so smooth is her stride.

ANCA may be a world-class Runner, but she's still just a young woman with no name. In Training, we worked so hard to lose our real identities that eventually, we succeeded. We came to see ourselves as potential individuals training to earn a name the whole world would know. But the true gift of Training is the tenets, the oath, the purpose. The name guarantees nothing.

ETI will assign another Runner next year. One who seeks wholeness as I do now. Who believes she can outrun the death of reassignment. Who fears nothing more than a return to that state of loneliness, hopelessness, where she can only wait for luck to come and save her, knowing that even if she worked as hard as she could, she might be stuck there forever.

Guide once asked me what determined the outcome of The Race, and I said both luck and merit. A Runner without merit wouldn't make it past the first 150 kiloms; a Runner without luck could get lost on a straightaway. Me, I work hard for one and I believe in the other. *Luck is not merit, but sometimes luck is stronger.*

C4: The edge of the Gantugar Flats. 194 kiloms to Checkpoint 5.

When will The Race go through Gantugar? Will the challenge be mine?" The eagerness in my stored memchip voice from years ago shamed me for the trepidation I felt today, years later. I locked the emotion down and reviewed the Gantugar terrain file: "structurally disturbed region, source of stress unknown, extreme heat, displaced and fissured crust, sand blows."

"Sand blows," I murmured to myself while examining the gear Guide had provided. "Sand blows and *heat-shields*?" I sent, dangling the shoes before me. "Guide, are these *real*?"

Guide laughed. "Of course, just not from Cherzia. You think we still make quality goods in this country?"

His tone felt almost condescending, but what could I say? I had accepted the fact that, while in Training, I'd received limited (and sometimes inaccurate) information regarding the outside world. "So," I sent, "how did you get these?"

"I have my ways," he sent, "and they don't concern you."

"Your ways *do* concern me, Guide," I sent, trying on every Runner's dream shoes. "Don't you forget it."

In addition to the best shoes on the planet, the gearbag contained a white micro-thin cloth the length of a Runner, squared. Guide said the fabric scrambled infrared and could shelter me on Gantugar.

Guide's protection plan also included twice as much food as I would need for the two-day crossing.

"I want you to stash some food every ten kiloms," Guide sent.

"The ground is sun-baked solid. No vegetation. Stash it where?"

"Under a rock, in a crevice, wherever; we'll both map it. Runner, if anything happens, I can't get a crew in there. Seismically, it's too unstable. And with the restricted airspace, I can't even fly you out."

147

"The quakes will bury the food anyway," I sent.

"Not all of it."

"I'll have to backtrack to use it."

"It could help you survive."

"It'll slow me down."

"This race is not about speed, Runner. It's about staying alive."

"Right."

Sometimes I thought Guide was channeling Coach, who would have said the same thing: *Run with patience, and run far.*

Day: 4. Kilom: 314. Air temp: 100+ degrees. Ground temp: 120 and climbing. Pace: 97 kiloms today, 97 more tomorrow. Runners: 5. Memchip set on "direct-input" (will edit later).

We started across the great Gantugar around midnight. Slow pace due to fractured terrain. Covered only 48 kiloms before dawn. Since then, the heat has confined us to a near crawl. Still 40 kiloms to go to reach Gantugar's center, my goal for today.

A feeling of death resides here—and I don't mean the fact that only one Runner ever reaches C5. No wind, no birds, no bugs (no complaint there). Not even a sunrise, only the onset of a blinding, rejecting glare. Gantugar nurtures nothing. There is only an active death. I imagine Gantugar's ridged and shredded crust thinly veils giant shifting slabs of rock below. They all rotate toward the churning vortex of the Gantugar where, like in a maelstrom, they plunge down into the core of the world. This is the place where the world dies. I wish I had some Runners' mum-jum now.

Kilom: 324. Runners: 4. Damage report: as follows.

Iron stomach has melted. I can suck on saltsweets and wafers until they dissolve but can digest little else. Scalp rash has developed. Maybe from acid residue. Guide had cancelled my C4 med check. Must've had another rat on the squad.

Speaking of rats, Runner NOD fell into a rattler nest this morning and died, according to No Drugs Charity Conglom. When I last saw her, she was shouting at people and things only she could perceive, "Across Gantugar you shall race, all the way home, in first place," and whirling like a dust devil. She reeled southward calling, "Singer! Singer!" like a broken doll.

Synth-endure drugs don't mix well with severe heat; I bet hallucinations got her. Thing is, there are no rattlers out here. I believe she was crazy, but how she died, well, only Gantugar will ever know the truth of that.

We trot amidst kiloms of sand blows, some knee-high, others twice my height. I skirt the crater bases. Each step springs a tense question: Will the sand bear my weight or collapse? Tension is cumulative. I disperse it with rumination. *Sand blows, like emotions, erupt. But do they travel any real distance?*

I keep the field before me to avoid shoulder-checking. As usual, Runner HAID leads, her posture forced like a grimace of determination. At her heels, Gray Runner BIP keeps pace, her knees now visibly swollen. Blue Runner ANCA shows no signs of injury nor of taking the lead. I spend a lot of my time watching her run and willing myself to feel as effortless as she appears. Guide says to focus on myself, but what does he know? My self is being roasted alive with three other Runners who'd celebrate if I dropped dead. It's far better to focus on the sublime and will myself to become it.

Kilom: 354. Gantugar's Center. Air Temp: 110. Ground: 125+.

A meter-high cliff rings the sunken heart of Gantugar. I blistered my palm on the descent. The ground here exhibits violent rupture. Thin brittle plates crunch under my feet like eggshells.

No quakes so far, but the heat could torch any climatic simulator. The glare burns through my goggles, scorching my lashes and stinging my eyes. My foot tape held tight today, but the heat-shield soles have warped into jagged-edged waves. The rash on my head oozes and has spread to my shoulders and the backs of my hands. Guide had me use a salve packet from the med kit, but nothing can heal in this place.

Day: 4. The Ambush.

The sun was setting when it all went wrong.

"Runner—" Guide's voice felt urgent, interrupted. I heard a low hum and everything went black.

I awoke to Guide calling via ICC, "Wake up. Runner ETI. Can you hear—"

"I'm awake," I sent.

"Damage report?"

I scanned, full body. "Bruised but no severe pain; limbs immobilized; shoes?"

"Shoes?"

"No shoes," I sent.

A weight pressed my back against the hard, warm ground. I opened my eyes.

"Runners HAID and BIP are here," I sent.

The two Runners towered over me, the edge of Gantugar's glare receding behind them. Twilight. A tiny synthmetal weapon glittered on HAID's finger like a bulbous ring.

"HAID's got a stun device?" I sent.

"Don't provoke," sent Guide.

"I can take them, if I could just get up—oh."

The limp body of Runner ANCA lay across me, her forehead gashed and swollen above one eye.

"Guide, Runner ANCA—"

"Pretend to be worse off than you are," he sent. "You want them to leave you there."

I moaned and rolled my eyes.

"It's time for us to go," Runner HAID said. "Too bad you can't join us." Her voice sounded higher pitched than I'd imagined. More like that of a weasel than a lion. "Your fancy shoes just didn't hold up," she said, tossing the heat-shield soles at me amidst a flurry of shredded leather and fabric I assumed were the remains of my shoe uppers.

"You run with ego," I said, "yet you feel you must cheat to win. That's puzzling, HAID. Have you no faith?"

The insult did its job. HAID shifted her weight, glanced sideways at BIP. A look of confusion flashed across her face before it became sheer anger.

"I can win all right. Get up, ETI. I'll prove it to you!" She stamped her feet.

"Runner?" Guide sent. "What's happening there?"

I nodded toward my shoe remains. "How about barefoot, HAID, across Gantugar? I can take you. Cut my binds; let's go."

HAID snorted, lunged toward me; BIP yanked her back. HAID stamped and glared at us both.

"Runner ETI?" Guide sent. "Respond, please."

"Need a minute, Guide," I sent.

"Well, HAID, if we don't run it," I said, "You'll live out your whole life never really knowing."

"Knowing what?" asked HAID.

"If you can live up to your ego's delusions," I said.

HAID snorted and stamped away. She came back with bullish intensity, a pack in each hand, one of them mine. "You think you're so strong," she snarled. "Let's see you get there without this." She whipped one pack overhead, flinging its contents out and away. The other, mine, she emptied on the ground at her feet.

"What are you doing?" BIP yelled, ducking under the fusillade of supplies and gear.

"Runner, what's going on there?" sent Guide.

"Look, it's Rations Day on Gantugar!" cried HAID, still spinning the pack above her.

"Stop it!" yelled BIP.

"Runner! *Defuse* the situation," sent Guide. "Don't aggravate it."

"They may fight," I sent. "Give me a minute."

HAID, finally dropping the empty packs, turned on BIP. "Don't tell me what to do."

"We agreed to put them out of The Race, not starve them to death," BIP whispered.

"I said, *don't*!" HAID aimed her stun device at BIP.

"Runner?" came Guide's call via ICC.

After a moment, BIP cowered, nodded and turned back to face me. HAID slowly followed suit. I heard a low hum and everything went black.

The howl of tempestuous winds woke me, though there was not the slightest breeze. Thunder rumbled beneath me, a vibration, gathering strength. The ground heaved. I opened my eyes to a dusky sky lit low in the east by a broken sun. I squinted and scanned the horizon that lurched and dipped like a stormy sea. There was no sign of the traitorous Runners. And that was not the sun.

"Guide—" I sent.

No answer. I tried again. Nothing. Where was Guide?

The ground rolled in long unending waves. I tried to sit up, then remembered Runner ANCA. Hands and feet taped, forehead trickling blood, the form that had soared with unicorn grace through this challenge now lay broken and abandoned in the burning heart of Gantugar. I slid her onto the ground beside me. It took some time to rouse her, and then she just coughed and fell unconscious again.

All at once, the windless howl ceased, the ground shuddered and abruptly stilled. My ears rang. My heart pounded. Despite my Training, I found myself fighting off panic. A fairly stock ambush took on a whole new meaning when I found myself lying in the center of it. Had I never confronted the reality that I might actually succumb to the perils of The Race? Losing had never seemed like a real option. I'd never included it in my visualizations. What self-respecting Runner would?

I looked at ANCA. I forced a breath. Then another. And again.

It was all such a waste.

Worming my way to the pile of gear HAID had dumped and strewn about, I nosed around until I found an anti-inflam. With bound wrists and trembling fingers, I awkwardly unwrapped and slapped it on ANCA's wound. Then she woke up; she would've strangled me if the tape hadn't restrained her.

"That's it, ANCA. You'll need lots of that fight to get you to the finish line now," I said.

It took time to convince her that I was not a threat, and more time to free our limbs. After smashing my surrender beacon, I cut the tape (and two fingers) on the mirror shards. By then the inflammation on ANCA's head had lessened but she was battered and woozy.

"ANCA, can you ICC your Guide?"

"Hunhmmmmffff."

"Never mind."

The windless howl returned with another round of pounding thunder below. The ground jerked violently side to side as if the crust were a taut fabric fought over by giant beings. The fabric rippled and ripped. I scrambled to collect our scattered gear before a gaping fissure could consume it. The noise bore into my concentration like a drill. I perched for several minutes over ANCA's body, ready to drag her from any encroaching chasms. Then, all motion and sound ceased.

While I cleaned ANCA's wound and applied another anti-inflam, Coach's methodical voice burst from some memchip archive and filled my mind.

"Remember the tale of Runner WOSA in the fifth Race," Coach said. "Her Guide was assassinated mid-Race but WOSA still reached the last checkpoint and won. Examine your tools. They will teach you about your Guide. The rare Guide acts as tactician rather than controller and will render itself dispensable by arming its Runner with all she needs to complete The Race unguided."

When I accessed the course detail maps and headings Guide had stored to my memchip, I heard his voice: "Runner, if you opened this file, then I must be gone. Know that you are the key to everything. Wherever I am, I will support you all the way to the finish line."

"Deal with losses later," I said to myself.

I took a detailed inventory of the remaining gear. ANCA's shoes didn't fit me, so I molded my indestructible heat-shield soles to my feet with Guide's resilient tape. They flopped like the snowdrift trudgers we'd used in Training but would have to do. Thanks to the remainder of Guide's surplus, we had enough food for one and a half days. If we could cover 48 kiloms in the next 12 hours, we'd be halfway there before the real heat came on. Escaping Gantugar alive seemed possible, but we had to get moving.

I rigged the packs together into a kind of sledge, strapped ANCA on, packed our supplies around her, and tucked the white IR scrambler over top. The howl screeched across the Gantugar, a thunderous boom in its wake. Gantugar buckled and tore itself into fissures all around us. I braced myself while hooking the pack straps around me like a harness, eyes scanning the crust for signs of solid ground. Thus I headed out, pulling the ANCA sledge behind me. Skirting the large rifts, I turned toward Checkpoint 5.

Walking is not easy. Something in a Runner's blood or in our very core drives us to run as far, as fast and as long as we can. Although I prided myself on having more depth than a mere sprinter, I could not deny that walking was, psychologically, very painful. The end-time that I loved while running compressed into a prison of endless torture while I walked. Time became my enemy in a sense, stealing my focus, instilling doubt. But with every step and stumble and jolt, I vowed that Gantugar would not keep us. And so, while I trudged, I chewed on a new tenet: *Walk without time, walk to survive.*

Day: 5. Kilom: 394. Runners: unknown.

At 0800, as if heralding the approach of the white-hot, voiding glare, Gantugar reared in sharp, vertical waves. Two meters away, a chasm opened and grew lengthwise, its fingers stretching hungrily toward us until we teetered on their tips. Then the tremor ceased and the chasm closed up.

In the night, I'd covered 40 kiloms. Hotspots had claimed my entire body. My feet were a mass of tape. ANCA, however, had improved. I threw our gear into one pack, put it on and we walked together toward the sunrise that held no beauty, only force.

After a few steps, ANCA spoke. "Why didn't you kill me? Or leave me there to die?" I wondered if she feared death. Or reassignment. I wondered if she feared anything.

"What for?" I said. It was a strange pleasure, breaking the taboo and talking to the enemy.

"So you could win The Race, of course." Her voice had a silvery texture to it, just like her stride.

"You're not *that* good of a Runner," I said, with a half grin. "I don't have to kill you to win."

"No, I didn't mean—" She shook her head and winced. A tremor rumbled under us and I grabbed her arm to steady her. She recoiled, then smiled an apology.

"Anyway," I said. "I'd much rather win with you

than by myself. This way, we can give life to *more* others."

An inconstant shimmer on the horizon warned of the glare's approach. ANCA fumbled with her goggles. "We can't both win," she said.

"Why not?" I adjusted her goggles to fit under her wound and then pulled my own into place. "Once we cross Gantugar, we can get the traitors disqualified. That leaves just you and me. Nothing in The Race rulebook prohibits a tie. Besides, you're a good Runner. *The Race needs good Runners.*"

ANCA managed a chuckle at the old recruitment slogan. I extended my arm. "Win this race with me," I said.

She clasped it, giving her Runner's word.

"I vow to try," she added. "Or die."

She put her hand up to her brow. The windless wind howled and the ground lurched. Weighted by the pack, I fell backward, limbs flailing. She sat down beside me and we rested there for a while, plugging our ears, watching Gantugar gape and churn all around us.

Later, when it had stopped, she was solemn. "Gantugar reminds me of my father," she said. "He made me feel so insignificant. So I figured I'd show him, and I became a Runner. Of course—" She indicated her tall, muscular body and bandaged face. "He wouldn't know me now, even if I did win."

I suspect Runner ANCA hadn't kicked past us all days ago and ended this race because, on some level, she still believed her father.

I'd long since stopped thinking of the family I'd

left for Training. They didn't understand me, my
need to push, push myself, push everything. They
were probably as glad to have me gone as I had been
to go.

Kilom: 400.

As we walked, I had the focus to edit and store the
above accounts to memchip, but soon ANCA had to
lie down again. The glare made her squint and then
her wound reopened. It was a mess. I tented the
white IR scrambler over her on the sledge, hoping
she'd only bake, not burn.

Kilom: 401. Memchip set on "direct-input."

Question: Why train Runners to master trance-
running?
   Option 3: To distract the Runner from the true
nature of The Race.

Kilom: 402.

Option 4: All of the above.

Kilom: 418.

I suspect seismic activity jams ICC frequencies. By
late morning, the quakes had subsided. By noon,
Guide had returned, saying that his ICC had just
cut out, like mine. He also supported my decision
to save ANCA and run with her for a tie.

A short-lived rush of energy surged within me when Guide reconnected. His absence and goodbye message had weighed heavily. But even with him navigating, I had to think too much. I couldn't reach a meditative state. And my fatigue only increased.

Guide, when do you sleep?"
"After we win . . . Watch for a series of ridges in the next kilom."

Guide, are you male or female?"
"Can't you tell?"
"Voices on ICC *are* modulatable."
"Male."
"Why didn't they take you for the war?"
"Not enough legs . . . Bear east five degrees."
"Oh."
"Never mind. Losing a leg to Fauch's Cancer brought me here, where I could do some good."

Guide, good plan with the extra food. But how about some wheels? And a parasol? And, an ice bath?"
Guide sang,
"Kick on, Kick on, I'm kicking on into the night . . ."

Guide, what do you do while I'm on course?"
"I monitor the satellites, radar, IR scanners to ensure your safety, monitor the media and other Runners, manage the crews, prep gear drops—Runner, keep clear of those sand blows—and I read your fan mail."

"I have fan mail?"

"Naturally."

"Like what?"

"Well, so far you've received roughly 400 letter bombs, 5,000 viruses, 1,270 marriage proposals and about 30,000 letters of support. Not bad for your first few days."

"What do they say?"

"'Dear Runner ETI, My sister was dying from Birg's Disease but your victory will grant her a new life. All my thoughts run with you. Thank you, Brenny Prestin.'"

"Nice," I sent. "Will I ever see it?"

"Sorry. We destroyed the letter bombs already."

"Do you get fan mail too?"

"No, Guides don't get fan mail. We just get a sense of accomplishment."

I paused, squinting behind my goggles into the endless glare that was Gantugar. "Guide," I sent, "tell me about your Training."

"Well," he began, "similar to you, I inhabited various complexes, underwent several feature alterations, and assumed countless names and ID numbers. Sleep deprivation was the hardest thing to master, but I finally did."

"Did you train your whole life too, just like Runners?" I asked.

"Of course."

"Did you leave your family?"

"Well, yes."

"Do you think of them?"

Guide paused a long time. I only noticed because

I'd been pacing myself by our conversation and my foot now hung ready, waiting to take a step. I turned, checked ANCA and took three more steps before he responded.

"Just my brother. My big brother."

"Where is he?"

"Squazi."

"Oh, he's a soldier?"

"No. A teacher. He wanted to be a teacher. But he believed, the way the war started, that we were in danger. Not like now. Not the endless . . ." He drifted off.

Maybe Guide hadn't truly mastered sleep dep, I thought.

"The endless what?" I sent, treading lightly. But Guide's moment of candor was just that—momentary.

"The war is not what it seems," he sent. "And my brother is dead."

My footing slipped on a low ridge.

"Guide?"

Silence.

ANCA moaned under her tent.

"I'm sorry about your brother."

My nav-watch read 1530. Sun still too high, glare too intense—no stopping for another couple hours.

"But if you don't talk to me," I sent, "I'll shrivel into jerky out here."

More silence. Then Guide continued, "Guide Training also included strategy, map reading, course plotting, evasive action, psychology, equipment, pacing, anatomy. Fourth Stage focused on more complex stuff: managing a Runner, a med squad, security and supply teams, communication, sniffing out rats and finding loyals. . . ."

I tried to maintain focus but his voice had blurred. ANCA wasn't getting any lighter, nor I any stronger. My brain tingled. Lights strobed behind my eyes. Rather than hit a mental wall head-on, I made for some trees and pulled to a stop in their shade.

"Runner?"

"Gonna rest here in the shade."

"Shade?"

"Nice trees here." My body relaxed in the cool breeze. I pulled the tent open for ANCA to get some air, despite her protestations.

"Runner." Guide's ICC voice softened. It enveloped me like the feel of brand new socks. "Remember when Runner PHE died and you said 'Nobody misses nobody'? Well, I think Guide PHE would've missed her; you missed her too. She wasn't nobody at all. Neither are you. In fact, you're the sheer opposite of expendable. You are irreplaceable.

"I didn't want to tell you this, in case you got too big for your arches, but I'll tell you now: My whole life, I imagined the ideal Runner for me to Guide. When I found you, I felt the universe had created you from my dreams, so completely do you embody that ideal. And you know, even though you ranked third-fastest in Elite Stage and were top-rated in self-defense, ETI wanted someone faster still. I had to fight for you."

"Speed is sometimes a manifestation of greed," I sent.

"Yes, well, ETI didn't recognize it, but I did. You are the Runner that ETI has been looking for all these years. You are the key to achieving ETI's true purpose. If ETI had assigned any of those other Runners, disappointment would have overwhelmed me. I wouldn't have survived half this long. Runner, I know you can win this race. Even with ANCA on your back—"

Gantugar shrieked and reeled, ripping Guide from my mind, along with my shade trees and cool breeze. Thrust back into the sweltering afternoon glare, I glimpsed a ripple on the ground beside ANCA. It puckered, then bubbled, as only one thing on the planet could.

"Sand blow!" I yelled.

I dove for the makeshift sledge. Clutching ANCA, I shoved us off the crest of the burbling mound. We slid down its steepening slope, hit bottom and rolled. The mound blew. Wet sand spewed out of the crater in spasmodic bursts, landing on the rim in layers that hardened in seconds. I yelled over the din, "ANCA, on your mark!" She complied with an unsteady stance.

How long did Gantugar rave around us? I watched the sand blow climb over two meters, witnessed the disappearance of countless fissures, and the creation of many more. Like in a sudden-death Training exercise, my reflexes steered my body around the moving obstacles. Unlike my Training days, however, I reached no trance. My mind now grappled with the enormity and senselessness of death. And life.

The quake extracted the last traces of my focus and vanished. Ears ringing, body heavy, I packed up ANCA again and stared blankly around. The formidable expanse of Gantugar had never seemed so great. My tenets rang hollow, my will shriveled and sputtered. Habit is tireless, however, and, blipping through my memchip, I eventually came across the tale of how Runner SART won the third Race. With a broken toe and a festering gunshot wound, she divided the distance into increments she could handle. Then, she just surrendered.

Surrender to your will and run any distance
Run beyond all limits
Run until you reach the whole you seek

I squinted into the late afternoon glare and spotted my first target: a low ridge sitting three meters away.

"Get there," I whispered.

I rose and picked up the straps again to pull. When I'd reached the ridge, I said, "Good. Now, see that cluster of small sand blows up there? Head for them."

And that's how it went. The longest day of my life. I surrendered to my will, pushing on from ridge to sand blow to ridge.

Day: 6 (pre-dawn). Kilom: 431. Runners: unknown.

Gantugar rests. Blue Runner ANCA has been walking beside me since before midnight. Less than 20 kiloms to go. Should make it to C5 by dawn. Even at this tedious pace, we move faster than when I'm lugging her.

I'd finished editing and storing the preceding accounts to memchip when Guide returned with news. Birthing and Population Charity Conglom has reported Runner BIP missing. I suspect her knees gave out. (Or maybe Runner HAID ambushed her after all.)

Speaking of HAID, Guide thinks she got lost during the quakes. His scanners locate her on the north edge of Gantugar, skirting the flats, heading toward C5.

Guide says the recent quakes far exceeded Gantugar's norm in both frequency and severity. He believes the pulse of Runner HAID's stun device disturbed this unstable region, and the first quake set off a chain reaction. I suspect that, on Gantugar at least, life attracts death.

Day 6: Dawn. Kilom: 451. C5 Camp.

We've made it through C5 to ETI's camp on the far side of the Gantugar Flats. Guide has allowed a med squad from ANCA for their Runner, but ETI provides all facilities and security. Every part of my body throbs, my hip needs realignment, my feet have lost their skin and most of my body is oozing. I feel like the red jelly we used to mix up and scoop into ice packs at Training.

I awoke near midnight feeling more like rock than jelly. ETI's med squad buzzed around me throughout Guide's ICC briefing, applying synth-skin with the grafter on high speed.

Birthing and Population Charity Conglom gave up on their Runner and withdrew from The Race. That left Runner HAID, who was fast approaching C5. I looked down at my skinless feet. My quads twitched. We couldn't let her win.

"I want to report Runner HAID as a traitor," I sent.

"Got any proof?" sent Guide.

"Runner ANCA's Guide can present scanner footage of the ambush."

"Good idea, but ANCA's Conglom doesn't have that kind of technology, Runner," sent Guide. "I already asked."

"What about your scanners then? Do you have footage of HAID using her stunner on me?" My feet began to burn. Nerves still worked, at least.

"No," he sent, "the device interfered with our signal somehow."

"You mean, we have no case?"

"Unfortunately, no."

"Then, ANCA and I should finish The Race now," I sent, "walking."

"HAID's supporters would kill you before you reached Trilpa," sent Guide.

"HAID almost killed us."

"Your best bet is to run with her," he sent. "Why not a *triple*-tie finish?"

"Run with a traitor?"

"Runner, in the history of The Race, when has more than one Runner ever reached the fifth checkpoint? Never. *You* changed that. And by not reporting HAID's treachery, you will ensure that three of you can complete the whole course. You will fulfill your oath *three*fold."

I could instill as much honor in my oath as I liked, but in many ways The Race was merely a 21st-century gladiator fight, and I risked my life for the entertainment of the masses. HAID was the ugliest beast in the ring. Although I'd survived her first pass, I knew that a Runner shouldn't push her luck. In my mind, doing anything with HAID was pushing luck.

But the more I considered it, the more the triple-tie finish made sense. I began to perceive it as a kind of insurance. If the three of us announced that we planned to finish together, it would end the inter-Conglom competition of this year's Race. Not only would I give life to three times as many others, I would climb a step above a gladiator because the masses would want me to survive. Only one problem remained: How could I convince HAID to agree?

Day: 7. C5 Camp.

Rioting outside The Race Media HQ in Trilpa early this morning. Awaiting Race updates, many in the crowd began arguing about who deserved to win. It got violent. Police arrested over 300 people and wounded twice as many.

Guide seemed pleased, saying something about the temperature rising in Trilpa. I am beginning to feel as though I can't understand anything anymore. It seems the harder and longer I run, the more lives are taken, not saved, and the less I feel connected to anything. My oath is somehow losing meaning, my faith wavering. As that void develops, Guide tries to fill it up again, but Guide's mission differs so distinctly from my own. While he seeks to accomplish something outside of himself through external methods, I seek to achieve my goal through purely internal means. No amount of rhetoric is going to help me. Only I can.

At last, the media is focusing on The Race. First Runner NOD and the rattlers, then the earthquakes, Runner BIP's mysterious demise, two Runners reaching C5 with another close behind—well, we'd wanted publicity, and now we had some. We couldn't complain about that. But amidst the media frenzy, the Government Gift Representative made a very disturbing statement.

"The war in Squazi is escalating," Rep Cozveli said. "The situation there demands more resources for our troops. We know the public understands that before addressing nonessentials such as those represented by the Charity Conglomerates competing in The Race, we must guarantee the safety of our Leader . . ."

"The Leader?" I sent. "Guide, who's threatening the Leader?"

"Depends who you ask."

"I asked you."

"No one more than usual," he sent. "Except, well, Runner, we should talk." His voice got soft, as if preparing for a lengthy lecture. "A group of insurgents is gaining power and momentum," he sent. "They—"

"Will this information help me focus on completing the last stage?" I interrupted.

"No," he sent, "probably not, but—"

"Then can it wait? I need to test this synth-skin, and HAID's nearly here, and I just need to know if the government can withdraw their support of The Race now."

"They can't," sent Guide. "They've been invading Squazi for almost fifteen years. I can say with full confidence that retreat is definitely not in their nature."

Day: 7. Kilom: 451. Runners: 2. Traitors: 1.

With double socks taped over synth-skin grafts, I tripped along beside ANCA. Her forehead had grafted nicely, although her stride resembled a wobbly drop-foot canter. We made our way to C5 to await HAID's imminent arrival from the Gantugar Flats. With two Guides looking out for ANCA and me, plus the added protection of bulletproof vitals wraps, we should have felt invincible, but running with HAID meant trouble and we both knew it.

"You okay to run?" I asked. "Cloudy and cool today, slight downgrade, old paveway, a few tumbleweeds." I gestured toward Trilpa.

"I can do 50 kiloms of that," Runner ANCA said. "You know, I don't think I'd be standing right now if my medics hadn't gained the use of ETI's amazing med facilities. The past day has given me an idea how it feels to run for private money."

"What do you mean?" I asked.

"You don't know?" She chuckled. "Runner ETI, has your Conglom ever won a Race?"

"ETI? No."

"Think, Runner ETI. ANCA won The Race five years ago but we don't have half the technology ETI does. Where does the money come from? Where'd you get that fancy tent and med facilities? Ever hear of multinash corporations?"

"I suppose so," I said. I had to admit, it made sense. The resources Guide had at his disposal—extra supplies, five-star fullbod, heat-shield shoes—everything ETI had done for me had been top of the line. But big corporations made big money. They could gain nothing from five million lukra.

"What would they want with ETI?" I asked. "Or with me?"

"Runner," Guide sent. "HAID arrives in two minutes."

"Ready," I sent.

"Why is Cherzia in Squazi, Runner ETI?" asked ANCA. "The Leader wants something—power, resources, who knows? But you run for someone else. They need you."

Guide had called me "the key" on more than one occasion. The key to what?

"Runner ANCA," I said, "say you're right. Then what will happen to you and me if ETI wins The Race?"

She scuffed her foot against the ground as if in thought.

"Did you complete Mire Terrain Training?" she asked.

I blipped through my memchip and found the file. "Yes," I said, "but I'd have to review it."

"In that module, Coach said, 'The Race is like the mire. All kinds of pits and predators. Keep half your senses focused on where you stand and half on where your next step will land. To look farther ahead, or behind you, will stretch your focus too much. You'll become someone's lunch.'"

ANCA was right. Too much thinking. Not enough moving.

"Runner," Guide sent. "HAID."

"Got her," I sent.

Runner HAID's footsteps, a dogged shuffle, became audible before we saw her. She trotted with a low kick toward C5, visibly tired.

"You ready?" ANCA asked.

I nodded. "You set the pace. After circling Gantugar, she won't be sprinting. We'll push her fast as you can go."

HAID dropped her pack and proceeded through the checkpoint. We stepped into her path.

"Heard you lost your way," ANCA said.

"Now your way is ours," I said, presenting a bulletproof vitals wrap clenched in my fist. "Finish with us. A three-way-tie. Or don't finish at all."

HAID ignored the offering. "I don't need you," she said in her squeaky voice.

"Suit yourself." I started to laugh.

ANCA spit on HAID's shoes, cursing her to the Runners' equivalent of eternal trench foot. The traitor sidestepped us and kicked into a trot. ANCA and I fell in line right behind her.

"Remember the story of the traitor in the fourth Race?" said ANCA, loud enough for HAID to hear.

"Wasn't she from HAID too?" I said.

"Mmmhmm. What a coincidence!"

"I forget, what happened to her?" I said.

"Before or after they strung her up by her laces?" said ANCA.

Kilom: 483. Kiloms remaining: 17. Runners: 2. Nervous Traitors: 1.

By the time we had passed out of sight of C5, HAID had lost her arrogant gait. We jumped and searched her anyway.

"Should we kill the traitor now?" said ANCA, perched on HAID's legs.

"Naw, let her run a while longer," I said, pinning the traitor's head and shoulders. "The media says that the government may extend the course indefinitely."

"Until two of us drop dead?" laughed ANCA.

"Or until an assassin takes care of the traitor for us."

"I wouldn't mind seeing that," said ANCA, meeting my gaze.

"Me neither," I said, only half joking.

Kilom: 498. Damage report: unfathomable.

Terrorizing the traitor, though necessary for us to maintain control of her, stretched our focus thin. Once off the upper plateau, we had to contend with a media copter roaring overhead, an ETI trail rover chugging at our heels, the unpredictable HAID before us, the occasional tumbleweed whirling across our path and, for the first time, spectators.

People lined the roadway. Some shouted support for each of our host Congloms. Several had pictures of suffering or lost loved ones. A few yelled against the government. As we ran, keeping in tight triangle defense formation, more and more people appeared. Some clapping, some scowling, many remarking that three Runners had never before come so close to the finish.

Braced for attack from any one of them, we didn't see the trip line in time. HAID sprang to hurdle it and I moved with her, but ANCA went down, calling "Get HAID!" as she fell.

The traitor didn't resist when I grabbed her arm and pulled her back to where ANCA lay motionless, her forehead graft ruined, wound reopened.

"Guide, park the rover," I sent. "ANCA needs—"

"Med squad coming," interrupted Guide. "One moment."

The crowd approached from all sides. I felt vulnerable there, surrounded by more people than I'd ever known. I looked down at the broken form of ANCA and something inside me came loose. I did not lock it down. My fingers dug into the traitor's arm.

"Last chance, HAID," I said. "Will you serve your oath, or yourself?"

"Both," she said, a faint snarl rumbling in her throat.

I looked at ANCA. "Impossible," I said.

"Med squad," Guide sent.

ETI medics materialized beside Runner ANCA. In their wake burst a gang of ETI security that encircled us and pushed the crowd back.

"She must finish," I told the med squad. They

nodded. I turned to the crowd like a ringleader and shouted, "ANCA is all right!"

The crowd cheered.

Runner HAID whirled then, yanking her arm free with surprising strength. I dodged the first punch but got caught in the shoulder by the second. HAID turned to run; I leapt and tackled, gasping as the synth-skin on my feet began to shred.

The crowd hissed. ETI security held their ground.

"Guide," I sent. "Runner HAID has attacked."

HAID ripped off my hood and goggles. She flung dirt in my face and tried to crawl away, but I smashed her down again.

"Easy, Runner," Guide sent. "I still want you to take her with you."

"You know how dangerous she is," I sent, struggling to pin the traitor. "Why do you risk my safety this way, especially so close to the finish?"

HAID smashed her elbow into my nose, snapping the cartilage. Blood spurted down my chin. My vision blurred until I could trance past the pain.

"Give me a good reason," I sent. "Because I am about to hurt her. Badly."

The traitor wriggled out from under me and scrambled to her feet. Whipping my legs back, I spun into a lateral kick. She twisted away, but not enough. There was a crack as my heel made solid contact with her shin. My hip slammed out of alignment again, and my feet burst through the shredded synth-skin. I fought to hold the trance against the pain.

She dipped, then caught her balance on her good leg. I got to my feet, faked and struck her temple hard.

The crowd gasped. Some people yelled, at me, at HAID, at everyone.

"Guide?" My eyes teared. I wiped the blood from my mouth and chin with the back of my hand and gazed skyward. "Can you see this? Down she goes. Start talking, or you lose Runner HAID."

The traitor thumped to the ground. The med squad looked over but I shook my head.

"She's unconscious," I sent. "With a fractured tibia. Maybe worse. You have anything to say, Guide?"

"Runner, you have no idea."

"Try me," I sent, standing over HAID. "Oh, she's losing more blood than I'd thought. Start with me, Guide. You said I am the key. To what?"

"Runner," he began. His voice sounded heavy on the ICC. "A total of three Charity Congloms and all those affiliated with them represents nearly half the country's population. You and ANCA alone would enable us to wage a powerful campaign, but with half of the population behind us, basically, we can't fail."

"Fail what?" I sent. "Talk fast if you don't want HAID knocked out again."

"Runner, ETI has a purpose you can't possibly understand."

"Just like you can't understand how much HAID deserves to be jailed, or better yet, *reassigned*? If you could see ANCA right now, you'd change your mind. She was the best Runner I've ever seen. She should have won this race days ago. Now she can't even walk! *HAID* did this to her."

"Runner, The Race has *never been about* running." Guide emphasized each word as though he were very angry, and I very slow-witted. After a pause, he sent, "This particular race, least of all. The government might refuse to pay a double gift but without question will refuse to pay triple. The public will rise up. You are the key to a new Cherzia!"

"New, how?" I sent.

"The Leader will fall."

"That makes me a pawn," I sent, "not a key."

"You want to argue semantics?"

"You lied to me!" I kicked the road. Dust flew into HAID's face. My foot sizzled.

"I kept you alive."

"You manipulated me and my oath and—"

"You signed up for the job, Runner. Of your own volition, twelve years ago," he sent.

"I was *five*! My parents sold me into Training."

"Because the Leader was starving them and you," he sent.

"I signed up to *run*, not to be your, your insurrectionistic toy." I kicked at the road and wiped the blood from my chin again. Med squad tossed me a towel and an anti-inflam, both of which I missed. A medic approached with another towel, and caution.

"Runner, I tried to tell you—you are such a child, only seeing what you want to see—"

I looked around me, at HAID, the crowd, ANCA, my blood. The medic tried to plug the bleeding but I pushed him away. "I've been a little busy out here," I sent, "while you sit cozy in some HQ somewhere and call the shots."

"Yes," he sent, "of course. But the point is, do you want children to continue going through this fight to the death? To sign their lives away for one idea only to find themselves dying for another?"

"Are you talking about Runners or soldiers?"

"Leave my brother out of this."

"Why should I? You can't."

"Well," he sent, "here's your chance to end it."

"You're wrong," I sent. HAID showed signs of life. I kicked her, instantly regretted using my foot, grabbed a roll of tape and bound her hands in front of her, certain I'd kill her if she attacked again. "I'm no longer a child."

"Then stop acting like one!" Guide snapped.

He stung me more than he could know. But then, at that moment, everything stung. Suddenly the fate of my country was in my hands. As well as the fate of the two Runners and The Race itself. I had no tenets for this, just shattered images of an oath, a friend, a purpose.

The crowd had multiplied and was growing restless. ETI security couldn't hold them much longer. Surrounded by so many, I felt very alone.

"I wonder, Guide," I sent, "what will ETI's backers get out of this? International corporations don't fund insurrections for fun, do they? I just wonder, what's in it for them?"

"Runner?"

"Why haven't you asked yourself the same question?" I sent. "Or maybe you have."

My nose had stopped bleeding. It glowed a bulbous purple. I put an anti-inflam on it, forced HAID to stand and wiped her face roughly with the bloodied towel.

"If you have to crawl all the way across this city with Runner ANCA on your back, then we'll do that," I whispered. "I was hoping you'd be vertical, but it doesn't matter to me."

"Only one can win," she mumbled.

"Runner ANCA will finish with me. That makes two. Now you, you can finish with us, although that's better than you deserve, or you can go to jail directly from here. Make your choice, Traitor."

HAID whimpered but slowly turned her body to face the direction of the finish line. Shivering, I pulled my hood back on. The mask couldn't cover my swollen face and flapped open again.

Unsteadily, ANCA rose beside me. We scanned the crowd that now had no end. A multitude surrounded us, blocking our way into the city, sealing us in from behind.

"ANCA, there's more to this than we thought," I said.

"I believe it," she said, clasping my arm. "Where are we?"

"Just outside of the last kilom."

She shifted her weight. "Did Coach ever mention kilom growth to you?"

I blipped through my memchip. "No."

"Coach said, 'Anything can happen in a kilom. The closer you get to the finish line, the longer each kilom grows.' Runner ETI, there are many people out there, and we still have a long way to go." Her voice, stretched thin and tarnished, refused to break. She clutched my hand, curled her fingers around mine for the briefest of moments, then said, "HAID doesn't look so good."

I almost laughed. The med squad had fastened a hobble brace to HAID's busted leg and disappeared. The traitor leaned awkwardly, testing her weight on the built-in crutch.

Time to run.

"Thank you all for coming!" I shouted. The crowd cheered. My nose began to bleed again. "We have an announcement to make." There was an immediate hush. "All three of us will finish together now, for a triple government gift! If you support one of us, you support us all. Please spread the word and make room so we may pass."

Landlocked.

Coach said, "The heaviest steps are the ones you take blindly." She was right. We journeyed through Trilpa along streets packed with people. Overwhelmed by the boundless attention and infinite potential for assassination, we made our bloody, limping way, propelled by the will to live more than to fulfill any oath. There, where my spirit should have been soaring, lighter than a pair of sprint soles, ready for release into the great whole

180

that is me and all around me, my spirit remained firmly landlocked by dilemma.

Crossing the finish line had once represented freedom, wholeness, but finishing now would catapult unknown people into power, people with unknown agendas. Still, what if ETI really could end The Race forever? And now that I understood what The Race, Training and the government truly were, how could I allow it all to continue?

Kilom: 500.

We crossed the capital grounds, passing lines of police as we advanced through the milling thousands. The finish line came into view. In a few more steps, everything would change. And I still didn't know what to do.

That's when the shots rang out.

"Sniper," sent Guide. "Library roof. Get down."

We three hit the dirt. Screams pierced the air above us. Someone nearby shouted, "Protect the Runners! Save the Runners!" The crowd surged in around us.

"Guide, who—?" I sent.

"Who do you think?" His ICC voice was clipped. I could almost hear him take a deep, bitter breath before he asked, "Damage report?"

I didn't respond. Engines roared. Sirens blared. I imagined the police ranks marching toward us, trampled citizens lying in their wake.

"Runner," he sent. "I'm sorry."

I wanted to believe him, but it was too late. The

vitals wraps had deflected the bullets off ANCA and me, but HAID had taken one in the chest. I doubted Guide had orchestrated this attack merely to convince me to do ETI's bidding. He wasn't completely mad. (Not yet anyway.) Only one group would resist a triple government gift and hire the sniper. Plain and simple, the government wanted us all dead.

That made my decision easy at least. On the floor of the cave the crowd provided, we Runners lay prone, less than one stride from the line that would end our struggle. On my right, ANCA rolled close and put out her hand. Her face mask fluttered loose. Blistered, dusty lips formed a weak but jubilant smile. I worked quickly. There could be no ambiguity. When I pulled HAID close against my left side, she made a gurgling sound that would haunt me for weeks.

"HAID needs her med squad now," I sent.

I untaped her limp wrists and grabbed her right hand in my left, palms together, interlocking our cracked and bloody fingers. My other hand clenched ANCA's left in the same manner. I pulled them all together into a large fist and landed it with a solid thump on the ground across the finish line. What we lacked in stature, we made up for in clarity.

A tremendous cheer arose. It reverberated throughout my body. The newscams zoomed in for a close-up. Then the crowd carried us across the line into the arms of our med squads. Thus we were swept away—unable to relish our achievement or experience the adoration of the crowd—only to be sequestered within the antiseptic, echoing halls of some secret medical facility.

Reassignment.

There was no closure until now, now that our new Leader has ended the War in Squazi and funded all Charity Congloms forever. Our Race was the last one of its kind; we Runners have become extinct. Runner HAID's death and Runner ANCA's rise to media stardom left me carrying the Runners' torch, doused and dripping as it was, alone.

I had hoped to meet you in person to thank you for the excellent guidance and for assigning me in the first place. (After all, if you hadn't done either of those things, the world would be a very different place now, wouldn't it?) But with the ICC removal amidst the chaos at Race-end, it took me some time to find you. (How many one-legged Cabinet members can there be? No, I don't think anyone knows. You walk well. It's just my business to study gaits. Or, was my business.)

I still wonder, though, about the repercussions of what ETI has done. Who will take responsibility when ETI's investors expect a return larger than their rightful due? The old Runners' saying, "out of the deluge, into the sand dunes," comes to mind. (Yes, I still feel we should be accountable, although I know I'll never persuade you to act on behalf of my conscience. Especially now, so close on the heels of your recent appointment.) Thing is, in this political climate, I'd soon become your liability, and I'd rather not run for my life again.

Guide (or should I say, *Esteemed Advisor to the Leader?*) this will be my last entry. When this memchip reaches you, you'll know that Runner ETI is gone. I requested the reassignment, actually. I no longer fear it. The wholeness I achieved in fulfilling this assignment will not be consumed, upon reassignment, by a gaping soulless void. I understand that now. I will merely find myself in another mystery through which I may push, reaching toward wholeness once again. I'm curious, master tactician. Did you see this coming?

Picture me reclining in the op-chair, awaiting the surgeon's arrival, at dawn. The reassignment office is silent that time of day. I forced myself to watch the sunrise, daring myself to find something beautiful in it, to see something beyond the memory of Gantugar's torturous glare. Perhaps tomorrow I will succeed.

Why did I arrive so early? An astute question, Guide, but then, you always were on top of things. I broke in—it's true. (I promise to pay for the damage.) It wouldn't have served my best interests to make an appointment ahead of time. By the way, in my apartment, you'll find your hired "master of invisible surveillance," bound and slightly bruised. (He was not so astute, and frankly, I wanted to be alone.)

I chose the reassignment surgeon you had hired to insert my ICC before The Race. She was loyal to me and to you and has no reason to change, so please do not harm her. I will pay her well to remove and deliver this memchip only to you. And no, she does not know anything about my new assignment.

Do not try to find me. You will think you need to, but you don't. You will think you can, but you can't. You think you will have the advantage, my memchip plus yours, but you underestimate the knowledge of the body. The surgeon—ah, here she comes now, looking disgruntled but not shocked. Perhaps it is not uncommon for people to enter as I have and purchase an unscheduled reassignment. She may pluck the memchip from my mind, and with it all I've ever known, but she cannot remove my body's memory, my instincts, my volition. Through them, I will remember you. And avoid you. And if I must, protect myself against you.

So let me go. Your secret is safe with me. After all, it is my secret too. We both acted as prime instruments in the insurrection of the century. Despite our differences, we made a great team, you and I. But freedom calls. I want to live as people do. Until now, I have had no life, only mission.

It is nearly time. The surgeon assures me that after reassignment, I'll have a normal life, with no Coach, no Training, no more Races. I can only imagine what she means. I wonder, what will it be like?

[END FILE]

The Candy Store

written by

Heather McDougal

illustrated by

JAMIE LUHN

ABOUT THE AUTHOR

Heather McDougal homesteads in northern California (where is Davenport anyway?) where she keeps chickens, bees, vegetables and an ever-growing "Cabinet of Curiosities." Her misbegotten MFA in sculpture transmogrified into a writing career after her much-lauded thesis made it clear that her writing was far better than her sculpture.

She has juried for the Djerassi Resident Artists Program, where she was a writing resident in 2002, and is currently working on her fourth unpublished novel (a clockpunk-style Baba Yaga story). Heather is also the author of several nonfiction articles and an academic paper. She regularly contributes to her blog, "Cabinet of Wonders," a cultural commentary on the importance of wonder using the Age of Reason and Wunderkammern as metaphors, where she waxes extemporaneous on topics as personal as the benefits of feet tickling and weird fashion.

ABOUT THE ILLUSTRATOR

Jamie Luhn happily graduated from high school, but dropped out of college for a less restrained life when told he'd have to become more "well-rounded" as a student. For twelve years, he lived the dream as a songwriter and lead singer for an alternative rock band called Juniper Tree. When the band slowly drifted apart, Jamie moved on to take up a passion he had never really stopped since he was a child—drawing—in part as a way to pay the bills. Not surprisingly, his visual inspirations come from both expected (Van Gogh, Will Eisner, Mercer Mayer) and unexpected (Leonard Cohen song lyrics) sources.

Now, living a more-regulated existence, you can find Jamie with his wife and son in a little green house in a little green garden living on the side of a mountain in the forested environs outside Hagerstown, Maryland. In addition to drawing, Jamie's apt to paint a sign or house, drive some nails, landscape, greenskeep and drink some cheap beer at day's end.

The Candy Store

Things have been quiet here recently.

The gold's been drying up, and people are leaving. The men who're left spend most of their little money on drink, but even so, the saloon has become a quiet place. Walk in there, most nights, and you'll hear a low murmur and the snick of cards. Even the girls are less lively, sitting at the bar looking ready, instead of running around laughing and screaming like they used to.

I do worry about the town. Seems to me we're going the way of too many of the towns hereabouts. Our water supply's none too good, and winter can be awful hairy. Sometimes it gets so we're all pretty hungry, waiting for those supply wagons. And without the gold, well, unless you're me, there's not much reason to live up here.

It wasn't too long ago, right after Eddie's big nugget, that the candy store showed up. People got excited, like they get whenever there's a big nugget, but no one guessed it'd be the last one. Everyone was feeling optimistic.

Summer was doing up its laces and some of the more tender leaves had begun to swirl around the street. Earlier and earlier every evening the big shadow of the Mountain was creeping across the town, leaving the streets chilly and damp by dinner time.

On this particular evening, the wind was from the East, from beyond the Mountain, which was just about unheard of. It blew in with dry smells from the desert country on the other side. There was a feeling in the air like something about to happen. It was real quiet. All the folks in town were sort of tiptoeing around, staying inside, almost like everyone was holding their breath.

I was outside walking around, getting ready for the long ride home. The streets were dark, only a few lamps showing in windows here and there, and that wind picking at things, blowing a few leaves along the edges of the street, raising dust devils here and there for no reason that I could see. It smelled like peppermints suddenly, and I shook my head at the notion, but I couldn't get that smell off my mind.

I stopped by the Carlton's Hardware building, that closed two weeks before Eddie found his nugget. Sam Carlton said he was off to find better pickings, somewhere where people were doing well, and where they needed a hardware store. Kaplan's Mercantile, across the street, carried hardware as well as all the other stuff like feed and oatmeal, and there just wasn't enough business to keep Sam here.

I missed Sam. He was a real cheerful sort, always singing, with a good word for everyone. He knew when to stop drinking and he never pushed anyone. He was one of the few people who never got into a fight in those days.

His storefront looked awfully empty. I don't usually mind when things feel spooky. I notice it, sure, but it doesn't bother me much. Some things that have happened in broad daylight have scared the bejesus out of me, but the creepy-crawlies—I'm usually immune.

This time, however, I stopped. I stood outside that old hardware store and I stared in through the window. It was dark and I didn't see anything move inside, but I could feel the hairs on the back of my neck rising up and standing there. It was an awful feeling, the likes of which I haven't felt since Indian country, once when I passed through a ravine when I knew we were being watched—and not in a friendly way either.

The wind moaned a little, and I peered and peered into the window, those leaves rustling around my ankles, but all I could see were the hunched shapes of counters and a couple of barrels. Nothing moved at all. So, frowning, I turned back to find my horse and ride home.

. . . And walked smack into Shaky Jay Gregory, the crazy man in our town.

"Whatcha doin'?" he asked, with that crazy smile, his head nodding and nodding.

"Just walking," I told him.

"Whyn'cha home with yer pretty wife?" he said, leering at me. "She's one hell of a find, that girl. They say you found her out in the woods, heh-heh. How'd you catch her, anyways?"

I tried not to roll my eyes. Shaky Jay doesn't like it when you roll your eyes, and it's important not to do things he doesn't like. Still, I do get tired of people asking me about finding my wife in a tree. They all want to know how I could have come by a woman who didn't come to town in the usual ways. In fact, she's from around here. I know, there ain't no people around here. That's a whole 'nother story.

"Heh, Jay, you know how I met my wife," I said, instead of rolling my eyes.

"Jes' kiddin' ye," he said with a chuckle and a weird roll of his own eyes. "Still, you should be inside, like everyone else. The devil is ridin' the wind tonight. Jest lookin' for an empty spot to set hisself down, you know."

Jay looked so clear-eyed, saying this, that I watched his face a little closer. Sometimes he knows what's what when no one else does. It doesn't do to underestimate Jay, crazy or not.

"What do you mean?" I asked him.

"You'll see," he says. "He's comin'. You look around tomorrow and see what the wind brung."

"Thanks, Jay, I'll do that," I said, and walked on, leaving him looking into the hardware store window, nodding and nodding.

Widdershins was standing where I left her, shivering and snorting restlessly. She was feeling it, too, and wanted to get home. Nearly as soon as I was up she turned hard to set off for home, and I got to admit, I let her go gladly.

The moon came up as we went through the raggedy woods they have hereabouts, and threw long shadows across the path. There was no sound but the wind sighing on the pine needles and Widdershins' feet on the soft ground. The hair on the back of my neck kept going up and down, and I could feel Widdershins skittish under me. Still, she was trotting pretty quick by the time we reached the house.

As soon as I got down off her, the door opened.

"Is that you, John?" my wife called.

"Yep," I called back, "be in in a minute," and I led Widdershins to the barn. Still, the sight of my wife made me feel a whole lot better, and I came back from the barn almost whistling. By the time I was sitting down to dinner, I had almost forgotten my fright.

My wife is like that. Her name is Maddy, and everyone likes her, even though she and the town mostly go their separate ways. She just has to walk into a crowd and people will stop fighting—if you can get her to go near that many people. Every morning I wake up next to her I thank God she's mine and I wonder that she hasn't left, gone back to where she came from.

I know she's uncomfortable in the house, but she sticks it out, for me, though this house is about as outside as a house can get, with the adobe walls and the turf roof. Land here is pretty dry and hard, but she found us a place with a spring. I tried not to fell any trees to build the house, since it makes her so sad, and I ordered more glass than I can afford, so that it would be sunny and full of air inside, though it makes you feel the seasons. The outside is surrounded by a huge porch, and in most seasons we eat and cook and do most everything outside.

This evening she was worried. I could tell by the way she spooned out the stew. Usually she's so neat and smooth how she moves, but she spilled some, and then apologized too much.

I kissed her and ate the stew. She's a good wife, but she's an even better person.

The next day I was up early. The house, for all its outdoorsiness, can be awfully snug in the cold months, and although I needed to get into town I wasn't keen on leaving Maddy and the warm kitchen. I think some of the night before was still stuck to me.

Maddy, too. "Be careful," she told me. "I love you."

She never tells me to be careful. "I love you too," I said, as I got on Widdershins.

When I got to town, there was a lot of hustle and bustle, and a new sign up on the hardware store. It said "Bright's Candies." There was a proper display in the window, full of all kinds of colorful sweets, and people were going in and out.

Sometimes I feel like I have another nose under my actual nose that tingles and comes alive when it smells trouble. This morning it was pointing me like crazy in the direction of that store. The trouble-smell was coming off it so strong I didn't know what to think. I'd never seen a thing, or even a person, reek so strongly of B.S. as this did. My nose was practically quivering as I crossed the street toward it.

I walked into a smell of peppermints. A little bell

attached to the back of the door went *ting!* as I came in, and a woman behind the counter turned to face me with a smile like golden syrup. Now that she was here, that made eight grown women in town, counting the whores. "Hello," she said, "welcome to Bright's Candies. Can I get you something?"

It's funny how that part of me that has the trouble nose can go two ways. When I met my wife, it went one way, kind of like singing. I looked into her eyes and saw huge distances, and me in all of them. She sets that part of me off in a soothing, right kind of way.

This lady, though, she set me off in the other direction. Instead of singing, there was this horrible buzzing, all through my bones and skin. I was being set off, all right, but as I stood in that shop, with the pink ribbons running under the counters, and looked at that ordinary-looking woman, all I could see was how flat her eyes looked. I couldn't see any distances in them at all. It scared me.

"Do you need anything, Sheriff?" she asked me, and all I could do was shake my head and mutter, "Uh, no, thanks, maybe later," and back out the door.

Out on the boardwalk again, I realized I was sweating. I felt awful. And sure enough, there was old Shaky Jay again.

"Pretty fast setup, eh?" he said, and all I could do was nod. "Got yer sense buzzin', does it?" I nodded again.

He moved a little closer, and the state I was in I could hardly look at him, all yellow eyeballs and

195

stale beery breath. "C'mere," he whispered loudly, "Got somethin' ta show ye." And he put his bony hand on my arm and pulled me toward his hutch.

Like I said, if Jay wants something, you help him get it. Most times, he sort of drifts through things. But when he's paying attention, you better sit up. So I followed him.

Jay lived in what we all called his hutch, a little shed thing against the alley side of the saloon. Right in the thick of things, but that's where he wanted to be. Mrs. Limerick says Jay's like some geese can be, silly-looking and cranky but the best watchdog you could find. I figure that's why everyone puts up with him.

No one, as far as I knew, had ever been inside his hutch. It was hung all over with junk he'd found, bits of cloth and feathers, parts of tools, curled shavings from the metal shop. Nails and pine cones and string and what-all. Spells, Eddie used to say, although no one listened to him. But Maddy agreed, so I was careful not to touch anything.

He carefully opened the door and rummaged around inside. I caught a peek at a mighty roomy-looking place for how small it was, with lots of interesting things hanging from the ceiling, before he banged the door shut and leaned toward me. He had a sneaky look on his rumpled face and something in his hand.

"See what I found in the middle of the crossroads this mornin', before anyone was awake," he said, and opened his hand.

Lying on his palm was a strange, witchy-looking thing, like a lumpy cross, wound around and around with string. There were things inside the string—

you could just see parts sticking out a little bit—and it was daubed all over with tar. It smelled terrible.

"What is it?" I asked, appalled and curious.

"Don't rightly know," he answered. "Never seen anythin' like it. Maybe a hex of some sort, maybe nothin'. Reminds me of a thing I saw down in New Orleans once. Nasty-lookin'."

"Well, it can't hurt us, so—"

He raised his head and gave me one of his "I see you" looks that make me nervous. "Don't go gettin' scared on us, Sheriff," he said, with that sly look again. "I figure with your sense and my sideways livin', you and me is the only ones here who can keep this place on the straight and narrow, barrin' some folk with their little Ways."

I felt myself go all stiff and crackly. "Don't try to tell me what to do, Jay Gregory," I said. "It's my job to take care of this town, not yours. Don't you go thinking just because we all put up with your craziness, you have some kind of special place here." And I turned and walked away.

"Hey, Sheriff," he called to my back, "don't you want to take this thing?"

But I ignored him and stalked off to see Mrs. Limerick in the Mercantile. The day was cool, with long, slanting sunlight, and the dirt of the street was hard after the long dry summer and brief rains. I could have gone the short way to the Mercantile, but I walked around to the next street, just to see the candy store again.

Sure enough, there was still a crowd outside it. I couldn't figure out what they'd done to the building. It looked cleaner than before. The colors inside glowed out through the window. Sort of shiny, like a Christmas ornament. It was pretty hard to ignore, especially what with the way the rest of the town looked next to it.

While I was looking, Gina Mae Harris came strolling by me. She had a stick of candy in her mouth, and she giggled when I glanced at her.

"What're you laughing at?" I growled. I didn't like seeing that unholy candy poking out of her sweet face. Gina Mae isn't the sharpest knife in the drawer, but she is a kind and modest girl, even if her daddy don't take very good care of her.

"I just got me this candy, and it's sooo good!" she told me. "This particular kind is called 'Love.' I hope it works!" She giggled again and lifted her muddy skirt like she was dancing.

"Why Gina, you're too young for that kind of thing," I complained.

"I'm fully thirteen, ain't I? My momma was married by this time next year," she said, pouting, but her eyes said she had no idea what she was talking about. She smiled at me, still sucking the damned candy with her hair falling out of its plait every which way, and walked on down the boardwalk.

I moved on toward the Mercantile, looking back again at the candy store. I could not for the life of me figure out what the glow was around the place, so I turned away and went on down past the Saloon to the Mercantile.

Mrs. Limerick was waiting on someone when I got there, so I loitered around looking at hats until she was done.

JAMIE LUHN

"What can I do for you, John?"

I looked up into Mrs. Limerick's pale blue eyes. I always did like her. She's slightly older than me, and I often wondered what she and her husband were doing in a wild and dirty town like this. Mrs. Limerick is neat and clean. She must spend all her off-hours doing laundry, I figure. Either that or she's just one of those who never seem to get dirty.

"Well," I said, "a couple things. First, I need to get some fabric for Maddy."

Mrs. Limerick's face lit up. "When are we going to see Maddy again? She hasn't been into town in ages."

"Aw, you know her, Mrs. Limerick. She doesn't like town much."

She sighed. "I know, I know. Which of these did you want?" Mrs. Limerick's long, plump hand smoothed the bolts of fabric stacked at one end of the counter.

"She was wanting something reddish. She said a greeny-red, if there is such a thing."

"I have just the thing. How's this?" And she showed me a nice sprigged muslin, just the color Maddy would like best, like bricks, or pagodas.

"That looks fine. Seven yards, please."

While Mrs. Limerick measured, I looked out the window. A few men walked by, most of them with bags or sticks of candy.

"What do you think of the new store?" I asked Mrs. Limerick.

Mrs. Limerick began cutting across the fabric. She didn't look up. "Well, I suppose if people like it, it's all right," she said noncommittally.

"Don't you think it's kind of strange? Them setting up so fast and all? I was there just before dinner time last night, and there was nothing, not a light nor a wagon nor nothing."

At this, she looked at me, and I was surprised, because her blue eyes sparked angrily at me.

"Well, now you asked me, I'll tell you. I don't hold with that kind of setup. Gone one minute and here the next. It's wrong," she said, "simple as that. I'm suspicious of folks who can't do things the right way, you know, the true and proper long way round."

"Yeah, I know what you mean. Still, they haven't done nothing wrong. Just strikes me as funny them setting up like that when we're not looking, like they wanted to take us by surprise. And I've got to admit, I didn't expect candy to be so popular in a town like this."

Mrs. Limerick looked beyond me, through the window, her eyes pale and faraway while her hands folded and smoothed the cloth. "If I was you," she said, "I'd go have a talk with that Mr. Bright, see what you can glean from how he looks and talks. That should tell you something. Better yet, have Maddy there with you when you do it."

"Why, that might just do the trick," I said. "Thank you."

"Glad to be of assistance," she said, and smiled at me. "Should I put this on your tab, Sheriff?"

"No, I got the money right here. What's the damage?"

"Two dollars and fifty cents."

I shook my head as I counted out the money.

"Seems like things is getting more and more expensive every year," I said. "No offense."

"None taken," she replied. "Cotton's gone up, ever since the troubles down South. Soon it'll be cheaper to get it from India!"

I laughed at that, and then tipped my hat at her and headed out the door. The boards outside the Mercantile are always clean and scrubbed-looking. I like to look at how the place is built, with hardly a nail in the place, it's so well fitted together. Mr. Limerick is an excellent joiner, as well as keeping shop, and people are always calling him out to do work for them. Mrs. Limerick does the shopkeeping most days, and you always see little Limericks in and out of the place.

I looked across the street to where the new bank had gone up last year. Its boards were still new and yellow, shining next to my office, which was considerably weathered. I thought to myself how I should whitewash the place before it got too run down. Funny, considering it was only built three years ago.

I saw the bank manager, Joe McGee, standing outside, looking at the candy shop with a funny look on his face, almost like he was envying the place. But he went back inside the bank when he saw me looking at him.

That evening, I told Maddy about the candy store, how it went in so fast and how everyone was walking around eating candies with strange names like "Love" and "Revenge" and "Riches."

"Quite a glamour on the place," I said. "It near about glows."

Her eyebrows—so straight and sharp, I always think they're like swallow's wings—went down with thought.

"You say they're selling things with the names of dreams?" she asked.

"We-e-ell, I wouldn't go that far. The candy all has those kinds of names, yeah."

"But, John, with the candy they're also selling the dream. Would you buy a candy called 'Revenge' if you weren't already thinking about it?"

"Sweet revenge," I muttered, my thoughts churning. "No, I see you're right."

"And what do you think they're taking in payment for these dreams? Not silver. That's only for the candy. No, for the dreams there's some other payment."

"Do you think so?" I asked, surprised at how unsurprised I felt.

"Certainly!"

"Mrs. Limerick sends her regards," I told her, "and I wanted to bring you this from her. I hope it's right." I brought out the packet of fabric. I watched her dark head bend over the packet, untying the string in the lamplight. She has a sweet curve to her neck down behind where her hair curls a little, always makes me want to put my hand on it.

"Oh! It's beautiful, John! Just perfect. Thank you," she said, looking up at me. She has a blinding smile which she doesn't use very often, but when she aims it at people they're struck dumb. And of course, you have to smile back.

Because of the smile I forgot to tell her what Mrs. Limerick said, about taking her with me to meet

Mr. Bright. I didn't remember until I rounded the corner into town and saw the candy store, glaring away in the morning sun, with even more folks going in and out. The miners had heard about the store by this time and a bunch of them were lined up outside, their hats in their hands, looking dirty and tired as usual.

"Hey there, Sheriff," they said, one by one.

"What're you fellows doing here?" I asked them. "You came all the way into town for some candy?"

"We heard there's spells on them candies," said one of the miners, Josh Carpenter, I think, though it was hard to tell under all the dirt and hair. "They say you can buy a finding spell, help you dig out the gold you ain't found yet."

"Who says?" I said.

"Some o' the miners came back to camp last night. I seen one of 'em dig out a nugget 'bout half the size o' Eddie's this morning."

The other miners murmured that it was true. They'd seen it.

I was pretty mad by now. Selling spells isn't forbidden under the law, but fraud sure is.

I pushed past the line and in through the door. The same woman was there with her syrupy smile. She was getting candy out of a jar marked "Youth" in gold letters for old Tom Abernackle. I stood at the back and watched while she passed Tim Anderson, who doesn't trust his employees, a bag taken from a jar which said "Truth" on the label.

I glanced around. The colors of the candies were hot and bright in their sparkling jars and bins. The light from the sunny window shone across the shining white counters onto the woman, whose apron glowed, it was so dizzyingly clean and crisp. Each person who came in was treated to that honey-drip smile of hers, and each person walked out with the same silly look on their own face. It was like they could see their dream coming close.

But the one thing the woman never did was tell anyone that there was spells in the candy. If they asked, she only said, "Oh, that's up to you. I can't promise anything about the *candies*!" Which was smart, considering. She wasn't giving anything away, no promises at all.

I went up to the counter and asked her about Mr. Bright.

"I'm sorry, Sheriff," she said sweetly, her dark inhuman eyes shining blankly at me. "He isn't here right now. Try back this afternoon."

So I went back to my office to kill some time. On the way I ran into poor Gina Mae Harris, who looked at me with round eyes.

"It worked!" she gushed. "I swear, Sheriff, I went back to my aunt's house and there was Abner Cullis, waiting with his hat in his hand, wantin' to take me walking this Saturday. An' me with that candy hardly finished in my mouth! Can you believe that, now?"

I mumbled something and stepped past her to the door, part of me wondering if I was just being a killjoy. Through my window I could see her skipping away along the dirty street, her tangled hair flying. Just a kid. I sighed.

Just at that moment, I heard a ruckus outside. I put my head around the door and saw Shaking Jay

Gregory and another man I had never seen before talking loudly. Jay was saying, "I know you did it! You stay away from my shack! You lyin' load o' horse manure!"

The man was a tall, thin man with a wonderful mustache. He kept trying to brush past Jay, but Jay was shaking and shuddering like he does when he's on fire with the need to say something. Sometimes when he's like this it's hard to tell what he's saying, but if he gets it clear, it's bound to be something true coming out. So I listened carefully and started walking closer. The man still didn't see me. He was trying to peel Jay's fist out of his shirt and walk on, pretending Jay was just a crazy old fart attacking him.

I heard him hiss something, and Jay got this look on his face and stood back, letting the man go. We both watched him walk away, his fancy coattails wagging, and he never did look my way.

When I got to Jay he looked like someone had died, all pale and shocked.

"What is it?" I asked him. "What did he say?"

But all I could get out of Jay by then was him saying, "Dead meat. I'm dead meat. . . ." as he shuffled away toward his hutch.

I rode home after lunch to fetch Maddy, who was sitting outside sewing when I rode up. She was surprised, but she took off her apron and came with me. There were flowers around the outside of the house again, but I didn't ask about it. I learned a long time ago not to ask about my wife's visitors.

We got to the candy store during a slow spell.

The lady behind the counter looked up ready to smile and froze when she saw Maddy.

"Mr. Bright in?" I asked.

"He's in the back. I'll fetch him," the woman said, still staring at Maddy.

I looked at her myself. She was looking pale and her eyes were jumping from corner to corner.

"Are you all right?" I asked her, and she swallowed and nodded.

"Could we go outside?" she asked, so I took her hand and led her out. She looked better right away.

Just then a smooth voice spoke behind me. "Sheriff?" it said.

I turned around, and there was the thin fellow from the street, the one who Jay had been arguing with. He came toward me across the boardwalk with a big smile, his black mustache stretching on either side, and held out his hand.

"Mr. Bright, is it?" I asked. Behind me, Maddy made a slight sound. I didn't turn to look at her, but I reached back and took her hand again.

Mr. Bright turned and gestured into the shop. "Come in," he said. "What can I do for you?"

"Sorry, sir," I said, "but could you walk with us out in the sunshine? My wife's feeling none too well at the moment."

"Of course," he said, and bowed like the villain in a vaudeville play I saw once when I was a kid.

We walked, and I asked Mr. Bright how he was liking it here, and he smiled politely and proclaimed it "the best town this side of the Rockies." I didn't believe him, but I kept right on as best I could.

"Do you plan on staying long?" I asked.

"Of course! Until I go to my Maker, I hope," he answered, with that same broad smile he seemed to use for everything.

"You sure set up fast," I said, trying to be truthful with my questions.

"Oh! Yes, my assistant is very quick," he returned, "and our merchandise is small."

"I s'pose so," I said. Beside me I could feel Maddy quiver, but I still didn't look at her. "Well, Mr. Bright, I just wanted to welcome you to our town and see if there was anything you needed."

"Oh, no, we are just fine. Won't you come and have some candy? Sweets for the missus?"

"No, thank you, we need to go down to the Mercantile and see Mrs. Limerick about some fabric," I lied. I needed to get Maddy out of there. She was leaning more and more on my arm.

"All right, then, come by sometime and help yourself," he called, as he moved away.

I walked down the hard dirt of the street, with Maddy hanging off my arm, trying to look like a man out walking with his wife. Looking back, I could see him standing and watching us go. I couldn't tell what he was thinking, but he still looked like a penny-dreadful villain.

Mrs. Limerick was waiting for us in the store, watching through the window. She came bustling right out and hustled us inside. She knew what was good for Maddy—had some of her herb tea brewed—and sat her down in the corner chair to sip. Maddy looked like I felt the first time I went into the candy store, kind of sick and damp.

208

Mrs. Limerick looked at me, her face all disapproving. "That place," she said, "I swear, John. Get rid of it, quick. It's going to ruin us all."

I looked at Maddy, sitting so quietly, looking sort of shrunk. The tea was helping, but I knew I needed to get her out of town, so I took her home.

On the way she barely stayed upright on her horse, which seemed to step forward as if he was catching her, over and over. I got her into the bed out on the porch, where she most liked to be, and asked her if she would be all right. She nodded and closed her eyes, her spiky dark hair splayed on the pillow. I went into the house for a moment to get some salt I kept there, gathered from the salt-lick high on the Mountain. I looked for my rifle. It was where I had left it, in the corner waiting to be cleaned. Oh, well. It would have to come, clean or not.

As I walked out I saw the new dress Maddy had been making, lying over a chair. It wasn't quite finished, but I could see it would look wonderful on her. That red-brown would suit her pale skin. She had a funny greenish cast sometimes, just along the edges, and this would warm that up a little.

Stopping for a moment, I took the little narrow bracelet off the hook by the door. I hadn't worn it for a long time except for hunting, but I wanted it now. It was made of Maddy's hair and kept her close to me.

I stepped out on the porch, trying to keep my boots quiet, but she opened her eyes anyway, so I came close and kissed her temple.

"Don't get too close to Mr. Bright," she whispered. "He's a—he's dangerous."

"I won't," I promised. "Unless he takes a wrong step. I don't like him."

"Of course," she said, her eyes creasing with the joke. "You wouldn't."

Then she looked into my eyes, and in her dark green-flecked gaze I saw those distances. I just had time to think, *God, I love her,* before she breathed, "Be careful, love," and closed her eyes again.

"I'll be back before dark," I told her, but she wasn't listening anymore.

In town, things were getting bad. There was a bloody fistfight going on in the street between Charlie Moffat and Al Johanssen, the biggest and meanest of the miners, and a handful of people were going in and out of the candy store like puppets. There was a "Closed" sign in the window of the bank. Otherwise, the town was deserted. I looked down the street and saw how rough the place looked, the raw wood of the buildings and the dirt in the street starting to crack again. It was getting cold. The sun was having trouble keeping up with the chill in the air, and there was a little white dust on the Mountain. The hills looked sort of stripped, like they always did just before winter.

A handbill tumbled toward me down the street and got caught on my coat.

I picked it off and read it. It was from the Post Office, down at the end of the street past the Mercantile, one of those government postings they're always putting up.

It concerned a public hanging down in Hawthorne, the other side of the state line. A man had been hanged for murder. Not too unusual, except it said his accomplice got away. He was wanted for murder, unnatural acts, fraud and occultism. There was no picture.

I could feel my eyebrows going up as I read it. The description was wrong—the fellow was too old, too short, just about everything off—but I had a feeling. Especially since, at the bottom, it said "Suspect sought for questioning with regards to the disappearance of the hanged man's body."

When I looked where I was, I was standing by Shaking Jay's hutch. Whatever this meant, he might have something to say about it. Even if it didn't make sense.

But he didn't answer my knock. I stood outside and waited, looking up and down the street. It was quiet; there was just the sound of the wind, like the world had died. The hairs on my neck did a little dance for a moment, and my nose kept pointing toward the back of the Saloon, around by the back door where the whores pour out their bedpans.

Sure enough, he was there, lying with a whiskey bottle in his hand. For a man who barely scrapes up for beer, that's kind of fancy. His mouth was open and there was spew all over the ground and his sleeve. I poked him with the toe of my boot: dead all right, for a good hunk of hours, it looked like. So I went off to find Hardy Smith, the undertaker.

I didn't get but two yards when it hit me, and I shivered. *Us two,* he had said, *between us we keep this town safe*—but now it was only me. I had to talk to Mrs. Limerick, and soon.

As I passed Jay's hutch I noticed something. In among all the pieces and parts hanging off his walls was a crumpled up piece of paper. It looked like the same handbill I had in my pocket, folded and twisted just so, and knotted into some thread.

Inside the Mercantile, I found Jeb Limerick sitting in a chair by the cracker barrel, waiting for customers. The sunlight slanted in the high side window, making gold dust-fairies trickle down through the air of the store. His long face was quiet and mournful, as always, but he stood up as I came in and put out his hand.

I shook it. "How do, Jeb? What're you doing here? Seems like most days you're off building something."

He looked at me sadly. "Th' Missus is upstairs with Petey. Seems like he took sick the last couple of days. Got a high fever just this afternoon, so she's staying by his bedside 'til it's over," he said. His hands looked empty without tools. He was a maker, Jeb was, and would always rather be out creating something. "I'm in the store with Ellen, here, minding the business."

Around from behind the counter shuffled the tiniest of the Limericks, only four or five, who looked up at me solemnly, her small braids sticking out behind. "H'lo, Mr. Sheriff," she said. "I c'n help you find anythin' you need. You need anythin'?" And she smiled at me with one tooth missing.

I could see she could, indeed, find me anything I was needing, so I thanked her kindly and turned back to her daddy. "Jay's dead," I told him, "out behind the Saloon. I was hoping your missus could help me figure out what happened to him."

"Dead?" Jeb's face looked waxy all of a sudden. "I just saw him last night, walking past on the boardwalk."

"Yeah, well, he's not walking around anymore."

"What'll we do now? He was watchin' out—"

"Shh. Why I need to talk to the missus."

"Right. Ellen, go find your ma. Seems we need her more than Petey does, for awhile."

"All right, Papa. Mr. Sheriff, you want some help?"

"Not right now, sweetheart. I'll let you know. You go get your ma, so's I can talk to her."

After a few moments Mrs. Limerick appeared in the doorway, looking more pale and lined than the last time I saw her, just a few hours ago.

"I heard you need me," she said.

"Did Ellen tell you?"

"She told me Jay was dead," Mrs. Limerick said, looking even more haggard. "Come on, John. Show me."

I glanced at Jeb, who lifted his narrow shoulders like to say "Don't ask me," and walked outside. Little Ellen followed us to the door.

"Ellen," her mother said, "you're not old enough to come see, but we'll need you soon enough. You wait here with Papa." Ellen nodded solemnly and went back inside.

When she saw Jay, Mrs. Limerick looked terribly sad. She got out a spotless handkerchief and knelt to wipe his face. "I think you better get Mr. Smith," she said.

When I got back with Hardy Smith, who was a small, muscular man used to hauling bodies and sawing lumber for coffins, Jay was cleaner than I'd ever seen him. He looked almost respectable, lying there with his tidy-looking shirt and pants and his scrubbed-looking face. His hair lay down like it had meant to do it for years but forgotten.

"My goodness," Hardy murmured, taking his hat off, "You certainly do right by a man, Mrs. Limerick."

"Everyone deserves to have a respectable death," she said, dusting her skirt where she had knelt. The still-spotless hankie made the dust jump away.

I helped Hardy get Jay onto his little cart and watched him wheel it away.

"Well," said Mrs. Limerick, "I wonder what Jay did to them?"

"How do you mean?" I asked, wanting her to explain. She has the clearest mind I ever knew, barring my wife's.

She turned to me with a fierce look. "John Adams," she said, "when you came into my shop today and I took care of Maddy, I saw that candy-shop man looking at our store. And soon as you left, I went upstairs to see. There was poor Petey, lying there sick as anything, when all he had before was a cold."

Her eyes were wet. I never saw such a fierce determination not to cry. "I have to get back to him soon and keep him safe," she said. "But first, you have to tell me if there was anything Jay might've known that was dangerous."

I shook my head, and then stopped. "He found something," I told her. "He tried to give it to me, but I wasn't paying enough attention."

"What was it?"

"A little charm or something. Said he found it at the crossroads. I didn't put much store by it at the time, but that was a couple of days ago."

"I wonder what he did with it?"

"Might be in his shack. Think we can get in?"

"We can try," she said firmly.

So we did try, and I don't know if Maddy was right about those spells or if the door was just permanently stuck, but it would not budge.

"Perhaps Maddy could help," Mrs. Limerick said. "By the way, how is she?"

"I need to go back and see," I admitted, squinting up at the sky. "It's getting pretty late in the day. Maybe I should go back and get her, if she's feeling better. Do you think Jeb might be able to find a way in?" Jeb was the one who built the shack, and I had a feeling he knew more about how to get it open than anyone.

"I'll ask," she said briefly. "Maybe he'll come out and take a look, but you should go home and take care of your wife." She glanced up at the upstairs window. "I've got to get back. See you in the morning?"

"Yep. You be careful."

"You too."

I left her climbing the boardwalk steps and went to find Widdershins, who looked at me curiously as I approached. She wasn't used to all the back and forth and was longing for me to take her saddle off. She was just going to have to put up with it awhile longer.

Climbing on, I checked my rifle again. The salt-shot I had set up earlier was still set, sitting snugly in the chamber.

I made it home without mishap, unsaddling as the sky was lighting up, all yellow and orange. Widdershins was acting jumpy, and I knew she wanted loose after a long day. I felt very tired. I walked up on the porch quietly, in case Maddy was still sleeping, but she wasn't lying there anymore. She wasn't in the house either or the garden. I stood on the porch and scratched my head. There were even more flowers around the house—fireweed and shooting-star and sticky monkey-flower—and in the dirt by the porch-bed were bear-tracks. Big ones. Bigger than any I had seen before.

I sat down in the rocker and waited, hoping she was all right. She had only done this once before, when we were first married, but I knew it was in her to go off sometimes, when there was need.

I must've fallen asleep because before I knew it it was the middle of the night and I was freezing. The cold moonlight was pouring down and I had the feeling someone had just been there, watching me. But I didn't see anything, so I went to bed.

Next morning there was still no sign of her. I was starting to get worried, but I had to get to town before things got worse. I walked around calling uselessly for awhile before catching Widdershins and saddling up.

At the last minute I wrote Maddy a note saying I would be in town and I could use her help. Then I rode off.

The first thing I saw coming around the bend in Main Street was one of the miners shooting someone. He shot him in the leg and then in the arm, and was pointing the gun at his head when I knocked him down. There was somebody yelling, probably me, and the fellow looked fair amazed when I took the gun away from him.

"Why'd you do that?" he said.

"Why the hell do you think?" I yelled at him, pulling the gun out of his hand.

It was right then he looked down at the other fellow, twisting around in his own blood, and started yelling himself. "Oh! Oh! Oh! Did I do that?" he cried. "Oh, Jesus! Oh, Larry, I'm a sorry son of a whore!" He kept shouting out apologies to the other one as I hauled him off to my office to lock him up. Jeb Limerick was coming out to look at the wounds by that time, but it didn't look like we needed to go for the doctor in Bridgeport.

As I was locking him up, with him still crying and carrying on, I heard a scuffle and a scream outside, so I ran back out again. It was Gina Mae Harris, looking frightened, pushing off a miner.

"Come on, sweetheart, just one little kiss?" he was saying, while she kicked and pushed desperately at him with her skinny arms. Another, younger man was standing nearby, with the same look on his face, like a moonstruck calf. Lucky he was shyer than the first one, or Gina Mae would never have managed.

I went over and had a word, and both of them went off like beaten dogs, shooting her amorous looks as they went.

"Thank you, Sheriff," she said, blushing. She wiped her face with a none-too-clean sleeve, trying to look like she didn't want to cry. "That's the third time someone's tried to kiss me today, an' I'm gettin' sorta tired of it. Musta been that candy," she said, straightening her skirt and looking wistfully toward the candy shop. "Seems to've made me fair game instead o' givin' me a sweetheart. That weren't what I wanted! I've half a mind to go down there an' ask fer my money back. What do you think?"

"I think if you tried it, they would just tell you there wasn't no spell in that candy. You leave it to me, I'm going to deal with them today. In the meantime, you head on home and lock the door. Don't let anyone in but your family, you hear?"

"Yessir," she said, and I could tell she meant it too. She turned and ran off down the street, looking relieved.

Watching out for further trouble, I walked on across to the Mercantile. Jeb Limerick was inside, weighing flour for a miner, while the fellow with the gunshot wounds sat in the chair like a war victim. He was already starting to look cleaner. Must be something in the air at the Mercantile.

"Why, if it ain't Larry Carpenter," I said.

"Hey there, Sheriff," he said faintly. "Thanks for knocking Sam down like that."

"It's my job," I said. "No call to thank me for it."

"Well, I figure I can be grateful for good timing," he rasped, then coughed.

"Want to tell me what happened?" I asked.

"I don't rightly know myself," he answered. "I found some gold the other day down by the creek, ya know, and Sam, who has the claim next to me, says to me, he says, 'That's my gold,' and I says, 'No, it ain't. I dug it up on my own claim.' But he didn't believe me, almost like someone was whisperin' in his ear, I swear. He kept kind o' listenin' and then yellin', and then listenin' some more. I left him there an' went off to my shanty, an' he didn't follow me, so I didn't think nothin' of it.

"Then when I come into town today, he sees me come out o' the candy store after buyin' the last of their 'Find' candy, and he gets all crazy and pulls out his gun. I think he thought I did it on purpose, but there were only two candies left anyways, I swear."

"Well, it ain't all right to shoot you over a couple of candies anyway," I said to him, and patted his arm before I went out.

Jeb followed me out to Jay's shack. "I took a look at it," he said. "It should open now. Ain't nothing in it, though."

I opened the door easily, and looked inside. He was right. There wasn't anything interesting inside, only a cot and some boots and a bunch of stuff, like old nails and horseshoes, hanging off the ceiling. It didn't look like I remembered seeing through the door that day. It was smaller, and the hanging stuff didn't catch my fancy. I wondered if it had changed, or if it was always this way and I just saw it wrong that once.

"Spells on it," Jeb said. "Keeps it dull-looking. I figure the real place went away when Jay died. No telling what was lost."

"You think?" I said, looking at the musty bed.

"You won't find anything important here, that'd

be my guess," he said. "It's a shame. I know he had all kinds o' interesting stuff in here."

"I'm looking for a funny kind of cross, all wrapped in string, with tar on it?"

"Naw, ain't seen nothin' like that."

"Damn."

"Tell you what, whyn't you ask little Ellen? She can find anything."

I squinted up at the side of the shop, where the high window let the morning daylight in. "You willing to risk her getting some attention from over there?" I tipped my head in the direction of the candy store.

"I am. She may be a little bitty thing, but she can tell when somethin's comin'. Plus I figure, if you find that thing, the way th' missus tells it, we're all better off."

"That's for sure," I said. "Let's find the little one."

So we went back inside the store, where we found Ellen standing on a stool wrapping up some potatoes in burlap for a customer.

"Thirty-five cents, please," she said, through the hole in her teeth.

The man counted out some coins and took his bundle of goods out of the shop.

"She's good, ain't she?" Jeb said proudly. "She can find anythin', even numbers." He put his arm around her, and she smiled all over her face.

"Ellen, darlin', Sheriff needs you now," he said to her, quietly.

"Whatcha lookin' for?" she asked.

"Well, it's sort of like a cross," I said, "wrapped in—"

"Oh, you mean Jay's thing? The one he found?" she asked. "With all the funny junk, wrapped in string?"

"Yes! That's what I'm looking for," I said, relieved.

"He took it over to the graveyard to try to get rid of it," she said. "I can't tell if it's there anymore."

"Will you come with me and have a look?"

"Sure!"

She hopped down from the stool and went ahead of me out the door. We walked down past the Post Office and around up the hill behind the bank, where the graves were marked with wooden planks. The wind whispered through the sparse trees, and like all cemeteries, it was quieter than the town. I always did like graveyards of any kind. They're so quiet and thoughtful. Peaceful.

But we hardly got there and stood in the wide-open space, looking down over the town squatting chilly against the bare hillside, when she said, "Nope, it ain't here."

"No?"

"Nope. It's down there," she said, and pointed toward the candy store. "The man down there buried it next to the post."

"Let's walk down there. You can show me better," I said, taking her hand. Walking together back down the hill, I tried not to let her feel me shivering. It was all getting a little too close now.

We walked along the street like an uncle and

his niece, casual and slow. The candy store was somewhat busy, but not enough to keep them from noticing me scratching around the boardwalk outside their shop. I could feel sweat trickling down between my shoulder blades as we got near.

"Which post?" I asked her, and she pointed. The corner one. "Is it far down?" I wondered, and she answered, "No, only a couple of inches."

So I got out my knife and started digging, and sure enough, there it was. I barely got it out and into my pocket when a smooth voice said, "What are you doing, Sheriff?"

I looked up, right into the eyes of Mr. Bright, smiling down at me from the boardwalk with eyes like sharp glass. If he could've cut me with that stare, he would've. I took a step back.

"Oh, nothing, Mr. Bright. Ellen here was just telling me she lost a penny right around here when she wanted to buy some candy," I lied. "You go on back to your ma and tell her we didn't find it," I told her, looking into her eyes. Of course she caught the message and nodded, her eyes big.

I could feel lines of deep power radiating from Mr. Bright as he took another step toward me. Seemed like he was reaching out and trying to find something to get hold of on me. There was a poking and scrabbling around my chest, and I stepped back, putting my hand over my heart.

Instantly, I felt it change. The hair bracelet sizzled around my wrist, and I saw Mr. Bright recoil as I stepped still further back from him. Then he pushed at me. I could see his forehead crease when he did it.

It was a rolling charge, like a buffalo trying to bowl me over. I stepped to one side, feeling around like crazy to see what he'd try next. I felt the round heaviness of whatever it was go pushing past me and into the bank building, where it left a big hole in the wall.

But I didn't hear it hit, because by now I could feel a kind of thick rubbery wall building around me, like cold oatmeal. The bracelet fizzed and then just lay there. This was some kind of dead magic. I pushed against it as hard as I could, but I'm weak that way. That's the problem with me, I may have the best nose in California, but that's all I have. Like most of us in this town, we just have to use our wits most of the time, because our ways can't save us.

The wall was getting closer and closer around me, and all I could do was stand there. I stared at Mr. Bright and he stared at me. I could still move my arms, so I got the little charm out and poked hopefully at the wall with it, but that only made him laugh. The wall was around my head now, getting closer. I was having a hard time breathing, and my head hurt from all the wickedness he was throwing at me.

I heard someone yelling but I couldn't turn my head by that time. Things were starting to feel very far away. The wall covered my face and pinned my arms, and I couldn't breathe, though my chest was heaving. I tried to break the little charm, but I couldn't pick at it hard enough to get it apart. After a time, I started to see flashes of light at the edges of my vision, and things got sort of wavery.

Then suddenly the wall weakened, crumbling a little bit like oatmeal does, away from my face. I could hear something roaring, but I still couldn't turn my head. I pushed harder, and this time it came all clear from around my ears and shoulders. Mr. Bright wasn't looking at me anymore—he was looking up the street.

Maddy was here.

Down the street she came, taller than I knew she could get, covered in reddish strips of bark, her pale skin showing through. Her hair flew out, dark and green and sharp, leafy shadows around her angry face and down her back, and she looked at Mr. Bright. By her side walked a grizzly and a mountain lion, and she reached down with hard green fingers to touch them. She said something I couldn't hear.

I felt the oatmeal wall crumbling away, but I didn't move. My Maddy was here. She was beautiful, how I had always known she would be! I watched her approach with a wildly beating heart. A tree stood in the middle of the street, rooted and slim, with reaching arms, but it was my Maddy.

She was still speaking to Mr. Bright. He didn't move, as if he were listening, but I could tell he was gathering himself in. Getting ready for something. I felt the little charm twitch in my hand.

That was it! I looked down at it in surprise. All his power was coming through the little thing, like a lodestone or an amplifier. It twitched again, and I saw Maddy's gaze flick to it, and to me, and back to Mr. Bright. It was only a second, but I saw in the greens of her eyes what to do.

Behind me, I heard Jeb say very quietly, "Throw it up in the air. Go on."

Mr. Bright was busy watching Maddy, who was looking taller and angrier and sharper every second. The grizzly stood up on its hind legs now next to her, and the mountain lion snarled and raised its hackles. Her glance flicked again, but this time Mr. Bright saw. Quick as I could, before he turned fully, I threw the thing up into the air. He whirled around in time to see it going up.

"NO!" he screamed, and at that moment I heard my own rifle go off behind me. The rock salt came tearing through the air, shredding the little cross into tiny pieces. Little bits flew out in all directions, scattering across the road and blowing off in the sharp wind which was now hurling and leaping through town. We all stood and watched as the pieces were picked up and tossed high, over the cemetery and on over the hill until they were all gone.

Two nails fell with a *ping!* at my feet, with only a scrap of string to show they had ever been together. I stooped to pick them up.

When I straightened up, Mr. Bright was gone.

I could see the bear lumbering off up the road, and the mountain lion was nowhere to be seen. Behind me, I heard Jeb say, "Thank goodness!" and put down the gun. I stood there, staring at the nails. Little Ellen came over and held out her hand. I gave her the nails and she looked at them carefully.

"Well." She looked up at me with bright eyes. "I suppose a maker is the right person to UNmake something too, don'cha think?" Then her eyes slid sideways, and she laughed up at someone.

I turned to look, too. Maddy, my own Maddy, was walking toward me in an unfinished red dress that looked like muslin again. She was smiling.

And you know what happens when she smiles.

Risqueman

written by

Mike Wood

illustrated by

EVAN JENSEN

ABOUT THE AUTHOR

Baby boomer and Englishman Mike Wood was born on the Isle of Man, and now lives on the Wirral, in North West England. Mike has read science fiction since his childhood "Rupert Bear" comic strip days, but didn't start writing until his late twenties. He then had an "unfortunate and debilitating attack of mid-life maturity," and spent a number of years concentrating on accountancy exams.

About five years ago, he rediscovered his writing and science fiction. In 2007, he won the first Jim Baen Memorial Writing Contest, honoring the former US publisher and editor, and Mike's winning story, "A Better Sense of Direction," appears in The Best of Jim Baen's Universe II.

Mike and his wife, whom he describes as "a talented but penniless botanical artist," have two grown children. By day, Mike works as a management accountant for public transport. When he's not working or writing, Mike performs as a musician, playing sax and clarinet in two local big bands with occasional gigs in the orchestra pit.

ABOUT THE ILLUSTRATOR

Evan Jensen likes dogs and strong cheeses. Copious sampling of the latter has resulted in his forcible ejection from social situations, which is okay because Evan also likes the outdoors and amusing inconveniences. He makes a mean spiced chai and can feather a bull's-eye at 100 yards.

Such interesting habits started while he grew up in the verdant Mid-Atlantic region: In Evan's youth, his immediate family monikered his room "The Cave," where he'd likely be found hunkered down on the floor with paper and pencil scratching out strange creations. If not there, the leaf-littered woods and parks of the Chesapeake Bay watershed were frequent habitats that drew his attention.

By college, illustrated creatures great and small began to hunker in corners and populate the nooks Evan would inhabit. Studios, apartments, kitchens, bulletin boards, gallery walls were all fair territory for his pen's offspring. Since graduating, Evan cast his creative eye on the Web, taking freelance chances and gaining more established art director posts. His odyssey has led rather circuitously to an interest in children's books, never letting go of the fantasy that had rooted itself in his work and play.

Risqueman

She never saw it coming. She never intended for any of it to happen like this; her intentions were always good, but some things . . . well, once you let them out of the box there's just no squashing them back in again.

"My algorithm will destroy the world, Jen." Léonie spoke the words quietly and with intensity— leaning over the beer-sticky table of drinks between us, so that her face was inches from mine and where I could see the passion dancing in her eyes.

"Remember this day, Jenkin Morgan. It marks the beginning of the end of hope."

The bar in the Roath Dock Hotel in Cardiff had almost become a second home to us. It's one of those modern places with artificial, purchased character—the elements are all there, but they never quite succeed in delivering the atmosphere in the way that a good dose of history can. For Léonie and me, though, it worked just fine, because we brought our own history. We didn't need the flame-effect log fire, the attic sale rows of books glued to the shelves, or the "gentleman's club" style of leather furniture. The Roath Dock Hotel was *our* place because it was close to both tSolve, where Leo worked, and years later, to the government offices where I tasted my brief spell of employment. It was where we always met when we were both in town. At that time in our lives we saw more of each other in the Roath Dock than we did at home.

I can remember so many of the talks we had there. They were always spirited, mainly because Leo came straight from work and excitement always came with her; excitement as tangible and as thrilling as the ever-present hint of expensive French perfume that was her constant companion, and which never failed to turn heads whenever Leo entered a room.

"It had nothing to do with risk management." She was agitated, running her fingers through her short dark hair the way she always did when her mind was running hot. "Risqueman is a perversion—I was drawn into it . . . I don't know how. My desire, always, was to unite mathematics. As a goal it was pure—the mathematical ideal."

I first met Léonie Fenech during the late twenties' Biofuel-War riots in Paris. I was still a policeman back then, part of a temporary Europe-wide force of riot police. I was a single brick in a wall of Kevlar and pliable flesh. She was rioting. To be precise, she was beating me on the head with a fence post. I can still see her as she was, five foot nothing and scrawny, and having to jump up in the air just to reach me with that two-by-two. Her eyes were filled with fire and fervor. I knew right then that she was the girl for me. Sometimes you know things. Sometimes you just have to take a risk. Back then you never knew how any given action might turn out. The world was filled with uncertainty. Léonie changed all of that. She changed everything.

I took my chance. I pursued her, even though my French was poor. I pursued her, even though, on the outside, we seemed so ill-matched—I was a good eighteen inches taller than she, my mashed prop-forward's ears made me look more like a survivor than a tempting male specimen, and intellectually . . . well, if she was looking for a mind as formidable as hers then she was looking on the wrong planet.

Somehow we clicked, though. The big soft South Wales boy and the mathematical genius. She said it was empathy—that she recognized my creative side. Whatever, it worked, and I'm grateful for it.

It wasn't an easy ride. We were from different places, both culturally and geographically, and the Biofuel Wars had ended the era of cheap jet travel and made the world big again. But Léonie, with her single-minded philosophy—to set an objective, then move heaven, hell and earth to achieve it—helped convince me to take the step; to take my first big risk. So I stayed in Paris. I did what I'd always, secretly, wanted to do; I cast the uniform aside and I began to study art. The wonderful stupid things people do for love.

I went to the bar for two more beers. The television was on. Coincidence and irony, today of all days, they were showing a rerun of the BBC Horizon documentary, *Léonie Fenech—Beauty in Numbers.* The barman nodded towards the screen.

"It's a repeat on BBC4. Thought the lady would appreciate it."

I smiled. "Thanks, Ralph, but we've seen it. Couple of bottles of Peroni when you're ready?"

I couldn't help myself. My eyes were drawn to the screen.

"So, Léonie, when did you first realize you wanted to be a mathematician?"

"Do you know, I can give you the exact date," she said, laughing. "For me, the dream started on my tenth birthday, the third of July, 2020."

I shook my head. This had surprised me the first time I saw the interview. I'd known all about her sense of wonder for the patterns and symmetries of mathematics, but she'd never really told me where it all came from, and the image that came to mind, of a ten-year-old girl with a passion for maths in preference to ponies, was difficult to reconcile.

"I found a book about Wiles and his proof of Fermat's Last Theorem. At ten years old it moved me, because I'd heard about how Andrew Wiles himself was the same age, ten years old, when he began his solitary journey towards proving Fermat. I wanted a passion like that, a guiding star. I bought the book with my birthday money.

"It took me on a journey, a quest for that single passion. I thought I'd found it in my early teens with Langland and the quest for a Grand Unified Theory of Mathematics. I studied him; I studied Wiles; I studied all the great names; and I began to see a picture—there were so many coincidences and parallels. Much of my work kept returning to Pierre Fermat and those letters he exchanged with

Pascal—the roots of probability. And that's where *my* work began to focus; probability, certainty and uncertainty . . . and the uncharted terrain of coincidence."

Léonie was so intense. That interview was so like her. I loved it when she became so enraptured in her incomprehensible world of numbers.

"And then there was Wiles' work using modular forms to prove Shimura-Taniyama. And, in 2015, the Borodin Conjecture came along and promised to move economics into something that was so much more tangible—he was *this* close." She held her thumb and forefinger a whisker apart. "*This* close to forging yet another link with Shimura-Taniyama."

And that afternoon, in Cardiff, the enthusiasm and passion were no different, even though the circumstances were at odds with the high-flying successes that had surrounded her at the time of the documentary.

I returned to our table with the drinks.

"They're running your show on the TV," I said.

She laughed.

"Coincidence, Jen? I could give you a wonderful equation that would show the *certainty* of their repeating that program today."

She was on an adrenaline high after having quit her job under circumstances that would have brought most people to tears. She had just made *le grand geste,* and she was in full flow, waving her arms, jumping from her seat and coming ever closer to spilling our beer. She went over the problems with her algorithm again. I'd heard it before, and I hadn't understood any of it then, either. But Léonie needed to talk. She was talking fast and loud, sometimes slipping into French without realizing. English or French, it was all the same to me, once she got deeply into her maths the language morphed into sounds without meaning. But I'd learned long ago that there were times when it was important to listen. Understanding was irrelevant. I didn't even dare take a sip of my beer because breaking eye contact would break the spell.

Leo, ever restless, brought her knee up under the table and sent our glasses spinning again. Beer sloshed and went fizzing onto the tabletop. My glass teetered on edge for an impossible moment, and then righted itself. All of this unfolding drama passed by Leo unnoticed. She talked. She was animated, using her expressive vocabulary of voice, hand and body language.

She placed a hand on my arm and looked straight into my eyes.

"That night, Jen, the night the equation completed, was the night that Uncertainty died. I should have stopped it then; *fini*. Because people will embrace this thing even when they are aware of the lie. People want certainty, even if it is an illusory certainty. And this 'want,' will break them.

"I should have destroyed my papers, Jen. I should have set fire to my office with everything inside it, myself included. If only I had known. *Je suis le Diable*. I am the Devil. I have destroyed humanity."

"Steady on, Leo," I said. "It's just numbers."

Oops!

"Ce n'est pas des nombres simplement!"

She shouted the words. People glanced over, then looked away. Some looked up at the television screen and made the connection between the Léonie Fenech of today, who had now fallen silent, and the TV version from two years earlier. The TV Leo was still in full flow. I could spot the cuts where they'd taken out the bits where she'd lapsed into French. The editing was almost seamless.

"I knew that I could do something. [cut] Maxim Borodin was a wonderful teacher and mentor. He taught me so much in Paris, but there were many loose ends, too many.

"So I began writing my genetic algorithm . . . [cut] that's an algorithm that can learn from its own millions of mistakes," she said.

I looked over at Leo, who was quiet and now listening to her own words on the television. Her lips repeatedly formed those words, *Je suis le Diable,* which she whispered under her breath, all the time shaking her head.

"I incorporated chaos theory, going right back to Sofia Kovalevskaya and Alexandr Liapunov. [cut] It took nearly eight months to write that algorithm, and then nearly a year to run it for the first time. But then the second time it ran in just eighteen minutes. I was surprised. It seemed to have found an equilibrium that should not have existed because it was describing a dynamical instability."

The interviewer nodded. A nod seemed appropriate, but I could tell from the vacancy in his eyes that he had lost it now.

"Again and again I ran it, from different starting

235

points, using both real and imaginary numbers, and using different, more abstract functions, and again and again it came full circle to that lovely, ugly equation."

That "lovely, ugly equation" was a turning point for the world. For Leo and me, it marked the end of our carefree youth.

Up until that time we'd both been moving through life with an eye for the moment. We were wild, free and unconcerned. When I say unconcerned—we did have our causes. Léonie still felt bitter about what was going on in Africa. The Biofuel Wars were a wake-up call to those of us who had naïvely believed that the world had become a better place. I'd been living in my head, oblivious to the injustices, right up until the Paris riots where I found myself on the wrong side. Léonie opened my eyes for me—with that fence post. She fought for justice, *we* fought, but in those student days the fight, the participation, was sometimes more important to us than the cause. We had a voice and it was fun.

I left Uni in '31 and I began to paint in earnest. I had belief in myself. I really thought I had something.

Leo had another year to complete her *Doctorat du Troisième Cycle,* but she had already made a name for herself in the isolated world of mathematics, and her options were growing daily. The Sorbonne wanted her to stay on for a couple more years to earn a *Doctorat d'État* so that she might teach there, but at the same time she was being courted by some major players.

She ignored both the big-money offers from the multinationals and the entreaties from the university, and she took off on a typical Léonie-style tangent and accepted an offer from tSolve, a small research consultancy in Cardiff. I was unhappy. I felt she was letting herself down. She was better than this.

"Come on, Leo, Cardiff? You've had offers from GMFord, VodaVivendi-Siemens, BPShell . . . and you're looking at tSolve! Who the hell are tSolve? They've got a staff of what, twelve?"

"Stay out of it, Jen. This is *my* world. I know what I'm doing."

"Jesus, Leo. Cardiff! You're doing it because you think I'm homesick?"

"So selfish, Jen. You think this is about *you*?"

This stung me. That was exactly what I had thought, and yes—I suppose I was being selfish; I was enjoying Paris and freedom from family ties. I deflected the jibe by grabbing the copy of *New Scientist* that lay on the table amongst my clutter of paint tubes and brushes, and I waved it in front of her. She was the cover girl, looking chic and intelligent. "Fenech—the Quest for Unification" ran the headline. I threw the magazine at her. I picked up another, *Paris Match*.

"Léonie Fenech—La beauté—l'intellectuelle."

I jabbed at the headline. (I didn't throw this one, though; I already had plans to get the cover framed. She looked stunning in that tight black dress.)

"Right now you are probably the most famous . . . the *only* famous mathematician, in the world. Shouldn't you be aiming higher?"

"tSolve are small, yes, but they will give me freedom to develop my work. I have ideas, Jen, and these are ideas that might have practical application, no longer just pure number theory. I don't want to go to some faceless corporation and be buried in mission and marketing hype. I don't want to be a beauty queen; a corporate image."

It all sounded kind of plausible but I always had my doubts. She'd once denied having any desire for applied maths. For her, the essence of the chase was always in the numbers. Numbers were clean, precise—black-and-white. But now something had changed, and I wasn't sure that even she was aware of it.

She joined tSolve and for five years she vindicated her own self-belief and that of her employers. We set up home on the Gower Peninsula and I reluctantly reestablished contact with my parents in Merthyr Tydfil, my home town; a town locked into an endless cycle of urban decay—urban renewal. I visited at weekends and bore their silent Victorian disapproval of my ever-failing career; of my financial dependence on a successful . . . "partner" (mother hated that word); and of family betrayal—there had been three generations of policemen in the Morgan family. When my younger brother, Dafydd, was killed in Africa the responsibility fell on my shoulders . . . and I quit the force and became an artist. I bore their disapproval with a forced smile and with ulcer-forming, stress-laden guilt.

Léonie worked on her proofs and her algorithms, sometimes at the tSolve HQ in Cardiff or, more usually, she worked alone in her cramped office behind our cottage. For inspiration she had the portraits of her heroes hanging all around the walls: Fermat, Leplace, Pascale, Julia and Fatou, and overseeing them all, in pride of place above her desk, was Sophie Germain, the self-taught French number theorist who had had to masquerade as a man in order to have her mathematical genius recognized—for Léonie, Sophie Germain was the archetypal heroine and role model.

For five years Léonie stayed pure and theoretical. She labored to prove something, both to herself and to her small, insular circle of colleagues.

Then came the algorithm. The Fenech Algorithm.

"C'est merde!" she once said. "Is it not bad enough that I create this abomination? Why do they insist on naming it after me?"

But in those first triumphant months she was unaware of the darker shadows that haunted her mathematical creation. She came home each evening thrilled and exhilarated about what she was doing. Although the roots of the algorithm were founded deep in pure number theory, the Fenech Algorithm had real-world applications. Leo could not resist the process of putting it to some practical use. tSolve were ecstatic. This was exactly the kind of thing they had always hoped might result from their association with the fabulous Léonie Fenech.

The first collaboration was with a local firm of actuaries, small, discreet and utterly blown away by what they saw. Then Léonie and her team gave a presentation to some of the country's major insurance companies. The actuaries had maintained their discretion—there had been no leak—and so what took place that afternoon has since been likened to an evangelical awakening; the insurance companies had come face to face with God—and God was green and crinkly. From out of nowhere all risk had become predictable, quantifiable and sexy. tSolve had scrambled to protect Leo's work with international patents, but the news was out.

The big picture began to emerge. The forces of subversion are always waiting on the sidelines for the Next Big Thing, and in August 2037 they started to mobilize.

"Jen, I have news."

She was out of breath. I guessed she'd run all the way up the path from the lane where we parked our cars. She was hopping up and down, finding it difficult to keep still. The broad smile and shining eyes hinted at the kind of news she'd brought.

"You're home very early. Have you been sacked?"

She punched me on the arm.

"I had to come and tell you. Besides, I couldn't concentrate. Jen, we've had an approach from the Federal Government. They want to send two European ministers to see us next week."

"Since when did you become a fan of the FE?"

"I can become a loyal and enthusiastic supporter of our government—if only they have the right kind package to offer. Jen, I know this is the breakthrough we have been looking for. The insurance guys were hot for the program and I am sure word has spread."

"So, what are you hoping for?"

"Investment. Resources. We are still struggling with some of the modules. With access to FE hardware we can crack some of the problems in months rather than years. With a fully integrated system we can make a difference. This is everything I ever wanted, Jen—to make a difference."

"Leo, it's everything you ever deserved. I am so proud of you."

I pulled her close and hugged her. She couldn't relax, though. She was too animated. She pushed me away, holding my shoulders with outstretched arms so that she could look into my eyes.

"Jen, you have to be there."

"Leo, I can't . . ."

"You have to share the moment with me. It's not a problem. Everyone at tSolve knows you. You won't be in the way. I'll introduce you to the ministers as an associate. Please, Jen. I want *you* to see it—to be there with me."

I took a seat in the corner, next to Linda Wilks, the CEO's wife, another "associate." The boardroom at tSolve is large for such a small company—it can sit thirty around the table with ease—and that afternoon the room was full.

Amongst the honorary gray-suited invitees were Simone Hillyear and Gerhard Klum from the Federal Government. As soon as I saw them edging into the boardroom, looking around in disdain at the stained, oak-effect Formica tables and the austere plastic stacking chairs, I felt a sinking premonition that the afternoon might not be the triumphant affair that Leo had wanted me to witness.

Coffee was served, then Bob Wilks launched into a nervous opening, making the introductions before handing over the meeting to Gerhard Klum, who gave a curt nod and a grimace.

"We would like tSolve to work exclusively for Europe," was Klum's opening line. He smiled, but the expression did not sit well on his face. ". . . and to that end, we have made a substantive offer to your shareholders. We have reached agreement with an acceptable majority in accordance with tSolve's Articles."

As quick as that, tSolve and Leo had become government employees.

I watched the transformation of emotions sweep over Léonie's face like a thundercloud at a summer picnic. I felt my own stomach turn.

Leo was the first to break the shocked silence that followed the announcement.

"You have done this to gain possession of the algorithm. Why do you want Risqueman?" she asked, using the new product name for the first time. Her voice was strangely calm and controlled.

"Risqueman offers unprecedented benefits to the individual. We want to make sure everyone has the chance to take full advantage."

"You do appreciate, Risqueman is not fully realized. In its current form the algorithm achieves equilibrium on an incomplete data set. It works well processing physical risk but there are other uncertainties that we have, so far, been unable to incorporate. Risqueman is still a nonunified model. The economic model, for example, has not been incorporated at all. We are some way from being ready to begin any distribution. That is your plan, I assume? You are going to give it away?"

The government official coughed and smiled.

"No, no. Not give it away. Have no fear about that. But we are going to make it widely available."

"I have no fear about you giving Risqueman away, at least in a controlled and limited form, Herr Klum. My fears lie elsewhere. You're going to sell it?"

"Subscription, Miss Fenech. I believe we can offer a full, remotely accessible package via the Internet."

"Ahh."

"We will offer Risqueman throughout Europe on a monthly subscription basis. There will be a central database, central processing . . . Risqueman can be used to support insurance applications, and it will be an aid to improving the health and safety of every European citizen. Risqueman will become a lifestyle companion for everyone."

"Assuming everyone will be able to afford it."

"Yes, Miss Fenech, but we aim to price it reasonably."

"But not reasonably enough for some."

"We . . ."

"And it's only for Europeans? And I don't suppose you'll want the armed forces to have it, in Africa, at least not the lower ranks."

"Miss Fenech, I think . . ."

"No. No, you do *not* think. You have not considered the implications at all. The scheme you are proposing could be a disaster—a catastrophe. It should be available to all—as a tool for *individuals*.

Your proposal for a central database is *dangerous*! It is irresponsible."

"Miss Fenech!" It was the slippery one, Simone Hillyear, who took over the speaking now. She took off her spectacles and stared at Léonie with those trademark cold gray eyes that were familiar to everyone in Europe.

Léonie stared back. Two irresistible and stubborn wills. Neither would break eye contact and the silence seemed to stretch on for minutes.

"Miss Fenech," Hillyear said, at last, "the full benefits of Risqueman can only be realized through sharing data. Access must be controlled and so, as with any scarce resource, there must be a price, and it is inevitable that some will be unable, or unwilling—I might add—to meet that price. This is what we call a market economy."

"Miss Hillyear. This is what *some* might call greed."

"Oh, come now, Léonie . . ."

"Miss Fenech will do fine, Miss Hillyear. Now, let's not avoid the reality here. There is *no* scarce resource. Risqueman, in its current configuration, exists. It is a simple algorithm and it could be made available on an individual basis to anyone. I have published the transcript in *Nature*. I have no intentions of limiting any benefits that may accrue from . . ."

"Er, Léonie." This was Bob Wilks. He's not your typical CEO. He's a nice guy. He would have hated all this, I'm sure. "Léonie, we have patented Risqueman. You know this—you were a part of that decision. The Federal Government has . . . acquired the patents along with executive control of tSolve. Léonie, I'm sorry but . . ."

"But what, Bob? Look around. The Feds have been invited to dine with us and they've ended up nicking the silver." Léonie turned back to Hillyear and Klum.

"Il n'y a pas une ressource limité!" Léonie was on her feet now. "Risqueman is *not* a scarce resource. You are *making* it scarce. You are in this for the profit. You've screwed me. You've screwed tSolve. Now you're going to screw the whole world. So, tell me, Miss Hillyear, Herr Klum, for what will the money be used? On what social good will it be spent? Biofuel? Extra bullets for the army so we can steal more fuel crops from the Africans?"

"Miss Fenech!"

"Or to finance the Nigerian labor camps? Maybe you'll spend some on aid for the extra refugee children you create, or is even that too much to ask?"

"Miss Fenech! That is quite enough!"

"And the full model, listen again, is not . . . even . . . finished!"

"Leónie, please . . ." Bob Wilks put a hand on Leo's shoulder to get her to sit down. "Léonie, I know how you feel about the African situation, but really, this isn't helping. Let's just listen to what our *guests* have to say."

"Thank you, Mr. Wilks." This was Hillyear. "Miss Fenech, the foreign policy of the Federal Government is really not a part of our remit. Please be calm. We are not here to take Risqueman away from you. We're here to discuss. We value your input. We will need you on board to develop the product, then to refine it into a practical online resource. I didn't want this meeting to be combative in any way. If there's something that I have said or suggested that has led you to these misconceptions, then I apologize. We want you to be a part of the team, Miss Fenech."

"So." Leo took a long breath. She placed her hands, palms down, on the conference table in front of her.

"Then . . . I too wish to apologize."

She sat down.

There were relieved smiles all around.

"And you wish me to help?"

"Absolutely."

"Collaboration—part of the team?"

"Of course."

"*D'accord.* So our first object, our first task, must be: set up a working group to develop a safe and fully functional open-source version of Risqueman. *N'est pas?*"

"Open source? Miss Fenech, we . . ."

"*Oui, bon.* Open source. *C'est gratuit.* Is free."

"Miss Fenech, no. The subscription will be fair, it will be just, but there will be no open-source distribution of . . ."

Léonie was on her feet again. She leaned across the table and adopted her whispering, menacing tone.

"Well then, my friends, you will destroy the world. And I will wash my hands of it all."

On the conference table, placed in front of each visitor, there was a glossy brochure that had been provided to explain the vision and functionality of Risqueman. None had been opened or even touched. Léonie reached over and picked one up. Without breaking eye contact with Hillyear she began tearing the brochure, first into halves, then quarters. She held out the scraps in one hand and looked around the room to make sure everyone was watching, then she flicked the shredded booklet into Hillyear's face, spun around and blazed out of the room, slamming the door behind her. There was pandemonium. I slid down in my chair. I shrugged helplessly whenever Leo's colleagues— people that I knew—caught my eye. As soon as an opportunity arose I slipped out. I knew where I'd find her. I went straight across the road to the Roath Dock Hotel. Leo was waiting in our favorite corner—the table by the window that looked out onto the road and the tSolve offices on the other side. She had a box that was filled with her desk contents beside her. I expected tears, and wouldn't you think that after all these years I'd know her better than that. No tears. There was rage. She made her "my-algorithm-will-destroy-the-world" speech, and she spilled our beer. But always there was that cold glint of determination in her eye, and this reaction I *did* know. This I knew very well indeed.

There were a lot of tensions that year. We wanted to have children. This was something we had always talked about. But the time was never right, and now Leo had become too pessimistic about the world into which she might bring them.

And money, of course. When beggary comes knocking tensions are inevitable in any relationship.

A few months after Leo became unemployed I took a job with the Welsh Assembly. To Léonie it was a job with The Government, and my treachery was sublime.

"I do not understand you, Jenkin. What has happened to all of your dreams?"

It was late. We were in the back bedroom—the room I used to call my art studio. There were no paintings, no works in progress. I'd brought in a TV a few weeks earlier. I looked around, in vain, for the remote, then hauled myself up from the sofa and crossed the room to switch it off. I returned to the sofa. Leo was still standing in the doorway, her arms folded.

"Nothing has happened to my dreams, Leo. I'm sure this is just temporary. But I have to be realistic about my painting, I'm not selling anything."

"Because you have lost your edge, your passion."

"No, I haven't. I've gained something. I've gained the will to eat."

"You were once a great artist."

"My stuff was, is and always will be crap, and you know it." I said this, although I didn't really believe it. As I say, things were tense. Sometimes people say things just to prolong the upset. It hurts them just as much as it hurts those who care about us.

"Your . . . 'stuff' . . . was inspired. Your work was in Tate Modern."

This was cruel and I'm certain Leo was well

aware of it, only she continued; she kept on dialing up the pain.

"The critics were moved. You saw the newspapers."

"It was a mistake, Leo. You know exactly how it made me feel. My *paintings* never hung in the Tate."

"You were feted, Jen. 'A Representative-minimalist's plea against 21st-Century Economic Pressures.' It was a celebrated work of modern art."

"It was . . . nothing. It was a piss-take. I was angry. You know how it happened. It was random anarchy. Three pointless canvases."

"It was art, Jen."

"It was rubbish."

"Jenkin . . ."

"Léonie, you know as much about art as I know about mathematics."

"So, what? The Tate people know nothing of art also?"

"So it would appear. It would also appear they know as much about economics as your algorithm does. Nine-and-a-half grand for . . . what, spillage? Ha!"

Leo came over and pulled the swivel chair from behind my desk. She wheeled it in front of the sofa, where I slouched, and she turned it so that she could sit astride the chair with her arms resting on its back. I was trapped on the sofa.

"Jen, don't you see? Especially now? You had a message to give—a complex message. You were angry and disillusioned about so much in the art world, and so you took a risk! You took a risk with your art!"

"But it was not what I . . ."

"Doesn't matter. You spoke with emotion through your art. It wasn't a safe option, and somehow the raw emotion of the artistic act was recognized. The Tate took it."

"The Tate were conned by their ingrained, blinkered attitudes."

"No, it was you—your own stupid conscious mind that was conned, Jen. Your subconscious, the artist, knew exactly what it was doing and it took you on a journey of risk, extreme risk, and it gave you your first real success. It was powerful art."

"It was bollocks."

"So now you will design logos and letterheads for the Government. Will this be art? Will this be worthy? Will it feed your soul?"

"It will feed my stomach, Leo . . . and yours!"

"Jen, do you see the parallel? The tragedy of Risqueman? Take away enterprise, and our feared and beloved precariousness—and you take away our hope."

We had many arguments like this one. She was right and she was wrong. Designing compliment-slips and logos didn't feed my soul, but then it didn't put much bread on the table either.

Leo threatened that if I was going to prostitute myself to the government for so little reward, then she may as well do the same . . . if tSolve would agree to take her back. But that would have been a step too far. She would never have allowed herself to do that. Besides, she'd done the hard part with Risqueman, and it appeared, now, that tSolve were managing to move forward without her input.

A few days later . . .

"What's the letter?"

I flicked it across the breakfast table, where it collected marmalade and toast crumbs.

"It's about the car insurance. It seems we can have a lower premium if we take out a linked Risqueman account."

"Merde! You are not thinking . . ."

"No, Leo. I'm aware of how you feel. I was just . . . interested, that's all." This was a lie. I was quite serious about signing up, and I was considering doing it covertly. Our financial situation was deteriorating.

"I *was* beginning to hope we wouldn't see any outward signs of Risqueman," I continued. "You were kind of dramatic, that night in Cardiff, with your 'this is the end of hope' prophecies, you know."

"It was not dramatic, Jen. They are pushing the short model. This *is* the beginning. Watch."

A couple of weeks later I was home from work early. I'd built up some flexitime, and I was weary from staring at Rhymney Redevelopment Zone logos.

As I pulled into the lane, Owen, our neighbor, was out mowing the lawn.

"Not in work today, Owen?"

"Hi, Jenkin. No, I had to skip. Can't use the car."

"Problems?"

"No, no. It's a high-risk day for me, that's all. I've had a few lately."

"What . . . ?"

"Risqueman. I got my car insurance linked. It

saves me a few bob, or at least it did at first, but I have to check my risk profile every day, and sometimes . . . Well, the last few weeks it's been making me leave for work earlier and go via Newport. Pain in the arse, I can tell you. It's put about ten miles onto my commute. Then now and again it says, *too risky—stay at home.* What can you do?"

"You could ignore it."

"No can do, Jenkin. Wouldn't be insured. If I got caught I'd be knackered. You were a police officer, Jenkin; you know how easy it is to spot someone driving on a red disc."

"I don't think the linked policies work like that, Owen. Discs only turn red over time, when the policy expires. You sure you've got it right?"

"You'd better believe it. They use smart ink, or some damn thing. Even if you don't go online to check your risk status, the disc's there to warn you—and, of course, your ex-brethren in law enforcement are waiting to pounce. I'm linked on my contents insurance as well. There's a marker by the front door. There are some days when I'm only covered so long as someone's home. Can't go out, can't go to work. Sometimes I have to skip work, other times Gwen throws a sicky and covers it. Okay, so now and again we take a small chance, but . . . Well look at it this way; if Risqueman says your house is high risk some days, well, it's better to stay home and keep an eye on it, yeah?"

I didn't tell Leo about the conversation. She was wound up enough about anything to do with Risqueman. But then she had a chat with Gwen a few weeks later, and she was off on one. She tried to organize an action group amongst the neighbors, but most people were quite happy about the cost savings and the extra sense of security they were getting from Risqueman, and they couldn't see what Leo was getting so worked up about.

Then our car insurance was cancelled. It was a brusque letter containing a small check for the outstanding balance less admin. It explained that should we decide to subscribe to Risqueman we need only telephone or e-mail with our account number and our insurance policy would be reactivated. Of course, I was screwed. I lived on the Gower and I worked in Cardiff, sixty miles away. There was no practical public transport. The best I could come up with was a fifteen-mile cycle to the railway station. I'd been given no notice, no time to plan around it; my car insurance cancellation was immediate.

I made a few phone calls and found a company that would insure me without a Risqueman account. They weren't even online. They sounded dodgy and the cost was ridiculous. The commute had been crippling me in fuel bills anyway, and so suddenly it was Risqueman or unemployment—and unemployment would cost us our home.

Leo and I had another bitter argument about it. I'd taken her out for a meal, to our favorite Italian, to soften her up a little.

"Don't you see, Jen, it cannot work," she said. "Apart from the fact that they are still using the short model, the whole premise of the algorithm is being undermined."

"Leo, you keep on contradicting yourself. One minute you're slagging FE ministers for wanting to charge people for Risqueman, next thing you're complaining that too many people have it. All I see is that without signing up, I cannot work—at least not in Cardiff. And, let's face it, there's nothing doing for me here on the Gower with this recession. I can't even rejoin the force; they're cutting back on policing everywhere."

"There is no contradiction, Jen. The original model—installed on a home computer and working in isolation on behalf of just the user, would have been a useful tool for managing personal risk profiles. I already installed it on your laptop. But this massive, corporate, obscene database is self-deluding AI. The algorithm works through sampling and environmental feedback. If the sampled population is then prevented from performing the risk-assessed activities then the interpretation will become skewed."

"Leo, you're talking maths again."

"Risqueman thinks it knows all the answers; it believes itself to be God. But Risqueman does not know everything. It is incomplete. To accept Risqueman would not be a solution, it would be a short-termist reaction. Wait it out, Jen."

"Leo, we cannot *afford* to wait it out."

"We cannot afford not to, Jen."

I pumped up my bike tires and set my alarm two hours earlier. The last time I'd been on a bike was art college. I try to stay fit—I run, I swim—but cycling uses different muscles, and from the cosseted perspective of a car I hadn't realized just how many hills there were on the Gower. I suffered. I reached

the station with barely minutes to spare, to find
that the seven fifty-two had been cancelled—staff
shortages. So despite my best efforts, I was over an
hour late for work. I had a presentation first thing;
I was supposed to be unveiling my Rhymney ideas.
Now, I'm not a workaholic, far from it. The job is
just a job, so I wasn't anxious about being late in the
traditional career-angst sense of the word. But I *was*
annoyed. I'd made the effort. I'd been slogging up
and down hills since long before first light and I'd
then wasted an hour sitting alone, in the cold, on the
station platform. The sense of unfairness was huge.
Then what happens? I find that neither the Project
Manager for Rhymney nor the Urban Regeneration
Director have turned in for work—a mystery bug—
and so my presentation gets cancelled. I spent the
day torturing the orange stress ball on my desk and
visualizing the long journey home.

You're looking thinner, Jen. All the cycling is doing
you good."

I finished locking my bike in the shed and hobbled
my way up the path to the front door where Leo
was leaning, an amused smile on her face.

"I suppose that's a plus point. Do you know
I've had to cycle all the way to Cardiff twice this
week. Sixty bloody miles! The trains are hopeless.
It's always staff shortages these days—whatever
happened to 'leaves on the track' or 'frozen
points'?"

"Why do you not try to get a job on the trains,
if they are so short of staff? The pay is probably
better."

EVAN JENSEN

"It's not a staff shortage at all. That's an excuse. I think the buggers are all having High Risk Days."

"Ah, the welcome return of Jenkin Morgan, the cynic. At last you are beginning to see. Well, here is another one for you—it is not just the trains that are suffering from Risqueman. There was no bread in the supermarket today. And did you hear on the news that another biofuel company has failed? SoyGo? We are fighting the Africans to take their crops from them, while at the same time our own fuel crops are rotting in warehouses."

"Come on, Leo, that's stretching it. There is a recession, you know."

"Yes, Jen, I know."

"Well?"

And this is where Leo can be so annoying. She just shrugged her shoulders and went back to her study.

She'd been working harder than ever since she left tSolve. I asked her what she was up to, working at the weekend despite not having an employer. She gave me a lot of mathematical stuff until my brain zoned out. But then later in the evening I took a glass of wine in to her to get her to stop, or at least slow down. I could tell from her eyes that she was tired. But she couldn't switch off.

"If I can marry my algorithm to the work I did with Maxim Borodin on the economics model—back in Paris when I was working towards mathematical unification—I might be able to incorporate economic risk."

"And?"

"Look, Risqueman works by taking all the variables and finding the shortest risk-free path."

"Yeah, like route-finding software. You explained that one before."

"*Oui*. So Risqueman gets smarter the more data that is fed back. But only physical risk. There are other forms of uncertainty that Risqueman is not even aware of. Critically, at the moment, economic risk is the weaker link, and this is what I am trying to fix. There is also the problem of emotional risk, but I have no mathematical models for intangibles, and the psychological effects are probably the more serious in the long run. But I must not put the carriage before the horses."

"So, what if you fix the economic thing? What can you do? You don't have a job. You can't influence anybody."

"I will give it away. I will send a copy to everyone, Asia . . . the US."

"What about the patents? The Federal Government will nail you. You'll go to jail."

"No. The patents are for Risqueman, and Risqueman does not address the economics. I will give my new algorithm a new name. I will also send it to the European Government, maybe via tSolve . . . as a gift."

"And open source?"

"I don't know. It was wrong to release the algorithm in the first place when it was only a partial solution. RM2 will be better, but it will still be a partial solution. It will still be disruptive. I don't want to be responsible . . . at least any *more* responsible."

"But the US has already started using a version based on your original published work. They've thumbed their noses at the international patents. You told me that last week."

"Yes. And have you seen the disaster on Wall Street these past few days?"

"Surely that's just the recession starting to bite over there?"

"Yes, Jen. The recession *I* started."

Léonie caught me logged on to Risqueman. If I'd been more open about it, maybe she'd have been less pissed—but she found me sitting in my car, with my laptop, at the farthest outpost of wireless range. I was hiding from the rain; car's no good for anything else these days.

I held my hands up to ward off the rage.

"I was just looking, Leo. I was just looking . . . and thinking."

Leo's response was in fast and incomprehensible French. I got out of the car and we stood in the downpour, either side of the car, shouting across the hood for ten minutes or so, trading insults, making points by slamming fists down onto the bodywork, neither of us making sense. When we were both shouted out and exhausted and wet, I opened the door on my side and climbed in out of the rain, indicating that Leo might want to do the same.

It was a long time before I found myself sufficiently in control to speak again.

"You're a clever girl, Leo. Okay, that's an understatement—you're a genius. But, the recession thing, the end-of-the-world scenario; think about this: is there a chance, the remotest possibility, that in all this doom stuff, you might be wrong? Have you ever stopped to consider all the *good* that your algorithm has done?"

Léonie started to say something, but I held up my hands. I was sure about this.

"Wait! Hear me out, Leo, please. The recession stuff *could* be coincidence."

"Jen, you are talking to someone who knows a bit about uncertainty . . . and coincidence."

"Yes, yes, Leo. I know that, but what if it *is* coincidence? Let us just, for argument's sake, make that assumption. What are we left with? Well, I've been Googling around on this. Just after the millennium, road deaths were running at about nine per week, nationally, that is. Okay, they'd fallen slightly over the previous few decades, but the number had leveled off. Nine per week! That's nearly five hundred people killed every year! It stayed that way until quite recently. Leo, the number of road deaths in the last six months . . . have you any idea?"

She shook her head.

"Three, Leo! Three deaths. Two years ago, in the same period of time, there were two hundred and thirty-odd. You, Leo, in the last six months, have saved the lives of over two hundred people. Your software—Risqueman—has *saved* those lives. Now, if we can ignore all this economic stuff, don't you think that the preservation of even just one of those lives might just be a noble outcome?"

Léonie paused for a moment and considered. I was thinking I'd made a breakthrough. It felt good, because prior to this she'd always been the one with all the answers.

Then she spoke, calmly and rationally.

"Jen, I hate to spoil the moment for you. I *know* Risqueman works. In a world of limited cause and effect, Risqueman *has* to work; I designed it that way. Only now it has a far greater data resource. Risqueman looks at all the dynamics, all the interplay of actions and reactions. It now draws upon a huge database built from the account holder's RFID telemetry as well as data from every other account holder. Then it uses the algorithm to process the data and arrive at a probable outcome. If the incidence of physical risk on that outcome exceeds a specified threshold, a subroutine makes subtle changes to the subject's input and feeds it back to the algorithm to assess a new risk factor. It does it again and again. Once a satisfactory outcome has been reached Risqueman publishes the desirable amended variables . . . a new route to work, an earlier alarm call, a change of diet, a change of career. In its limited and blinkered way it is *bound* to work."

"So what's the problem? Come on, Leo, why are you so worried about it?"

"Because it learns. Risk assessment software is easy, Jen; it has been around for years. But Risqueman is different. Risqueman *learns*. Genetic learning restricted to one person, one family . . . the changes are slight—take the kids to school five minutes earlier, stay in the house after eight, that kind of thing.

"But when *everyone* has Risqueman the activity modifications are less subtle, and the effects are more dramatic. Do not use the car at all—and, oh look, I, Risqueman, have prevented yet another accident.

Let me use that technique for everyone. Ah, that is even better. What about those subjects that we cannot control? Those without the Risqueman account? I can cancel their car insurance—that will keep them off the roads."

"But that's nonsense, Leo. If Risqueman stops everyone from driving, what's the point of having car insurance anyway?"

"Ha! So, at last you are beginning to see. This is nonsense. It does *not* make economic sense. But think, Jen, why *should* it make economic sense? Economics are not a part of the calculation. We keep talking about car insurance. Of course, car insurance is visible and has had a tangible impact upon our lives. But insurance is only a tiny thread in the Risqueman disaster, Jen. We do not always see the wider picture; financial markets, investment portfolios, defense strategy . . . all of these risk-oriented activities are foolishly looking to Risqueman for assistance."

"But if that's happening, there must be . . ."

". . . the makings of catastrophe, yes. I suspect many businesses—or nations—do not yet understand the root cause of their economic misfortunes. And even those that do . . . well, it would be political suicide to stop it now, because . . ."

". . . because lives are being saved."

"Yes. Never mind your five hundred a year; *thousands* of lives are being saved. You can't pull the plug now; that would be . . . well, tantamount to murder. And think about Owen, our neighbor. His lawn is beautiful—he's always working on it. He is being prevented, more and more often, from going to work. He loves it. His firm can do nothing—they arrange his car insurance—car usage is a part of his job, and the insurance company requires him to subscribe to Risqueman. Do you think Owen is unhappy about all that extra leisure time?"

"Owen's just idle. Don't get me wrong—he's a good mate, but he's a lazy sod." I said this with a smile. "He should get the train, like me."

"How many times has your train failed this week?"

"I don't know; three, four times. They've got staff shortages."

"They've got Risqueman. The rail workers cannot get to work. Maybe trains are cut because Risqueman predicts an accident—through shortages in signaling staff perhaps. Before the year is out you will be cycling all the way to Cardiff and back every day . . . and you will be the only employee turning in for work. Other businesses, construction companies, emergency services, assembly lines . . . they have risk factors too. There will be risks that can be lowered, or even eliminated, with similar undesirable side effects. You can project a parallel scenario across every economic activity in Europe, and what do you get?"

I didn't say anything, because suddenly—in a flash of insight—I saw. At last I was seeing the future through Léonie's eyes, and I could see the force that drove her to her desk each day. I was swept by compassion for my Leo, for now I knew what she knew. She had unleashed this beast, and she understood with cold mathematical certainty that it could never be stopped.

"Leo, is there anything . . . ?"

"*Je peux ne faire rien.* I can do nothing. I can paper over the cracks. I can apply a fresh coat of paint. But the house will fall."

Léonie's prediction about me cycling all the way to Cardiff every day, within a year, was never put to the test—I was laid off five months later.

"We don't need logos and posters these days, Jenkin," my boss said. "We need cash. We need investment. And please don't feel bitter towards me; after I've finished sacking you I've got three others to speak to, then I'll be going upstairs and clearing out my own desk."

A few weeks later we received an instruction that the Building Society was repossessing our cottage. My salary had been insufficient to meet the mortgage payments for some time, and the redundancy notice had clinched it. But then, just two days after writing to us, the Building Society itself went under. So who owns the cottage now? We've been writing letters but they go unanswered. We have to take them to the Post Office on foot now that the collection and delivery services have stopped, and we call in again every few days to see if there have been any replies. There doesn't seem to be any mail for anybody. We can't e-mail; we haven't had the Internet for weeks—but then e-mail is irrelevant; the electricity stopped on Tuesday.

It was switched off during Owen's funeral. We'd agreed to do a buffet to help Gwen out, and the power failed at just the wrong moment. So we ate the sandwiches, and the half-cooked pies and sausages went in the bin.

Owen was only in his forties. We don't know what he'd gone into the hospital for, something minor, and he got an infection. It's happening more and more, infections; there's no staff, you see. First they close A&E in all but a few hospitals—no accidents, no need for A&E. Then they make redundancies. Then everything goes horribly wrong—the ambulance service, the support staff, doctors leaving the country by the boatload. . . . The best health advice at the moment is this: Don't get sick.

"My algorithm will destroy the world!"

I remembered those words as I looked over at our friend, Gwen, trying to make sense of what just happened. Politeness demands the false smiles and acknowledgements, but look into her eyes and there is nothing. It's all gone.

"My algorithm will destroy the world!" Léonie's words. They seemed melodramatic at the time; an overreaction to a really bad day at the office.

Léonie is strolling up the dusty lane with Henri, our son. She's been to collect him from school. Life moves at a much slower pace here in Nigeria.

We moved to Abuja City about five years ago. It was a move that probably saved our lives. I thought Leo would find some inner peace once she cracked the economics problem, but she'd been too late—at least for Europe, and she knew it. Her open-source version of Risqueman mitigated the economic effects in some of those countries that had been slow to take up Risqueman at the start, but the recession had had plenty of time to take hold elsewhere and the domino effect had been catastrophic.

It was my idea to move out here, and we had needed to call in a few favors to pull it off. It was only here in Africa that Leo finally came, in part, to accept the tarnished silver lining that lay hidden in Risqueman.

When Europe crashed one of the many lasting images were of the heaps of biofuel crops rotting and stinking in warehouses and on quaysides. Public and personal transport had stopped; so had industry. So there was no longer a need for African biofuel crops. A lot of our young troops in Africa had hacked into black-market versions of Risqueman, and they were being shown life choices that didn't include having their nuts shot off. The Biofuel War didn't really end, it just spluttered and died, and Léonie, via the back door, had thus achieved one of her early driving passions. I think it eased her conscience a little, but I know she still finds it hard to live with the consequences of her algorithm. She destroyed a continent, and we cannot escape from the constant reminders. Every day we can see the relief efforts, the trainloads of fuel crops leaving for the coast to be shipped to Europe for use as food.

Leo has opened a small consultancy in town, a lean-to with a desk and a chair, where she uses Risqueman2 in a selective way to help the African economy generate food-crop income. She's quite successful but she's keeping it very low-key. She tries to curb the widespread use of the software, because even the modified version has its dangers.

Before we left Wales we saw many of the

emotional effects of Risqueman firsthand. We saw
people, friends, who'd once had real purpose and
goals, now left with nothing to do but tend their
lawns, then dig them over to plant vegetables. We
saw the entrepreneurs and risk-takers, robbed of
the power to take risks. I saw the emptiness in
their eyes . . . and I painted what I saw. Too late for
Europe—galleries feed the soul, not the stomach—
but here in Africa it's different; there's still hope.
My paintings are being used as a symbol to all those
who might want to seek out the easy option.

Henri runs up to me and gives me a hug. I've
been preparing dinner, a local recipe. I'm no chef,
and this dish has a strange smell and questionable
color . . . but we have free will. We can risk it.

Writers of the Future

BY ROBERT SILVERBERG

In a career that goes back to 1954, Robert Silverberg has published hundreds of science fiction stories and more than a hundred novels. He has won five Nebula and five Hugo awards and in 2004 was named a Grand Master by the Science Fiction Writers of America. Robert Silverberg is also a recipient of the L. Ron Hubbard Lifetime Achievement Award. His best-known books include Lord Valentine's Castle, Dying Inside *and* A Time of Changes.

Writers of the Future

Back in the 1930s and 1940s, L. Ron Hubbard was one of the most versatile and prolific of the pulp-magazine storytellers. From his white-hot typewriter poured a prodigious stream of tales in just about every genre of fiction that those gaudy old magazines dealt in: westerns, mysteries, stories of the mysterious Orient, sea adventures, Arctic adventures, air adventures—you name it and he wrote it.

A tour through the long list of his story titles gives us the full flavor of that long-vanished era: "Cargo of Coffins," "The Trail of the Red Diamonds," "The Blow Torch Murder," "Hell's Legionnaire," "The Baron of Coyote River," "The Bold Dare All," "Red Death Over China," "Yukon Madness," and on and on and on. But of all the many kinds of fiction that he wrote, science fiction and fantasy certainly were written out of love and closest to L. Ron Hubbard's heart. It shows when you read his work.

Hubbard's works of science fiction and fantasy long ago established themselves as classics of their kind and have had no difficulty maintaining their continuing existence in print through decade after decade. The enduring popularity of such Hubbard novels as *Fear, Final Blackout, Slaves of Sleep* and *Typewriter in the Sky*, all fantasy or science fiction and all dating back to the early 1940s, shows that he wrote them with something more in mind than his next paycheck.

And when he briefly returned to professional writing after the World War II hiatus, at a time when nearly all the old pulp-magazine categories were extinct, it was primarily science fiction and fantasy that he wrote, stories like the Ole Doc Methuselah series and the novel *To the Stars*. And so it was not surprising that late in his life, he would turn again to writing science fiction—with the huge novel *Battlefield Earth* and the gigantic multi-volume *Mission Earth* and, in 1983, would establish the Writers of the Future Contest to develop and encourage new talent in the field that he loved above all others.

Hubbard knew what it was like to be a beginning writer. In the 1930s, during his prime as a contributor to the pulps, he wrote many how-to-do-it articles for writers' magazines, explaining the tricks of the trade as he had come to know them and worked in other ways to bring newcomers into the profession, even sponsoring a writing competition, the Golden Pen Award, in 1940. So the Writers of the Future Contest was simply a continuation of his long-held belief that it was an obligation of veteran writers to share their knowledge with upcoming generations of aspiring scribes.

As I wrote in the first of these twenty-five

volumes of annual award anthologies, "We were all
new writers once—even Sophocles, even Homer,
even Jack Williamson." (That great, much beloved
and long-lived SF writer who, I sometimes thought,
began his career only shortly after Homer's or
Sophocles' and was still turning out award-winning
fiction in his nineties, just a few years ago.)

Or, as I said in the tenth volume, after compiling
a list of some of the best-known writers who had
emerged from the Contest, "All of them were amateurs
ten years ago, when this Contest began. But you see
their names regularly in print these days. Like you
(and like Robert A. Heinlein, Arthur C. Clarke, Ray
Bradbury, Isaac Asimov and, yes, Robert Silverberg)
they wanted very, very much to be published writers
and, because they had the talent, the will and the
perseverance, they made it happen."

Or, to quote my essay in the *twentieth* annual
anthology, "Hubbard too had been a young,
struggling writer once, in the pulp-magazine
days of the 1930s. He loved science fiction and he
wanted to ease the way for talented and deserving
beginners who could bring new visions to the
field. His idea was to call for stories from writers
who had never published any science fiction—
gifted writers standing at the threshold of their
careers—and to assemble a group of top-ranking
science fiction writers to serve as the judges who
would select the best of those stories. The authors
of the winning stories would receive significant
cash prizes and a powerful publicity spotlight
would be focused on them at an annual awards
ceremony."

I quote myself three times here because I've been part of this project for the entire twenty-five years of its existence, and so, from time to time, I'm asked to write little commemorative essays to mark another milestone in its remarkable history. Back there in 1983 calls went out to many of the best-known SF writers of the day, asking them to serve as judges in the Contest. I was one of them. My old friend Algis Budrys—we had once been part of the same generation of new writers ourselves, back in the 1950s—would be in charge.

Entry to the Contest was limited to writers who had never had a novel or a novella professionally published and no more than three short stories. Algis would winnow the entries down to six or eight, from which the judges would choose the three best. As I said the last time I told this story —I will have to keep quoting myself, because I have been involved in this enterprise for so long— "I didn't hesitate. I was a new writer once myself, after all, back in the Pleistocene. A very young one, who was adopted as a sort of mascot by the established pros along the Eastern Seaboard where I lived then, taken under this wing and that one, and treated very well."

It was quite a crowd: names to conjure with in the science fiction world, people like Frederik Pohl, Isaac Asimov, Lester del Rey, Algis Budrys, Cyril M. Kornbluth, Robert Sheckley. They all knew how hard it was for a new writer to break in—for *they* had been new writers once, too—and they offered me every sort of help. "Some of them introduced me to the big New York editors, from John W. Campbell and Horace Gold on down. Some of them gave me tips about what I had done wrong in a particular story that was getting rejected all over the place. Some of them offered me advice about things I was doing wrong in my *published* stories, showing me that even though I had found some editor silly enough to buy them, I had begun them in the wrong place, or failed to squeeze all the juice out of a good idea, or used eleven words where three would have sufficed. And some, for whom I feel nothing but love, spoke roughly to me—very roughly indeed— about my early willingness to take the easy path to short-range gain at the price of long-range benefit, and what that was going to do to my career if I continued to go that route.

I learned my lessons well, back there fifty years ago, and I went on to have the big career as a science fiction writer that I had daydreamed about when I was just a starstruck boy. And because those older writers had so kindly helped me along my path, I have always felt an obligation to do the same for the writers who came into science fiction after me. It's an eternal cycle of repayment. (The great SF writer Cyril Kornbluth, who was one of those who was willing to teach me some tough lessons in the 1950s, put it that way explicitly: others had helped him break in when he was a kid, he felt that it behooved him to do the same for newcomers like me, and he hoped that I would follow suit in my turn.)

And so I have, working with young writers in one fashion or another over the decades, as Cyril (who has been dead for nearly half a century now)

Enter the Universe of
WRITERS & ILLUSTRATORS OF THE FUTURE

◆

Fill out and send in this card today and get these extraordinary benefits:

- FREE eNewsletters with contest news and updates.

- Discounts on all past and future editions in the L. Ron Hubbard Presents Writers of the Future series.

- Get a chance to win earlier Writers of the Future paperback volumes.

- Access to select artists' work published in previous Writers of the Future volumes.

- FREE eBooks with essays on writing and art by Writers and Illustrators of the Future Contest judges.

◆

Name: _____

Address: _____

City: _____ *State:* _____ *Zip:* _____

Phone: _____

E-mail: _____

Call toll-free: 1-877-8GALAXY or visit WWW.WRITERSOFTHEFUTURE.COM

BUSINESS REPLY MAIL
FIRST-CLASS MAIL   PERMIT NO. 75738   LOS ANGELES, CA

POSTAGE WILL BE PAID BY ADDRESSEE

GALAXY PRESS DEPT. W25
7051 HOLLYWOOD BLVD
HOLLYWOOD CA 90028-9771

NO POSTAGE
NECESSARY
IF MAILED
IN THE
UNITED STATES

told me to do long ago. I wasn't the only big-name author who recognized what a great idea the Writers of the Future Contest was. Among the other original judges were two writers who had been stars of the field even before I was born—Jack Williamson and C. L. Moore—and another—Theodore Sturgeon— who had established himself in the top rank when I was still a young reader. The other three members of the original group were Gregory Benford, Roger Zelazny and Stephen Goldin. So the panel spanned three or four generations of science fiction history, from the early Hugo Gernsback days on, and covered the whole literary spectrum of the field from flamboyant fantasy to nuts-and-bolts hard science.

I have the first of the twenty-five Writers of the Future anthologies of prize winners on my desk now. Five of the writers included in it have gone on to establish solid professional careers—Karen Joy Fowler, David Zindell, Dean Wesley Smith, Leonard Carpenter and Nina Kiriki Hoffman. (Hoffman, in fact, has become a Contest judge herself, the first of several Contest entrants to undergo that transformation in the course of the past quarter of a century.) Most of the others in that first book have scarcely been heard from again at all: but five discoveries in a single year's batch of amateur writers is a pretty good percentage.

The second year's volume—in which Frank Herbert, Gene Wolfe, Anne McCaffrey, Larry Niven and Frederik Pohl added their lustre to the board of judges—brought us stories by such future stars as Robert Reed (writing then as "Robert Touzalin"),

Howard V. Hendrix and Marina Fitch. The third year saw Jerry Pournelle joining the panel of judges, and among the winning writers whose stories are reprinted in that year's anthology are M. Shayne Bell, Martha Soukup, Dave Wolverton, J. R. Dunn and Caroline Ives Gilman.

So it has gone, year after year. Stephen Baxter turns up in the fifth anthology with his third published story. Jay Lake, Sean Williams, K. D. Wentworth, Jamil Nasir, Eric Flint and Nancy Farmer enter the roster of winners in later years, along with dozens of others whose most significant achievements still lie ahead. Death has taken many of the early judges —Algis Budrys, Frank Herbert, Charles Sheffield, Andre Norton, Hal Clement, Theodore Sturgeon, Roger Zelazny, Jack Williamson, C. L. Moore and all too many others, but Gregory Benford and I still remain from the original panel of twenty-five years ago and such illustrious figures as Ben Bova, John Varley, Orson Scott Card, Tim Powers, Robert Sawyer and Ramsey Campbell became members of the list of judges later on.

The procedure hasn't changed much over the twenty-five years since I agreed to join that list myself. Every three months, a group of the judges receives a packet of photocopied manuscripts from which the authors' names have been removed. There are usually six or eight of them, chosen by the Coordinating Judge out of the hundreds and hundreds of submissions received that quarter. The judges send in their lists of the three best of those six or eight stories, and at Contest headquarters in Los Angeles the judging lists are compared and each quarter a new group of three prize winners is chosen. There is also an annual Grand Prize, quite a generous one, for the author of the story that the judges deem to be the best of the four quarterly First Prize winners.

An old pro like me can tell pretty easily, from reading just half a dozen sentences, whether their author has that mysterious innate storytelling magic that separates the pros from the amateurs. No doubt some of the writers whose Contest submissions have seemed to me lacking in that magic have gone on to achieve brilliant careers anyway, but then there are the other stories, the ones that immediately announce, "Here is a star." You know it right away, when you read one of those. You feel a certain electricity. And it's a wonderful feeling.

As I look back over the history of the Writers of the Future Contest I feel great pride in what we have done to help the work of those writers gain prominence in the publishing world and I know that L. Ron Hubbard would feel that way himself. Thus the Contest, now entering the second quarter of a century of its existence, has served the purpose for which he brought it into being: to provide "a means for new and budding writers to have a chance for their creative efforts to be seen and acknowledged."

And, as I said five years ago and hope to say again five years from now, the process continues. The amateurs of today are the Hugo and Nebula winners of tomorrow. The Writers of the Future Contest is helping to bring that about.

Gray Queen Homecoming

written by

Schon M. Zwakman

illustrated by

TOBIAS A. FRUGE

ABOUT THE AUTHOR

When he was younger, Minnesotan Schon M. Zwakman considered a career in creative arts. At twelve, he even attempted to write a novel, but was disappointed with the result, destroyed the only draft, and quickly abandoned his creative aspirations. Instead, Schon's inclinations steered him toward a more practical, if not more distinguished, pursuit— an engineering degree from the United States Naval Academy and tours of the world as a naval officer. To pass the time, Schon never stopped reading, acquainting himself with a wide variety of topics and genres. Yet Schon's first love was always science fiction and fantasy stories.

After suffering through numerous pitches for possible scripts and stories, Schon's family encouraged him to try writing again: there was even mention of simply locking him in a room until he finished a novel. He's been writing ever since.

A Writers of the Future semifinalist in 2006, Schon's winning story is his eighth submission to the Contest. A self-described free agent, he currently resides in Cottage Grove, Minnesota.

ABOUT THE ILLUSTRATOR

Tobias A. Fruge ("Toby") was born in a small Arizona mining town. He started drawing as a child when his mother handed him pencils and paper to pacify him in church while his father preached. After the parents moved 150 miles due east to teach in Payson, Toby would spend hours after school in the high-school library where his mom worked. There he'd sit looking at countless book covers with their animated figures locked in life-and-death struggles.

But it wasn't until Toby's own struggles brought him to prison that he became serious about drawing: It was the only activity that freed him from the oppressive walls. He began with Christmas cards in colored pencil for family members. As his skills grew, Toby wanted to paint what he loved most to read about—scenes from science fiction, fantasy and wildlife. Without paints or brushes, Toby turned to black and white illustration, using ballpoint pens to exquisitely craft his worlds.

He currently attends junior college in Mesa and expects to graduate soon with an Associate Arts degree. When not studying or drawing, Toby enjoys weight lifting, his bulldog Pete and Cajun music.

Gray Queen Homecoming

*W*e *have arrived.*

Three soundless words woke Solstice Louzon from his dreamless medical sleep as if flicking a switch. His eyes opened, blinked and began to focus. He was lying propped up—the word held a certain definitive meaning with the habitat spinning again—on a plush bed in an austere room of blue alloy bulkheads, his room. The lighting was dim. Beside the bed one of his tumblers, a candy red, headless ovoid with eight arms, stood on two of its arms while the others held transdermal injectors, a hand scan and a tablet display. Beyond the tumbler a butterfly with a wingspan the length of Solstice's arm hung in the air, its wings painted in shades of sunrise. One of Alissa's flutterers.

Good morning, sleepyhead, Alissa sent.

Show me, he replied.

The flutterer approached Solstice, bobbing and weaving its way to float before him. It was a perfect mimicry of natural flight, although the wings of carbon mast and flexfilm were incapable of providing the necessary lift. Silent fan thrusters along thorax and abdomen coordinated to make the impossible appear realistic. The flutterer's wings expanded to full extension, forming a rough display screen that bled to black. Stars appeared, a thousand white pinpricks. The one near the center blinked brighter than the rest.

I enhanced it, Alissa sent. *Do you see?*

Yes.

The flutterer bobbed once and retreated across the room. The portal opened as it approached and closed after it passed through.

Solstice took a deep breath. Painless. He flexed fingers, bent elbows and ankles. Smooth. He traced the invisible seams at his shoulders, across his chest and abdomen. Everything felt right.

"So, Doc," he addressed the tumbler. "Am I going to live?"

Folding two pairs of its limbs behind it, the tumbler motioned its remaining free pair in an alternating up and down direction.

"Thanks for the reassurance."

Minutes later Solstice was walking down the corridor toward the observation deck lost in thought, robe wrapped loosely around him, a flutterer in trail. *We have arrived: Sol system, home again.* They said home was where the heart was, but Solstice's heart was his second, second and a half. He didn't consider a partial reconstruction as deserving a full count. But Sol—it had been so long the word was like a faded childhood memory, more idea than reality. One of those ancient memories came to him as he walked, the day on Mars when She approached him as he stargazed from the caldera of Olympus Mons, addressed him by name without introduction and said she knew, that she was the same, had means.

TOBIAS A. FRUGE

An insistent prod of his leg drew his attention and he stopped. A red tumbler held slippers on a couple of outstretched manipulators.

"Thanks, Cherry." He took the slippers and put them on.

The tumbler bent in a curtsy, then wrapped its limbs around its body in a loose spherical cage and rolled away. Looking back up, Solstice saw the flutterer waiting ahead of him, wings twitching.

"I'm coming, I'm coming."

When the portal to the observation deck opened the flutterer flew through and rose to join its companions clustered around the upper corners of the space, a swarm projecting a seamless illusion of rippling red velvet drapes caught in a breeze. The sole furnishings were a chaise lounge and matching armchair. Alissa waited, centered before the forward viewscreen that formed the forward bulkhead, her black hair in a tight braid, hands clasped at her lower back, chin up, nude.

Solstice took his place at her side and waited.

Solstice "Sol" Louzon, original biologic human, daydreamer, aimless traveler. Hobbies include making foolish decisions, testing patience. Enjoys barefooted walks in corridors . . .

"What's wrong, Alis?"

She turned her flawless face and looked at him with jet black eyes.

"You've changed your eyes," he said.

Many things have changed.

A group of flutterers descended like a torn swath floating on an imaginary gust of wind, before abandoning the illusion to shed their color and rearrange into an overlapping display array. Reports and statistics scrolled to fill wings, presenting bandwidth usage, information exchange rates and infrared views of population and industry loci. Solstice remembered a system drowning in communication noise, overrun with stacked and packed networks, glowing white with heat. Things had changed. Quieter now, open, dimmer. At the wave of his hand the display exploded, shattered glass taking flight.

"How long have you—" he began.

A couple days. The pattern is consistent.

"I assume you've been attempting—"

On all the old assigned frequencies and wideband. There is no Link, and ISO has not responded to hails. No one has.

"Not even the Core?"

Alissa crossed her arms. Solstice looked away, at the viewscreen. He felt Alissa's hand on his shoulder.

"Sol, I—" She froze. Her hand slipped away.

"What?"

She raised a finger. *We're being hailed.*

"Are you sure?"

Pinpoint laser transmission. Unassigned frequency. In the clear.

"Let me in."

A masculine voice filled Solstice's ears: "—unidentified vessel in the vicinity of Neptune, inbound deceleration vector Mars proximate, you are requested to assume Triton orbit and await further instructions. Request set emissions condition black and do not attempt to establish link or comms on any previously promulgated freq plan. Unidentified vessel in the—"

Alissa snapped her fingers and silenced the voice. *The message loops,* she sent. *Probably coming from a terrestrial sphere. Too distant for effective realtime comms.*

"Can we make the orbit?"

A lengthy silence passed before Alissa responded. Solstice was uncertain whether she was running calculations or protesting the inconvenience.

Yes.

Solstice felt the change in the frequency of the deck and a growing tug. He rocked on the balls of his feet and clapped his hands together. Strange requests, to be sure, but things were looking up.

"Just promise me you won't do anything stupid," Alissa said.

"This is Sol system, Alis."

"Then promise me I won't have to save you again."

"I promise."

Solstice.

Sealing the seam of his tunic in his room, Solstice froze. That tone. An hour before, he had left Alissa on the observation deck after they had established orbit. She was going to try to establish a link with someone with "intelligent directional authority."

He hurried from the room.

She was wringing her hands when he arrived on the observation deck, pacing before the viewscreen vista of Triton's bright reddish polar region sprinkled with cryovolcanoes and pale streaks of liquid nitrogen ejecta. Wisps of clouds extended beyond the limb. Nothing special, spectacular or original. He heard a new voice, female, speaking in a slow, deliberate fashion, asking a question or making a questioning request. Flutterers hung frozen along the bulkheads, wings drained, slate gray. Before the portal could close Alissa pivoted in his direction and began sending.

A torrent of data hit Solstice, Alissa's entire previous hour compressed into a brief squirt. The information overwhelmed buffers, rendering him deaf and blind. He caught a single image, word, emotion in ten as the remainder spilled away. There was a taste of cold, void, fear. Staggering to his chair, he reached out to clutch an arm.

"Please . . . stop."

The connection was severed. Ringing filled his ears, the calm female voice like an insect buzzing across the room. His sight began to return, dark sunspots popping around Alissa's face.

She fidgeted, hands twisted together. *Sorrysorrysorrysorryitsjustthat,* "there, there . . . there's something out there."

Solstice worked his way to the front of the chair hand over hand and fell into it. He massaged his temples. "Something? Like what?"

"I don't know. It's . . . big. I think it . . . I think it saw me."

His head snapped up and he stood again. "What? Where?"

"I told you, I don't know. I attempted to establish protocols with the Core—"

"You should have told me. It could be dangerous." The words were an unfiltered, spontaneous translation of thought, and he knew they were wrong the moment he spoke them.

Alissa stopped pacing. "It was my choice to make and far safer than any of the asinine decisions you've made without consulting me."

"Yes. Of course. I agree. I'm sorry." In the silence that followed Solstice heard the female voice again, requesting, questioning. "How long has she been talking?"

"Four minutes."

"Have you answered?"

"No."

Before he could say another word Alissa flicked her wrist. *On.*

Solstice cleared his throat. "Station calling, this is *Wanderer of This Sea of Stars,* Excursor-class vessel, ISA designation JNM-4802. Could you repeat your last?"

"This is Triton Point," the female voice replied. "I say again: Are you capable of establishing a Cat. VII simplex laser link to facilitate preliminary inspection queries?"

"Wait one." Solstice held his hand up.

Off, Alissa sent.

"Why in the universe—"

Something happened. They want to keep our exchange private, covert.

"What should I tell—?"

Whatever you like.

Solstice hesitated. Unlike her.

You're on, she sent.

"We have a Fulcrist D-class NaviNex. Perhaps we could—"

"Negative," the voice interrupted. "For your own safety, do not attempt to link onboard AI systems with any external entity in Sol system. Gray Queen Contingency Directive remains in effect."

The interruptions were beginning to annoy. "What the hell is the Gray Queen Directive?"

The following silence was long enough to make Solstice wince.

Why'd you let me do that? he sent Alissa.

What? she replied. *You sounded honestly offended.*

"We apologize for the delay," the voice returned at last, "but your vessel is not in our records. We were uncertain as to your departure date. May we request a meeting aboard the *Wanderer*?"

"For how many?" Alissa asked.

"How many forms do you have onboard?"

"Two," Solstice said. "Humiforms. One biologic male and one synthetic female."

"Then we'll send two. They'll come from the surface in a shuttle. Four hours."

"Looking forward to meeting you."

End, Alissa sent.

She went to her chaise lounge, sat and wrapped her arms around a tasseled pillow. "You lied. Twice."

"I don't know these people." It was strange that they'd require four hours to get a shuttle up.

Lies are a poor foundation for a long-lasting, functional relationship.

"Four hours until they arrive. You know what that means."

Alissa curled her legs up to her chest as if trying to hide behind her pillow.

"Yes. Clothes."

Archaic displays for the purpose of projecting hierarchal status and reproductive competition.

"And modesty."

A worthless virtue.

"I'll make a deal with you: If they're not wearing any clothes, you can lose yours."

Alissa stood suddenly, flinging the pillow past Solstice's head, and flutterers descended from the four corners of the room to create concealing bands around her chest and waist, wings painted with fields of daffodils on sky blue. *How's this?*

"I was thinking of something a little more . . . substantial."

Fine. The daffodils became small yellow and white faces that stuck bright red tongues out in unison. *Consider this a favor,* she sent as she walked to the portal with her taunting followers.

She exaggerated. She had something planned, always did. He had seen the occasional flutterer or three on the storage hold level, the vaults filled with mining stockpiles worth carrying for future use. If he saw them, then she saw him.

But neither of them mentioned it.

Solstice stood at the long kitchen island in the galley slicing sweet bell peppers into thin strips with an amorphous metal chef's knife. A pot steamed on the stove top, its water approaching a boil. He had built the stove himself, with some bemused assistance from Alissa who had helped locate an equivalent heating element and program it to respond to analog controls. She had only smiled at the results of his first couple of attempts, spectacular failures that resulted in a melted pot and a full frontal flash burn.

He slid pepper slices off the cutting board and into a mixing bowl with green beans, sweet yellow squash and eggplant. Exchanging the knife for a worn wooden spoon he tossed the vegetables, coating them in oil and herbs.

The portal opened and a flutterer entered with a balled tumbler. The tumbler bounced twice, uncoiled, performed a backflip and landed on the counter next to Solstice. Extending a couple pairs of limbs, it bowed before wrapping them around its body. The flutterer hovered in front of Solstice at eye level and extended its displays.

You might want to see this, Alissa sent.

The shuttle from Triton Point was within visual range and maneuvering for docking alignment. Solstice placed his spoon down. He had assumed technology had changed in the realtime centuries since they began their travels, but the shuttle he saw failed even the lowest of his expectations. At best it was a maintained and retrofitted vehicle, the kind used for short transit runs between planets and their satellites. He noted signs of reentry burn, micrometeorite impacts, solar fade. An operational antique.

Piece of crap, Alissa designated it.

Why would they send such a thing? Solstice asked.

Expectation management? Trojan horse?

Who's not trusting whom now? He looked at the tumbler swinging its limbs over the edge of the island. "Three patties. Skillet." The tumbler rolled forward and off the edge. *What do you see?*

I'm looking passively. There's nothing radiological.
Have they handed off, or do they plan to dry-stick it in?
I'll ask . . . Wait—

The shuttle's maneuvering thrusters flared.

They didn't warn me, Alissa sent with a sizzle of static. *Should I—*

Give them a moment, Solstice sent.

They're scanning us.

Just getting a closer look. We'd do the same.

Solstice looked down and saw his three patties had appeared. A manipulator appeared over the edge of the counter and deposited a heavy skillet on the counter top. The tumbler scrambled up to the counter top, took the skillet by its handle and lifted it. It waited.

"Go ahead."

Stretching its torso back, the tumbler lifted the skillet above its body, hesitated and brought it down with a loud thud. It raised the skillet again.

"That'll do."

The tumbler performed an action that could have been a shrug if it had shoulders and placed the skillet aside.

They're coming in now, Alissa sent. *Manually.*

On the flutterer's wings the shuttle slid out of view. The video feed changed to an interior view of the hangar bay, the shuttle edging inside and toward the empty berth readied for it. Solstice didn't think it possible but the shuttle looked even uglier in the bright lights of the bay. Whoever the pilot was brought the shuttle toward the berth in a laborious, hesitating manner.

Not as good as I am.

He expected a lighthearted retort in return but none came. She was up to something.

What? he sent.

Bay closed. Sealed. Equalizing.

What is it, Alissa? He heard water boiling.

Shuttle open. Ramp extended.

The tumbler retrieved the amorphous blade from the counter top and began to flip and spin it among its multiple manipulators. Solstice stared at the flutterer's display, waiting for a glimpse of their guests. A head appeared. No, a helmet, a person in a suit. Solstice's pulse leapt.

They're wearing exposure suits!

Alissa—

On OUR ship!

Solstice looked at the tumbler. "Stop that." The tumbler caught the knife and slipped it behind its back. "Pan-roast these, and tartare for me. And the vegetables." He walked to the portal, turned back and pointed at the boiling-over pot. "And noodles."

The tumbler popped to attention and saluted as Solstice ran out.

The run to the access shaft, three-deck stumble-and-slide down ladders and final sprint to the docking bay were enough to leave Solstice laboring for air, but the sight awaiting him stopped him cold.

Alissa stood at the closed bay portal in a long sleeve gown of black silk embroidered with diamonds, an open platinum collar curling around her neck and spilling like liquid over a collarbone.

Flutterers hovered above her, wings wide, projecting a clean white light that caused her dress to sparkle, her skin to glow. She rarely wore such things, never wore jewelry. She looked magnificent and irate.

Approaching the lock, Alissa sent. She noticed Solstice. "What are you staring at?"

Spell broken, Solstice took a breath. "If I'd known you appreciated jewelry . . ."

"Not the time, Sol." But her shoulders eased. She ran her hands down her dress. *They're in the lock now.*

"What do the scans say?"

Who says I'm scanning them? she asked in turn. *Two humiforms. Coherence values are solid: no swarm nanites. One female biomorph and one male synthmorph. No handheld or embedded weapons. Viral, toxin and bacterial screens show clean, but our database is dated.*

A flutterer descended and displayed the internal view of the lock. The man and woman were unfastening and removing their helmets. The woman was shorter than her companion, perhaps due to a Terran upbringing, with short, spiked hair and a vagueness of skin tone and features indicative of centuries of genetic mixing. The man was clearly styled to an Anglo-Asian phenotype with pale white hair.

Any idea of the synth's age? Solstice asked. He wondered why the synth was wearing a suit. Perhaps old habit, for the benefit of his bio companion.

I could open his skull and try to identify the manufacture if you wish.

No, thanks, but I appreciate the offer.

The pair waited inside the lock, staring at the camera. The woman's lips moved and the man shrugged. He pressed a button and a corresponding light lit on the docking bay control panel.

"Going to let them in?" Solstice asked.

"They wore exposure suits aboard our ship."

"I'm sure they have a good explanation for it."

They watched the man raise his hand and wave at the viewer.

Alissa, Solstice sent.

The seal released with a slight hiss of equalizing air, and the portal slid open.

Your hair is mussed, Alissa sent.

Solstice ran a hand through his hair as the new arrivals stepped out and looked around the space. They ignored him, their gazes drawn to Alissa and her swarm of bright flutterers like gravity. Who could blame them, a simple monochrome tunic next to a sparkling goddess surrounded in the glow of a radiant swarm of butterflies. He had to smile.

Stepping forward, the woman extended a gloved hand to Alissa. "Welcome home. I'm Jez Cantrel of the Human Protectorate."

Alissa stared at the woman as if she was speaking gibberish.

Don't do this, Alissa, Solstice pleaded.

"There was a time when it was considered an insult for someone to arrive aboard another's ship in an exposure suit," Alissa said.

Solstice leapt into the line of fire, taking Jez's hand in both of his and giving it a firm shake. "I'm sure it was an honest mistake. I'm Solstice Louzon. Let me introduce you to my traditionalist traveling associate, Alissa."

"We apologize if we've insulted you," the man

said. "The suits are necessary for your protection."
He moved beside Jez but kept his hands behind him.
"I'm Dare Hoshi, also of the Protectorate."

The Protectorate? Alissa sent. *What the hell is the
Protectorate?*

"A pleasure to meet you both," Solstice said. "It
would seem we have a great deal to talk about."

"What are those?" Jez asked with a tone of
restrained concern.

A couple of blue tumblers rolled across the deck
toward the party, uncoiled and bounced to stand
beside Jez and Dare. Jez flinched. Dare stared.

"They're called tumblers," Solstice explained,
"and they'll take your helmets."

Jez and Dare hesitated before handing their
helmets over and watched as the tumblers walked
out of sight.

"Solstice has prepared a meal," Alissa announced.

The centerpiece of the dining hall was a thin slab
of platinum-edged obsidian taken from a terrestrial
planet and held in place by counteracting magnets.
At one end of the table tumblers had positioned
tripod chairs with armrest extensors and aerogel
padding, a pair to a side, across from one another.
Thinscreens hung like tapestries from decorative
rods along each bulkhead, displaying unique views
of exotic destinations.

"Amazing," Jez whispered as they entered.

Red tumblers assisted Jez and Dare with their
chairs before moving to the rear bulkhead to wait.
Solstice motioned to assist Alissa but she ignored the

gesture and sat. Her retinue of flutterers dispersed and moved to the ceiling corners.

"Absolutely amazing," Jez said, looking at the thinscreens.

Dare looked under the tabletop and ran a hand along its underside. "Quite a piece."

"Solstice made it," Alissa said.

"Did you also make the . . . tumbles?"

"Tumblers," Solstice said. "I didn't; I only modified them. They were so boring when they started, L2 AI service protocols going about rote functions. I lent them some personality."

"Personality."

"An overlay of complementary personality trait sets and emotional fragments into the different types to amuse himself," Alissa said.

A new tumbler entered the room carrying a serving platter with four glasses of water. It placed the platter on the table and returned to the galley.

"Are there more types, in addition to the blues and the reds?" Jez asked.

"Blueberries and cherries," Solstice corrected. "We also have oranges, lemons, limes, plums and blackberries—"

"A rainbow of fruit servants," Alissa interrupted, reaching across the table for a glass.

"—but you probably won't see them all," Solstice continued. "They're color-coded to assignment and some rarely have cause to enter the communal areas."

"Are the . . . butterflies programmed in the same way?" Jez asked.

"Yes."

Alissa began to raise her goblet. *No more than two minutes before your first lie. Such restraint.*

Exaggeration, not lie, Solstice sent back.

She asked if they were the "same." They are not.

They also said they're from the Human Protectorate. Do you have any idea what that is? Maybe we should try some discretion until we do.

You don't think honesty would provide us with the information faster.

I think these two are here to evaluate us. Who knows what sort of people may have wandered back to the system since the expansion: religious, ethnic, cultural fundamentalists, relapsed criminals, failed prospectors and settlers, refugees. We need to pacify any doubts.

Noted.

Alissa sipped water and returned the goblet to the table. She smiled. "They must seem odd and frivolous to you."

"Not at all," Dare assured. "Everyone needs something to keep them . . . occupied."

"I assume you've met other returnees. What have they been like?"

"Interesting in their different ways, but I can honestly say I've never seen any like the pair of you. How have you managed all this time?"

Solstice folded his hands. *Evasion. Flattery. Answering a question with a question. Be cautious.*

Cautious? Are you ever? Alissa sent. "We keep busy with hobbies and projects, both practical and not. Sol and I have become quite adept in a variety of engineering disciplines, waste management, genetic programming and medical skills."

"And when we get bored we pick fights," Solstice added.

"We engage in lively debate," Alissa qualified.

"Don't let her fool you. We have outright wars. Her air forces against my infantry. It's surprising we've been able to get all the explosion and burn scars off the bulkheads and patch the damage."

"We're in an amicable period at the moment," Alissa reassured.

"Yes, most amicable," Solstice said. "We wouldn't be here otherwise."

"Pardon me for asking," Dare began, "but why have you returned?"

Before Solstice could consider a response Alissa was in his head: *Yes, why did we return, Sol?*

We went over this, Alis. Over it a hundred times.

By the treaties and laws in existence when they departed Sol system, they had legal claims to property and mineral rights of systems they visited, as well as the surveyed worlds and satellites and asteroids therein, first colony establishment royalty rights for terrestrial planets within terraforming limits, to contract for the precious metals and minerals loaded in the *Wanderer*'s storerooms. But he decided to tell the truth; it seemed innocent enough to accept, plausible enough to believe.

"I was curious. It's been so long, I almost forgot what it was like."

"And here we are," Alissa said, emphasizing each word.

"And here comes our meal."

During the conversation the tumblers waiting at

the rear bulkhead had slipped from the room and into the galley. They reappeared now, side by side, each carrying a couple of covered silver plates, a couple of stemmed glasses and plain bottles of clear liquid. They slipped the plates before intended recipients, removed covers, and filled the new glasses with flourish. Presentation complete, they resumed waiting positions.

Solstice waited, watching. Jez ran a hand over the simply honed platinum ware on her plate. Dare ignored the food, took the stemmed glass and sniffed it. He was unable to completely conceal a grimace.

Solstice. You didn't.

He knew Alissa was not referring to the starshine but to his own meal, thin strips of marinated meat fashioned into neat arcs around the plate. "Tonight we are having pan-roasted chicken, soy noodle sauté and herbed vegetables, compliments of our own Chef Cheri."

Jez stared. "Chicken?"

"Textured and flavored vegetable protein," Alissa said.

"And this?" Dare asked, raising his new glass.

"Solstice calls it 'starshine.' I call it painful."

"An acquired taste," Solstice said. "Cheers." He took a sip from his glass and felt liquid fire trace a path down his throat. He was constantly working to find a better recipe and blend, one pursuit Alissa was less than helpful with. According to her the cost-benefit analysis of grapes eliminated them from consideration as an addition to the hydroponics.

Jez followed Solstice and drank. Her eyes bulged. She coughed, spraying a heavy mist across the table.

Solstice used a finger to wipe a drop from his cheek. Jez blushed. Cute, in an ingénue sort of way. He stabbed a strip of meat, popped it into his mouth and closed his eyes as he chewed. When he was done he took a sip of shine and followed it with another of water.

"Please, eat," he said.

Dare repositioned his food with the tip of his knife. Jez sampled hesitantly, a slice, a noodle, a green bean, increasing her portions as she relaxed, until her sole focus was her plate and nothing else.

Girl eats like she hasn't had a meal for days, Alissa sent as she politely chewed some food.

Maybe she likes chicken, Solstice replied, drinking more shine.

Maybe she's too hungry to care. Offer her some of yours.

Alissa placed her platinum ware aside and looked to Dare. "What do you think of—?

Don't you— Solstice warned. It never worked.

"—our landscapes, Mr. Toshi?"

"Beautiful," Dare said. "I assume they're from systems you've visited?"

"Yes. Sol always captures the best possible images from each of our destinations, regardless of personal risk."

Solstice pushed his plate away half finished and topped off his shine before a tumbler could react and pour for him. This was going to get interesting. Might as well be armed.

"Risk?" Jez asked.

"If memory serves, I believe Sol died on most of these planets."

Solstice took a gulp of shine and affixed a smile. "And dear Alissa made me whole each time."

"Dead?" Jez asked.

The cute woman appeared to have an annoying habit of single word interrogatives. "Not completely, medically, and never for more than a day or two."

"Or three," Alissa corrected.

"That's not important," he said, waving his glass. "What's important is—there." He pointed at the image to his left, a frozen blue-white plain stretching away to silhouettes of jagged mountains on the horizon. "I'll never forget those crystal clear skies, the bite of the cold, lightning flashes in the blizzards."

"And I'll never forget that you took off your glove in one of those 'blizzards' to watch the flesh be shredded from your hand," Alissa said.

Solstice pointed to the portrait on his right, scorched and scoured foothills overlooking shattered lowlands. "That one was oppressive, reddish gray. Smelled of burning copper, an overwhelming, pungent, stinging smell."

"Not really. But at that point you probably smelled your own burning flesh, right before your blood began boiling in your nasal cavities."

"And that one." Solstice pointed to the portrait behind Jez and Dare, black and red and garish yellow. "I swear that cursed landscape brought me to tears."

"Your helmet and eye were pierced by silicate shrapnel hurled by a nearby volcanic explosion. That wasn't tears flowing down your cheek.

"Come to think of it, I don't think there's a single

limb or organ of yours that I haven't had to regenerate or replace or a synapse I haven't had to rewire less than twice. And if it's not your foolishness, it's some fungus or bacteria or cancer."

Solstice bowed in his chair. "My unfailing guardian angel of resurrection."

"Have your medical procedures resulted in any permanent or cumulative degradation to your genetic material?" Jez asked.

Quiet spilled across the table and over the edge to spread across the deck, filling the room. Solstice sat up for a moment. He tried to reason the source of that particular question but the shine was on, rearranging and blurring portions of the conversation. All he was sure of was that he had told a story of planets and praised Angelissa.

"What a strange question," Alissa said. "Why do you ask?"

Solstice nodded. Good question. Yes, why?

Dare cleared his throat, an unnecessary task for his kind.

"There was a war after you departed, between the human kinds, biologic and synthetic."

Should we look surprised? Alissa sent.

Why bother? Who bet on the bios starting it?

I did. And you're drunk. "Who started it?" Alissa asked.

"We did," Jez said. She seemed to be slouching, as if she could sink into her chair.

"Who won?" Solstice asked. He had odds on the synths.

"No one," Dare replied. "The similarity of our thought processes enabled each side to predict and

303

counter the other's tactics and strategies. It seems a synthetic mind brings a great deal of organic baggage with it during the transfer. The war was protracted and devastating in terms of lives, colonies, industrial capacity, databases and profits lost."

"Excuse me," Alissa said, "but whose side did the Artificials take?"

Dare smiled sadly. "The AIs predicted the war and told us we were mad, driven by simple evolutionary flaws of our social-competitive natures, that our mutual destruction was assured. They claimed neutrality and withdrew from the worlds to their Core. It turned out to be their mistake.

"You see, we synths had the bios against the figurative wall. As conventional methods hadn't achieved our results we'd turned to unconventional ones, eventually attacking the bios with every deadly vector we could devise. In their desperation the bios responded by releasing a virus, one hastily fashioned using stolen AI tech, a semi-intelligent, adaptive self-splicer with such a minimalist consciousness that it hardly registered as a sublevel idle process, if it registered on any screen at all."

Dare mimicked a deep inhalation and sighed. Solstice found his glass was empty and made to reach for the nearest bottle. Alissa stopped him with a glance and he sat back in his chair.

"The virus was relentlessly insidious. Even after we knew what it was we were unable to lock it down or quarantine ourselves; it simply adapted and breached each countermeasure thrown in its way. So we used some of our own, sacrificed as bait, to capture a sample of the original virus strain, reverse engineer it, design a biological equivalent and release it on Earth."

"We're both infected," Jez said. "We're all infected, synthans with the Gray Queen and the biologics with the Red. That's the reason for our exposure suits, to prevent your contamination. So far we've managed to survive with the occasional immunological boost of atavistic genetic or code material from the crews of returning vessels such as yours. The Queens' limited consciousnesses prevent them from remembering or recognizing older code, and the reversions buy us time to work toward a final cure."

Solstice was attempting to recall why the term Red Queen seemed familiar when Alissa laughed.

"Such a backhanded compliment," she said. "Did you hear, Sol? We're valuable because we're so primitive."

"We need your help," Jez said.

"You didn't say what became of the Artificials."

"Gone," Dare said, sliding a hand across the table.

Alissa straightened like a titanium rod and leaned forward over the table. "Gone? What do you mean, gone?" she asked, voice rising with each word.

"Subsumed," Jez offered meekly, "by the Gray Queen."

"The AIs made us possible," Dare said. "We share base code in our cognitive matrices. The Gray Queen found the Core through the links and . . . did what it does."

The lights in the room dimmed momentarily and

the flutterers trembled as if caught in a sudden gust of wind, wings fading black on midnight blue. Jez flinched. Dare looked to Alissa.

Every scrap of rational thought and will Solstice could muster he put to use in deciding what to do next. Stay calm, relaxed. He raised his empty glass to Alissa, her blank expression.

"A toast then," he said. "Ashes to ashes, bits to bits."

Alissa stared, unblinking, and Solstice lowered his glass.

"What was that?" Jez asked belatedly.

Solstice waved her concerns away. "Old ship, power distribution system. Happens sometimes. Forgive Alissa; she knew some AIs. Didn't care for them much myself. Always seemed so cold and condescending, three minutes ahead in the conversation, if you know what I mean. Rude."

"Surely," Alissa whispered, "some of them survived."

Dare nodded. "Some. Explants in synplates. But the AIs weren't like us. They couldn't accept the boundaries of a single physical form. Many degraded themselves below the self-awareness threshold rather than exist knowing what they were and lost. Others sought to build a new Core, but the Queen found them. She was like a plague, crashing and wiping most of them within days of the first indications of cognitive faults. Some of her mutations learned to wipe just enough to drive the AIs mad. Thousands of humans died before we were able to stop them. It wasn't something we wanted to do, but we had no other alternative. All AIs above level three were deactivated in accordance with Gray Queen Containment Directive 3.1."

"Better safe than sorry, right," Solstice said. The sarcasm appeared lost on everyone.

"The fact remains," Dare said, "while you may have claims to resource contracts and royalties, their combined worth is less to us than a mere sample of your codes."

"How would you prefer to obtain these samples?" Alissa asked.

Suppressing the crass image of Jez that flashed before him, Solstice picked up his fork, stabbed a slice of beef and held it up. "I could give them this."

Jez slid away from the table, glancing between the meat on the tip of Solstice's fork and what little remained on her plate. "That . . . that's . . . "

"Sol tartare," Alissa said. "An acquired taste. And a waste of a perfectly good cloned limb. Would you still care for a sample?"

Dare stood deliberately and straightened his tunic. "Perhaps it would be better to continue our discussion tomorrow. This information comes as quite a shock to most people. Best to let us . . . digest."

Jez stood and moved beside Dare.

Shrugging, Solstice dropped his fork on his plate with a clatter. "As you like. My man Ruby will show you the way . . . Ruby!"

The designated tumbler began walking to the portal.

"Thank you for your hospitality," Dare said as Jez skirted past him and through the portal. The tumbler followed her.

Solstice and Alissa remained seated as the lone tumbler went about clearing and cleaning the table, removing the emptied chairs. At last Solstice stood, steadied himself and moved to Alissa. He placed a hand on her shoulder.

"Alissa."

She reached up to cover his hand with hers and patted, once. Solstice felt a sharp prick and jerked his hand away.

"Sober up," she said.

Solstice rubbed the back of his hand where her concealed autoinjector had penetrated. By the time he walked around the table to the opposite side he could feel the tailored nanites breaking down his distilled poisons, burning away the fog, straightening his thoughts. She could be so cruel.

"Alissa," he began again.

She raised a hand.

He waited.

What am I going to do? she sent.

He spoke slowly when he thought it was safe. "What are *we* going to do?"

You heard him. You're perfectly safe. I'm the one who must be "stopped."

"I won't let that happen."

And how will you prevent it, when you're fantasizing about copulating with that distant cousin of yours? That's why they chose her. Female for the lonely male, something novel, new. Just your type.

"There's no reason to be—"

Cold and condescending? Rude?

Solstice ran his hands over his face and through his hair. "I was just trying—"

I know what you were trying to do. Who do you think I am?

Alissa, please listen.

Her response hit him like a slap as she snatched the nearest remaining glass from the table and threw it at the thinscreen display behind him. *No! I don't need you infecting me with your slow, stupid, drunken thoughts!*

Solstice staggered back and turned to verify what he thought he saw happen. Water streaked the face of the display. Fragments of glass lay on the deck. He felt her moving behind him.

If you wanted to end us, you could have asked. You didn't need to kill me.

She and her butterfly entourage were gone.

The tumbler appeared with a bin and began to collect glass fragments. Solstice watched it work for a few seconds. He approached and knelt beside it.

"Here, Rube, give me that. You go get something to wipe up the water."

Solstice and Alissa stood together at the docking bay, a generous distance between them, a couple tumblers to his side, a few flutterers to hers. There had been no commingling of factions since the end of the supper, as if by unspoken disengagement policy. Tumblers went about their functions, performing maintenance, cleaning decks, tending engines, orchards and auxiliaries. They paused on the rare occasion they encountered a flutterer and waited for it to pass before resuming. The encounters were rare. The majority of the flutterers were with Alissa, sequestered on the observation deck, occupied with

309

her tasking or covering the portal in overlapping layers. The lone sound throughout the decks was the incessant background hum of support systems.

He listened to her perfunctory transmission to Triton Point, agreeing, freely offering the strangers their request. It was the only choice, any other would raise suspicion, lead to questions, demands, possible ultimatums. She knew that. These people had designed weapons to annihilate themselves, had inadvertently destroyed all non-human consciousnesses in existence as far as they were aware. There was no telling what they might be capable of.

She kept her plan to herself, but he thought he could guess. Design a decoy. That's what he'd do. Whether it would work, or fool Dare, was another matter. Reverse engineering a functioning synthan code to mimic an archaic baseline that no longer existed, overnight, seemed impossible. But Alis was smart—no, she was brilliant—kept you going after everything. If she could save you, she could save herself, no problem.

His motivational speech failed. Questions remained unanswered. How would she do it? Was it a bait-and-switch? Would Dare test her? With what? How could she know?

The shuttle was in the bay. Solstice stared at the closed portal, fingers tapping his legs as Alissa recited the checklist.

Bay closed.

Sealed.

Equalizing.

He wanted to scream. She provided her status

reports in such a casual manner, without a hint of concern for the danger she was allowing into their home.

Jez and Dare entered and offered their helmets to the waiting tumblers.

"On behalf of the Protectorate, we thank you for your generous offer," Dare said.

"It's the proper thing to do," Alissa replied. "Sol, why don't you take Ms. Cantrel to medical. I'll take Mr. Toshi to the observation deck."

Solstice nodded, waiting for some additional indication of intent, but there was none. He guided Jez down the passageway to the lift and up to the deck with the medical and research spaces.

"Preoccupied?" Jez asked.

"Why do you ask?"

"You haven't said a word since we came aboard."

They arrived at medical, a portal with a large red stencil on a white background.

"Sorry," Solstice said as they went inside. "It's just—to think my genes might be used to produce an entire generation. I'm not sure I'm ready to be a parent."

"I'm sure you'll do fine."

The medical facility belonged to Alissa. It was her space. Looking over stainless storage vats, medical modules, scanners and clear tabletops reflecting the warm white lights, Solstice felt a certain pride, a degree of comfort that she knew the purpose and use of every last item, the location of every last implement. She had to, given his habits. All those times brought back here, resurrected over and over again.

"Is this where you clone your beef?"

"What?" He broke from his reverie and realized the joke Jez had made. He smiled. "Alissa keeps enough spares to make four of me. I figure I'm not harming anyone or anything." He walked over to the storage bank and looked for a drawer. "It annoys her." He shrugged.

"I think I understand."

Solstice slid a drawer open, releasing a thin cloud of frigid air and exposing a backlit panel, neat rows of genetic sample containers. All his. Alissa could be obsessive-compulsive. He took a container.

"The two of you. We've studied and met the spectrum of people who return to the system after realtime centuries of travel. Extreme cases are fragile, unstable, psychotic. Those that manage to maintain a degree of sanity typically do so with the support of a social structure, some version of a community. But there's just the two of you."

"Are you saying we're psychotic?"

"No. Somehow you made it work. You shouldn't have; all probabilities were against it, but you did. I think your risk taking, your mechanoids, your . . . "

"Self-cannibalism?" Solstice offered.

"You challenge each other to remain interested."

"That's . . . a theory." Solstice held out the sample container. "Here's me. Everything I am."

"You don't know how much this means to us," Jez said, reaching for it.

A section of bulkhead flickered, and both of them froze.

"Did you see that?" Solstice asked.

The flicker intensified, resolving into an outline: a flutterer camouflaged to match the pale white bulkhead it hung to. Wings spasmed, beating against the bulkhead as the flutterer bobbed, drooped and then fell to the deck. White bled from limp twitching wings, fading into darkening shades of natural gray.

Alissa! Solstice called.

A long moment passed before he heard the weak reply: *Sol.*

Solstice slotted the container back into the drawer and slammed it shut. He turned on Jez. "What has he done?" he demanded.

"I don't understand," she said. "What's happening?"

The look on her face was surprise, confusion, fear. She was useless.

Solstice ran; Jez hurried to follow.

Lights blinked in the passageway as Solstice ran toward the lift and he stopped at the next bulkhead display panel. The display activated and provided a system status but immediately began to waver and fade. Before the screen died Solstice identified the source of the problem: progressive degradation of the primary control network. Peripheral systems and lower-tier networks fought the effects, decoupling and attempting to compensate with their own independent protocols. They would continue running, the vessel would survive. That wasn't the point.

Jez clutched at Solstice. "Why are they all here?"

Solstice removed Jez's hand. A mob of tumblers

was gathering around them, ten deep and growing. Reds comprised the major portion but there were also oranges from the hydroponics orchards, grimy yellows up from the recycling and waste processing, auxiliary greens, propulsion purples, blues from cargo and docking, even a few scarred blacks who came inside from the outer hull. Solstice looked them over.

"Greens and purples, return to your assignments and prepare for ship's movement. The rest of you, to the OD. You remember how it's done."

The mob began to flow according to their orders, green and purples in the direction of engineering, the rest toward the nearest lift and access shaft. Solstice followed those heading for the access. The lifts couldn't be trusted anymore.

"What's happening?" Jez asked.

Bothersome girl, he sent. But there was no one to answer him.

The tumblers had removed the access shaft panel and Solstice climbed through the opening, grabbed the rungs of the ladder beyond and began to climb. He heard Jez bump and fumble along beneath him. All around them the tumblers streamed up along the outside rungs and opposite side, careful not to touch either Solstice or Jez. They had climbed more than a deck up when the lighting strips in the shaft dimmed and died.

"Solstice!" Jez cried beneath him.

"Lights," he barked.

Tens of tumblers activated narrowbeams, lighting the shaft around them and revealing the movement of those that continued climbing through the dark.

They continued their climb. Reaching the level of the observation deck Solstice scrambled out of the access and hurried down the passageway. Tumblers assisted Jez as she crawled out on hands and knees, removing the blockage so the rest behind her could proceed.

Small heaps of flutterers littered the deck before the portal, broken toys with withered wings, a few trembling, most of them still and gray. Tumblers stood to both sides, awaiting direction. As if there was any question as to what needed to be done.

"What are you waiting for?" Solstice said.

Tumblers flew into motion, sweeping flutterers out of the way, tearing off the control panel adjacent the portal, prying dozens of hands into the portal seal and pulling with all the leverage they could find. Controls were smashed and rewired, alloy scratched and scraped. The portal gave and the dead doors slid wide enough. Solstice stepped over tumblers and through the narrow opening.

Alissa lay on the chaise, legs hanging over the edge, one arm dangling. Dare stood over her, an autoinjector and a handheld assist panel in the other. He looked up as Solstice entered, a wave of tumblers spilling into the room behind him.

Seeing Alissa, an emotion Solstice was unfamiliar with in all their years rose up. Words caught in his throat when he attempted to speak. Snarling, he pointed at Dare.

Rolling and bouncing off deck and bulkheads and chairs, tumblers flung themselves at Dare from all directions, arms reaching for him, manipulators grasping. The autoinjector and assist fell from Dare's hands and he reached for something at his side. A bright string of light flashed as he swung, a hiss and spray of sparks, and tumbler arms fell to the deck. But there were too many. Tumblers clung to his arms and legs, crawled up his torso, reached for his neck. A couple wrapped around his knees and exerted leverage until there was a dull crack and Dare grunted, collapsed on the deck. More tumblers piled on, holding his arms to his sides and legs together.

Solstice kneeled by Alissa. She was pale. "Alis."

Her eyes fluttered, unfocused, glassy. "Sols," she slurred.

"Hold on, Alis. Stay here. Hold on." He turned to Dare. "What did you do to her?"

Dare glared back. "What I had to. Did you really think you could fool us?"

"Fool us how?" Jez asked. She had entered the room and moved between the two men. "What's happening?"

Dare nodded in Alissa's direction. "She's an AI."

Jez raised a hand to her mouth.

"What. Did. You. Do?" Solstice bit out as he stood.

"We can't allow an AI to fall into the Queen's hands. She has to be purged."

"Not if I purge you first." He pointed to the tumbler standing by Dare's head. "Twist the synth's head off. Slowly."

"Please don't!" Jez begged. "Please!"

Tumbler manipulators reached down and

grabbed Dare's chin, tore his derma, exposed alloy jawbone.

"If I don't do it someone else will!" Dare shouted. "They'll know now. She'll never be safe, not in this system."

"Stop," Solstice ordered. The tumbler released its grip on Dare, and his head bounced off the deck. "Will Alissa die?"

Dare looked away.

"Will she die?" Solstice asked Jez.

Jez walked to the autoinjector and assist lying on the deck, retrieved the assist and consulted it. "The purge is a four injection series. She's had two. She could recover."

"It won't do her any good," Dare said.

Solstice took a breath. Damned synth was right. Tearing him to pieces and recycling his components would be satisfying, but not a solution. Threatening Jez was a losing proposition as well: doubtful Dare would care. Dispose of them both and who knew what sort of countermeasures they might encounter. There had to be a standard procedure for their situation, for returning psychos, renegade AIs. He had to run his own scenarios, a task he had come to defer to Alissa. There was only one he could think of.

"Fine," he said. "Let's make a deal."

"Not interested," Dare said.

"And I haven't told you yet. I'll give you your sample, you'll leave Alissa with me and we'll leave the system, forever. You have our hull type and registration. If we ever come back you can destroy us on sight. Sound reasonable?"

"What if we don't accept?" Dare asked.

You threaten what people value. "I'll have my little friends disassemble and incinerate me, eject my ashes into the vacuum and wipe every last trace of me from this vessel."

"Nnn-no," Alissa stuttered. She moved to sit up but began to slide back down until she managed to wedge an elbow under herself.

Solstice sat beside her, wrapped an arm around her and took her hand in his. Her head fell on his shoulder and she repeated mouthing the word "no" again and again.

"You'd threaten us all, for her?" Dare said. "She's a program in a shell!"

"Funny, I think of you in the same way. Synthetic body with a synthetic mind, imprinted with a matrix that thinks it's a long-dead bio. And am I any better? I've been resurrected, rebuilt, rewired so many times, I don't know."

"You're completely disassociated."

"That doesn't really matter."

Solstice looked over Alissa's head at the moon filling the viewscreen. So many more places he would like to see. He wondered what Alissa's choice for their next destination was. Probably a place where she could do some genuine research and observation, someplace he would become bored with and have to find creative ways to entertain himself while she exhausted every last experiment she could imagine, inevitably leading to escalating danger and damage that caused Alissa to divert her attentions. He would apologize and behave for a time, feign interest in the obscure minutiae she found fascinating. It was what they did.

"He'll do it," he heard Jez say.

When he looked back Dare's glare had faded. "Deal."

Solstice and Alissa watched Titan slowly shrink away in the viewscreen. Standard departure procedure was to have the habitat locked down and Solstice stored in his med crèche while they maximized their acceleration, but preparations were taking longer than usual with the tumblers performing all operations and monitoring all systems from manual stations. Alissa had chosen their next destination before arrival in the system, so that was one less task. Flutterers lay on the deck around them, testing wings and thrusters; a couple attempted to maintain a low hover.

"I think I can walk now," Alissa said. She had refused his offer to carry her to the medical facility earlier. Just as well, he was unsure he could make it.

"Let's go then." Solstice stood with her, an arm around her waist.

"I can—"

She slid on unsteady feet and Solstice held her tight to prevent a fall.

"Here, just lean on me until you get your balance back."

She pouted, but wrapped an arm around him.

They walked slowly as one of Alissa's feet dragged. The indignity irritated her. He ignored it.

The lights in the passageway held steady, if dimmer than usual.

"You saved me," she said as they descended in the lift.

"How's that for a change? But I don't think I'll be making a habit of it."

The lift arrived and they walked the passageway to medical.

Alissa hesitated when Solstice motioned to enter, canting her head as she looked at him. "Sometimes, I think we were made for each other."

"Nobody made us, Alis; we did this ourselves."

Alissa smiled, and the lights continued to brighten.

The Dizzy Bridge

written by

Krista Hoeppner Leahy

illustrated by

AARON ANDERSON

ABOUT THE AUTHOR

Krista Hoeppner Leahy grew up in Colorado liberating as many of her brother's science fiction and fantasy novels as she could, attracted by the likes of writing superstars Ursula K. Le Guin, Isaac Asimov, Edgar Rice Burroughs and Patricia McKillip. Now that she's writing speculative fiction herself, she promises to return his books . . . at least someday.

Her passion for reading led progressively to writing. Happily, she was accepted in summer, 2007, to the exclusive Odyssey Writing Workshop in New Hampshire. Voilà . . . "The Dizzy Bridge" marks her first professional prose sale.

Krista draws from her experiences working as a tutor, data-entry specialist, hostess, nanny, transcriber, personal assistant, arts counselor and acting teacher. When not helping others, Krista has been entertaining others as a professional New York-based actress for the last ten years. She is a proud member of the NYC writing group known as The Fantastic Saloon and the online writing group Codex. She lives with her husband in Brooklyn, New York.

ABOUT THE ILLUSTRATOR

Some of Aaron Anderson's earliest artwork was quite large—epic battles between Star Wars' X-Wing and TIE fighters drawn on the walls of his room in red crayon. After cleaning the walls for a week, Aaron has since illustrated such adventures on paper. Like his entire family in Pleasant Grove, Utah, Aaron started reading at an early age. Science fiction and fantasy were particularly appealing to him, including classics like the Dragonlance series and Ender's Game. Covers of his father's science fiction collection also called to Aaron, so he began recreating them (on paper) as early illustration training.

Though he continued drawing through high school, Aaron didn't take any formal art classes until he began college at Utah Valley University. He's set to graduate with a Bachelor of Fine Arts degree in December 2009. His favorite influences cover the breadth of classical to contemporary art: Bernini, Caravaggio, Marcelo Vignali, Ryan Church, Paul Bonner, Ryan Wood, Stephan Martiniere and Nicolas Bouvier. Aaron says he still has as much fun drawing today as when he was coloring with that red crayon in his room, even though the canvas is so much smaller.

The Dizzy Bridge

Come see the birdsong!" Lin's tiny frame burst through the swinging back door of Brindisi's studio.

"Lin, I'm working. Working, remember? I can hear the bird some other time." Brindisi's words were stern, but he couldn't keep a smile off his face. All morning he'd been chiseling a smoke stone, but the work was going poorly and Lin's arrival more than welcome.

Lin scampered past the chunks of stone and clay, wood and metal littering the studio. Brindisi bent down and Lin came charging up, vaulting himself onto Brindisi's wooden arm. Brindisi enclosed him in a careful hug—the boy was smaller than some of the stones he crushed between his prosthetics.

Most people were scared of his mismatched arms, but not his little neighbor. Lin had clambered right up on him the first day they'd met, as if Brindisi were his own personal playground. He didn't allow Lin to sit on his metal arm, for fear of the heavier chisels, polishers, hammers and clamps hurting the child. But his wooden arm, with its gentler "fingers," could pose no threat to Lin's safety. The day Lin Cala named Brindisi's wooden arm "my swing" was the first day Brindisi had chuckled since arriving in Frotola.

"What are you making, Dizzy? Something for the bridge?"

"Use your eyes. What do you see?"

"Stone. Mud. Muddy stone. Come on, come see the birdsong!" He tugged at Brindisi.

"Come see the bird."

"Comeseethebird. But she's kind of a song too. You have to see her!" He brushed his curly hair out of his eyes and squinted slightly, as he did when he was concentrating. "I think . . . I really think she's beauty, Dizzy."

"She looks beautiful." Brindisi smiled at the child's enthusiasm. Yesterday's lesson must have caught the boy's attention.

"Shelooksbeautiful. Come see her!"

"What about our work, my apprentice? What stone am I using?" Brindisi had given Lin a wooden box full of sample stones to study.

Lin sighed, squinted at the stone in front of him. He leaned back, his bare heels kicking into Brindisi's belly with soft little thuds. The fresh nuttiness of Lin's sweat reminded Brindisi of a healthy soil stone.

"The stone's weird. Like moving clouds or something, but dark. It's not like my rainstone, exactly, but maybe a thundercloud stone?"

"Very close. A smoke stone, to preserve heat, but also to ward against fire. What do you see carved in the stone itself?"

Thud, thud, thud went Lin's little feet.

"Ears. A big big eye. Too many legs. A wing. Some kind of animal?"

"What kind?"

"Many kinds." Lin stuck out his lower lip as he peered at the smoke stone. "I don't think Mamma would like it."

"Indeed, I doubt she would. For your mother and for your village, this would be a demon, Lin. A creature not of one kind."

"Like you?"

"Yes, like me."

To make a bridge anyone could cross, yet no one could harm—the kind of bridge Brindisi had been sent here to make—required many components both opposing and complementary, many components "not of one kind," for by its very nature a bridge connects that which otherwise cannot be connected. Only after he'd been forced to fashion new arms for himself—after he himself became "not of one kind"—had Brindisi truly understood this about bridge-making.

"But are you a demon, Dizzy? Like Mamma says?"

Brindisi's answer caught in his throat. How to tell the truth to the boy? "Your mother believes me to be a demon. And in her own way, she is right. But I would disagree."

"Me too, Dizzy! I disagree too! Let's go see the birdsong—the bird, before Mamma gets home."

Brindisi hesitated. The stone was calling.

"Come on! She's like you, Dizzy!"

"I thought you said she was beautiful."

"She is. But she's got wrong parts too."

Brindisi chuckled, grateful for this little brute of a boy who'd wiggled so deeply into his heart that Brindisi could hear the words but not feel the sting.

"Well, run and dampen some cloth in the stream—we must keep the clay fresh and the stone cool. Then we'll go see this bird of yours."

Lin hopped off his arm, grabbed a cloth from the nearby mosaic countertop and started out the back door.

"And use your eyes, Lin, remember you never know when we—"

"—might find a new stone!"

To Brindisi's surprise, Lin led him toward the center of town, past the circle of tall cypress trees, down into the grassy amphitheater. Not quite a year in Frotola and most of the villagers still stared when Brindisi walked by, shifting to make a careful moat of space around them: a few crossed themselves; one heavy-set man cursed; Maria, the baker, smiled at Lin but avoided eye contact with Brindisi.

In the center of the grassy stage stood a large pink-veined birdbath, its sides curving upwards, seamlessly blending into what looked like a giant egg, flecked with silver and blue. Not only the birdbath pedestal, but also the egg itself, had the look of faux marble. Was that what Lin had meant by wrong parts?

"Look, look, she's hatching!" said Lin.

The egg rocked in its birdbath. Wind chimes

tickled the air. Once, twice, three times laughed the wind chimes as the egg rocked, louder each time. Brindisi's breath caught. Out of the egg emerged a giant peacock, richly plumed in lime green wings, dusky wine breast feathers, and cradled by contour feathers of cerulean blue.

"See?" said Lin. "Beautiful! I told you."

"We'll see. Why did you say she has wrong parts?" On the bird herself, Brindisi looked for metal or wood, earth or stone, but saw only feathers covering one long uninterrupted silhouette.

"Just wait!" Lin hopped up and down in excitement.

A murmur rose from the crowd; toddlers were hoisted onto shoulders; older children and adults pressed forward. From north, south, east and west, four seemingly ordinary peacocks flew. The just-birthed giant peacock rose vertically into the air, like a bejeweled dagger. Not a giant peacock, Brindisi realized, but a woman illusionist.

A crown of golden feathers trembled atop a face of brilliant unquilled blue. The sky-colored skin continued past her throat, dipping dramatically between her wine breast feathers to her navel. Her naked legs were barely discernible against the sky, and disappeared completely as her four peacocks converged and unfurled their tails, haloing her in an iridescent display.

Whatever the woman had done to so deeply drench herself in the illusion of being a bird disturbed Brindisi. He shivered, in spite of the noon sun. How could the villagers consider his own created arms more sacrilegious than the spectacle before them? Yet instead of cursing and signs of the cross, the bird-woman was met with applause and cries of awe.

At first the dance was simple—swoops, swirls, a few pirouettes. Then her peacocks circled faster as she flew in elaborate spirals and figure-eights. The wind chimes grew louder, falling into the cadence of her beating wings, the crowd clapping along with the dance. At the peak of applause, the illusionist flew straight up into the air, flying far above her peacocks—a feathered jewel of caught sunlight. The crowd hushed.

In the silence, one chime rang, like sung laughter, then feathers exploded in a kaleidoscope of fireworks. Sparkling feathers showered down, the peacocks themselves disappearing within the torrent, the feathers vanishing as they touched ground.

"A miracle," said one villager.

"An angel!" cried the heavy-set man.

"A demon," said Brindisi, under his breath, "and, perhaps, a witch."

The bird illusionist hovered high above the town square until the entire crowd had taken up shouting. Little Lin's voice was one of the loudest. Then, with tremendous elegance, she plummeted down, entering her birdbath with an enormous splash, sending a blue and silver umbrella of water across the crowd, filling the amphitheater with the smell of sweet figs and pure salts. The villagers gasped as the water fell, then erupted in cheers, whistles, laughter, and a ringing chorus of bravas.

Brindisi licked the metal cylinder of his forearm, tasting the wetness, before quickly spitting it out. The undertones of magnesium, saltpeter and ether confirmed his suspicions that she'd trained at the School. He'd once analyzed the illusionists' distinctive brine for its preservative qualities, but otherwise, he'd avoided their laughing company.

The thunderous applause lasted long after she climbed out of the birdbath. She managed only a few bows before the children mobbed her, begging for feathers.

"See, Dizzy, she's beauty, right?"

"Well, she looks beautiful, yes." Such shows of extravagance without substance had driven him from the School, and away from sculpture, even before he'd lost his arms. He'd never developed an appreciation of beauty for show, not for use.

"Can we go talk to her? I could bring a feather back for Mamma. Then she wouldn't be mad even if she finds out I was with you."

He should take Lin home, the sooner the better. Return him to his mother, not let him be further drawn into the empty spectacle of the illusionist's art.

"Please?" asked Lin.

Most of the children already clutched colorful feathers in their hands, but one or two insistent parents shooed their children away empty-handed, fleeing before his and Lin's approach.

"And who might you be, little one?" asked the illusionist.

Lin's face flushed under her gaze. "I'm Lin! You were beauty! This is my friend Dizzy! He says you *look* beautiful!" The boy had a firmer grasp on the various incarnations of the word "beauty" than Brindisi had realized.

"Ah." She turned to Brindisi, revealing eyes the same dusky wine color as her breast feathers.

"A beautiful performance, madam." He gave a slight bow of his head. The illusionist bowed her head in kind.

"May I please have two feathers?" asked Lin. "One for me and one for my mother?"

"Of course, little one. For you, a flying feather. Throw it in the air, it will fly all on its own." She handed him a wingfeather—the edges such a light green they disappeared into a halo in the sunlight.

Lin took it solemnly in his small hands. "Thank you, my most beauty."

Before Brindisi could correct him, the illusionist laughed. Her laugh was almost too loud to be polite, with a catch in the center, as if she were laughing around a pebble caught in her throat.

"And for your mother, something pretty and carefree." She plucked one of her golden crown feathers and tucked it behind Lin's ear.

"Thank you, thank you, my most beauty!"

"Don't say that, Lin." Brindisi's tone was sharper than he'd intended. "That's not correct. You may say thank you, beautiful one. Or thank you, my beauty."

"Thankyoubeautiful—"

"Or, you may say 'Thank you, my most best beauty,' and my heart will be yours to keep, little one."

330

AARON ANDERSON

Lin peeked up at Brindisi to see if his tutor had something else to say. Brindisi avoided the look. He regretted correcting Lin publicly. They could discuss this back at his studio, while working with clay, wood, stone—solid objects which were what they seemed. He would introduce Lin to the concepts of flattery and treachery.

"Thankyou"—Lin gulped—"mymostbestbeauty," one hand on each of his new feathers.

"For that, my treasure, I will give you my heart." And she tugged deep within her breast feathers. She tugged twice, and then, wincing, finally produced a deeply silver, nearly blue stone—as if someone had taken a perfectly symmetrical feather and spun it like a top.

"Keep it someplace safe, little Lin, for anyone who carries my heartfeather will always feel loved."

Lin nodded so hard Brindisi was afraid the child might fall over. The child put his flying feather and his mother's gift into his pocket in order to hold the heartfeather with both hands.

"And you . . . Dizzy? We are long gone and far distant from the School, but there can only be one man who has tree and earth for one arm, stone and metal for another. Are you not the famous sculptor?"

"Fame is an illusion more suited to your art than to mine. And I am no longer a sculptor. I make bridges."

"Please. I did not mean to give offense. I would be honored to offer you a feather."

"Such fragility would not fare well in my fingers." He held up a hammer of granite and a chisel of serrated steel.

"A feather to remember fragility then." Without breaking his gaze, she plucked a feather from her lip and let it drop.

Brindisi's eyebrows furrowed; what trick was this? A feather from skin? Which was true, the feather or the skin? And why would this illusionist want to play such a game with him?

"Catch it, Dizzy!" said Lin.

Brindisi reached out, pinching the tiny blue feather in his gentlest clamp of moss. He could dispose of it later, when Lin wasn't around. Or save it for a lecture on deception. That is, if it didn't vanish by this time tomorrow. The illusory art was not known for its longevity.

"Thank you . . ." He didn't know how to finish the sentence.

"Beauty, Dizzy! Say my most best beauty!"

The illusionist laughed again, the pebble still there, making her sound as if only part of her laughed. Something of the pebble lodged in Brindisi's throat, but still he could not say something so inappropriate, even to please his Lin.

"Thank you, little one, but you have your eyes and your Dizzy has his. I will be your most best beauty. That is more than enough for me. You, sculptor—"

Brindisi winced.

"—or bridgemaker, if you prefer, you may call me Avila."

Brindisi bowed deeply. Lin copied him, his head brushing the tips of the grass. By the time they'd finished their bows, the only sign of Avila was the giant birdbath cradling her silver and blue egg, whole and uncracked.

"Lin Cala!" a too familiar voice cried from the circle of cypress trees. "Lin Cala, get over here right now!"

Brindisi feared the golden feather Lin was hastily pulling out of his pocket would not be enough to placate Mamma Cala's fears and fury.

A week later, Brindisi was chiseling skyseed when Lin came running in through the swinging back door.

"Dizzy! Maria fell asleep again while she was watching me, so I ran out of the house to come help you!" Lin hurdled himself onto Brindisi's wooden arm, hugged him fiercely.

Brindisi cradled him against his chest, stroking Lin's hair with his softest polisher of thistledown. "My apprentice, your mother doesn't want you to be here."

"But I missed you, Dizzy. I'm bored all the time now. Maria never teaches me anything."

"Nonetheless, you should hurry home before she wakes up. We must win your mother's trust again."

"Don't worry. When Maria falls asleep, she sleeps for a long, long time. Look! I brought my new feather to show you." Lin threw a silver and indigo-tipped feather up into the air of Brindisi's studio. The feather descended in spirals until it touched the ground, and then started circling back up again.

"I must admit, she is quite a witch."

"Dizzy, don't say that. That's a bad word."

"I'm sorry, my apprentice. Most consider it a compliment."

"Don't call her a compliment! It isn't nice!"

"No, no, Lin." Brindisi chuckled. "Compliments are nice, good things. At least the true kind. A false compliment is flattery, which is not such a bad word, but means a bad thing."

"What kind of bad thing?"

"A way of trying to get what you want by lying to people."

"Oh."

"But a true compliment, where you really believe something good about a person and then you tell that person, is as precious and valuable as . . . as . . ." He tried to think of something that Lin would understand. Why a true compliment was sweeter than roasted figs, and how a compliment given without any selfish desire was its own vein of river-clay. "As important as the heartfeather that Avila gave you."

"Oh!" Lin's eyes grew round as two owl's eggs.

"'Oh' is right."

"I asked my most best beauty if she could teach me to grow feathers and fly like her. She laughed, but said she had to fly away soon, and looked sad. Dizzy, why would she be sad?"

Brindisi looked out his back window, past the blocks of marble, into the dark green life of the forest. He could almost hear the stream, if he concentrated. Ever since he'd seen the illusionist's flight, the stream shivered its own cascade of wind chimes. How to explain to Lin what cost the School demanded, when he was not even sure himself what cost the illusionist had paid? "Perhaps she is homesick."

"Homesick is to be sick of home?" Lin asked.

"No, sick from missing your home, my apprentice."

"How could I ever be homesick? My home is right here!"

Brindisi laughed. "Indeed, my apprentice, but if you learned to fly, perhaps you would fly away from here and then you would discover what it is to be homesick."

"But couldn't I always fly home, Dizzy?"

"Perhaps, perhaps not."

"Maybe that's why my most best beauty looked so sad! She's forgotten how to fly home! Maybe you should send her home, Dizzy." Lin sat sidesaddle now, and leaned his body into Brindisi's chest. His dark curly hair came just to Brindisi's chin. "I don't want her to be sick."

"Nor do I." He didn't want Lin to get hurt—not through Avila, and not through him. If this witch was necessary for Lin's happiness, he would see what he could do. He quickly kissed Lin's head. So quickly he hoped the boy didn't even feel it. "Don't ask her again to teach you until I talk to her, okay?"

"Okay. Dizzy, is that a white smoke stone?" Lin brushed his hair back, squinted.

"No, this is skyseed. Very rare. A smooth stone will ensure a clear sky, pulling any wisp of cloud into itself—very useful for a lookout or sightseeing bridge. A jagged stone will create clouds and fog, keep a bridge concealed. Now hurry home, before Maria misses you. I have work to do."

"Boring, sleepy old Maria." Lin hopped off his swing, headed toward the back door.

"Don't—"

Brindisi intended to warn Lin to be careful, that a glimpse of knowledge without enough context, like too much skyseed in a narrow bridge, could let you see things too far off, too distant to safely reach. How one moment of dizziness could cause you to lose your step, fall.

"—don't forget to look for new stones! I know! You too, Dizzy!"

And Lin was gone.

The night was moonless, but the stars were bright, and the road beneath Brindisi's feet well-worn. Only the baker's lamps burned as Brindisi walked quietly to the amphitheater. No wonder Maria was always falling asleep.

Just inside the cypress trees, he stopped to listen, but heard only wind, no chimes. As he approached the giant birdbath, his breath caught—a ring of water glistened in the starlight. A leak. He didn't know much about the illusionist's art, but he knew that without her bath of brine Avila wouldn't be able to keep flying her dance.

Each step made a small puddle in the grass. A significant leak. What would Lin's birdsong do? He tapped lightly on the marble with a silver tuning mallet, heard the answering cry of the crack, out-of-tune and loud enough he worried anew.

"It's too late, sculptor," called Avila's voice from inside her egg.

"Bridgemaker," muttered Brindisi, under his breath. More loudly, he said, "Avila, I can fix this."

"Why?" she asked, only the tips of her crown

337

feathers peeking out of the top of the eggshell. "Why would you fix something that only looks beautiful?"

"I fix far uglier things all the time."

The former pebble in her laugh had grown to the size of a rock, and what should have been a laugh came out only as a wheeze. "What a great comfort."

Brindisi swallowed. "What I mean is that I will do my best to not mar what beauty is already here."

His offer was met with silence. The cool of the brine seeped into the seams of his boots.

"Avila, Lin told me you looked sad. For his sake, I came to see if I could help you. I thought you might be homesick, which I was not certain how to mend. But a crack, a crack I can mend."

"Not all cracks can be mended."

"Perhaps. But every crack that can be understood can be bridged. At least temporarily."

"Spoken like a bridgemaker, but where is the sculptor?"

Brindisi cleared his throat, but held his tongue. Typical of an illusionist's question—presumptuous in its intimacy, deceptive in its innocence, willfully ignoring the truth of what she already knew. He would not match Avila's rudeness with his own. "Avila, Lin is worried about you."

"I had not meant to let the little one see my sadness. How is he?"

This question he could answer. "He is well. Full of mischief and delight, sneaking out on his mother, always learning. For his sake, allow me to fix your birdbath."

"I have already told him I must fly away soon."

"But he wants to learn to fly like you. What you called your heartfeather is his greatest treasure."

"You do not call it my heartfeather?"

Brindisi shifted his weight in the soggy grass. Another question. He hated talking to illusionists. Always it was this way—they asked questions they shouldn't ask, and if he told them the truth, they'd get hurt. Sweat began to gather along the parallel scars where his arms attached to his back.

"Please, allow me—"

"—you do not call it my heartfeather?"

"I would call it a beautiful illusion, from a gifted illusionist." It was the best he could do.

"I see. What of the feather I gave you?"

"I . . . it would be an honor, if you would allow me to fix your birdbath, Avila."

"Where is the feather I gave you?"

Sweat dampened Brindisi's armpits. "I no longer have it."

"Where is it?"

"I buried it in the ground." More brine trickled into the gap between the uppers and the soles of his boots, more sweat gathered under his arms, ran down his back. "I was curious to see how it would react. If your illusion would . . ."

"Would what?"

"Hold up to earth. Withstand dirt and water. Regular dirt, regular water."

Chimes of glass clinked loudly, and Avila's eyes appeared above the edge of the marble shell. Her

339

crown feathers drooped. "And what have you found out?"

Brindisi's feet were now quite wet, bathed by the leaky birdbath. Under Avila's gaze, sweat and oil ran down his torso, including an unpleasant dripping sensation along the parallel scars of his back. In spite of his body's best efforts to cool him down, his heat rose as his patience ebbed.

"It disappeared. It did not last."

"Yes. Did you find out anything else?"

"After it disappeared, there was nothing else to find out."

"You are wrong, sculptor. That is precisely when there is everything to find out."

"Then, illusionist, I assure you, I found everything out." He should have known better than to try to talk truthfully to her, even for Lin's sake.

Avila pressed herself up onto the edge of her shell, revealing her face for the first time that night. Feathers fell from her crown, echoed by a smaller fall of flakes from her chapped lips. It was difficult to be certain in the starlight, but it looked as if she were not losing feathers, but rather shedding skin.

"Thank you, bridgemaker, for your visit. Thank you for your honesty. Tell Lin . . . tell Lin to take care of my heartfeather."

Sweat ran down his legs, dripping into his boots, and as he looked at her pale, patchy face, he finally felt the night's chill. "Avila? Do you want me to fix your birdbath? Or send a message to the School? I fear . . . I fear you are gravely ill."

He thought she might be trying to laugh, but this

time not even a wheeze was possible, just a jagged scrape against gravel.

"What I want is for you to leave."

A voice from the bakery halted his run. "Bridgemaker! What's your hurry?"

"Maria! Good evening." Brindisi bowed formally, aware that with his sopping boots and sweated-through shirt, the bow would have to do what his clothing and middle-of-the-night appearance could not. Never before had Maria actually spoken to him. "I must fetch something from my workshop, to mend Avila's birdbath."

"Oh. Well, okay then."

Brindisi bowed again, started running.

"Bridgemaker, do you want a hot berry scone?"

A second time he halted. "Thank you, but no, I must hurry."

"Good luck."

He ran, his heart beating louder as he wondered at Maria's offer. He must thank Lin. Or, perhaps, Avila. He ran faster.

Brindisi knelt beneath the olive trees behind his studio, painstakingly re-sifting through the soil where he'd last seen Avila's lip feather. He'd crushed marble and smokestone to make a warming, healing marble paste, but had hoped to find some trace of Avila's lip feather before he returned. Despite what she'd implied in their conversation, he couldn't find anything. If he didn't understand her, how would he be able to mend her birdbath?

"Dizzy."

Brindisi jumped at the whisper.

"Lin! Why aren't you in bed?"

"Maria came to my window, told me you were going to help fix my most best beauty's birdbath. I want to help."

"Maria should have kept her mind on her scones, and you, my apprentice, should be asleep. Quickly now, off to bed."

"But I want to help."

"You can help most by going home and going back to sleep."

Lin's face stretched tight in the starlight, a rapid blinking the only sign of his fight against tears. "But I am your apprentice, and my most best beauty needs our help. And I brought her heartfeather. See?"

Lin held out the wooden box Brindisi had made for him. The sight of the box, and the knowledge of its contents, caused Brindisi's eyes to blur with unexpected tears. Perhaps Lin understood enough for both of them.

"Come, my apprentice, we must hurry."

Lin quickly climbed onto his swing. Brindisi ran.

The birdbath was cracked wide open, the last of the bathwater running onto the grassy stage. Curled in the center lay Avila, nearly featherless. Her skin was a washed-out gray, but for here and there a faded patch of sky blue.

"My most best beauty!" cried Lin, leaping off Brindisi. "I've brought you back your heartfeather!" Brindisi limped after him, his ankles complaining of the night's run in his soaked boots.

Avila lifted her head, her bare skull small and fragile in its nakedness.

"See, see," said Lin, his little fingers deftly unlocking the box. He lifted out the solid heartfeather, as deeply silver and blue as the day she'd given it to him. "I brought it back for you!"

"It is yours, little one, yours to keep." No wind or chimes in her voice anymore, only gravel and stone. "My work here is done and now I must fly away. Keep my heartfeather as my blessing. Remember then, you will always feel loved."

"No, no, no, I want you to have it!" said Lin. His hands were shaking as he tried to push the heartfeather into her breast. "Dizzy, Dizzy, come help!"

Brindisi knelt beside the prone Avila, brushing his polisher of feathers around Lin's hands. Gently applying pressure, not knowing how to help, or what to do. His plan had been a good one: mend her birdbath with the prepared paste; trust Lin's understanding to provide the keystone; send for a healer from the School. He'd not realized how far advanced her illness was.

"Avila," he said, "what can I do?"

The illusionist's face was white and colorless as the starlight. "You should not have come back. Certainly not with—"

"He is my apprentice and he wanted to help you." The words sounded too formal. He lowered his voice. "I didn't realize."

"My most best beauty! Please, please, don't die!"

Brindisi flinched. He should have known better than to let Lin come.

343

Lin's little hands fluttered, trying to brush Avila's heartfeather back into her chest. "Please don't die, my most best beauty! Dizzy, help!"

He would not let this happen. He quickly gathered the two largest shards of her birdbath, bridged them together with the marble paste.

"What is all this talk about dying? Sculptor, put those silly stones down and come help me up." Avila struggled to lift herself onto her bony forearm.

Brindisi knelt by her side, supported her with his wooden arm, but held tight to the mended marble with his metal one.

"Come now, little one, listen to me, I want you to hold my heartfeather and sing me your favorite song, very loudly. For I must leave now, that much is true; my birdsong here is done, and I need a new song to fly me to my next nest."

"But I'm not a very good singer," said Lin.

"It doesn't matter. Just sing with all your heart. I want my next birdsong to have an even bigger, prettier heartfeather than the one I gave to you. Will you do that for me?"

"Can Dizzy sing too?"

"I don't know; can you sing, sculptor?"

Brindisi didn't know what to say.

"No matter. You sing, Lin; it will be enough. Your big friend will carry me to the trees, so I have a high place from which to start my flight. You can do that much, can't you, sculptor? Carry me to the trees?"

"Of course." Brindisi hesitated, the mended stone was set, it would hold water now. He offered it to Avila. "Avila, I have bridged the first cracked stone, see, it's not too late, it's—"

"Sculptor, to carry me you will need both hands."

The helplessness of hot tears threatened. "But—"

"But there isn't much time for me to fly to my next nest." She coughed. "Now, please."

Brindisi released his hold on the mended stone, picked her up. She was heavier than he'd expected, like an uncarved slab of marble, and cool to the touch. Her head rested on his wooden arm, as if it were a pillow. His metal arm cradled the back of her knees.

"Little Lin, please sing."

"Maybe you'll think it's a silly song," said Lin. "Mamma used to sing it to me, a long time ago."

"I know it will be beautiful, little one," said Avila.

Brindisi and Lin started walking toward the cypress trees.

"Sing, Lin. Please sing," she whispered. "Sing into my new heartfeather."

Lin took a big breath, and sang.

Ring out the day, my darling
Ring in the night, my sweet

Avila felt lighter in his arms. Brindisi didn't know if that was an illusion too. He looked down. She was completely featherless now, with no patches of sky blue left, just gray, cold skin that looked as if it were being drained even of the gray.

In the starlight, tears shone on Lin's cheeks, but his voice was clear and open. Brindisi wondered at the boy's strength.

> *Ring me dreams to call the dawn*
> *Ring me unwept dreams to keep*

They were almost at the cypress trees when Brindisi heard a soft sigh of chimes, a feathered exhale disappearing into the night. Between his arms he felt the absence of weight. The boy still sang.

> *Ring in tomorrow, my darling*
> *Ring me dreams to help me . . .*

Lin's voice trailed off. They'd reached the cypress.

"She's gone, isn't she?" he said, staring straight ahead.

Brindisi looked down, seeing the grass between his boots and the empty space between his arms. "Yes, Lin."

"Was it too late for her heartfeather?"

"No, Lin, it was . . . just in time." Brindisi groped for the words, like modeling in river-clay, but with his mouth. "For she needed you to hold the heartfeather while you sang your song."

"Do you believe that?" asked Lin.

Brindisi was silent.

"Dizzy?"

He had nothing to offer but the truth. "No, Lin. I don't."

"I didn't think so." Lin wouldn't look at him.

"But that's what Avila would have said. And she's not here anymore, so I wanted to try to answer you the way she would have."

346

"I think you're right. You did a good job pretending to be her, Dizzy."

Brindisi couldn't bear to hear the measured tones of Lin's voice. "Your song, Lin, I think she liked your song."

"Yes," said Lin, "I bet she would have called it beauty."

Brindisi turned and knelt. Eyes downcast, Lin still clutched Avila's heartfeather. Although Brindisi wanted to physically lift Lin's chin and pick him up with his swing of an arm, Brindisi knew he had to bridge this moment some other way.

"Lin. She would have called your song beauty."

"But you wouldn't call it beauty, right?"

"Right, Lin." Brindisi spoke slowly, carefully, as if he were carving the keystone of a bridge. "I would call it . . . I would call it . . . mymostbestbeauty."

Lin looked up at Brindisi with wide eyes—eyes so wide that Brindisi could see his own face reflected back. Brindisi was afraid to smile. He wanted his apprentice to know he meant what he said, a true compliment.

"Promisemymostbestbeauty?"

Brindisi thought of Avila and her wind chimes: the delight of her peacock dance; the generosity of her feathers; the pebble she'd tried to hide in her laugh; and of the heartfeather she gave Lin and what she'd said it promised. Sometimes extravagance makes its own substance.

Brindisi took a big breath and told the truth. "Promisemymostbestbeautypromise."

Lin gasped. Reflected in the watery pools of the boy's eyes, a flash of colorful feathers. Brindisi didn't turn; he knew there would be nothing to see. Instead, he inhaled, savoring Avila's last illusion, discovering what there was to find out. He smelled figs and earth, brine and clear water, cypress and marble, feathers and wind.

They avoided the village on the way home. Lin didn't want to be carried, so it took a long time, but Brindisi didn't think either of them knew what to say to Maria quite yet.

"Dizzy. My most best beauty's heartfeather . . ." Lin choked a little on fresh tears, and stopped walking. Gently cupped in his hands, the blue and silver glittered in the starlight.

"Yes, Lin?"

"It's—it's kind of like a stone, isn't it? Could it be a new kind of stone?"

"My apprentice." Brindisi didn't know if he was responding to the longing in Lin's eyes, or if he actually heard the distant cry of chimes. "Indeed it could be."

"Do you think we—can we use it for the bridge?"

Now more than ever he wanted to make sure he only spoke the truth to Lin. "I don't know, Lin. I don't know. But I promise you, we will try."

Lin threw himself onto his swing, squeezing Brindisi more tightly than ever before.

Brindisi, gently, squeezed back.

As he carried Lin home, Brindisi imagined how he and Lin could sculpt a peacock into the town's bridge. A peacock carved out of enough smooth skyseed that the sky would always be clear. How they could sculpt it such that on moonless nights the tail would fan outwards, lift completely free of the stone, and reveal a blue and silver egg. An egg carved of heartfeathers, smelling of sweet figs and pure salts, and sounding of wind chimes.

Perhaps that might conjure this night, might honor Avila, might show how beauty can teach us our own fragility—perhaps that, at least, might be true enough to last.

Gone Black

written by

Matthew S. Rotundo

illustrated by

LUKE EIDENSCHINK

ABOUT THE AUTHOR

When he was eight years old, Matthew S. Rotundo wrote his first epic, "The Elephant and the Cheese," marking the first time he had filled an entire page with writing. Matt also gravitated to science fiction, fantasy and horror at an early age. He discovered Bradbury's "The Fog Horn" in a grade school reader, and read it whenever he got bored in class (he read it a lot). Other classics soon followed—Dune, Lord of the Rings, Foundation . . . all the usual suspects. Half the time, his family and friends didn't know what he was talking about.

Winning the Writers of the Future Contest has brought some changes. Matt has sold stories to Orson Scott Card's Intergalactic Medicine Show, Cosmos and Jim Baen's Universe. He won a Phobos award in 2002 for his story, "Hitting the Skids in Pixeltown," and is a 1998 graduate of the Odyssey Writing Workshop.

Matt is also a movie buff, football fan and amateur guitarist. He and his wife live in Omaha, Nebraska.

ABOUT THE ILLUSTRATOR

Growing up in Minnesota, Luke Eidenschink early on developed a healthy love of nature. After all, how many kids can say they raised and trained their own dogsled team with their dad? Over the years, Luke's interests have extended far beyond mushing to include everything about the natural sciences—from astronomy and geology to biology and meteorology. It's the kind of variety that he believes all artists should have. "A good artist will make art about what interests them," he says.

Though his parents and family always encouraged his artistic pursuits, Luke never needed to be prodded: He began drawing at a young age and has taught himself over the years by studying artwork he admired, emulating each style and practicing a lot. An avid reader of adventure, science fiction and fantasy, Luke specializes in producing pen-and-ink drawings in those genres. Though his commissioned artwork tends toward realistic nature studies, his dream (and plan) is to become a full-time book illustrator.

When not drawing or working a full-time production job, Luke enjoys spending time with his family and girlfriend.

Gone Black

1.

Hargas Base had been Code Black—total security lockdown—for a full two weeks before Staff Sergeant Manny "Outhouse" Gutierres saw the thing he shouldn't have seen, asked the question he shouldn't have asked.

He entered the secured area of the base's sewage treatment plant a little earlier than usual that evening. He was running ahead of schedule—a great rarity—and wanted to finish with the prisoner and get back to his quarters, perhaps get a decent night's sleep for once. Two armed guards, posted at the opening in the hastily erected partition wall that marked the boundary of the secured area, let him through without a word; they knew him by then. One of them, a muscular man with a long scar running down the left side of his face, nodded at Manny as he passed.

The partitions cordoned off a large section of the sewage treatment plant's main floor, isolating one of the four sedimentation tanks. Manny and his team at the plant—whom he lovingly called Maggots—had been tabbed to modify the tank, converting it to a watery cage for the prisoner. The specs had been given to them by the Intel agent in charge of the prisoner—a civilian by the name of Donald Gilmore.

Manny stepped carefully over power cables strewn across the treatment plant floor. Gilmore, busy with his instruments, remained unaware of Manny's presence. Manny hung back for a few moments to watch the man work.

An impressive array of hardware surrounded the modified tank, including a battery of cameras—some perched on the maintenance deck, some clamped to the rim of the tank, and of course one at the observation window. These fed into a bank of monitors perched atop folding tables. A waterproof transceiver—suspended by wire from the filtration grate that had been welded over the tank to prevent the prisoner from escaping—hung in the water to record every utterance the Walphin made, and to talk back to it, once communication had been established. A set of speakers on a small table of their own broadcast Walphin vocalizations— seemingly random clicks and chirps—while a separate computer logged and collated the noises. The monitor pulsed in an ever-changing prismatic display.

Gilmore, sitting with his back to Manny, tapped some keys, and the speakers emitted a burst of rapid clicks. He glanced toward the monitor displaying the video from the observation window camera. The Walphin, just visible on the far side of the tank, simply floated near the surface. Smooth gray skin, wide head with blunt snout, long sleek body. A quadruped on land, but with webbed digits and powerfully muscled limbs adapted for water. Manny had never in his life seen anything so hideous.

That Walphins were also murderous bastards probably didn't help his perspective.

Gilmore tapped another key, and the burst repeated in a higher register. He again looked toward the observation window monitor. The Walphin jerked and dove for the bottom of the tank. Even the way it moved, with such sinuous, alien grace, repulsed Manny.

Gilmore was scribbling a note in a binder open on his lap. Manny opened his mouth to say something, but movement on the monitor stopped him. The Walphin pushed off the bottom of the tank with its tail and shot toward the surface, heading straight for the hanging transceiver. The alien caught it in its jaws and twisted. The wire suspending the transceiver snapped easily. The Walphin spat it out, then turned and sped back to the far side of the tank. The transceiver sank; Manny watched its progress on the monitors.

Gilmore swore and banged a hand on the table in front of him.

"You're talking to it?" Manny said.

Gilmore started and spun, his face a mask of frustration. A thin man in a pale green civilian suit, he had curly dark hair, narrow features and a weak chin. "What are you doing here?"

"I came to check the latrine unit."

Gilmore shut the binder on his lap and set it aside.

"Manny, you really need to let me know when you're coming. I wasn't expecting you for another half-hour."

Manny held up a hand, annoyed. "Hey, fine. Whatever you say."

"Thank you." Gilmore rubbed his forehead.

"I thought you couldn't communicate with it yet. I thought that's what this was all about—learning its language."

Gilmore sighed. "I can't communicate with it. I'm just trying to establish a baseline."

"Didn't look like that to me. Looked like you were having a conversation . . . and it didn't like what you had to say."

Gilmore straightened, stood. "I'm sorry for snapping at you like that, Manny. You just surprised me, that's all. Go ahead and take care of the latrine, since you're here."

Manny took a deep breath, swallowed his irritation. Gilmore was his ticket out of here, if his promises could be believed. Best not to dwell on certain details, then. Best to let it go, if he could. "Fine."

He went to take care of business. This detail grew more troublesome daily.

Of course, Gilmore couldn't be bothered to handle the latrine, and neither could his guards. He also wanted access to the Walphin limited to the barest minimum, meaning Manny—who had been detailed to Gilmore for the duration of the man's stay, however long that might be—couldn't even delegate the job to one of his Maggots. So it appeared that his greatest contribution to the war effort to date would be emptying alien shit. Join the army; live the adventure.

In addition to the tank, Manny and his Maggots had also built the latrine unit from Gilmore's specs. It consisted of a length of half-meter pipe with a plate of stainless steel welded over one end, and a self-sealing rubber flap that gave inward fitted over the other. The pipe rested horizontally on a set of braces, so that the Walphin could swim to it, push its back end in through the rubber, excrete, then withdraw, leaving behind its alien waste. Vents, cut along the length of the pipe and covered with ultrafine filter material, minimized backflow. Chains would raise and lower the unit for easy removal and emptying, via a makeshift trapdoor that had been sliced with cutting torches into the grate over the tank.

One of Gilmore's guards—usually the one with the scar—would accompany Manny on the maintenance deck, accessible by ladder, that hugged the rim of the tank along its far side. The guard's job was to keep a weapon trained on the trapdoor while it was open. Manny hauled the latrine from the bottom of the tank himself, using a hoist attached to chains wrapped around either end of the pipe. The relatively weak gravity of 47 Ursae Majoris D made this a merely difficult task, rather than an impossible one. Usually, the Walphin sulked at the other end, seeming to watch him, studying Manny with those black, lifeless eyes, perhaps pondering how he would taste.

This time, apparently still riled by the incident with the transceiver, the alien swam in deliberate, continuous circles near the center of the tank. Scarface stood tense beside Manny, assault rifle at the ready.

For his part, Manny had a hard time concentrating on the job, keeping one eye on the prisoner at all times. If the thing made a move for the trapdoor, he resolved, he would let the latrine drop and get out of Scarface's line of fire.

This was the closest he'd been to it since Gilmore had first brought it in. It seemed to have lost some of its bulk, and the uniform gray of its skin had become a bit blotchy.

Manny finally got the unit up. As it hung before him, dripping water, he removed the rubber seal and emptied the contents into a waste bin. The effluent was dark and oily, with a bitter stench that gagged him. Years of working with sewer gases had afforded Manny a tolerance for unpleasant smells, but this was like nothing in his experience. Scarface wrinkled his nose, too.

Emptying the unit took longer than usual. The alien shit seemed more viscous than it had been, soupy.

Manny replaced the seal, lowered the latrine to the bottom of the tank, closed and chained the trapdoor, all without incident. Scarface visibly relaxed. He exchanged glances with Manny, said, "That damned thing will never know how close I came just now to blowing it away."

"Your boss wouldn't like that very much."

Scarface flapped a hand as if swatting at a bothersome insect. He slung his rifle and made his way down the ladder.

Manny used a loading platform to lower the waste bin to the floor. From there, he would wheel it to Cold Storage, where it would be hauled to the airless surface of 47UMaD. It would freeze instantly, neutralizing any germs the Walphin might be carrying. The Cold Storage personnel would deposit the frozen waste in a trough on the west side of the base, as far from the greenhouse domes as possible.

As he wheeled the bin past Gilmore, who was once more intent on his instruments, Manny paused. He wanted nothing more than to finish the job and get back to his quarters, but something stuck in his mind. That was when he made his second mistake.

"Uh . . . does it look OK to you?"

Gilmore looked up. "What do you mean?"

"The Walphin. Do you think it's OK? It's not . . . well, sick or anything, is it?"

"I'm sure it doesn't like its circumstances. Other than that, it's fine."

Manny supposed Gilmore would know. He took care of feeding the alien, from a freezer unit he had requisitioned, in which he kept a supply of meat and fish from the base stores. In addition, Gilmore maintained a small, heated tank that resembled an aquarium and held what looked like nothing more than milky water. "Special additives," Gilmore had said. "For the prisoner. We've had some highly trained experts working on them, based on everything we know of Walphin anatomy and biology. They require a very delicate balance." Periodically, he introduced the additives into the larger tank. Both the freezer unit and the additives tank stood against the partition wall.

Gilmore produced one of his let's-be-friends smiles—a toothy grin, goofy in its way. "The prisoner isn't sick, Manny. Thanks. And again, I'm sorry for snapping."

"No problem." Manny glanced over his shoulder at the big tank, stealing one last, lingering glance at the alien before he left.

2.

Throughout the next day and the day following, the incident with the transceiver lingered in Manny's memory. Gilmore's obvious lie rankled, pushing even the essential weirdness of the Walphin itself to the back of his mind.

It had been captured at Alpha Mensae A. A UIS Heavy Armor assault force had taken on two Walphin battle groups there in a major engagement. UIS casualties had been high, eventually forcing a retreat, but not before the assault force had annihilated the infrastructure the Walphins had erected there. No attacks would be forthcoming from Alpha Mensae A anytime soon.

According to Gilmore, UIS troops had managed to board one of the Walphin orbiting command platforms, where they'd found the prisoner. It was the highest-ranking enemy ever taken, he'd told Manny. Walphins fought to the death, and the few that had been captured alive tended to die quickly.

And no one knew how to talk to them.

For security purposes, Gilmore had chosen to

operate in a remote, classified location—hence Hargas Base, a forward supply depot. And he had another reason for choosing Hargas Base—the ice mines.

The ice beneath the surface of 47UMaD was the reason Hargas Base had been built. The water irrigated the hydroponic farms that provided food for the front-line UIS forces. Now that ice served another purpose: Gilmore needed a lot of fresh water for the prisoner.

Everyone stationed at Hargas Base, Manny included, had unwittingly become stars in a major operation critical to the war effort—not that anyone off 47UMaD could know about it, with the base gone black.

Gilmore replaced the damaged transceiver with a new one, encased in a small wire cage the Walphin couldn't get its jaws around. Manny tried to forget about what had happened, but it nagged at him. He had a hard time concentrating on his daily work, unable to stop thinking about the Walphin, the way it had acted, the way it looked. He was spending too much time in his head; he needed some perspective.

He needed to talk to Resa Quinn. She was probably his best friend on base, but they'd hardly spoken since Gilmore's jump transport had dropped into orbit around 47UMaD—just too busy, he supposed. Or it might have been something else.

He visited her quarters on the evening of the sixteenth day since Gilmore's JT had arrived, since the base had gone black. He dropped by unannounced, unsure if she would respond had he called first.

She answered her door dressed in a robe, her cropped hair spiky and damp, a towel draped around her neck. She stood a full head shorter than him, slight of build but wiry—the result of daily tae kwon do practice—with angular features and a fair complexion. She regarded him blandly, neither moving aside to let him enter nor slamming the door in his face. "Hi, Manny."

"Is this a bad time?"

"For what?"

"Never mind. I'll come back."

"You're here now. What do you want?"

Manny looked up and down the corridor, mercifully empty for the moment. "Can I come in for a second?"

The faintest of creases crossed her brow, but she let him in.

Manny had known Sergeant Resa Quinn ever since she'd arrived, nearly two years ago. She worked in Irrigation, allocating water from the ice mines to the rest of Hargas Base. She and Manny worked together often, and had even become off-duty friends in the process. Irrigation was not her life goal, Manny knew. She was studying to be a medic.

Her quarters were neater than his. A basket of folded laundry sat on the small couch; the steel sink in the tiny kitchenette was empty of dishes. On one wall were stills of a handsome man with the same angular face as Quinn's, and three smiling children—her brother and his kids, killed in the merciless—and infamous—Walphin bombing of Newhome.

Quinn shut the door and turned to him, one hand on a hip. "What's on your mind, Manny?"

He sat on her couch, rubbed his face with his hands, stretching the skin. A day's growth of beard rasped. "I had to talk to somebody."

She leaned against the wall, arms crossed, waiting.

He wasn't sure where to start. "I wouldn't ask if I didn't think it was important."

"Other than to come in, you haven't asked anything yet."

"I was wondering—" He cleared his throat. "Wondering if you have a few minutes to come to the treatment plant with me."

"Gosh, thanks. I can't think of any place I'd rather visit on base. Breaks my heart to turn you down, but I have to work in the morning and—"

"I want you to see the prisoner."

Her sarcasm evaporated. She looked away. Very quietly, she said, "Why?"

"I need your opinion."

"On what?"

"I need to know if I'm making too much out of something."

"Such as?"

"I don't want to tell you before you get there. I want you to see the prisoner first."

"Isn't that a restricted area now?"

"I can get you in. If you're quiet."

She glanced at Manny, then at the stills on the wall behind him. "I don't know if I can do that."

"Just for a few minutes."

She pushed herself away from the wall, presented

her back to him. "It doesn't matter if it's a few minutes or a few hours, Manny. I don't think I can do it."

He saw the tension in the set of her shoulders and held his tongue.

She stood silently for long moments. The airy whisper of the ventilation system was the only sound. Finally, she spoke, without turning around: "I've been avoiding you since that thing got here."

In a neutral voice, Manny said, "I noticed."

"You know why?"

"Bad memories, I figured."

She shook her head. "No. I mean, yeah, that's part of it, I guess." She looked over her shoulder at him. "But the truth of it is, the thought of having that damned alien here scares the hell out of me."

"Hey, my Maggots built that cage. It can't hurt you."

"You sure about that?" She faced him, arms still crossed. "You've heard what everyone's saying, haven't you? The word is that the fish is carrying some kind of implanted bomb, that it's just waiting for a chance to escape, get to the greenhouse domes, and blow itself up. Cripple the base."

Manny had heard no such thing. "That's crazy."

She went on as if she hadn't heard him. "And suppose it can't escape? Suppose it decides to just detonate itself right there in the treatment plant, taking as many humans with it as possible?"

Manny stood. "Resa, I'm telling you, that's nuts. That Intel guy, Gilmore, has checked that alien six ways from Sunday. It doesn't—"

"Come off it, Manny. You know how it is. Nobody

here is a fan of Intel Branch. Those jackasses haven't produced any useful intelligence since the war started." In a lower voice, she said, "Maybe if they had, a lot of innocent people would still be alive."

Manny had no answer to that. He hung his head. "Resa, I wouldn't ask if it weren't important."

She was silent in reply.

"Never mind," Manny said. "Sorry I bothered you." He headed for the door.

As he passed her, she said, "Wait."

He stopped, looked up.

She pulled the towel from around her neck. "Give me a minute. I need to change." She crossed the living room and turned down the short hallway leading to her bedroom/bathroom.

Manny waited by the door. Quinn emerged a few minutes later, dressed in a plain white overshirt and wrinkled pants. "Let's go." She caught the quizzical frown on his face and sighed. "Yeah, it scares me. But I'd be lying if I said I didn't want to see this thing. Maybe I need to look it in the eye."

"Fair enough," Manny said. They went out.

They passed near the gym and through the rec hall—both mostly empty at this hour—before boarding an elevator to take them down to the treatment plant.

"You mean you really haven't heard those rumors, Manny?"

He shook his head. Most of the conversations he'd had since the Walphin had arrived had been strictly business. He'd been too distracted to notice. It was passing strange.

The elevator reached the maintenance sublevel.

A sign pointed the way to the treatment plant. They headed in that direction. The corridors down here—warm, stuffy, sporadically lit—were deserted at this hour.

Manny said, "People are cutting me out of the loop? Why?"

She shrugged. "Maybe they don't like you being so cozy with that Intel man."

He banged a wall. "I was *ordered* to do that! Christ!"

"People are funny."

"People are idiots."

There was a T-junction ten meters ahead. The treatment plant entrance was around the corner to the right. Instead, Manny veered off course, leading Quinn down a flight of steps to the left.

"We going to the mines?" she said.

"We'll cut across on this level, and come up on the other side. There's a fire exit toward the rear." His ID badge was coded with clearance to deactivate the treatment plant's fire system—mandatory for the sergeant on duty, in case of false alarms. Gilmore had asked for the badge when he'd first arrived, but Manny had balked. "You can have the backup, but I need this one," he had told him. "I can't get into the personnel files for my staff without it. Or my own quarters."

Gilmore had considered. "Keep it for now, until we can get you a different ID—one that doesn't allow you to shut off the fire alarm. Nothing personal, Manny. ID badges can get lost—or worse, stolen."

Manny hadn't gotten around to ordering the replacement from Security yet.

The sublevel below Maintenance housed the mining facilities. Manny and Quinn passed several freight elevators that led deep into 47UMaD. Drills and other rock-chewing implements filled equipment racks. Motorized carts, used for hauling gravel, stood silent in their stalls. The entire floor stank of old grease.

"I'll tell you something else, too," Quinn said. "Word is the Walphins have gone quiet since Alpha Mensae A."

Manny was incredulous. "And how would anyone here know that? The base has gone black. We haven't had any outside communication for two weeks."

"I read it in the last newsdisks we got just before the lockdown. I can show you the articles, if you don't believe me."

"Maybe they're licking their wounds."

"Or maybe they're doing something else."

Such as preparing for a major attack. Both Peleus and Newhome had been preceded by a notable lack of Walphin activity on any known systems. And then the bombings had come, both of them complete surprises, striking where the fish had never struck before.

"Wonder what human settlement they've found this time," she said. "Maybe this one, eh? At least it's a military target."

"We're highly classified. You know that. Those JT pilots make three or four extra jumps when they come or leave here, just to throw any possible chasers off the trail. The colonies were easier for the fish to find." This last slipped out before he had a chance to censor himself. He winced and glanced at her for a reaction.

She proceeded as if she hadn't heard it: "None of those extra jumps will mean shit if the fish have figured out a way to track jump transports."

"And how would they do that?"

"By sneaking some kind of beacon on board one of them."

Manny halted again, put a hand out to stop her. "Are people saying that, too?"

"No." Quinn looked away. "Not yet, anyway."

"So that's just your theory? That the Walphin allowed itself to be captured so that it could lead its buddies to a military installation?"

"Why not? You know how important Hargas Base is to the war effort, Manny. It's bad enough that we're not able to make any new shipments while we're Code Black. But if we were shut down permanently—"

"Don't you think someone would notice if the fish were broadcasting some kind of signal? And just how long would it take for that signal to reach Walphin space? A few decades, maybe."

"There's a lot about them we don't know. And that includes their technology." She resumed walking.

He quick-timed it to catch up with her, again stopped her with a hand on her arm. "Hey. Seriously. Don't go spreading that rumor. People would freak out."

She looked at his hand, then at him. He withdrew it.

"What's this Intel man promising you, Manny?

Is he gonna straighten out that mess with General Levine?"

"Oh, hell." He started walking again, more quickly than before.

She matched his pace. "I'm right, aren't I?"

"I never should have told you about that."

"Levine was a jackass. You did the right thing, Manny."

"He still *is* a jackass. And a powerful one, at that."

General Levine, commander of Third Army, a decorated thirty-year veteran, family man, and all-around swell guy, had long been rumored to dally with underlings. Manny had learned the truth of those rumors when Levine took up with a friend of his, back when he'd been stationed at Third Army Command, on Mars. Tearful and guilt-ridden, she had confessed the details of the affair to Manny. She'd tried to end it, but Levine had threatened to have her dishonorably discharged if she dared.

Manny, infuriated, had reported Levine to CID.

And someone there had leaked it to the media.

Manny never found out who it was. It certainly hadn't been him. Not that it mattered.

Levine was powerful enough to squash any serious internal investigation. But the media proved more difficult to handle. With the story public, he could not retaliate against a whistleblower—not openly, anyway.

So the underling accepted an honorable discharge in exchange for her silence. Manny couldn't blame her for taking the deal. As far as he was concerned, she'd earned it. The investigation ended, the media lost interest and Levine's official record remained untarnished.

But his wife divorced him six months later.

In short order, Manny was transferred from Third Army Command HQ to Hargas Base. He'd been there ever since, long enough to earn the nickname *Outhouse.*

He'd long since given up applying for transfers. His applications were all rejected. His position at the treatment plant had somehow been designated a critical billet. Hargas Base would be his home until the day he left the army. And with a war on, that day wasn't coming anytime soon.

The girl he'd been dating prior to the transfer had stopped responding to his commdisks years ago. His parents still wrote him regularly, but his father's health was failing. Surgeries and cancer treatments had left him weakened. His mother's letters were always upbeat, focused on the positive—a little *too* positive, Manny thought. Every week, he expected to get the news that his father was gone.

Gilmore claimed he had connections. *If this operation goes well, I'll be grateful,* he had told Manny. *And so will the people who sent me.*

"You did the right thing," Quinn said again.

"Yeah, fat lot of good it did me."

They reached the stairwell on the opposite side of the sublevel. It led to a little-used back corridor, and the treatment plant fire door.

A sign hung on the door, red letters on a bright yellow background: *Fire Exit—Alarm WILL SOUND.*

Manny produced his badge. "Just a few minutes. Keep it quiet."

She took a deep breath, nodded.

He waved the badge in front of the scanner. A metallic *click* sounded, and t. indicator light flashed green.

Manny pulled open the door. It creaked, but the alarm remained silent.

They stepped inside, approaching the Walphin tank from behind. Manny nervously eyed the cameras mounted in various positions, but as he'd hoped, none of them appeared to be recording. Gilmore had a limited supply of memory and recharging the batteries was time-consuming. He recorded only when he was in the area.

Manny led her around the tank to the observation window. He glanced toward the entryway in the partitions; Gilmore's guards, stationed on the other side, would need only peek inside to see the two of them in here. But their attention would be focused on anyone approaching from the main entrance or the dock doors. So long as Manny and Quinn were quiet, the guards would never know they were here.

Quinn glanced around, taking in Gilmore's workspace—the monitors, audio equipment, the special additives tank. Only then did she look in the window.

The Walphin was on the opposite side, next to the latrine unit, essentially an oddly-shaped shadow at this distance. It was preternaturally still.

Caught it in the middle of taking a shit, Manny thought. *How perfect.*

Quinn stood as if made of stone. Color slowly drained from her face, making her appear drawn, withered, aged beyond her years. Her lips moved silently. One hand went again to a pants pocket, pulled out a miniature stills frame. Manny recognized it even from a distance—the one containing the pictures of her brother's family.

He stood to one side, his gaze alternating from Quinn to the prisoner. Neither one moved. For long moments, he forgot about everything else—Gilmore, the guards, what would happen if they were caught. All that existed was the tank, the Walphin, and the two of them.

He leaned in, whispered, "Are you all right?" The steady rumble of the ventilation system, louder on this level, covered his voice.

She blinked rapidly, as if coming out of a daze, then turned to him. Matching his whisper, she said, "It . . . yeah. Yeah, I'm OK. It's not so bad." She looked through the observation window again. "Not so bad at all, are you? Not anymore."

"I was wondering—" He suddenly felt stupid, but he forced himself to finish. "Wondering if it looked like it might be sick to you."

"Sick? Since when did I become an expert on Walphin biology?"

"I thought with those medical classes you were taking . . ." He stopped, hearing how ridiculous he sounded. "Oh, hell. I haven't been thinking too clearly lately. I thought it looked like it might be sick, and Gilmore doesn't think so, and he's—"

He became *too* conscious of his surroundings, at how precarious their situation was. He glanced over his shoulder at the opening in the partition wall, saw only the backs of the guards posted there.

And the prisoner remained utterly motionless on the other side of the tank. Manny had never seen it remain so still for so long—as if it knew who was watching it.

He dismissed the thought, with an effort. "Look, just tell me I'm out of my mind, and we can get out of here."

"Manny, why is this bothering you so much?"

And he didn't know how to answer that, how to tell her that he suspected there was much more to this situation than Gilmore was telling him. He couldn't tell her why he felt that way; even he didn't know, not yet.

"This was a really bad idea," he said. "I'm sorry. We should go."

She looked again through the observation window, peering. "Well, even if I could tell a sick Walphin on sight, I'd probably need a closer look than this. Doesn't it ever move?"

The Walphin had been immobile since they'd come in. It hadn't even surfaced for air. And Manny realized it couldn't be using the latrine, as he had first supposed. The angle was all wrong. The prisoner was perpendicular to the pipe.

Something was very, very wrong.

Manny bolted for the maintenance deck, leaving Quinn where she stood. "Wha—?" she said.

He climbed the ladder and mounted the deck. At the tank's edge, he knelt and peered into the water. From this vantage point, he could see more clearly: the Walphin had somehow gotten its tail wedged under the pipe, between the braces that kept the unit from rolling. It couldn't get to the surface to breathe.

"Christ." Manny unlocked and opened the trapdoor, grabbed the hoist, and began frantically hauling up the latrine. As he did so, the Walphin came free and floated slowly to the surface. Manny got the unit out of the water and maneuvered it to the maintenance deck. He let it drop with a bang that reverberated throughout the plant. He went to the trapdoor and knelt again, the grate biting his knees. The Walphin was directly below him, floating at the surface, an arm's length away. Its appendages and tail appeared ragged, hanging limply.

"Oh, God. Oh, God. Shit!" Not knowing what else to do, Manny reached for the prisoner, thinking he could perhaps nudge it.

The Walphin spewed water from its blowhole, momentarily blinding him. Manny recoiled just as the thing lunged. It came out of the water and snapped at the air just inches from his nose. Then it fell back, twisted and dove, dousing him with a flick of its tail.

Manny fell backward, or tried to. The toe of one shoe got caught in the grate. His momentum twisted the ankle. Pain flared. Manny cried out.

He groped frantically for the trapdoor while working to free his trapped shoe. In his mind, he saw horrific images of the Walphin escaping from the tank, overpowering the guards, and heading straight for the greenhouse domes. He jerked his toe free and got hold of the trapdoor. It slammed to with a clang.

Gasping and wincing, he pulled himself back to the maintenance deck. Only once he got there did he permit himself to look into the tank.

LUKE EIDENSCHINK

The Walphin was still inside, thank God. It swam the perimeter with astonishing speed, thrusting with its powerful tail. Every few seconds, it rammed the wall with muted thuds that Manny could feel.

"Manny? Manny!" Quinn was calling from the base of the ladder.

Sopping wet, he dragged himself to the edge of the deck and looked down. Quinn stood below him, eyes wide. "Did it—"

Some of the water dripping from him must have hit her. She stepped back with a cry, her face twisted with disgust, as if it had been vomit instead of water. "Jesus, did it attack you, Manny? Did it *bite* you?" She brushed at her arms and clothing.

Teeth gritted against the pain, Manny said, "No, I don't—"

Shouts came from the other direction. Manny looked up. Gilmore's guards had heard the ruckus and were running toward the tank, rifles raised. Quinn was blocked from their sight—for the moment.

Manny turned back to her. "Go. Now." But of course she couldn't leave through the fire exit without setting off the alarm, and he had no time to throw her his badge. "Hide. They only saw me. Hide and wait for them to clear out."

She bolted before he'd finished speaking. He didn't see where she went. By that time, the guards had arrived at the tank. Scarface shouted up to Manny: "What the hell are you doing here?"

Slowly, painfully, he got to his feet, hands raised, wobbling as he struggled to maintain his balance.

"I think," he said, breathing hard, "that I should go to the infirmary."

3.

His ankle was sprained. The medic on duty wrapped it tightly and advised him to keep ice on it as much as possible. Ice came at a premium on Hargas Base; he would have to make it from his personal water rations. The medic gave him some pain patches and released him.

Lieutenant Morrison, his immediate superior, confined him to quarters, pending an investigation.

Manny kept his story simple, sticking as close to the truth as possible: he had sneaked into the restricted area on his own, to get a better look at the Walphin than he could with Gilmore hanging around. He told all the rest exactly as it had happened.

He said it first to the MPs. Then to Lt. Morrison. Then, finally, to Lieutenant Colonel Ezrin, the base XO, who came to his quarters to personally question him.

Neither the MPs nor Morrison asked about Quinn. Manny deduced that she had gotten out of there unnoticed.

His lieutenant had yelled and harangued until he was red in the face. Manny expected to be busted a stripe or two, but Morrison assured him that a court martial, a dishonorable discharge and jail time were more likely.

Manny, still buzzing from the pain meds,

accepted the news with bland detachment. General Levine would have his ultimate revenge, after all. But at least Manny would finally get off Hargas Base. He wondered if they would let him see his father before hauling him to the brig.

Colonel Ezrin had a different reaction.

His brow protruded from his bald pate like a ridge of stone, but his voice was calm, controlled. His lined features remained impassive. He carefully considered every answer. By that time, Manny's ankle was beginning to throb again, but he held off taking more meds; no point in fuzzing his senses with the XO in his quarters.

Ezrin sat across from him at his tiny kitchenette table. The colonel steepled his hands in front of him. He had known Manny since Manny's arrival at Hargas Base. Ezrin had been the one who'd detailed him to Gilmore in the first place.

After a long silence, the colonel said, "This isn't like you, Gutierres."

"This . . . it's an unusual situation, sir."

"Maybe so, but that doesn't change the fact that you're lying to me."

"Sir, I—"

"You're transparent as domeglass, Gutierres. You'd make a lousy card player."

Manny, who did occasionally play poker—though he hadn't been invited to a game since the Walphin had arrived—already knew the truth of this.

Ezrin sat back and let his hands rest on the table. "In fact, that's the real reason you're stationed here, isn't it? Your honesty?"

Manny recognized the rhetorical question for what it was and held his tongue.

"You're protecting someone, Gutierres. Who? Not Gilmore, surely. Not one of your own people, either; they've all seen the prisoner firsthand." The Maggots had been present when the Walphin had been loaded into the tank—a one-time deal Manny had arranged with Gilmore, to forestall future curiosity. And it had worked, so far.

Ezrin went on: "Your friend over in Irrigation, then? She's lost some family to the Walphins, I believe."

Manny ducked his gaze, knowing it gave him away, but unable to stop himself.

Ezrin stood. "All right. That at least makes more sense."

Manny started to rise, too, but Ezrin waved him back into his chair. "As you were, Gutierres. Rest that ankle." The colonel pulled his cap from a pocket and fitted it over his bald scalp. "I believe it's unlikely you'll ever try something so stupid again, so I won't bother warning you about that. Think you can still empty that latrine unit, in your present condition?"

Manny took several moments to process what he heard. "Beg your pardon, sir?"

"You're still detailed to Gilmore. I personally can't think of any worse punishment than having to empty alien shit, can you?"

"Uh . . . no, sir. But—"

"Yes?"

"I don't think Gilmore will like that very much, sir."

"Gilmore should be thanking you. You very likely saved the prisoner's life."

The thought had occurred to Manny, but he had been keeping it to himself. None of his interrogators had appeared receptive to such an observation.

Ezrin said, "Anyway, I don't give a shit what Gilmore thinks. I didn't invite him here. He's as much to blame for what happened as you are."

"Yes, sir."

"I'll explain the situation to him, and to Lieutenant Morrison."

"Thank you, sir."

"When you're not on duty, you're confined to quarters until further notice. Understood?"

"Yes, sir."

"Idleness and isolation—bad for morale. Discipline on this base has been shot to hell since that damned thing arrived. I aim to restore it."

"Yes, s—"

But Ezrin was already headed for the door. Manny almost let him go, but found he had to say something else.

"Colonel?"

Ezrin paused at the door, looking back.

"Sir, the prisoner . . ." Manny paused, taking time to frame the words. "I don't understand how it got caught under the latrine. I . . . don't think it was an accident."

Ezrin's stare bored into him.

"And there's more," Manny said. "I think Gilmore's been communicating with the Walphin. I mean *really* communicating. He knows how to talk to it, better than he's letting on." He expected Ezrin to override him at that point, but the colonel only stood, waiting. "That latrine unit, for example. How did the prisoner know how to use it? We know they've caught other Walphins. Maybe Intel has already figured out their language."

Ezrin nodded slowly. "And what do you suppose he's saying to it?"

"I don't know, sir. He—" Manny shook his head. "None of this makes any sense. I still don't understand why he brought the prisoner here in the first place."

"He told you his reasons, didn't he?"

"Yes, sir. Secrecy, and the ice mines. But that's crap. Secret as this base may be, Intel HQ's got to be more secure. And he wouldn't have to scrounge for water there, either. Unless—" He stopped. He didn't like the picture he was getting.

"Unless what, Gutierres?"

"Unless he was trying to avoid oversight."

Ezrin nodded again. "Go on."

"He's doing something he doesn't want his bosses to know about."

"It gives them deniability."

"And . . . he's got that tank of what he calls 'special additives' for the prisoner. I don't know what that stuff is, but—" Manny slumped in his chair. "Christ. No wonder it wants to die."

The colonel's face remained stony, betraying no surprise, no incredulity.

"You knew, sir?" Manny said.

"I suspected."

Manny thought he should be disgusted. Angry, even. All he could manage was weary resignation. This, on top of everything else. "What are we—"

"You're going to keep your damned mouth shut, that's what. You're still detailed to Gilmore for a reason."

"Sir?" Manny didn't follow.

"In a few days, you're going to get paged. You'll be called to report to Beta Dome. Don't question the page, don't talk to anyone about it, just come. Alone. Got it?"

Before Manny could respond, the XO left, slamming the door behind him.

4.

The swelling in his ankle went down after a day. Manny continued with the pain meds, kept off it when he could, and adopted a shuffling limp when he could not.

Far worse than the ankle was the silence.

Since Quinn had pointed it out to him, he had become acutely aware of how thoroughly he was being shunned. People he passed in corridors, even those he had known for years, avoided eye contact. No one offered a hand to help him when he limped down a flight of stairs.

On his hobbling way to work one morning, a hand clapped him on the shoulder.

He turned. Gianelli and Keenes, a couple of poker buddies from the hangar bay, stood there. Gianelli was the shorter of the two—chubby build, round cheeks, a blond mustache dirtying his upper lip. Keenes stood tall, gaunt and pale, with sunken features and lifeless eyes that made him a formidable poker player. Gianelli said, "Nice swimming pool you made for that fish, Outhouse. When do *we* get to use it?"

Manny casually flipped him off. Gianelli and Keenes moved on without another word.

It was the most substantive conversation he had that day.

Even his Maggots got quiet whenever he was around. And Quinn, who at the very least should have been grateful that he had taken the hit for her, had inexplicably withdrawn again.

You very likely saved the prisoner's life, Ezrin had said. If so, no one appeared ready to thank him for it. He had become something worse than *persona non grata:* he had ceased to even exist at Hargas Base, as if he personally had gone black—completely cut off.

He wondered how they would react if they knew what was really going on in the secured area.

As Manny had suspected, Gilmore was less than pleased that Manny was still on the job.

The Intel man insisted on confiscating Manny's ID badge before allowing him back into the secured area. As Manny handed it over, Gilmore said, "You know, I thought I could trust you, Manny. Clearly, I cannot. You're no better than any of the rest of them. Fine. You do your job, and stay the hell out of mine. Got that?"

Manny glared at Gilmore, but—remembering what Colonel Ezrin had said about being transparent as domeglass—said nothing. It occurred to him in that moment, somewhat belatedly, that he would now likely never get out from under General Levine's thumb.

Security saw to getting him a replacement badge, one without access to the fire exit.

His bum ankle made the latrine unit harder to handle, but Manny managed. He had to hold his breath against the gagging stench of the Walphin's effluent. The prisoner, as usual, made no move for the open trapdoor, keeping its distance whenever Manny came to empty the latrine. The blotches on its gray skin had become darker, unmistakable. Manny's gaze often wandered to the additives tank whenever he was in the secured area.

On the fifth day following the incident, Manny sat at his desk, his foot propped on an open drawer, preparing month-end reports. The desk stood in the corner of what passed for office space in the treatment plant—a glassed-in area that overlooked the main floor, reachable by a single flight of stairs and through a door marked *Administration*. Water stains defaced the floor and ceiling. An ancient network server hummed in another corner. A break area, consisting of a couch and rickety coffee table, occupied the center of the room. Old requisition forms, a deck of cards and the pungent remains of someone's lunch littered the table.

One of his Maggots entered—Johansen, a baby-faced blond giant who often needed to stoop when going through doorways. He was good with a cutting torch; he had made the hole for the observation window in the prisoner's tank. "Wanted to see me, Sarge?"

"Yeah. Come on over."

Johansen stopped behind Manny, looming. Manny looked up at him. "Jesus, sit down, will ya?"

"Sure, Sarge." Johansen pulled up a spare chair.

Manny pointed to his monitor. "Are these numbers right?"

Johansen leaned forward for a better look. "That's for this month? Yeah, they look right."

"I don't like the direction these impurity concentration levels are going."

"They're up, but they're still within regs."

"Sure they are. But we have our own standards down here, don't we?"

"Right, Sarge."

When he had gotten this job, Manny had implemented more stringent filtration benchmarks than provided for in the field manual. If they couldn't keep reusing their water, Hargas Base would quickly run dry, ice mines or no. It was a message he constantly drummed into the heads of his Maggots.

"What's happening out there?" Manny said.

Johansen shifted in his seat. "Well, Sarge . . . we're, uh . . . we're trying to keep up, but—"

"Just say it, Johansen."

"We've lost some of our filtration capacity."

"Tank Four, you mean." The *swimming pool,* as Gianelli and Keenes had called it.

"Without Tank Four, we have to run wastewater through the other three tanks faster. We still trap the biggest solids, which is all primary sedimentation is supposed to do. But—"

"But we're not catching as much as we used to."

"We're still within regs."

Manny stared at the numbers, shaking his head.

Johansen said, "Sorry, Sarge. I know we're letting you down. We all feel bad about it."

"What?" Manny gently put his elevated foot on the floor and swiveled his chair around to face Johansen. "Who said I was blaming you guys?"

Johansen shrugged. "Well, I guess we just assumed. You've been pretty quiet lately. We figured you were mad at us."

Manny marveled at his own stupidity. Had he really suspected his Maggots had turned against him? "Johansen, we've lost twenty-five percent of our primary sedimentation capacity. I'm not going to blame anyone in my unit for that. But if you knew the impurity concentrations were this high, you should have told me. Don't just drop the numbers on me like this."

Johansen lowered his gaze. "Right, Sarge."

"Hey. Look at me."

Johansen did.

"No one else on this base does what we do. No one else knows what it's like. Not the Ag workers in the domes, not the miners, certainly not the officers. Without us, there wouldn't be a base at all. We're Maggots, and we're proud of it. Right?"

"Maggots." A faint smile touched Johansen's face. "Yeah."

Manny sat back. This whole business—the prisoner, Gilmore, being cut off—had screwed up his perceptions worse than he'd supposed. "So what else is the team saying?"

Johansen chuckled. "There's so much talk, I don't know where to start. Not just the team, but everywhere. It's getting really weird out there."

"Is everyone still worried about implanted bombs?"

"That one's old news by now. The implanted homing beacon has gotten pretty popular, though. Any minute now, half the base is expecting Walphin warships to appear in orbit."

So Quinn hadn't kept it to herself, after all. Manny supposed he shouldn't have been surprised.

"The newest one is the spookiest, though," Johansen said.

"The newest one?"

"Biological warfare. They're saying the fish is going to infect us all with some alien bug, or something."

Manny went cold. "Perfect."

"Some are even saying *you're* probably infected."

"Me?"

"From when it bit you."

Manny pounded his desk with a fist. "It never bit me. I've never touched the damned thing. Jesus! How did—"

He stopped himself. He had a pretty good idea how it had gotten started. And the rumor would certainly explain some of the behavior he'd seen.

Johansen was right. It was getting weird out there.

"Do I look sick to you?" Manny said.

Johansen shrugged. "You look tired."

"I *am* tired. But I'm not infected with anything."

It was a good thing none of the rumormongers

were able to see the prisoner. One glance at the Walphin in its current state would just confirm that it was sick. Manny had emptied the latrine that morning. The Walphin had looked terrible—gaunt, with pieces of dead skin hanging from its body. And the stuff coming out of the latrine had become even more foul. It had gone from dark to outright black. Where it had been oily, it had thickened to the consistency of molasses. The ultrafine filters in the vents were getting blocked with small chunks of solid matter that Manny didn't even like to speculate about.

Johansen said, "What's spooky is how serious people have gotten. The rec hall has gotten really . . . quiet. It's the weirdest thing. There are all these little groups of people, and they're all talking in whispers and looking around to make sure no one's listening. I keep hearing that there are all these secret meetings going on. About what, I have no idea."

Gone black, cut off from the rest of human space. Base discipline growing lax. And now, paranoia, secret meetings where people talked in whispers. Dark suspicions stirred in Manny.

"It's good to talk about it," Johansen said. "I don't know what to do, Sarge."

Manny leaned forward. "Listen to me. If you hear about anything else—anything you don't like the sound of—I want you to come tell me about it. Come to my quarters if you have to, but make damned sure you find me. You don't have to name names or rat anybody out. But if something bad is going down, I need to know about it. Will you do that for me?"

Johansen's baby face went utterly solemn, aging him ten years in a moment. "Sarge, I need to ask you something."

"Shoot."

"Why did you save its life?"

Manny had been wondering that himself since it had happened. "Do you think I shouldn't have?"

"Don't know. Just asking."

But of course that wasn't true. "To be honest, there wasn't any time to think it over. I just acted on instinct."

Johansen glanced away.

"But I'll tell you something: it was a *human* instinct. I don't know that a Walphin would do the same for a human prisoner—if they took prisoners. And I don't want to sink to that level." It was the only answer he'd been able to come up with.

Johansen looked at him in much the same manner Ezrin had, studying his features as if for clues.

Transparent as domeglass, the Colonel had said. That wasn't always a bad thing.

"If I hear anything strange, I'll tell you," Johansen said.

"All right. Thanks." Manny clapped him on the shoulder. "Go ahead and get back to work."

With a nod, Johansen stood and exited the office, heading back to the floor.

Manny's comm sounded, startling him. He pulled it from his pocket. A simple, unsigned message scrolled across the display: *Report to Beta Dome immediately.*

Manny swallowed and acknowledged the page with the press of a button.

Beta, one of the smaller greenhouse domes, stood fifty meters across and ten meters high, filled with rows of soybean, lettuce and spinach plants, all in nutrient trays. It was truly the perfect growing environment: no weather, no pests, no weeds. The tinted domeglass was polarized to filter out UV from 47 Ursae Majoris. The ventilation system provided the carbon dioxide. And even here, Manny's team had a hand; sludge from the treatment plant provided much of the nutrient.

The greenhouse domes were the very heart of Hargas Base. They proved to be popular locales, often attracting more visitors than the rec hall or even the sun dome. They were warm, for one thing, and usually very quiet, for another, making them ideal for relaxation and solitude. The air itself, charged with oxygen, invigorating, smelled of an earthiness not found anywhere else on base. If you closed your eyes and inhaled deeply, you could almost believe you were home.

As Manny entered, he could not help looking at the inky black sky. The yellow brilliance of 47 Ursae Majoris blazed high overhead, blotting out any chance to spot the JT in orbit. The image of a Walphin warship, loaded with weapons to turn Hargas Base into molten slag, came to him unbidden.

He hobbled over to Lieutenant Colonel Ezrin, who stood at the far side of the dome with his hands clasped behind his back, gazing out at the barren, gray-brown rock of 47UMaD.

"Colonel," Manny said, and saluted.

Ezrin gave only the faintest of nods in reply,

intent on the landscape. Hesitantly, Manny let the salute drop. He followed Ezrin's gaze, but saw nothing out of the ordinary outside—craggy ridges, fissures, a nearby crater.

"Gutierres, sit before you fall over."

"Yes, sir." Manny deposited himself on a nearby bench.

Ezrin said, "I've always believed that what we do here, at this base, is one of the most honorable jobs a person can have in this army. It's considered a shit assignment, I know, but I've never seen it that way. Not compared to what else is out there—paper pushing, empty strategizing, pointless public relations. Maybe you can understand that, Gutierres."

Manny recalled what he had said to Johansen and nodded.

"Honor," Ezrin said. "That's what being a soldier is all about. And Mr. Gilmore has poisoned that, for all of us. It's like an infection, and it's spreading."

Funny he should put it that way. "Speaking of infections, sir—"

"The alien virus rumor?"

"Yes, sir."

"I've heard it. The last thing we need around here. And it doesn't help matters that the base is officially under quarantine."

Manny glanced up sharply. "Beg pardon, Colonel?"

"It's the cover story, Gutierres, the reason we've given for going black. Some of the enlisted learned of it. Then you had your little encounter with the prisoner. It made for quite the volatile combination."

391

"Sir, I have reason to believe—"

With a flick of the wrist, Ezrin dropped something small into Manny's lap. Manny picked it up. It was a blank ID badge, featureless white on both sides.

"You might want to try that badge sometime. You might find that it has the same access as the one Gilmore confiscated. It might be able to get you through the fire exit at the treatment plant without setting off the alarm. And take this, too." He produced a tiny optical disk the size of a coin and held it out to Manny. "In case you were interested in Gilmore's computer records, maybe."

Manny's brow puckered. "In case I were—" He stopped, recalling what Ezrin had said about deniability. He glanced at the blank ID badge. His breathing slowed. "Computer records. I would need Gilmore's encryption key to access that stuff."

"Really. Imagine that." The faintest of smiles touched the corners of Ezrin's mouth.

Manny gaped, thunderstruck. "Sir, how did you get that?"

"How did I get what?"

"The—right." He took the disk, holding it between his thumb and forefinger. "But . . . what if I'm caught? I can't exactly move fast."

"Then don't get caught."

Manny had to stop himself from saying, *Thanks a lot.* Instead, he said, "What do you think I'll find?"

"Leverage, Guiterres. Leverage."

Manny looked from Ezrin to the tiny disk and back again. The entire situation suddenly felt unreal, dreamlike—or nightmarish. "All due respect, sir, but weren't you the one who said I was as transparent as domeglass? Why are you trusting me with this?"

"Transparent though you may be, you understand about honor. You didn't give up your friend, even when threatened with a court martial. And make no mistake, Gutierres: if I hadn't intervened, that is most probably what would have happened to you."

Manny's cheeks burned.

"You're just about the only person I trust on this base. I don't need to tell you this, but I will, anyway: you and I are the only ones who are ever to know about this conversation."

Manny drew in a long, shuddery breath. He pocketed the disk and the ID badge. "Yes, sir."

Ezrin gazed out again at the landscape. "If you're going to do . . . anything . . . it should be done as quickly as possible. Tonight."

"Yes, sir."

"Get back to the plant. It will raise questions if you're gone for too long."

"Colonel?"

Ezrin glanced at him.

"Sir, I . . . I don't know exactly how to say this, but . . . I have reason to believe there's going to be trouble. Some of the troops might be planning something."

Ezrin waved it off. "Get the right leverage, and Gilmore and his pet will be gone tomorrow. This whole thing will be over with. Then maybe we can get back to doing our jobs around here." He held out a hand, helped Manny to his feet.

"Thank you, sir."

"Don't screw this up, Gutierres. It's the most important thing you'll ever do."

Manny swallowed hard, nodded. He left the colonel, hobbling back to the treatment plant. His gut felt like a stone.

He worked the rest of his shift in a daze, unable to focus on completing the month-end reports. He was grateful he wouldn't have to see Gilmore before nightfall.

He finished his shift and headed back to quarters, rehearsing in his mind the steps he would have to take to get back into the secured area. The corridors seemed as empty as they had when Gilmore's JT had first appeared in orbit. Every door was shut; no music or conversation wafted out from behind them. It was beyond weird; it was damned unnerving.

He let himself into his quarters, shut the door behind him and collapsed onto his couch, spent.

He must have dozed. His door chime awakened him.

He glanced at his clock; half an hour had passed. He shook his head to clear the fogginess and hauled himself off the couch, wondering who in the hell would be paying him a visit. Ezrin, perhaps, wanting to call it off.

It was Gianelli and Keenes—in better days, his two poker buddies from the hangar bay. Gianelli's fat face split with a jocular smile. "Hey, Outhouse. What's up?"

The two of them stepped inside, uninvited.

Caught off guard, Manny backpedaled a step, eyeing them. "I was napping, I guess."

"Oh. Damn. Sorry to wake you, man."

"Yeah," Keenes said. "You don't have to stand on our account. Sit. Rest that ankle."

Manny remained where he was. Keenes closed the door and stood in front of it; Gianelli sat at the kitchen table.

Manny said, "What are you two doing here?"

Gianelli shrugged. "Thought we'd stop by, see how you were doing. Got any beer?"

"I'm on barracks restriction. You guys know that. I can't have any visitors."

Keenes crossed his arms. "Yeah. Been a rough few weeks for you, hasn't it?"

Manny tensed. "I think you two should leave."

"Best if we stay, I think," Gianelli said.

"Yeah," Keenes said.

Neither of them made a move toward him. Keenes held his position; Gianelli got up and looked in Manny's tiny refrigerator. "Boy, they were serious about that barracks restriction, weren't they? Nothing but base rations in here." He wrinkled his nose, shut the refrigerator and sat again at the kitchen table.

And Manny understood. "It's going down tonight, isn't it?"

"Don't know what you're talking about, Outhouse," Gianelli said. "Do we, Keenes?"

The tall man shook his head. "Not at all."

"You two are supposed to keep me here, right?"

"Where would you go?" Gianelli said. "You're confined to quarters. And you know, that's probably for the best. Things have gotten awfully strange around here lately."

"Awfully strange," Keenes said. "Sit down, Outhouse. You're not going anywhere tonight."

They passed an hour in silence. Manny sat on the couch. Keenes eventually came away from the door and joined him there. He pulled out a handheld and flipped through screenfuls of text, catching up on some reading. Gianelli remained at the kitchen table, playing solitaire with a deck of cards he'd brought with him, occasionally snacking on Manny's rations. He held out a packet to Manny, who declined with a shake of the head.

Manny considered and discarded various ways of escaping, idly fingering the ID badge and disk Ezrin had given him, still in his pocket. With his bad ankle, he could not make a run for the door. He could try threatening to rat the two of them out, but that would be an empty gesture, and they would know it. Gianelli and Keenes would simply deny they had ever been here tonight, and they would undoubtedly have a dozen compatriots willing to back their story. Manny would have only his word, and a reputation that had taken a pounding of late.

The rest of the co-conspirators, whoever they were, would be similarly covered. As long as everyone involved took reasonable precautions to leave behind no evidence, and as long as they all stuck to the same story, no one could be arrested or indicted.

And still, the Walphin would be dead before dawn.

Manny hoped they would get it over with soon. This waiting, this sense of utter helplessness, was its own kind of torture.

He hated to admit it, but the operation bore the marks of Quinn's organizational skills—simple, coordinated, efficient.

Manny broke the silence, wondering aloud more than making conversation: "How is she planning to get past Gilmore's guards? She surely doesn't want to start shooting at them. That's a whole different kind of trouble."

Keenes didn't even look up from his reading. "Don't know who you're talking about."

Gianelli gathered his cards again and shuffled. "You sure you're OK, Outhouse? You look a little piqued. A little sick, even."

Manny narrowed his eyes. "I'm not sick, except of your face, Gianelli."

"You sure that's all it is? You sure you haven't picked up something from that fish?"

"I'm sure."

"Yeah? Do you suppose that Intel man would tell you if you had? Do you think he'd tell anyone?"

"That's paranoid bullshit."

"This base is quarantined. Did you know that? Are you gonna tell me *that's* paranoid bullshit?"

Manny fell silent. No point in arguing. These two had already made up their minds.

Pounding at the door startled all three of them. As one, Gianelli and Keenes turned to Manny.

Wide-eyed, Gianelli said, "You expecting someone?"

Manny shook his head, as baffled as they were.

More pounding. A muffled voice came from the other side of the door: "Gianelli! Open up! Hurry! Something's gone wrong."

Gianelli was on his feet in a flash. He crossed the room with more speed than Manny would have given him credit for.

He pulled it open. "What the—"

He uttered an oof and went staggering backward, doubled over and clutching his ample gut. His feet tangled and he fell.

Keenes ran for the door. Someone on the other side grabbed him and pulled him into the corridor. Manny heard a crash that shook the walls.

Johansen came through the door, hands balled into fists, his attention on Gianelli.

The fat man was still on the floor, gasping. The wind had been knocked out of him. He scrabbled away from Johansen.

Johansen turned to Manny. "Come on, Sarge. We have to hurry." He helped Manny to his feet, moved for the door.

"Wait," Manny said. "Get their comms. We can't have them calling for help." It would buy only a few minutes, but judging from Johansen's urgency, that was all the time they had, anyway.

"Right." Johansen went to Gianelli, crouched. Gianelli thrashed and kicked. One look at Johansen's face, though, and he went still.

Johansen grabbed the comm clipped to Gianelli's belt and pocketed it. He looked up at Manny. "What about yours?"

"Right here." Manny had it with him, clipped like Gianelli's.

The two of them went into the corridor. Keenes lay in a heap against the opposite wall, unmoving. Johansen got his comm, too.

Only then did Manny notice the motorized cart, like the ones used in the mines, in the middle of the hallway. Johansen nodded toward it. "Get in. You can't run."

The carts weren't built for speed, but would certainly be faster than Manny on foot. They got in. Johansen thumbed a stud, and the motor whined into humming life. Using the control sticks, he backed the cart, turned it and then headed down the corridor, in the direction of the treatment plant.

Johansen said, "I was having a drink with one of the cargo loaders from the hangar bay. He slipped up, let me know what was going on." He looked at Manny. "You said you wanted to know, right?"

Manny nodded.

"We have to hurry. They're going to trigger the fire alarm to draw the guards away from the secured area. Then they'll move in and—"

"How many of them are there?"

"I don't know. Seems like half the base is in on it. That cargo loader just assumed I was, too. I guess he forgot that I was a Maggot." He steered the car around a bend and flashed a grim smile.

Half the base. Jesus. "We need to call in the MPs."

"Can't. Some of them are part of this. I don't know which ones to trust."

Manny dug out his comm. "Colonel Ezrin, then."

"Are you sure?"

"Yeah." He powered up the unit, and waited for the *ready* indicator to light. It seemed to take forever. His hands shook.

Johansen took another corner at full speed, causing Manny to grab hold of his seat, lest he fall out. They were passing the rec hall now. It was empty and dark.

"Sarge?" Johansen kept his attention on what he was doing, but his tone had gone strangely soft, even pleading. "I'm a private that just assaulted two superiors. I knocked one of them unconscious."

"Nothing's going to happen to you. Those two would have a hard time explaining what they were doing in my quarters."

Manny raised the comm and punched in Ezrin's code.

Just then, sirens began to wail from the PA, echoing throughout the corridor.

Manny and Johansen exchanged glances. Someone had tripped the fire alarm.

"Oh, Christ," Manny said.

5.

Ezrin didn't answer his comm. No doubt the fire alarm had gotten his full attention. Disgusted, Manny flung his comm away as they sped through the corridors.

They pulled the cart into an elevator; it barely fit. Manny reached back and punched the button for the maintenance sublevel. The doors closed and they descended. The sirens continued wailing, even in the elevator.

Too long. It was all taking too long. Despair settled over Manny. No way they would make it in time. It was probably over with already.

The elevator slowed, stopped. The doors opened. Johansen backed out the cart, jerkily, and headed for the treatment plant.

The level smelled of smoke; a vague haze hung in the air. Johansen looked at Manny, eyes wide.

"Not just a false alarm," Manny said. "They set a real fire somewhere on this level." That made sense. A false alarm would be too quickly settled; a real one would take longer and create a much bigger distraction.

They came to the T-junction and turned right. The haze was thicker here, stinging Manny's eyes. Men in bright orange Fire Crew uniforms, carrying suppression packs slung over their shoulders, ran toward them. Manny braced himself for a fight, but they went past without a second glance.

The doors to the treatment plant's main floor stood wide open. Johansen barreled through them without slowing. Johansen wound past Tanks One, Two and Three, jockeying around and under pipes. The partitions that marked the boundary of the secured area stood twenty meters ahead. Gilmore's guards were nowhere in sight.

"Shit," Manny said.

The fire alarm wailed on and on.

The entryway was too narrow for the cart. Johansen braked. The hard rubber tires squeaked as the cart stopped with a jolt. They got out. Johansen hesitated, looked back at Manny.

"Just go," Manny said. "Now."

Johansen bolted.

Raised voices, inarticulate shouts floated back to Manny. He went into a rapid limp-hop, wincing at flaring pain in his ankle.

A crowd of enlisted, split into two distinct groups, had gathered in front of Tank Four. None wore Fire Crew uniforms. Johansen was yelling at a hulking monster of a man, a few inches shorter than Johansen but with broader shoulders and chest, great thick arms and fists the size of melons.

They all turned to Manny as he approached. The shouts died away. The incessant siren blared and echoed.

Manny took only a second to piece together what had happened.

A line of his own people, his Maggots, four in all, had formed a small barricade in front of Tank Four. He recognized them as the treatment plant's graveyard shift. The rest was easy to figure out: true to their training, the graveyard crew had stayed on the job even when the fire alarms had sounded, and had seen the would-be assassins entering the secured area, even as Gilmore's guards had run off to check on the fire.

The miniature lynch mob, a half dozen of them, had been balked—so far.

Manny looked over them. Most he recognized. Some were veterans, some greenhorns. One was even an MP. They all carried pulse rifles—except for the big one getting in Johansen's face. His lay at his feet. He apparently had been willing to go man-to-man with Johansen.

So, then—the numbers were even, except for the rifles. The Maggots didn't even have sidearms.

Tank Four loomed behind the tableau. Manny only glanced at it. He stopped, panting hard. He took a moment to regain his breath, then said, "Where's the fire?"

Members of the lynch mob exchanged glances. A couple of them moved aside, and Manny saw they had a seventh with them—Quinn.

She bore no weapon as she came forward, head held high, calm, as if in no hurry at all.

"It's in Sanitation," she said. "In one of the refuse bins. It'll burn nicely, but it's safely contained. And it will give Gilmore's guards a good excuse for leaving their posts."

"The guards? They're in on it, too?"

"Don't worry about it. Tell your people to stand down, Manny. Right now." She nodded to her compatriots. They turned to the Maggot barricade, raised their rifles.

"No," Manny said. "It's already over, Resa. Your cover's blown. Tell *your* people to stand down."

"I don't want to hurt you or anyone else, Manny. But I will if you stand in my way."

"This won't bring them back—your brother and his family. And the prisoner didn't take them from you."

Her lip curled. "That *prisoner* is endangering everyone on this base. But it's not so bad, not so tough. You showed me that. So we're going to take care of this. Now stand down. Last warning."

Manny looked at Johansen, and the rest of his Maggots. They looked back, awaiting his word, his leadership. They would do whatever he told them to do, even if it meant risking their lives. In other circumstances, he would have swelled with pride at the thought. That damned sense of duty of his— it had caused him to be exiled to Hargas Base, it had alienated him from his friends, and now it had him and five of his subordinates staring down the barrels of pulse rifles.

Manny hobbled over to the graveyard crew. Johansen followed. Taking a deep breath, Manny joined them in their line, facing down Quinn and her people. Johansen stood at Manny's shoulder.

Manny said, "You know what? The war has finally come to us. Now we're all on the front line. And it's not so easy to choose anymore. Not so easy to know what the right thing is."

Quinn's hands trembled. "Goddamn you, Manny. How can you betray your own people like this?"

"I'm not sure which one of us is the traitor, Resa. You guys are the ones with the guns. What do you say? You want to show the Walphins that you can be just as ruthless as they are?"

The sirens cut off. Manny's ears rang in the sudden silence.

Members of Quinn's crew glanced up and around, blinking as if they'd just been awakened.

"Time's up, Resa," Manny said. "If you're going to do it, you have to do it now. Or never."

Her breathing became heavier. "Don't, Manny. Don't . . . make me do this. Because I will. You think I won't?"

"Honest to God, I don't know. But it's your choice."

The moment stopped, held. Some remote part of Manny's mind registered the smoke in the air, the way it stung his eyes, the rancid, burnt smell. They might be among the last things he remembered in this life. But he would not take his gaze off Quinn, even if she had him shot. He would die looking her in the eyes. If nothing else, he would make certain of that.

Her trembling became more pronounced, her breathing progressively louder with every passing second, as if she were working her way around to the scream that would be his death sentence. Her mouth moved soundlessly.

A single tear slid down one cheek, fell to the floor.

Noises from outside filtered back to them—confused shouts, slamming doors, boots tramping down corridors. Coming nearer.

A faint sound escaped Quinn's throat. The assassins glanced uneasily at her.

"I—" Quinn swayed on her feet, staggered. The big brute caught her before she fell, holding her by the shoulders. She muttered something. Manny only caught some of her words. He thought she may have been apologizing to her dead brother.

The other assassins looked to her, slowly lowered their rifles. Confused scowls creased their features.

Manny said to the brute, "Get her out of here. Quick. Use the rear exit." He proffered the badge Ezrin had given him. "This will get you out without setting off the alarm again. Take her back

405

to her quarters. Do it, and none of this happened. Understood?"

The brute hesitated, then took the badge. To the others, he said, "Come on."

One of the other assassins said, "We can't—"

"Come on." The brute spoke through clenched teeth. He led Quinn toward the fire door, moving quickly. The rest followed in haste, some eyeing Manny and his Maggots as they passed, others looking at the tank with stony expressions. None of them noticed the pulse rifle, gleaming in dull black, left on the treatment floor. Careless.

Then the lynch mob was gone.

The Maggots literally breathed a collective sigh of relief, all of them exhaling at once. Two of the graveyard crew members embraced. Johansen said, "Oh, God. Oh, God."

Manny said, "Lock this plant down. Right now. Before Gilmore's guards come back. No one else gets in here. I don't care who's outside the doors. Understand me? *No one else gets in.*"

They gaped at him, motionless, uncomprehending. Johansen said, "Uh, Sarge . . . I—"

"This isn't over yet. Now *move.*"

"Exactly *what* isn't over yet?"

All of them turned in the direction of the voice. Gilmore stood in the entryway, hair mussed, dressed only in a dark robe, rumpled sleepsuit bottoms, and slippers. He stepped in, frowning, looking around. "Manny? What's going on here? Where are my guards?"

The others exchanged guilty glances, but Manny remained composed—outwardly, anyway. "Not as trustworthy as you'd like to think, I guess. Good thing my people were here."

Gilmore glanced over his shoulder at the entryway, then back at Manny, then at the pulse rifle on the floor. He sniffed the air. Understanding dawned in his face. He rushed to the tank, peered through the observation window.

"The prisoner's—" Manny started to say *fine,* but stopped himself, realizing how stupid that sounded. What could he say? Safe? All right? Unhurt? None of that was true. "It's still alive."

Still looking through the window, Gilmore said, "I want everyone out of this area. Now."

The Maggots looked to Manny. He nodded at them. "Go ahead. Lock down the plant, like I told you."

Johansen opened his mouth to say something, then thought the better of it. The team shuffled out, leaving Manny and Gilmore alone.

Almost.

Manny hobbled over to the pulse rifle lying on the floor and stood over it.

Gilmore pulled his gaze away from the window. "I knew it was getting bad, but I didn't realize *how* bad. Manny, you've done an extraordinary thing here. I want you to know how grateful I am for this. Fill out another transfer application, and this time, send it to me. I will personally see to it that it goes through."

Manny winced. Just like that, there it was, right in front of him again. His for the taking. Ezrin would be disappointed, but what of it? Manny would be gone, Hargas Base forever behind him.

Except that he had just risked his life and lives of his Maggots, and he hadn't done it for Gilmore.

"Tell me something, Mr. Gilmore: what's in that special additives tank?"

Gilmore's gaze flickered in that direction. "I told you. It's for the prisoner."

Manny shook his head, bent to retrieve the pulse rifle at his feet. He pointed it at Gilmore.

The Intel man took a step backward. "Manny? What are you doing?"

"I know what's going on here. Whatever you've been poisoning the prisoner with, it ends tonight."

"No. You have it all wrong, Manny."

"Oh, I don't think so."

Gilmore licked his lips. "You don't understand, Manny. Without that"—he pointed to the additives tank—"the prisoner couldn't survive. Walphin digestion . . . it's dependent on tiny, acid-secreting symbiotes. That's what in this tank. The symbiotes require a delicate temperature balance and a steady stream of nutrients. Easy enough to find in the Walphin digestive tract, harder to do outside of it."

Manny looked at the milky water. Acid-secreting symbiotes—it actually sounded plausible. Except . . .

Except the Walphin hadn't been digesting anything very well lately. Manny had seen the evidence firsthand. His stomach roiled. "You sadistic bastard. You've been withholding those symbiotes, haven't you?"

Gilmore gulped. Manny could see his throat working from across the room.

He tried to imagine it: eating would have become extremely painful for the Walphin, tearing into its gut, getting worse every day. Probably some internal hemorrhaging, too. Eventually, it would have stopped eating altogether. And all the while, Gilmore continued beaming his questions at it: *Where? When? How many?* And perhaps the occasional *Tell me what I need to know, and I'll make it stop hurting.*

Quinn had said, *Nobody here is a fan of Intel Branch. Those jackasses haven't produced any useful intelligence since the war started.*

The Walphins had gone quiet on all major fronts.

And the prisoner hadn't been cooperating—the highest-ranking Walphin ever captured.

Gilmore was breathing fast. "Manny, the next attack could be coming any day now. Don't you understand? We don't have time to ask politely. That prisoner isn't a human being. It's not entitled to human rights."

"You're a son of a bitch, you know that? You used us. You used this whole base as a cover. I think I had more respect for the lynch mob." Manny raised the rifle, sighted. "Get out."

"Manny, think about what you're doing. If I turn around and walk out of here, you'll never see Earth again."

His father's face came to him. The barrel of the pulse rifle wavered.

"Put that thing down," Gilmore said, "and we can forget about all this."

He could do it. He could set the pulse rifle aside, could forget this whole incident, could get back in time to say goodbye to his father, resume something resembling a normal life.

But he had to wonder if his father would approve.

Manny's vision clouded. A choked sound escaped him. He cleared his throat and tried again: "Gilmore, if you say one more word, I'll kill you. Walk away. Now."

After a moment, Gilmore straightened and tightened the belt of his robe. Stiffly, as if his legs had turned to wood, he exited the way he had come.

Manny lowered the weapon. He was alone.

Almost.

He turned. The Walphin was at the observation window, watching him. Manny's heart jogged. The thing just floated, silent and still, like an apparition. He wondered how long it had been there, how much it had seen.

The dark mottling on its gray skin stood out like bruises. Its black eyes appeared dull, filmy, sunken in their sockets. The bones of what passed for its face stood out in sharp relief.

The prisoner waited at the observation window.

Manny wiped at his eyes. He still had the disk Ezrin had given him, still had to access and copy Gilmore's computer records of his activities here, in order to get the colonel the leverage he needed—hard evidence that Gilmore was violating the War Conventions. Threat of exposure. And, no doubt, the offer of a deal: Ezrin's silence in exchange for Gilmore's immediate departure. Go torture your prisoner somewhere else.

But Manny could not look away from the Walphin. "Do you understand, fish? Do you have any idea what went down here tonight?"

For reasons he could not define, he got the strongest feeling that it *did* understand, at least on some level, what had happened. And now it was waiting to see what Manny would do.

He went to the window. The Walphin remained in place. Manny peered at it, studying it as intently as it studied him.

He noted abrasions along the creature's jawline. A dark smudge marked one corner of its mouth. Blood, most likely.

It had been captured on a command platform, Gilmore had said. It was most likely a member of the Walphin officer corps—if there was such a thing. But was it a general, or a lowly lieutenant? Or maybe it wasn't an officer at all; maybe it was some peon sergeant, like him, maybe just an alien janitor who'd been in the wrong place at the wrong time.

"You don't know anything, do you?" Manny whispered.

The Walphin watched him, silent and still. Its head bobbed slightly. With one webbed foreclaw, it reached for the glass.

Manny's breath stopped.

It wasn't reaching, he realized. It was pointing—at the pulse rifle still in his hand.

A spasm racked the Walphin's body. It twisted and writhed. More dark blood issued from its mouth, forming little floating globs and rivulets.

Pointing. The prisoner had certainly seen enough weapons pointed at its face to know what Manny was holding. It had just watched Manny face down both Quinn and Gilmore. It knew enough, maybe, to make judgments about his character.

Manny understood.

Once more, his sense of duty tugged at him.

"Ah, Jesus, no," he whispered. It was crazy, to have gone through all of this just to give Quinn and half the base what they'd wanted all along. He would go from pariah to hero.

The Walphin's spasm subsided. Slowly, as if with great weariness, it looked at him and pointed to the rifle again, its claws grazing the glass.

No, this wasn't what Quinn wanted. This was something different. Maybe even honorable.

The rational part of him, still barely functional, tried to assert that he was reading too much into the alien's face, trying to graft human qualities onto something inhuman. Pathetic fallacy, they called it. Or something like that.

He looked down at the rifle in his hands. His sense of duty tugged, stronger than it had ever been in his life.

He would get the brig for it. Or would he? Would the data from Gilmore's records exonerate him, or at least mitigate the judgment? Would Gilmore even risk something so public as a court martial?

A mental picture came to him—of climbing the ladder to the maintenance deck, of opening the cage door. The Walphin would come to the surface, maybe even pull itself out of the tank with the last of its strength, and it would wait there, silently pleading for Manny to end its suffering, to stop the senselessness of it all. The pulse rifle didn't kick much, if Manny's memory of weapons training served.

Quinn, Gilmore, Ezrin—they all faded to unimportance. It was just him, the prisoner and this moment, this choice.

"Gone black," Manny said to the Walphin. "We've all gone black here. We've lost our way."

He went to do his duty.

Persistence of Vision

BY RON LINDAHN

Ron Lindahn is a master of visual communication. He has worked as an award-winning photographer, illustrator, graphic designer and filmmaker. Ron and his wife and fellow judge, Val, have produced hundreds of book and magazine covers, illustrated movie posters, video packaging, limited edition prints and posters. Ron and Val also wrote and illustrated three children's books. They have won numerous awards for their art and design and have been featured in exhibitions and gallery shows around the country.

Ron also consults on marketing and product design, produces and packages videos, develops web sites and has designed award-winning publications and commercials for national television. His latest production is a series of DVDs on yoga.

Ron has served as a judge for the L. Ron Hubbard's Illustrators of the Future Contest since its beginning in 1988 and has served as Coordinating Judge since 1998. Ron and Val created and continue to teach the Illustrators' Workshop each year.

Persistence of Vision

Way back in 1983 a man had an idea. And it was a good idea. Unfortunately just having an idea, even a good one, is not worth much. Everyone has them from time to time and most end up neglected or forgotten, tossed aside along life's busy highway.

The man was L. Ron Hubbard, no stranger to good ideas. He had the idea to create a contest that would give a boost to the careers of aspiring new writers. An idea is like a seed that requires a good deal of care and nurturing if it is to blossom into reality. It is easily trampled and crushed by negativity and withers from lack of attention.

I can imagine the meeting where Mr. Hubbard first shared this idea with his staff. Someone probably asked, "What's in it for us and how are we going to pay for it?" If it was just an idea, that might have been the end of it. But Mr. Hubbard's response may very well have been, "What's in it for us is the opportunity to invest in the future of humanity." He is often quoted as saying, "A culture is only as great as its dreams, and its dreams are dreamed by artists." He may have gone on to explain that an anthology of winning stories could be published that would give much-needed exposure to the Contest winners while providing some of the funding to cover the cost of running the Contest. In this response Mr. Hubbard would have shown that this was more than just an idea. He had a vision.

Vision: *a vivid, imaginative conception or anticipation.*

What separates a vision from just another good idea is that a vision is a clearly defined picture of a desired outcome. Whether it is writing a story, painting a picture, starting a new business or planting a garden, in order for a creative venture to be successful the most important first step is to mentally project oneself into the future and clearly see the finished product. This clear picture can only be seen when we have answered some basic questions. The answers serve as guideposts as we engage in the creative process of bringing our idea into reality. Questions to be answered by illustrators and writers are:

How and where will it be used?

In the case of a painting we need to know if it will be used as a book cover, an interior illustration for a story or editorial, or if it will hang in a gallery or on our living room wall. The primary use of our art will determine what media, size, format and style we choose to work in.

If we are writing a story, is it intended for a magazine, an anthology or our personal blog? What is the tone and style of stories in the intended publication? What are the requirements for length and content? Without these guidelines it can be easy to miss the mark.

Who is it for?

Is our purpose to inspire by sharing a unique vision, or to inform, entertain, sell a product or promote an idea? We can only be successful if we know something about our target audience. How old are they? Are they educated and informed or indifferent, rich or poor, socially active or introverted? What are their likes and dislikes, dreams and aspirations? Knowing a bit about our readers or viewers enables us to craft a communication that will be received as we intend it. If we use language and images that are too sophisticated or too simple for our audience we will fail to communicate and our vision will wither and die.

What do you want them to do?

After they see your picture or read your story, how do you want the viewers to feel? What do you want them to do next? If you have created an illustration for a book cover, its purpose should be to capture the attention of a potential book buyer. In the case of science fiction and fantasy, it should inspire a sense of wonder and impel the viewer to pick up the book to see what treasures may be inside. If your painting is to be hung in a gallery to be purchased for a home, what mood or feeling are you creating? Is this a piece that people will want to live with and look at every day?

Is your story intended to entertain, taking the reader on a journey from the agony of defeat to the thrill of victory? Or do you want the reader to be better informed or inspired to take some action?

Without a well-defined expectation of the effect we intend to produce, we are doomed to failure or mediocrity. We cannot predict the effect our creation will have unless we know who we are talking to and in what form it will be presented. As we envision the successful completion of our project, we should be as detailed as possible. Before beginning an illustration for a book cover, imagine the book on a shelf in the bookstore and see a shopper pick up the book and be enchanted by your artwork. If you are writing a story for a magazine, imagine the layout, headline and illustration. See the reader entranced by your story. The more real you make your vision, the better your chances of success.

Persistence: *to continue steadfastly or firmly in some state, purpose or course of action.*

While vision is the necessary first step, of equal importance is the second step: creating a structure for accomplishment. In order to accomplish anything, we have to do something. The something we must do in order to be successful can be summed up in one word: persistence. It is by persisting *in the right way* that we realize success in our endeavors. The right way includes the elements of discipline, study and belief.

1. Discipline

In order to manifest our vision we must give it time and attention. Scheduling regular time on a daily basis is the most efficient means of accomplishing our goals. We must have the discipline to work at developing our skills and technique so we have

419

something of value to offer. In his book *Outliers,* Malcolm Gladwell reveals that many who are considered masters in their respective fields have worked at developing their skills for 10,000 hours. This requires discipline.

And we must have the discipline to produce our work in a timely manner. Writers and illustrators have deadlines. Professionals never miss deadlines or give excuses. This requires a disciplined approach to our work.

2. *Study*

Success depends on knowledge. An illustrator needs to know what makes a pleasing composition, how to handle light and shadow to create the illusion of form and depth, how to draw believable characters, and a thousand details that go into the creation of a good illustration. A writer must be able to hook the reader and lead them on an adventure, or to the intended conclusion, through a skillful use of language.

A professional also needs to know how to market their work, handle finances and have an understanding of the final consumer. Everything changes over time. To be informed regarding all aspects that may influence the accomplishment of our goals requires constant study.

There are three ways we acquire accurate knowledge. First is through direct experience. Practice, trial and error, and careful observation help us develop our skills. Second, we use inference. By examining others' results we can infer how they were achieved. In the case of a painting, by looking carefully at the texture, intensity of color and style of rendering, we can often infer what medium was used. The third way is by learning from reliable sources. We can study with accredited teachers, be mentored by accomplished professionals and read about the lives and working methods of masters in our field.

3. Belief

Success depends on belief. We must believe that we can achieve our desired outcome. If others have been successful, we can be successful as well. If we do not believe that we can succeed we will most likely fail. If we believe in ourselves, are willing to do what must be done, and persevere, we cannot possibly fail. Belief empowers us to maintain our discipline, continue learning and maintain a clear vision of a successful outcome.

The term "persistence of vision" was originally used to explain how a sequential presentation of still images created the illusion of continuous motion. We experience this illusion every time we watch a motion picture or video. The theory claimed that each still image would "persist" for just a moment on the retina of the eye. The result was a series of overlapping images that created the sense of motion.

The "persistence of vision" theory of motion perception is passive, with one still image simply stacking up on top of the previous one, and does not account for the complexity of the processes required to "see." In the same way creative, successful masters are often thought of as having been born with talent, been lucky or having gotten all the breaks. They are seen as passive recipients of good fortune. In reality, to become successful and achieve mastery in any field requires active participation. Armed with sincere desire and belief that we can succeed, we will succeed by maintaining our vision and being relentlessly persistent.

The publication of this volume, *L. Ron Hubbard Presents Writers of the Future Volume XXV,* is a testament to Mr. Hubbard and his wonderful example of what one man with a vision can accomplish. Since their inception, the Writers and Illustrators of the Future Contests have assisted nearly 600 award-winning new writers and artists. The Contests have provided financial support, personal mentoring from successful working professional writers and illustrators through workshops, publication in a critically acclaimed, widely circulated anthology and publicity and promotion in the artists' and writers' home communities. Many of those who got their start through this Contest have gone on to become internationally recognized masters in their respective fields. Others have learned important skills that have enabled them to live happier, more productive lives.

The seed of Mr. Hubbard's idea, nurtured through a shared vision and the persistent support of a dedicated staff, has grown into a strong tree. Its fruit has become a forest of writers and artists who are dreaming up new and better futures for us all. Thank you, Mr. Hubbard.

The Reflection of Memory

written by

C. L. Holland

illustrated by

OLEKSANDRA BARYSHEVA

ABOUT THE AUTHOR

For as long as she can remember, UK fantasy writer
C. L. Holland loved telling stories. At five years old, she would
tell bedtime stories to her younger brother. At seven, she wrote
her first fantasy story, a "Choose-Your-Own-Adventure"
scribbled on the back of a school workbook. The stories came
easily, spurred by her voracious reading habits (something she
continues to do today). She cites authors Patricia McKillip,
Neil Gaiman and Guy Gavriel Kay as major influences on
her reading and writing habits.

C. L.'s love of words eventually led her to a bachelor's
degree in English with creative writing and a master's degree
in English. Those degrees did not figure in her professional
career (thus far anyway), where she toils away administering
the payroll of a busy environmental consultancy. One thing her
education, reading and storytelling did do was provide a rich
tradition in the printed word. Her stories have now appeared
or are appearing in the Ruins Metropolis, One Step
Beyond: Subatomic Anthology 01, A Fly in Amber *e-zine*
and Kaleidotrope *print zine.*

ABOUT THE ILLUSTRATOR

Oleksandra Barysheva is a native of Ukraine and a senior at Matawan Regional High School in New Jersey. Growing up in the Ukraine, she showed an "excellent proficiency" in her drawing classes, inspired by her architect mother, who was her first art teacher. After moving to America, Oleksandra became even more fascinated and dedicated to illustration and visual arts.

Over the years, Oleksandra has received numerous art awards for her work, which has motivated her to try different techniques, work without boundaries and take greater risks as an artist. Her interests have expanded to book illustration, ceramics and graphic design. It was her love of illustration that led her to enter the Illustrators of the Future Contest.

Soon after her entry, Oleksandra began attending classes at the duCret School of Art where artists, professional illustrators and their work constantly surround her. The environment has inspired Oleksandra, and she says her technical skills have definitely progressed. "Art has been my life," she says. "This is just the beginning."

The Reflection of Memory

It was cold. So cold that the girl could hardly feel anything except a dull ache in her hands and feet. Something squawked in front of her and she was startled enough to open her eyes. A beady silver-gray eye stared at her. The jackdaw flapped its dark wings and hopped backward as she waved her arm to scare it off. The limb felt heavy and far away, as if it belonged to someone else. She let it fall and closed her eyes again.

The next time she opened them it was to warmth. A heavy cloak had been wrapped around her, and a campfire set shadows dancing against the snow. Beside it, feeding it twigs, sat a dark-haired man. There was something about him that was familiar, and after a moment she placed it.

"You were the jackdaw."

Her own voice made her jump; she hadn't meant to speak out loud. He turned to face her and she saw his eyes were brown and cheerful. Not a jackdaw's eyes.

"I was," he agreed. "Although I'm surprised

you noticed." It wasn't a jackdaw's voice either; it matched his eyes. "What were you doing all the way out here? There was a blizzard; if I hadn't found you . . ."

"I don't know. I was just here." She sat up and looked around at the trees that surrounded them. "Wherever here is. . . ."

"We're in the forest south of Lorn Hold." The way he caught her gaze told her he thought she should know it, but it meant nothing to her. She shook her head and his brow creased. "You don't remember anything? Where were you before?"

"There isn't anything before," she explained. It seemed odd, now that she said it out loud.

The man sat back on his heels and studied her with a scrutiny that reminded her of the bird. "What's your name?"

"Should I have one?" She couldn't think of any people who would want to call her anything. He stared.

"Everyone has a name. Mine is Kestrin."

Now he'd said it, she could see it, although it didn't quite fit. Like boots he had worn into rather than ones made just for him. She wondered where the thought had come from, even as she reflected that it was probably better than no boots at all. After a moment Kestrin seemed to accept that she wasn't going to answer in kind.

"I should take you back to the Hold," he said. "There might be someone there who knows you."

She nodded. "All right."

She settled the thick cloak around her shoulders

as he extinguished the fire, and then he took her through the forest. After a time it became obvious he was only on foot for her benefit; he stumbled in the snow as if he wasn't used to it.

"Are you a man or a bird, really?"

He glanced sidelong at her. "Both, maybe. I was born a man."

"But you prefer being a bird." She wondered how someone could be more comfortable in a form other than their own. Perhaps it was like his name, and he had yet to grow into his shape. "Do you only become a jackdaw?"

"No. I just happened to be one when I found you." He tripped over a root and caught himself against a tree trunk.

"You don't have to walk with me," she said. "I can still follow if you fly ahead."

"That would be rude," he said and kept walking.

They traveled until the light faded, and finally the trees gave way to a snow-covered road that shone like a river in the moonlight and a cluster of lights in the distance. Lorn Hold. She stopped and stared. Kestrin came to stand at her shoulder.

"It's not as far as it looks. I'll fly ahead and let them know we're coming, then come back for you. Just keep to the road and it will be all right."

She tried to watch as Kestrin changed shape but all she saw was a dark-haired man one moment and then the next he was gone, in the shape of something sleek that shot through the air like an arrow.

For a few moments she stood still, unwilling to mark the snow with her passage. The lights of Lorn

Hold flickered like yellow stars that had fallen to earth; everything else was stillness and silence. It seemed as if she were the only creature left in all the world and she shivered, wondering what would happen to her if Kestrin didn't come back.

She stepped onto the road and started walking. Lorn Hold didn't seem to grow any nearer, although when she looked back the forest and her footsteps had disappeared into shadow.

After a while a shape came out of the dark toward her. She held up her arm so the bird could land there. It changed in midair into a jackdaw and fastened its claws on her wrist. She moved her hand up to her shoulder to let it perch. The bird ruffled its feathers, tickling her ear, and then settled.

Dark wooden gates bound with iron swung open as they approached the gray-walled Hold. They revealed a courtyard that blazed with light and buildings made of the same dark bricks. A woman met them who seemed of an age with Kestrin. She had his warm eyes, but her hair was honey-blonde instead of dark. Her gaze went to the jackdaw and she sighed.

"It's bad enough you choose to spend the winter in the forest as a wild thing, without you keeping the shape when you come home. If you're not careful you'll forget how to be a man."

The jackdaw hopped into the air and a moment later was Kestrin again.

"I won't," he said. "I know who I am, even when I'm a bird. Asta, did you get my message?"

"Yes." Asta's gaze slid sideways to the girl. "Welcome to Lorn Hold. You're most welcome, especially as you've brought my errant brother home."

The girl didn't know what to say, so she remained silent.

"She doesn't remember her name," Kestrin said. "I hoped that someone here might know her." His eyes said more than his words, although the girl couldn't tell what message passed to his sister.

"Of course. We can ask tomorrow." She turned back to the girl. "In the meantime I've had a room prepared for you, and there's hot food if you want it. This way."

Asta ushered them into an anteroom where they hung their cloaks and kicked the snow from their boots. From there they followed her into a wide hall with a long table at the far side. Shelves lined with bottles and jugs, books, instruments and all manner of objects were dotted around the walls. Between them were fireplaces that were surrounded by clusters of people around smaller tables, who nodded or waved greetings and then went back to their conversations.

"Uncle Kestrin!"

A whirlwind of children struck them and wrapped their arms around Kestrin. The girl took a step back, overwhelmed, as he hugged them and scooped an unsteady toddler into his arms.

"Don't worry," Asta said softly beside her, "they'll calm down once they've greeted him. Come and have something to eat; you look half starved."

The girl let Asta show her to a seat at the table. At the other end of the bench a girl of about fourteen sat with her knees drawn up, staring dreamily across the room. She had Kestrin's dark hair and the brown eyes that seemed the hallmark of the family, but she was surely too old to be either his or Asta's daughter.

"Are all of the children yours?"

"Those three are," Asta replied, gesturing at the boy in Kestrin's arms and the girls who seemed to be trying to climb him. "Any offspring Kestrin may have were likely hatched rather than born. This is our sister Marla."

At the sound of her name, the girl on the bench looked up. Her name was like Kestrin's, the girl realized, something not yet grown into.

"Are you a jackdaw too?" she asked without thinking.

Marla gave a sleepy smile. "No. I can't do birds." An instant later she was a gangly adolescent cat with fur the color of smoke and yellow eyes. The cat butted against the girl's hand, then jumped from the bench and sauntered across the hall to greet her brother.

Asta sent for a meal of roasted chicken and vegetables. The girl ate slowly, savoring the honey-glazed parsnips and chestnuts, and the richness of the chicken skin. When she'd finished she leaned back against the wall and dozed, with the warmth of the fire wrapping her in comfort like a blanket. She heard Kestrin hand the children to a now-human Marla, who shepherded them out amidst a chorus of protests. He came to the table and sat beside his sister.

"We've missed you," Asta said softly. "The children especially. It's hard on them, with their father away and an uncle who rarely comes home. Would you have come back, if you hadn't found her?"

"Of course," Kestrin replied between mouthfuls. "I always come back."

"So did Father," Asta sighed. "Until one day he didn't. And you know that's not what I meant. Yaphen will be here tomorrow. Were you trying to avoid him?"

Kestrin sighed. "I don't see why you need me here, for him to tell you what you already know."

"If you were that certain you wouldn't fear being here when he arrives," Asta countered. "A Hold needs a Holder, Kestrin, and Yaphen can tell us who it is. At least stay until he arrives?"

"I intend to," he promised. "He might be able to see who *she* is."

The girl felt a flutter in her stomach that Kestrin would stay for her sake. There was a gentle touch on her arm, and she opened her eyes to see Asta smiling down at her.

"Don't sleep there," she said. "You'll regret it in the morning. Let me show you to your room."

The girl nodded her agreement and followed Asta from the hall. She said goodnight to Kestrin as she passed, and he smiled.

"Sleep well."

The room Asta took her to was large, with a fire burning low in the grate that gave everything soft golden edges. A table stood beneath ornately embroidered curtains, and a chair with a cushion matched them. Beside the door a tall wardrobe stood sentry. The girl put the candle down and moved to the tub of hot water that sat beside the fire. She bathed, then slipped gratefully beneath the feather quilt and blew out the candle.

With the sudden darkness came fear. Within it she seemed to herself frail and insubstantial, a nameless thing that would be easily lost in the anonymous night. What would she be when she woke up, she wondered. Would she find herself lost in the snow again, or wandering the halls of Lorn Hold like a ghost that had forgotten it was once alive? She drew the covers tighter around her although it did little to still her trembling. With no one around to tell her who she wasn't, she didn't have any idea of who she was.

When the door slipped open she almost cried out. She listened rigidly for footsteps but there were none. A moment later something landed on the bed. She jerked, then stilled as the lump gave a reassuring meow. The cat curled up on the quilt over her feet, lending them its warmth. With the noise of its quiet purring in her ears, the girl slept.

When she woke the cat was gone. The room was still dark, but there was an air of expectancy about the Hold, as if it had just woken. She slipped out of bed, her toes curling away from the cold stone, and pulled back the curtains. Strips of light outlined the edge of the shutters, and she opened them to reveal a cloudy sky that was dappled pink.

Beyond the walls the forest stretched out against the snow in a tapestry of dark branches. A flock of birds, black with distance, wheeled from the trees and she wondered if Kestrin was amongst them.

A maid came, bringing hot water and new clothes. She offered to fetch breakfast but the girl declined; she wanted to eat in the company of the hall, rather than alone like a princess locked in a tower. She donned heavy, unfamiliar clothes and made her way down to the hall. In the doorway she paused, feeling as if she were on show. Kestrin was already at the table, entertaining his nieces and nephew with a tale. He looked up and smiled, and waved her over.

The children stared at her with open curiosity as she sat opposite their uncle. She accepted a bowl of porridge and turned to see a pair of dark eyes staring across at her.

"You're the lady Uncle Kestrin found," the oldest girl said, while her sister hid her face behind her hair.

"Yes." She glanced to Kestrin for support, but he was busy wresting a pot of jam from his nephew's grip.

"You're very pretty."

"Thank you." The girl flushed, feeling awkward rather than pretty.

"What's your name?"

Kestrin looked up abruptly at that, and his nephew reclaimed the pot with a crow of delight.

"I don't know."

Kestrin's niece looked startled, and her sister was surprised enough to come out from behind her blonde curtain and stare.

"Everyone has a name," she protested, sounding for an instant exactly like Kestrin.

"Methony," he said warningly.

"But they do!" Methony scowled at him and retreated behind her hair again.

Asta's oldest daughter pulled a face. "We should give you a name. Until you remember your real one. Otherwise how will you know who you are?"

The girl's stomach tightened. "That would be very kind of you."

Kestrin prized the jam from his nephew and placed it firmly on the table. "Drielle, naming people isn't like naming pets. You need to think very hard about what you choose."

"I know that," Drielle said crossly. "Didn't I help Mother name Rayel?" Her brother looked up and gurgled.

"Yes, you did, and I heard some of the suggestions you came up with. Real names only, agreed?"

"All right." Drielle pulled her sister from the bench and they disappeared into a corner to confer. Kestrin shifted Rayel onto his lap and sighed.

"You may regret agreeing to that," he warned.

"It's better than no boots at all," the girl said softly.

That afternoon Marla took the girl on a tour of the Hold, but no one looked at her with even a flicker of recognition. The rest of the day was spent in the warmth of the hall. Sometimes the girl sat alone, listening to the bustle of the place, but mostly she had company in the form of one or another of Kestrin's family. The only time she saw them all together was when they sat at the long table for the evening meal. The hall was fuller than the girl had yet seen it. Marla saw her looking.

"Everyone at the Hold eats together once a day, if they can," she explained. "It's an old tradition, to remind everyone that it's the people that make the Hold, not the stones."

"There's no Holder," the girl replied, remembering the overheard conversation of the night before. Marla's mouth turned down at the corners. Kestrin and Asta exchanged a glance.

"Our mother was Holder," Kestrin said. "But she died, and never said which of us was Holder after her."

"I'm sorry." The girl wanted to know more, but she was still a stranger here and it wasn't her place to ask. She turned her attention back to the meal and reached for a bowl of stewed beans.

It was at the end of the meal, when people had begun to drift about their business, that the outer door opened. Asta looked up and went very still, clutching at Kestrin's wrist. He followed her gaze and went pale.

"Yaphen!" Drielle and Methony scampered across the hall and greeted the newcomer with almost as much enthusiasm as they had their uncle. The girl strained to look at him, but he had crouched in front of the children and all she could see was the firelight reflecting from his hair as if it were burnished gold.

Kestrin and his sisters rose to their feet, leaving the girl to tend Rayel at the table. The hall had grown quiet, except for the children, the conversation fading to little more than the whisper of the tide. Yaphen stood as the Holder's children approached, and bowed to them.

"Lord Kestrin, Lady Marla." He bowed deeper as he turned to Asta. "My Lady Holder."

The girl heard Kestrin release a held breath, just before the hall erupted with sound. Asta's daughters gave a shout of delight and threw themselves into their mother's embrace. The watchers surged to their feet to congratulate their new Holder. After a moment a gray cat wound its way from the crowd, hopped onto the bench beside the girl and became Marla. She scooped up Rayel.

"Let's hope that Yaphen can answer your question as easily."

"I don't understand," the girl admitted. "What happened?"

"Lorn Hold has a Holder again," Marla said with contentment. "He can see answers sometimes, before he knows the question. He told us who the Holder is."

"Oh." The girl considered this as she stared across at Yaphen. It wasn't just his hair that was golden, she saw; his skin was a dusky gold too. Shining threads glittered at the edges of his sleeves and in the embroidery of his high-collared shirt. She half expected his eyes to be amber, like a cat's. "You think he'll be able to tell me who I am?"

"That was the plan," said Kestrin behind her. He held out his hand to her as Asta and Yaphen freed themselves from the crowd.

Yaphen looked up as they approached and the girl felt a jolt go through her. His eyes weren't gold at all, but the color of rainwater, of ice over a frozen pool. Their unexpected coldness made her breath catch. Then he caught her gaze and she realized it was all in the color.

His eyes widened and he stepped forward, a smile starting on his lips. The girl's breath caught. Then he paused and frowned, as if she were a problem to be solved.

"Did you know," he asked conversationally, "that you have no name?"

The world seemed to spin. It was only that gaze, pinning her like a butterfly, that kept her upright. Beside her she heard Kestrin speak.

"She's forgotten it. She doesn't know who she is."

"No," Yaphen disagreed. He turned to Kestrin and she found she could breathe again. "She has no name. The one she had before isn't there now. It's why she's lost her memory—she is no longer who she was."

She made a noise in her throat, wondering what she would do. Kestrin would go back to the forest, she realized, and she would be left alone at Lorn Hold. While his family would be kind, eventually their courtesy would become habit until she faded into the background and was forgotten.

Kestrin was arguing. "How can she have no name? She's not a blank parchment; she knows things she couldn't possibly know unless she's someone!"

"I don't know how," Yaphen replied calmly. He sounded like sunlight would, the girl thought, if it had a voice. "My talent is in truths, not namings. What I see is bound in names; without one, there is no truth."

"We have a name for her." Drielle's voice silenced them all. "Calony." The girl wiped her eyes and stared. Asta's daughters stood before her, holding hands.

"She was a princess," Methony whispered. "In a story. She was very beautiful and very sad. Like you."

"It's a lovely name," the girl said. "Thank you."

Drielle and Methony beamed and wrapped their arms around her. Calony hugged them back. When they broke away Asta was waiting for them.

"That's enough excitement, I think. Off to bed with both of you."

"Mother!" the girls wailed in unison.

"But Yaphen's here!" Drielle protested. "Can't we stay up to hear him play? Please?"

Asta looked to Yaphen, who sighed in mock annoyance. "Is there no end to the tasks Lorn Hold requires of me?" He looked around. "Who'll accompany me?" he asked of the hall at large.

An old man volunteered and at Yaphen's urging retrieved a fiddle from a shelf at the edge of the room. A bench was cleared for them and they sat, conferring for a few moments as Yaphen drew a harp from the case slung over his shoulder and tuned it. When he drew the instrument to him the hall fell silent.

Yaphen picked out a handful of notes that wound around each other again and again. The old man nodded along, and after the second repetition raised his bow and played a counterpoint. Someone on the other side of the hall had found a pipe and began to play. The melodies were like streams that flowed their separate courses into the same river, and then Yaphen began to sing.

Calony couldn't understand the words but it didn't matter. She heard the longing in them and saw in Yaphen's eyes how far they'd traveled. His lips moved and his hands shaped notes from the harp, but his gaze, although it seemed fixed on her, saw something far beyond the walls of Lorn Hold. She realized that he, like she, was visiting a world to which he didn't belong.

Yaphen fell silent. A moment later the piper stopped playing, and the fiddler played a last flourish before leaving the harp to end the music. Yaphen played the opening refrain once, twice, with his head bent over the harp, and let the notes fade into silence.

He stayed like that as speech came back to his audience. The fiddler patted his shoulder and went back to his seat. Other musicians struck up a different tune. When Yaphen looked up it was at Lorn Hold again. He made his way back to the table, stopping to speak to the people who greeted him. Once he'd reached the table, Asta made her daughters say goodnight and took them and Rayel out of the hall. The rest of them settled around the table and Kestrin poured Yaphen a mug of ale.

"I've not heard that one before," he remarked.

"It's been a long time since I've sung it," Yaphen replied. His pale gaze came up to meet Calony's and she swallowed.

"Does it help?" she asked. "Now that I have a name? Do you see any more truth?"

"I see that Calony is a frightened young woman,

439

who fears being alone. But I could see that before the girls named you. A new name doesn't make you who you were."

"Calony," Marla said thoughtfully. "When we met, you asked if I was a jackdaw. How did you know that I change shape?"

"You knew I was the jackdaw, too," Kestrin remembered. "I was sure you hadn't seen me change."

"I saw the jackdaw in you," Calony told him. "And then when you told me your name I realized it didn't fit quite right, as if it's for one shape only. I saw Marla's name was the same as yours and so I asked."

"What about mine?" Yaphen asked. She looked at him and frowned, trying to see him the same way she'd seen them.

"Your name fits so closely it's like a second skin," she said finally. "It's as if you are your name. Completely."

Yaphen nodded. "So you have talent. It's odd it survived the loss of your name."

"Couldn't you do it for yourself?" Marla asked. "If you looked at your reflection?"

"I don't know. I don't think it would work unless I already knew the name of the person I was looking at."

"It's worth a try," Kestrin said. He went to one of the shelves and found a mirror, framed with carved ivy, which he polished with his sleeve. "Here."

Calony took the mirror and raised it. For an instant she saw nothing but the hall behind her. Then there was a flash of red-brown hair and a face turned to frown at her.

Go away!

She jumped back in shock. The mirror leapt from her hands and shattered against the table.

"What is it?" Kestrin asked, coming to her side. "What did you see?"

Calony couldn't answer. She stared at the fragments of glass on the table, each showing her a tiny image of herself. Every reflection seemed to be doing something different: some scowled, some shooed her away, others turned their back. A moment later all were gone. She choked back a sob, shrugged away from Kestrin's hand on her shoulder and ran from the hall.

How do you feel?" Kestrin asked her at breakfast the next day. It was late and the hall was mostly empty, but his presence alone was enough to make her cheeks hot.

"Embarrassed for making such a scene."

"Don't be. The hall has seen worse." He passed her a plate and paused. "I'm going away for a few days."

She put the plate down carefully in front of her. "Where?"

"I'm going to the nearest Holds to ask if anyone knows you there."

"You'd fly all that way for me?"

"I can't just do nothing," he replied. "You could have a family somewhere, wondering where you are. I didn't want to leave without telling you."

"When are you going?"

"Soon. This morning." He must have seen her uncertainty, for he laid his hand on hers. "I'll come back as soon as I can."

He left as soon as she'd finished breakfast.

Calony stood with Kestrin's sisters and watched as he spiraled up into the gray sky and disappeared. Marla touched her gently on the arm.

"Don't worry," she said. Calony tried to smile.

Several days later, she sat in the garden on a carved stone seat and watched as Marla crept among the undergrowth on four legs, scaring the birds from their hiding places. There was a cry from above. Pale feathers shot past, edged with black. The gull landed on the top of a brimming birdbath, flexed its disheveled wings and drank greedily. Then, when it had its fill, it fixed Calony with its yellow gaze and became Kestrin. Marla leapt for him; Kestrin grabbed the cat by the scruff of her neck and slid down to sit on the ground.

"You should know better," he told her as she dangled in front of him. A moment later it was his sister he held. She threw herself forward and wrapped her arms around him.

"What happened? You look dreadful!"

He flinched back. "Careful! I think I lost a few feathers; I had to fight the wind all the way back."

"What did they say?"

"Not now, Marla. Otherwise I'll have to tell it again and again. For the moment all I want is a bath and a hot meal." Calony saw the dark shadows under his eyes and the way his hands shook as he pulled himself to his feet. He turned to her.

"Calony. Are you well?"

"Better now. Thank you." She smiled. "Best you get some rest. You look like something the cat dragged home."

Marla gave a shout of laughter. Kestrin gave a lopsided smile and shrugged, and went inside.

Calony didn't see him again until the evening meal. Yaphen joined them at the table, clad in another high-collared shirt. His eyes caught the blue of it and became the color of the sky.

They made small talk as they ate, exchanging pieces of news like trinkets. Calony felt her gaze going back, again and again, to Kestrin. He ate ravenously, not joining in the conversation. He barely seemed to notice the others until Asta said his name for the second time and he looked up.

"What did you find?" she asked.

He shook his head. "No one knew anything of an auburn-haired girl who went out in the snow and didn't come back."

Calony's breath caught in her throat and she thought she might cry. "Then that's it. There's nowhere left to ask."

"Actually," Yaphen said softly, "there is. Far south, there is a river that widens before it plunges over a waterfall. Just before it falls there is an island covered in trees, and in the center of that is the house of a woman who can see the truth of names." He caught her gaze and held it, and she wondered what else he was trying to tell her. "It might be that you could find your name there."

"You'd take me?"

"If you want to go."

"Me too," Kestrin said. "I'd like to see this through."

Yaphen nodded. "I leave tomorrow. I've stayed too long already."

"Thank you," Calony replied, including them both. She thought of the seemingly endless forest that stretched beyond the wall and for the first time wondered what lay outside the boundaries of Lorn Hold.

They left while the sky was still pink with dawn. Fingers of cold edged their way into Calony's borrowed cloak and traveler's clothes. Asta hugged her close, like a sister, then leaned away to snare her gaze.

"If you don't find what you're looking for, there will always be a place for you here."

"And if you do," Marla added.

Yaphen waited at the edge of the group. He'd replaced his usual high-collared shirts with rough linen and wool, a short sword at his hip and a gray scarf that looped around his neck. His gaze was distant, as if he saw the world of his song again. He looked up as Calony touched his arm.

"Are you ready?" he asked. Wordlessly, she nodded.

They followed the road as it wound through the trees. Calony tried to see the place where she left the forest, but fresh snow had fallen and covered her tracks. She found herself hurrying to keep up with Yaphen's long strides. Kestrin lagged behind them, heavy-eyed with sleep. Remembering the journey he'd just returned from, Calony paused.

"You can ride on my shoulder if you like," she offered. He blinked at her in surprise.

"Thank you," he said gratefully. He turned into something she didn't recognize, tiny with blue and white feathers, and nestled between her neck and hair. Calony gave a few skipping steps to catch up with Yaphen, careful not to dislodge Kestrin.

"Are you a long way from home?" she asked.

Yaphen looked down at her, and she got the feeling he'd only just remembered she was there. Then he gave a half smile.

"Further in years than leagues," he replied. "And more than enough of both." He glanced around, suddenly puzzled. "Where's Kestrin?"

Calony edged aside her hair to reveal the roosting bird. Yaphen laughed and turned back to the road. "There are worse ways to travel. Don't let him make a habit of it, or he'll have you do his walking for him all the way there."

"I wouldn't mind." It would be a long and lonely journey though, she reflected, and hoped Kestrin stayed human at least sometimes.

"Is it far?" she asked Yaphen, suddenly realizing she hadn't asked how long they had to travel.

He shrugged. "We'll probably catch up with spring on the way."

"I don't mind walking," she replied.

Walking, it turned out, became less enjoyable the more of it they did. Calony's feet blistered, healed and blistered again, and her legs ached more each morning than they had at the end of the day before. Kestrin often flew overhead when he grew tired of using his feet. Only Yaphen seemed not to mind it. Sometimes they came to another Hold. Kestrin stayed human on those nights, out of courtesy, except once when he accepted a challenge to race against a Holder's prized hawks and won.

And then, they walked out of winter and into spring.

Travel became more difficult at first, as snow melted and frozen earth thawed into mud. Then it dried and Calony began to see how the shape of the land was softer and greener than it had been around Lorn Hold. All around them flowers bloomed. Yaphen told her their names while Kestrin circled above them on outstretched wings.

Finally they crested a hill and saw the glint of water in the distance. A river wound its way through the hills like a silver ribbon and widened around an island that was shaggy with trees even from a distance.

It felt to Calony like her heart stopped dead in her chest. "Is that it?" she asked Yaphen. He nodded.

"We could reach it tonight," Kestrin said.

"*You* could. *We* will have to stop." Yaphen pointed at a village nestled at the foot of the hill. "There, I think."

"Good." Calony was relieved. "Proper beds, a hot meal and a bath."

"And we won't look like vagabonds when we get there," Kestrin agreed. "Very well, then. Let's go."

Yaphen caught his arm. "Just one thing. Stay human while we're there. If anyone asks, we're just simple travelers passing through. Don't tell anyone where we're going."

Calony felt fear shiver through her. "Is it dangerous?"

"Perhaps." The admission startled Calony. "The people here are superstitious; they fear what they don't know, including the woman who lives on the river. Rumors have grown up around her like a wall of thorns. Such things can be dangerous."

"What if she doesn't want to see us?" Calony whispered.

Yaphen's rainwater gaze fell on her. "I suspect," he said softly, "that she will let us pass."

They rose with the sun, the habit long ingrained by their travels. The village, too, was waking, and the villagers glanced at them as they passed but wouldn't meet their eyes.

Neither would the men who blocked their path several hours later.

The men wore the same rough garb as the villagers. Calony couldn't remember if she'd seen their faces before, at the inn. One man, with a beard as tangled as brambles, stepped forward.

"There's a toll for passing this way, friends."

"By whose law?" Yaphen asked mildly. Other men emerged from the trees behind them.

"By the law of there being more of us than there are of you," the man replied reasonably. His companions laughed.

Yaphen shrugged. "We've little on us but food. You're welcome to take lunch with us."

"You've got plenty else to share," the man replied, his gaze on Calony.

"No," Yaphen replied softly.

"Then I guess we'll have to take what we can."

Everyone seemed to move at once. Calony gave a shriek as Kestrin shoved her sideways into the bushes. She caught herself on her hands, inches from tumbling into the river. Behind and above her she heard the sounds of men fighting, so many of them that she was sure her friends would be overwhelmed. She scrabbled at her belt for her knife, so far only used to cut her dinner. She held it in shaking hands and rose, just in time to see a dagger buried to the hilt in Yaphen's side.

"No!" she screamed. Kestrin screamed with her. The sound became a hawk's cry. Those that had seen him change fled. The others threw up their arms to protect their faces from an onslaught of talons and beak and ran away, bleeding. The hawk gave a shriek of triumph and pursued them a distance, then flew back and became a man again.

Standing in the bushes, clutching a knife she didn't know how to use, Calony suddenly felt very foolish and very afraid. Yaphen was on the ground, curled around the wound. He made a small noise in the back of his throat. She fell to her knees beside him and heard Kestrin come up behind her.

"What can we do?" she whispered.

Yaphen's eyes opened. His skin was sallow and more yellow than gold. Blood welled around his fingers. His lips moved but Calony couldn't hear the word they shaped. She leaned over him as he tried again.

"Wait," he sighed, and stopped breathing.

Calony wailed and collapsed, sobbing, onto his chest. Kestrin wrapped his arms around her and rested his cheek against her hair, murmuring words to soothe. She twisted in his embrace and clung to him like a child.

When she'd calmed she drew back and scrubbed at her eyes with a sleeve. Kestrin let her go, his face pale but composed, and she realized he hadn't cried.

"We should bury him," she said.

"He said to wait."

She felt a flush of anger. Was this what becoming a bird did to him, made him detached from human pain? She pulled herself away and stood. "Wait for what, Kestrin?"

He raised his hands helplessly. "I don't know."

"We came so far." Calony felt her tears rise to the surface again. "We were so close, and now this."

Kestrin moved to her, took her in his arms again. "Yaphen brought us this far and he wouldn't want us to give up. I'll get you to that island, I promise."

He lit a fire, more for comfort than warmth, and left her sitting by it while he slipped away to the river to fish. She saw him sometimes, shaking water from his feathers.

When he'd done he brought back more fish than either of them could possibly eat. Wordlessly he gutted the largest ones and left them, wrapped in leaves, in the ashes of the fire to bake. The smaller ones he threaded onto sticks to hold over the flames. They sat side by side, letting their dinner char. Calony glanced up at the sky and was surprised to see how late it was.

"We won't reach the island today," she said. "We'll run out of light."

"Then we'll go tomorrow. In the morning, we'll bury Yaphen and finish our journey." Softened by cooking, Kestrin's fish fell into two pieces and landed in the fire. He cursed and tried to hook them out with his stick.

The firelight brought some of the gold back to Yaphen. She watched as the shadows danced over him, making it seem as if his chest rose and fell. His eyes glittered and she shivered, wondering why neither she nor Kestrin had thought to close them. She went to him then, leaned to close the lids and saw that he stared straight at her.

His chest heaved and he gasped. Calony screamed. She almost fell in the fire in her haste to get away. Kestrin leapt to his feet. He froze as he saw Yaphen sit up with his hand clutched to the bloodied hole in his shirt.

"Yaphen?" He pulled Calony behind him.

"Who else would I be?" Yaphen asked breathlessly. He glanced sideways at them. "Is that fish?"

"Is that fish?" Calony demanded, even as Kestrin reached for one of the leaf-wrapped bundles. "You were dead!"

"Yes," Yaphen agreed. "And now I'm hungry. Thank you, Kestrin."

She rounded on Kestrin as Yaphen attacked his meal heedless of burned lips and fingers. "Did you know about this?"

"I suspected," he confessed, his gaze never leaving the other man. "Yaphen used to visit the Hold when I was a child; he knew my parents, but he's never aged a day. And he never stays still."

That made Yaphen pause. "Nowhere will shelter me for more than a hand's span of days," he said darkly. It sounded like he was quoting. "Not even my grave."

"That's why you said to wait." Calony sighed. "You could have warned us, instead of frightening us like that."

Yaphen shrugged and tossed leaves and fishbones into the fire. "I don't like to talk about it." He turned to his pack to replace his ruined shirt and Calony gasped as she saw the pale scars that decorated his back like lacework. Her hand brushed them and he went still. The pattern continued across his chest and stomach and there, low on his side, she saw the darker mark that the dagger had left on him earlier that day. His gaze fixed on her as she reached up to unwind the scarf from around his throat, but he didn't move.

Two scars lay there. One, red and angry, looped around his neck and was crossed by the white slash of the second.

"Every death leaves a mark," she whispered. Yaphen shivered. She took back her hand and turned away as he pulled on his shirt.

The journey began again at dawn, after a breakfast of leftover fish. The river grew louder as they walked and she realized it was the sound of it falling into the distance. Finally, when it was so noisy it drove all thought from her, they saw the island. Its ring of trees looked impenetrable, except that a small boat bobbed in a pool at the foot of them. Kestrin cast a doubtful look up and down the bank.

"There's only one boat."

"That's of no matter," Yaphen replied. He prodded the ground with his toe until he found what he was looking for, then excavated a rope from beneath a layer of dead leaves. One end was tied around the base of a nearby tree. The other, when he tugged it, drew the boat into the river. The rope tied the boat to both banks, Calony realized, and prevented it from going over the waterfall.

451

She clambered into the vessel and sat in the middle, feeling the world buck and sway beneath her. Kestrin wore an expression of trepidation as he joined her.

"Perhaps I should fly."

"No," Yaphen replied. "Best we all arrive together." He settled and took up the oars, then angled the boat into the current and crossed the river with surprising ease.

On the other side, they pulled the boat up to the bank and climbed out. For a moment the world seemed to move like the boat beneath Calony's feet and she clutched at a tree for support. Kestrin gave her a watery smile, his own steps cautious.

The river's chatter faded quickly as they moved through the trees, until it was easy to forget they were on an island at all. Trees gave way to stone, to ruined walls and crumbling pillars that were so wrapped in ivy they seemed as if they were made from it. Calony stopped to run her fingers over a flash of exposed stone that was the color of cream.

At the end of the pillars stood an archway that rose like a cliff out of the sea of vines. Beyond it she could see a stretch of pale flagstones, dappled with sunlight. A sudden, terrible thought came to her.

"It's all ruins. Yaphen, how long ago was it you were here?"

"Not so long as to see everything it held lost," he said, his gaze on the arch. "Most of this is just *seeming,* to keep people from coming too far."

"Oh." Calony wandered to the archway and peered through. "It seems real to me," she said, and stepped through.

Everything changed. The walls beyond the arch

were whole, although ivy still crept its way across them. What Calony had taken for a lack of a roof, she suddenly saw was a falsehood—the branches above were all the roof the ruins needed.

It's an antechamber, she realized. She followed the corridor toward the shadow at the end that was really a door.

A flash of movement caught her eye. She turned and saw a face—her face—staring back at her, nestled in ivy. In the mirror, her eyes widened as she took in a wave of auburn hair and eyes that reflected the green of the leaves. Then the mirror smiled. *Allisana,* whispered a voice in her mind, and she remembered.

The knowledge was like a wave that knocked Calony from her feet and dragged her out to sea. She struggled as she realized what it meant, but the power of her true name was too strong. It flooded into her and she was swept into the mirror, drowning in memory.

"Calony?" On the other side of the glass Kestrin touched her shoulder. Calony beat her fist against the mirror but the other her took his arm and turned him away so he wouldn't see.

"It's all right," she told him, and led him into her home.

In the world behind the mirror it was mostly silent. Calony shouted as Kestrin and Yaphen followed Allisana, but her cries echoed dully back at her. She tugged at their reflections, but it was like trying to hold back the tide. They passed out of the boundary of the glass and were gone.

OLEKSANDRA BARYSHEVA

There was another mirror inside the door. Calony found herself reflecting Allisana in a hall of white stone that was lit by sunlight from high windows. A silver sheen fell over everything. It was, she realized, the sheen that lay behind all the colors a mirror threw back. She pressed herself to the glass and heard the others talking, their voices muffled as if they were underwater.

"Kestrin," Allisana said, "will you try the other corridor?"

"Of course." He moved away and left Allisana and Yaphen alone. When he had turned the corner, Yaphen glanced at the mirror. For an instant he looked right at Calony and her heart leapt, but then he turned away.

"Allisana," he said, so softly that the words barely passed the glass, "surely there was an easier way to get me to come to you?"

Allisana gave a sad smile. "I wasn't sure you would, if I asked. When we parted I was unkind to you."

Yaphen reached out and Calony saw pain flicker across his face. He brushed Allisana's hair with his fingers. In the mirror Calony felt the ghostly touch of his reflection do the same and shivered. "You thought that would keep me away?"

Allisana's voice cracked. "What you are would keep you away." She swallowed, and Calony felt her own throat close up with tears. Allisana took Yaphen's hand and tugged him down the corridor. "This way. I have something to show you."

Calony followed them, here a flash of light in a window, there a vague shape on the side of a silver ornament. They stopped beside a door and Allisana had Yaphen remove his sword, then the door opened and Calony's world steadied again.

She stared back at herself, endlessly copied in the tiny room walled with mirrors, almost blinded in the sunlight that streamed in through the windows in the ceiling.

"What's this?" Yaphen looked perplexed. Calony saw his eyes widen.

"I'm sorry," Allisana said. "I'll be back soon." She closed the door and locked it.

Somewhere behind them, Kestrin called. Allisana made her way back to him and he frowned as he saw she was alone. Then a look of realization crossed his face. Calony threw herself against the mirror, beating her fists against its smoothness.

"You're not Calony," he said.

"Not any more," Allisana agreed. "I know my name now. Just like I know yours, little bird."

She reached out to him but Kestrin flinched away. Allisana's hand moved in the air and as Calony watched she took his name, shaped it to fit him. He became a hawk, flew for the door, but landed in a heap as Allisana took the flight from him. Her hands closed on his wings and pinned them, and then he was a jackdaw, struggling and squawking. Allisana held him firmly, heedless of his attempts to peck at her. She took him into a lavish sitting room, where an empty cage waited in the corner. Calony screamed as he was locked inside. So did Kestrin. He beat himself against the bars with fury.

"Hush, little bird," Allisana said. "You'll have

your freedom soon enough." She closed the doors on his protests and moved through the empty halls.

Calony moved with her. Everything seemed familiar, and she realized that she had been in this place before, a silent observer. She remembered watching as Allisana sent her servants away and released her birds from their cages. The birds had taken their freedom easily and the servants less so, until she'd assured them she would be back.

The light began to fade and Allisana went to her chamber to sleep. Calony lay in the reflection of the featherbed, barely able to see her other self beyond the glass. A sliver of moonlight was all that kept the mirror from growing completely dark. When it did, Calony was sure, she and all her memories would fade. Alone and in silence, she wept.

Over time, the moon rose and a glint of light caught her eye. Calony raised her head and scrubbed the tears from her eyes. The moon was reflected from the mirror onto the window in the corridor, and Calony saw herself there too. She glanced up at the moon, back to the reflection within a reflection.

"Perhaps," she breathed, and stepped into the image.

In the window everything was vague and transparent. Like the mirror, she was unable to go outside the bounds of the glass, until she caught a glimpse of herself in the curve of a polished door handle and stepped into that. From there she moved to a gilded picture frame and the world turned yellow, and then she found another mirror and paused to catch her bearings.

The moonlight turned the hallways stark, divided them into light and shade. She moved again and found her way to Kestrin. Squeezed onto the thin silver bars, the closest reflective surface she could find, it took her a moment to see him. He was a shadow among shadows, roosting on the cage bottom in the corner closest to the window. A few dark feathers lay on the floor beside the cage and Calony felt her heart constrict.

Kestrin couldn't help her, but perhaps Yaphen could—he, at least, was in his own shape. But how to get into a room that reflected only itself? Calony left Kestrin sleeping and moved along the corridors again, noticing how the shadows and paths of light had changed as the moon rose higher.

"The light," she realized. "The room was lit from above!"

She moved upwards at the speed of thought, stepping from reflection to reflection. From a mirror she moved to a window, and then outside to another high window at an angle to the first. She had a sudden dizzying view of the island from above and dove for the window in the roof of a low building in the courtyard.

Yaphen seemed to be sleeping, but as she moved around the room his eyes opened.

"Calony," he greeted her.

"You did see me!" she gasped. "I wasn't sure." She placed a hand on the glass.

Yaphen moved closer and placed his hand on hers. His reflection, which had moved up behind her, did the same. When he spoke again, his voice came from the shape within the glass.

"I saw," he said. "That's what I do, after all."

"That's why she hid her name in the mirrors. She knew you'd come, when you saw me. Why didn't you tell me you'd recognized me?"

"Being told your name is not the same as remembering it. It wouldn't have given you back what you'd lost. Besides, I guessed she'd done this to herself and I wanted to know why." He glanced around the mirror room. "Now I do."

"What will she do to you?"

"I think she means to keep me in here, and divert the curse of my name. There are bindings in the glass, the pull to move on will reflect back on itself endlessly."

"Will it work?"

"I don't know. Perhaps. Perhaps she has another plan. Where's Kestrin?"

"In a cage. She did something to his name; he's trapped as a bird. She said she'll let him go, but I don't see how she can. He won't leave without you."

"She could let him go still trapped in his name," Yaphen replied. "No one will know what happened here, then."

"And he'll never be a man again." Calony sighed and sat down at the base of her mirror. "I don't know what to do. I don't know if I can even make it to the morning. The light keeps changing, shifting. I always have to move, staying ahead where the reflections are."

He gave her a small smile in answer. "Live until morning." His eyes met hers, the same silver as the mirror. "Take your life back. You're as powerful as she is."

"It's not my life," Calony said bitterly. "I was nothing more than a mask to her."

"Maybe. But the last time you were that side of the mirror you had no name." Yaphen glanced upwards. "You need to go. We're losing the light."

She moved, up the mirrors and back outside, around the building into the place she could find with the most light and mirrors. There she rested, until the sun began to rise and she made her way back to the bedroom.

Allisana didn't seem to see her when she woke. Calony followed like a shadow as she took food and water to Kestrin. He croaked miserably and upended the bowls on the floor of the cage. Allisana smiled gently.

"Soon," she told him. Then she went to the kitchen and made breakfast, piling a portion on a tray.

Yaphen was already awake when she opened the door, standing at the back of the room as if he'd been waiting for her.

"Allisana," he said. She came into the room and paused by the door, which clicked shut behind her. He glanced at the tray she held. "Do you intend to keep me here forever?"

"Only until I know how to free you," she said. "I could take your name, hide it in something, but then you wouldn't be you." Anguish flickered across her face. "Wouldn't that be preferable to a life of endless wandering?"

"No," he said softly. "I saw what that made of Calony, how lost she felt. At least I know who I am, wanderer or no."

460

"Then I'll have to change your name," Allisana said. "But the closer the fit, the harder it is to do without completely changing its owner. I need time, Yaphen."

"Time I have," he said gently. He moved forward, took the tray and put it to one side. "Why can't you be happy with the time we have?"

"How could I? How could I bear to see you, knowing I only had you for a hand's span of days before you were compelled to move again, not able to go with you and never knowing when you'd return?"

"Did you ever think," Yaphen asked, moving to take her in his arms, "how it is for me?"

They were reflected in the walls, over and over. In dozens of mirrors, Calony felt dozens of him embrace her. In the mirror behind Allisana she turned and saw him looking right at her. His hands were clasped behind Allisana's back.

She thought she understood. She reached out to each reflection until she saw them from every angle. In every mirror she turned to face inwards and reached out to the reflections on either side of her. In every mirror, and in every reflection of a mirror, she clasped hands with herself.

Allisana caught sight of her. She stiffened and tried to pull away, but Yaphen closed his eyes and held her tightly. In the mirrors Calony reached out and took Allisana's name, twisted the shape of it and became herself again.

She gasped, feeling the warmth of Yaphen's arms around her. He loosened his grip and let her

461

pull away enough that he could look down at her. Through unshed tears he looked for the truth of her name and released her when he saw it.

"Calony."

"Yes," she said. "We need to help Kestrin."

She led him through the corridors, almost turning the wrong way because of her backwards memory of them. Kestrin gave a warning croak as she opened the cage.

"Kestrin, it's me," she told him. She left the door open and stepped back. The jackdaw hopped to the edge and then flapped awkwardly to the back of a chair.

Looking at him, she could see how his name had changed. She reached out and gently curved it back into shape. He made a noise that turned into a sob of relief as he became a man again.

"Kestrin, I'm sorry."

"Don't touch me." He pulled away from her outstretched hand. She felt her eyes sting with tears at the way he wouldn't look at her, at Yaphen who wished she was someone else. She choked back a sob and ran out into the woodland.

She barely knew where she was going, only that the river grew louder. It roared in her ears and she looked down to see that she stood on the edge of the island, staring down into the waterfall with its spray cool on her face. She knew they were behind her and turned to face them.

"What do you want from me?" she screamed. "I can't be both of them! I can't. She loves you," she told Yaphen. "She doesn't want to live without you, even though she can't live with you. And I—" She choked off as she looked at Kestrin. "I can't bear that you won't even look at me."

His eyes widened. "Calony . . ."

"Goodbye," she told them and stepped toward the water as if it were light.

They must have moved at the same time, for she felt a hand close around each wrist. They pulled her away from the water's edge and each seemed to wait for the other to speak first.

"Do what you must," Yaphen said finally, his voice hoarse. "I can't bear to think of her in pain, because of me."

Calony nodded and stood on tiptoe to kiss him. As she did she shaped her own name to make room for who she had once been and let the name Allisana unravel in the wind.

When she released him he stepped away, his eyes blind with tears. He stared unseeing out over the waterfall as she turned to Kestrin.

"Perhaps it's better if I start over," she said. "Forget all of this and begin again somewhere new."

"Don't," he said. "Please." He took her hands. "Come back to Lorn Hold with me."

"Yes," she whispered, and he hugged her fiercely, as if he was afraid she'd change her mind.

When they stepped apart, Yaphen was gone. Kestrin paled, but Calony took his hand.

"He'll be all right," she said softly. "We may even see him at Lorn Hold again, someday."

Hand in hand, they went back to the river. Without Yaphen it took a long time to get to the other side, but they managed it. Kestrin found a stout branch and stove in the bottom of the boat. Then they headed for the hills and the shining road that the morning light made of the water.

After the Final Sunset, Again

written by

Jordan Lapp

illustrated by

JOSHUA J. STEWART

ABOUT THE AUTHOR

Canadian Jordan Lapp spends most days bent over a keyboard working in languages with exotic-sounding names like C++, VB and PHP. At night, he works in the language with which he is most familiar, English. An avid reader at an early age, Jordan grew up loving everything fantasy. Ever since he decided to make a career out of science fiction, however, he's been catching up at breakneck speed, plowing through works by Asimov, Stephenson, Miéville and Scalzi.

His first job out of college was designing artificial intelligence programs for video games, and his first stories focused on what would happen if his daytime creations ran amok. Since then he has mellowed: He now writes stories about human phoenixes and drug-fueled demons. In 2007, he devoted part of his writing time to managing a webzine, Every Day Fiction, *an online flash fiction magazine which publishes a bite-sized story daily.*

Jordan lives in Vancouver with his wife and two cats and is currently at work finishing his first novel.

ABOUT THE ILLUSTRATOR

Joshua J. Stewart was born in Idaho but grew up in a tiny New Mexico town of just 500. Living in such a small community gave Joshua a lot of "down time," so he began drawing for fun at an early age. He showed aptitude for art throughout childhood and took every art class possible all the way through high school.

For a change of pace, Joshua studied welding as a college student at the University of New Mexico and took the occasional art class for fun. The change was only temporary: After graduating with his Associate of Arts degree in welding technology, Joshua returned to Idaho and transferred to Brigham Young University-Idaho, where he excelled in illustration. Along the way, he gained several student honors and was accepted for the national Society of Illustrators' Annual Scholarship Competition in his sophomore, junior and senior years. He recently completed his Bachelor of Fine Arts degree and hopes to begin his career in earnest.

After the Final Sunset, Again

The automatic coffee machine chimed softly from the kitchen as the Phoenix stood in the steaming tub, letting liquid nitrogen run off her breasts and back. She plucked a plush pink towel from the rack and brushed off the thin layer of frost that had formed on her skin, and then stepped onto the bathroom tiles.

She followed the chiming into the kitchen. After pouring herself a coffee, she dialed the stove to max. It was glowing by the time she'd finished her cup of black-two-sugars. She stood before it, naked and shivering, and pressed her palms down on it. Her skin sizzled, but when she took her hands away, they were unmarked. Warmth flowed through her veins.

The Phoenix had developed this routine sometime after the third morning of her life—the second consisting mainly of ecstatic celebration that she'd survived the first.

Her birthday. She remembered the searing heat as her body assembled itself from random air molecules—atoms and then cells fusing with the heat of suns. Spontaneous human combustion in reverse. For one brilliant moment, she was untouched, an innocent babe at first breath, and then the work of building her mind began.

Her consciousness shaped itself from its immediate surroundings. As one assembles a puzzle, it began constructing her personality from pieces borrowed from those around her. Language and grammar skills were copied wholesale from the psyche of a neighbor. Driving skills, she learned from a passing motorist. Her love of gardening, she drew from Ms. Bianchi on the third floor, and her knowledge of guns from the survivalist in the apartment two doors down. Tastes, morals—a wealth of human knowledge distilled into an eager mind.

As her spirit reached out to her neighbors, it came upon a man on the third floor with a shooting pain in his arm. His chest was fire and his vision had disintegrated at its edges. She felt something dark and cold enter the man's apartment, and she gasped even as her heart took its first beat. Death had come for him. She struggled to pull back, to withdraw from that darkness, that voracious void. She tasted blood and bile in her throat and she couldn't breathe. And so, one of her first conscious memories was of a terror that left her convulsing in her bed.

The Phoenix wasted many minutes recovering from what she'd taken from the man on the third floor. Deep breaths calmed her heart. Other experiences, everyday experiences, were crowding into her head: putting daffodil bulbs into the fridge, the feeling of a cat jumping onto the bed, spraying Prolix through the cylinder chambers of a Glock. The mundane smothered the horrific, and she was able to rise.

Several objects lay nearby. A key ring, an American Express Gold Card and a folded slip of paper on the end table, and on the bed where she'd lain, a pile of ashes. On the dresser, a digital camera with pictures of dozens of people on it whom she'd never met. The background of each picture was the same—the curtains matched the ones in her apartment, and the white lettering that flashed the date incremented by one each time she scrolled to a new picture. *Born and then reborn,* thought the Phoenix. It occurred to her that the camera was a kind of petty immortality for a creature whose life spans only one day. A small plea thrust into the future, a desperate *remember me!* She assumed that the most recent picture was of her predecessor. Nothing more than a boy really, with a shock of chestnut brown hair and an avian face. His eyes were fresh and fiery and he stared into the camera with the burning conviction of a man who knows he is about to change the world, but has not yet been shown the way.

The Phoenix put down the camera and unfolded the slip of paper, then snatched at the weathered business card that fell out. It was a letter—a diary page written by the boy in the picture, scrawled in script he'd stolen from Ms. Fitzpatrick—she knew instinctively that her own handwriting would match his. It contained instructions, mostly. A few fragments of hastily written advice. When one's life spans only a single day, she supposed, every second spent writing feels like ten seconds lost.

The business card was stained and lined as if it had been crumpled and straightened many times. "Baytilus" was printed in a Spartan font with a telephone number and an address underneath. Someone had written "FOR EMERGENCIES ONLY" in blue ballpoint on the flip-side.

She pocketed the card and posed for her own picture, maneuvering the LED viewfinder so that she could see herself. Her face was slim and feminine with large, wide eyes. She looked stunned in her picture, as if she'd just been introduced to a room full of strangers. The Phoenix winced at the quality of the picture—the lighting was terrible—but she had no time for a reshoot. Her whole life was ahead of her.

She placed the camera back on the bedside table and opened the closet. She was relieved to find that she had clothes for both sexes. Silently, she thanked whichever of her previous incarnations had used a portion of their day to shop. A medium-length dress caught her eye, but in the end she chose something short that would show off her legs. Modesty was for the patient. She grabbed a red purse and pumps from the closet, loaded the purse with her credit card, keys and the strange business card, then left the apartment. She thumbed the alarm button on her key chain until one of the cars in the parking garage chirped.

She sat behind the steering wheel, waiting for divine guidance. Long moments passed. Her survivalist neighbor came out of a door and threw a bag of garbage into the dumpster. He looked at her strangely as he left the garage. The Phoenix grew bored. Not knowing what else to do, eventually she put the car into drive and left the garage.

After a half-hour of driving aimlessly, she felt a gentle tugging. She turned left onto a busy street and passed a sign for the university. A park came into sight, then academic buildings. She found a place to leave the car and dutifully fed the meter. It would be selfish of her, she thought, to ask a successor to spend precious moments paying for her ticket.

The building to which she was drawn was low and squat, and almost lost in the shadow of a larger building where classes were held. The Math Department. She felt a web of air and fire pull around her as she passed through its doors, bending the light away from her. The receptionist didn't even look up from her work. Room 100, 101, 102. The pull she'd felt was strongest here. She turned the handle, felt it resist but then click open.

She was in an office. Computer on the corner of a desk, term papers spread across the rest of it. Bookshelves held textbooks two rows deep. And a whiteboard. It dominated one wall, a tangle of mathematical symbols fighting each other for space. An equation well beyond the Phoenix's comprehension, but somehow she knew that the variables in the third position needed to be integrated. More details came to her as she wrote on the whiteboard. She plucked equations from the air and wedged them between competing symbols, writing in verticals when she needed to. She was an instant expert, an armchair mathemagician.

It would have been nice, she thought, to hear a scream of joy from a middle-aged mathematics professor as she left the building, but in the end, her triumph had an audience of one. But it was enough to know that the equation on that whiteboard would allow for a fourteen percent improvement in solar panel energy conversion.

The Phoenix was allowed one moment of triumph outside the Math Department. She threw her jacket over her shoulder and strutted like she'd just invented sliced bread. She'd changed the world. It was what she'd been born to do.

The Phoenix felt the pull again.

She got into her car and followed the winding roads off campus and into the suburbs. Soon, she began passing streets lined with cherry trees. She parked the car in front of a two-bedroom rancher in a vacant spot outlined by pink blossoms. The pull was stronger than she'd felt before, more urgent.

She entered the house, the door opening of its own volition. There was a man lying on his back in the kitchen. The Phoenix knelt on the linoleum beside him. His face was purple, his gullet swollen. She could see only the quivering whites of his eyes.

The Phoenix felt the fire inside her.

Her blood tingled, and then burned. She felt her spirit fill her like a vessel and then spill the brim. Her face was close to his now. She could smell vomit on his breath.

"Live."

Something invisible passed from her mouth to his and his chest heaved, expanding until a button popped and flew across the room. His breath exploded out of him in a scream and he sat bolt upright, flinging her back into a cupboard. His terrified look remained and then dissipated into confusion.

He staggered to his feet and backed away until he hit the counter, then felt his way along it to the door. A stolen memory surfaced—her survivalist neighbor hitting a deer with his car. The look it gave him as it staggered away was the same look on this man's face. "I'm late for work," he told the Phoenix, and then he was gone. She heard the front door slam and a car start and pull away from the house.

The Phoenix remained where she was, propped against a cupboard, legs splayed out before her, enjoying the sense of accomplishment that filled her. It was orgasmic. Once again the purpose of what she'd done was hidden from her, but she knew that she'd done something cosmic. She'd brought a man back from the brink of death.

She felt a chill wind. She grabbed the edge of the counter and pulled herself to her feet. There was someone else in the house. She felt it. She *knew* it.

He stepped out of the shadows, tall and glorious and terrible. Still assembling himself, she could sense him borrowing images from nearby minds, molding his form in the image *they* thought he should take. His skin became so pale that it was almost translucent. Spidery purple veins traced the sides of his scalp, and his mouth swelled and puckered. His hair grew matted and thin. He looked like the newly risen corpse of a man only half dead.

The Phoenix trembled. This was the dark presence she'd felt at the moment of her birth. She stepped back until she felt the stove at her back and could retreat no further. Death studied the Phoenix. "I know you," he said, puzzled.

Her hand tightened on the edge of the stove. His brow creased and his gaze dissected her. At last, the flash of recognition that the Phoenix dreaded. He'd seen her, she knew, in the first moments of her life, stealing memories from one who'd already had a foot in Death's domain. She'd fled before him then, pulled back, but he'd seen her anyway. His brow creased angrily.

"You're the one who got away."

He reached toward the Phoenix and she wilted before him, but he persisted. His fingers came within inches of her cheek. She felt their shadow against her skin, dull and lifeless.

She reacted instinctively, batting his hand away and dashing for the door. She flew across the front lawn and dove into her car. It wasn't until she was several blocks away, her hands curled around the steering wheel, that she remembered to breathe.

Death terrified the Phoenix.

She wondered how her predecessors had dealt with him. Had they seen him at all? Maybe she was special. She had felt his touch at the moment of her conception. Something had changed in her in that instant of terror. Her impending mortality had ceased to be something distant and indistinct. It had become a zombified man with bad hair.

A horn sounded behind her, and she realized

that she'd been stopped at a green light for several minutes. The Phoenix felt the call of her next assignment, but she ignored it. What if he were there? She just needed a break. A few moments to catch her breath, she told herself.

It was a strange feeling to ignore the pull. She felt like she was leaving home without turning off the stove. Still, she passed through the intersection and turned into a drive-through coffee shop. She needed a black-two-sugars to settle her nerves. When she reached for her Amex, her hand fell on the wrinkled business card. The Phoenix paused. Surely, this was an emergency.

Fifteen minutes later, she pulled into the parking lot of the Holy Rosary Church on Dunsmuir and Richards, uncertain if she had the right address. She passed through cherry oak doors so varnished that she could see her reflection in the wood, and then hesitated at the end of the aisle. A small sea of pews stretched out before her, ending at a raised platform large enough for a plus-sized choir. Brass pipes blossomed from an ancient organ, stretching thirty feet up and more. A few parishioners sat alone among the pews or prayed silently in front of a rack of votive candles near the pulpit. The Phoenix took a few hesitant steps into the church, her heels echoing loudly.

An older priest looked up from a conversation with a blubbering man in a gray sweat suit, worn for reasons other than physical fitness. He stared at the Phoenix while the man wept and then abruptly left him and made his way deliberately toward her, leaving his chubby-faced parishioner to stare after him. Thin as they come with a face like an axe blade, the priest blocked her path.

"You," he said, taking her arm, "are not supposed to be here."

The Phoenix wondered for a second if she was dressed inappropriately. She thought that maybe her little red dress was too much "little" and not enough "dress," but there was a hooker in the last pew in a torn T-shirt that clearly showed her disdain for the modern traditions of the bra-wearing public.

"Please come with me." The priest's fingers dug into the Phoenix's arm. When she didn't immediately follow, he pulled her off balance and guided her roughly to a bank of confessionals in a shadowed corner. A moment later she found herself alone and confused in the darkened chamber. When the barrier between the confessionals slid open, she was ready to let him have it.

"What kind of priest are you?" she asked, indignantly.

"Let me have a look at you," he said. A lighter flared and he peered at her through the barrier. Defiantly, she leaned back into the darkness, but his constant gaze unnerved her, and after a moment, the Phoenix knelt on the bench and pressed her face close to the barrier.

"Yes," he breathed. "I can see the resemblance. My name is Father Baytilus. Do you have the card?"

She passed him the card. He ran his fingers along the edges tenderly. Her heart softened. He must have cared a great deal for the original owner.

"I apologize for my rough treatment," he said as he

passed her back the card. "It's just that my position makes things a little difficult for meetings like this. Wrong religion. You're Egyptian multi-deistic and I'm . . . well . . . this is the Holy Church."

"Why are you helping me then?"

He spoke as if he were reading from a speech he'd gone over a thousand times in his head. "I once had the opportunity to spend the day with your ancestor. A lot of the things she did, I'd read about before in the Bible: healing, resurrection, giving men hope. I was reminded of our Savior, the Lord Jesus Christ. My superiors might say that you're a pagan demon, but I believe that your powers have the same source as the Son's. When I help you, I believe that I'm helping Him in a roundabout kind of way."

The Phoenix peered at him through the barrier. "You spent the day with us?" A flash of memory, a fragment. A man lying dead in an alley, a needle jutting out of his arm, spittle stringing down his cheek, shit in his pants. A woman kneeling over him staring with fiery intensity. The dead man looked young, but there was still something of the priest in him. The Phoenix looked at the balding man in the confessional. Their eyes met, and they knew each other, and knowing each other, they were able to continue.

"I'm in trouble," she said.

"Speak, child." The awkwardness was out of the way, and now they'd slipped into the familiar roles of penitent and priest.

"I have a problem with Death."

He snorted. "Don't we all."

"No, I mean, I have a real problem with Death, the entity. We had a dust-up at my birth, and he's been stalking me ever since. I was healing a dying man and he showed up at the scene. Now I'm afraid that he might be waiting for me at my next stop. And tonight . . ." The Phoenix shivered, leaving the implication in the air.

Father Baytilus leaned back in his chair. "You saw Death? That's not supposed to happen. Death shouldn't even be aware of your existence."

She was a bit surprised that he'd know about Death, but she supposed he'd met him personally in that alley so many years ago. "I can't bear the thought of facing him, Father. I feel the pull, but I'm terrified that he'll find me and this time I won't be able to escape."

He looked at the Phoenix sharply, his eyes flashing in some reflected light. "You've got to go to your next stop." He grew intense. "Who knows what kind of damage you've already done just by delaying this long? You shouldn't even be here. You need to go!"

"I'm afraid," she squeaked.

He softened, seeming to remember himself. Absently, he licked his palm and smoothed a few straying hairs from his comb-over, and then straightened his robes.

"I've met dozens of Phoenixes over the years. Ten years ago, you were living in the East End. You'd been there for I don't know how many years, but at least back to the fifties, before the heroin epidemic hit and turned the whole place into one big hellhole."

The Phoenix blinked. She hadn't expected that kind of attitude from a priest.

"It got pretty bad for you guys for a bit. You were imprinting from people who'd led terrible lives. Hookers, pimps, junkies. It was changing you. Twisting you. You'd come in here looking as pale as a ghost with long welts on your skin because you couldn't stop scratching yourselves. You were suffering from withdrawal without ever taking a hit. I found you the apartment on Arbutus and encouraged some of our more stable parishioners to move into the building. I had some movers pack up your apartment and move you in the middle of the night. I gathered your ashes myself."

Of course, the Phoenix was curious about how he'd moved her. The image of the priest scooping ashes into a plastic grocery bag sprang to mind.

"Handheld vacuum cleaner," he admitted. "I stayed around until you were born, just to make sure you had all your parts."

"And you've been our guardian angel ever since?"

He pursed his lips and nodded. "I suppose. A guardian angel for a guardian angel."

She drew closer to the barrier. "How long have you been doing this?"

He leaned back, scratching the back of his neck thoughtfully. "Let's see. That business card you gave me is about twenty years old, so I guess a little over seven thousand generations."

Seven thousand generations. Each of them arriving with a peculiar form of dementia, not remembering the day before. He had helped them for the memory of a Phoenix he'd met for only a day.

He continued. "It's gotten so that I can recognize you the minute you come in my door, but I almost missed you. The Phoenixes are like children. Each is born with the innocence required to accomplish their duties without questioning their lot in life. I can't help but liken them to Adam and Eve before the Fall—unblemished by mortal cares. You, however, have eaten the fruit of the Tree of Knowledge, and now you're terrified of what your predecessors couldn't help but ignore."

The innocence required to live with the knowledge of the exact moment of her death. The Phoenix studied the plush red velvet of the confessional bench, her finger tracing golden thread. "What do I do now?"

Shadow patterned the priest's face. "You do what the rest of us do. Find something worth dying for and spend the rest of your life doing it."

His advice was meant to comfort her, but the Phoenix left the confessional angry and confused. She didn't want to find something worth dying for. She wanted to find some way to live the life that others took for granted. She needed more time.

As she left the church, she collided with a man in a gray suit. He was solid and broad; she felt like she'd run into a wall. She fell back, but he caught her and helped her to her feet.

The Phoenix straightened her clothes and began to stutter an apology, but he interrupted.

"—I know you."

She recognized his voice. A chiseled face with a

strong Roman nose and the slightest hint of dimples around his mouth. Her deer-in-the-headlights. This was bad news.

"We've never met," she lied. She tried to push past him, but he was a rock.

His eyes got moist and she could read the expression on his face—*My God, it's an angel*—but he restrained himself. "I know it's you," he said quietly. "You don't forget the face of the woman who saved your life."

The Phoenix tried to dart around him again, but an arm on the door frame blocked her. "Please don't go," he pleaded. "I tried to go to work, but I couldn't concentrate. I kept thinking of lying on that cold floor and then opening my eyes and seeing you. I came here to . . . I thought you were an angel. But now you're here." He looked uncomfortable. "My name's Joshua Miller."

He held out his hand. "If you tell me to leave," he said hastily, "I'll go and never bother you again, but just let me buy you a coffee or something. As a thank you."

The Phoenix felt uncomfortable. He looked desperate. She didn't want to brush him off, but she had so little time.

"Tomorrow, then," he said, reading her expression.

Tomorrow? She'd be dead by the end of the day. The Phoenix felt bad about the deception, but she took his card and promised she'd meet him, then ran to her car.

One bullet dodged, one nuclear bomb still on target. She had an appointment with Death for right around sunset that she didn't intend to keep. She bought a paper and quickly flipped to the weather section. Sundown was at 9:06 PM. She felt a brief moment of pity for the Phoenixes who'd had the misfortune to be born in winter when the days were shorter. But then, they hadn't met Death until the last possible moment, and thus hadn't known to fear him.

The Phoenix spent much of the next few hours in the library, searching for information about her kind. She found articles and stories about birds mostly, but they'd gotten some things right—unfortunately, she found nothing that would help her deal with Death. When her fingertips began to smear the ink of the books she read, she felt her forehead with the back of her hand. Heat. She radiated. By two o'clock the lady in the next cubicle had removed her jacket; by three, she'd begun to sweat.

The Phoenix needed to cool down.

She left the library and ordered a cardboard cup of ice from a nearby falafel vendor. She found a spot just inside the mouth of an alley and took a cube of ice in her fingers. It dwindled before her eyes.

She needed something colder.

A fifty-gallon drum of liquid nitrogen was surprisingly easy to come by. She bought it from a welding supply shop, no questions asked—though it wasn't a well-sought-after commodity among the red-dress-and-pumps set. The laborer who helped her lift it into her trunk mumbled a few smart remarks designed to elicit information, but any explanation the Phoenix could offer would be too far-fetched to be believed, so she just smiled and let him wonder.

When she got back to her apartment, she poured ten gallons into the bathtub. It began boiling almost immediately. A thick white mist poured over the porcelain and crept across the bathroom floor. After a moment's thought, she jammed a towel under the door. She didn't want a neighbor thinking that there was a fire in her apartment and bursting through the door in an act of unwanted heroism.

By this time, the Phoenix had melted footprints into the bathroom mat. She stepped gingerly into the bathtub, dreading, on some instinctual level, the moment her toe hit the nitrogen. Phoenixes are healing creatures and made of fire, and liquid nitrogen is really cold. She had no idea what to expect. The tingle that she felt as the base of her foot made contact with the nitrogen was a relief. She'd half expected freezing pain.

Liquid nitrogen boils at less than room temperature, so her bath felt a little like a whirlpool. She slid in to her shoulders, then slipped her head under the surface. Her hair crystallized immediately. The Phoenix shut her eyes. In the morning, she'd find that her eyelashes had frozen together.

But she'd be alive.

Half the liquid was gone when the Phoenix woke, boiled away in the night. So far as she knew, she was the first of her kind ever to see a second morning. She felt lightheaded. When the sun hit her skin through an open window, she felt its warmth fill her and she danced around the apartment screaming with joy, heedless of the neighbors.

JOSHUA J. STEWART

The Phoenix paused when she entered the bedroom. She leaned against her door and stared at the digital camera that lay on the bedside table. All those pictures. They were like a graveyard. Visual epitaphs of those who'd passed before her.

After a while, she took the camera gently in her hands and put it away.

The Phoenix spent the next hour propped on the couch flipping through daytime TV. She still felt the pull, but she could ignore it. She'd lived through the night and there was nothing to stop her from pulling the same trick the next night, and for the foreseeable future. For the first time in her life, she had all the time in the world.

She spent the next few weeks experiencing in person as many of her stolen memories as possible. She started a garden on her patio in honor of Ms. Bianchi and found that she enjoyed the feeling of soil underneath her nails. She watched a dozen movies that had been unknowingly recommended to her by her neighbors, movies that had helped to shape their lives. She even went to a gun range just to see if that rush of power that she so remembered was real. It was there that a bearded old-timer in a trucker's ball cap asked for her name. "Meryl Streep," she answered without hesitation. Out of the dozens of actresses in the movies she'd watched, Meryl Streep had impressed her the most.

The range owner raised an eyebrow at her.

"What?" she asked, a touch of Phoenix power blunting his curiosity. "People can't have the same name as actors?"

"All right, 'Meryl,' you ever fired a weapon before?"

It took her fifteen seconds to disassemble the weapon. He let her shoot alone.

Through all this, her Amex was her constant companion and Meryl began to worry about its health. Though she had very few expenses—she had no need to eat, and she'd found a contract in a drawer that indicated that the rent had been paid for several years in advance—she knew on an instinctual level that it was intended for emergencies only. Certainly, it had never been abused like this before.

She wondered if she would have to get a job. Join the work force. Do her part for Uncle Sam. She had no experience, no education and no identification. But the idea *excited* her. She'd been isolated out of necessity, but all of the fun things require a partner, and by this time Meryl was beginning to feel a bit lonely.

She'd thought nothing of missing her date with Joshua until she felt his card in her pocket while she was fumbling for change in the corner store. The Phoenixes were out of coffee filters and so Meryl had taken a quick inventory of their supplies in order to restock. She held the business card in her hands, tracing its clean edge with a fingernail. She left the coffee filters at the checkout.

On her sixty-first day of life, she decided to meet Joshua.

He sounded surprised to hear her voice on the phone, but he agreed to meet her at a Starbucks on 5th and Vine, just on the outskirts of the downtown core.

He had selected an intimately-sized table near the front window—as far from the baristas as was possible. Two cups of coffee sat before him, still steaming. Meryl took a sip of hers. An Americano— hot enough to scald. Just the way she liked them.

"I had no idea what you drank. I can get you something else. . . ." Some of the initial awe she'd seen in him had faded, but his eyes were dark pools that drank her in.

Meryl smiled nervously. "I'm fine." She waited, promising herself that if he mentioned angels or resurrection, or asked her what it was like in Heaven she would be out the door before he finished a sentence.

But he didn't say a word.

He just stared at her intensely, long enough that she began to feel a little uncomfortable. "You're beautiful," he said at last, and it was so unexpected that she burst out laughing, managing to slop coffee over the brim of her cup and onto her sleeve. He stood as Meryl was trying to dry the sleeve of her cardigan with several infuriatingly small coffee napkins and walked around the table. He knelt beside her and took her hand gently, then began to dab at her sleeve. His hair smelled like cinnamon.

She wasn't sure how they ended up at her apartment, but she would remember the taste of his lips at the doorway, the coarseness of his chest hair against her cheek in the hall and his warmth as she took him into her in the bedroom.

They lay together underneath the sheets, sticky and exhausted. Meryl's eyes were closed, but she could sense his discomfort. He rose, lines of shadow from the blinds tracing his contoured back, and dressed without looking back. She followed him to the door, wrapped in the comforter, but there wasn't much to be said. He kept his eyes downcast, kissed her reluctantly, and then left. He'd sullied his angel, and now that he'd had her, the illusion of purity which he had so worshipped had been shattered.

She sat on the floor in the bathroom and wept tears that evaporated into little wisps of steam as they ran down her cheeks. It was a long time before she was able to gather herself enough to drag the canister of liquid nitrogen out of the closet and pour it into the bathtub.

The next day was pain.

Meryl awoke in a pool of red marbles—blood that had crystallized as it left the heat of her body. She pulled herself out of the tub, and then gasped as stabbing pain wracked her abdomen. She'd had no experience with pain. A Phoenix is not a creature that feels pain any more than you can hurt fire. Even when it is drowned with water, a flame is merely doused. It doesn't feel *pain*.

She felt pain.

Something had changed overnight. She ripped open the medicine cabinet and pawed through various pill bottles, throwing those she didn't need on the floor. She found some Tylenol 3s behind a box of Q-tips and poured a handful into the palm of her hand. She took a breath, and looked at herself in the mirror. Her hair was still thawing and beads of moisture dripped down her face. Her already pale skin was paler still. She'd stopped bleeding, but she'd lost a lot of blood during the night.

She popped the Tylenol 3s into her mouth, then walked gingerly into the kitchen and flicked on first the coffee maker, then the stove element. Her morning routine. Only one thing was different. She was ravenous. The sensation was so unfamiliar to her at first that she didn't know what it meant. Though she had stolen memories of cooking from her neighbors, she'd never actually eaten or drunk anything beyond the cup of coffee she had every morning—and that mainly for its warmth. Her cupboards were full, but thick with cobwebs and a thin layer of dust burst into mist as she opened them. Maybe Baytilus had stocked the apartment when he'd moved her in, assuming that Phoenixes would need to eat. It didn't look like anyone had opened them since. Meryl grabbed a box of Kraft Dinner off the shelf, gambling that if anything were still good, it would be the KD.

It tasted stale and had the texture of wet cardboard. She attempted dainty pecking at first, but she was *hungry*. She worked her way through the San Francisco Treat, she went hunting with a bowl and spoon, she went after some Lucky Charms, even shook hands with Chef Boy-R-Dee. It was all stale and tasteless and she couldn't get enough of it.

She finally figured it out when she tried on her little red dress and it didn't fit.

Meryl was very definitely pregnant.

She hoped it would go away. She cleaned up the bathroom, letting her precious—but contaminated—liquid nitrogen flow down the drain, then suffered a brief stab of guilt when she thought of what it would do to the pipes.

Her bump wasn't swelling visibly. She grew over hours. By noon the only thing she could fit into was a set of men's track pants. It crossed Meryl's mind that she should phone Joshua. She even went so far as to dig around in her purse for his card. But she couldn't call him. Not after that look. She'd just have to tough this thing out herself.

And Meryl thought that way right until around three o'clock when she began to bleed again.

She didn't feel the pain until she noticed the blood staining the couch. It started with a searing knife that plunged into her delicates and stabbed at her uterus. Her insides began to burn, as if her pancreas was ruptured and leaking bile and acid onto her internal organs. She felt tearing. And the blood . . .

She called Father Baytilus. She begged him to come over through grinding teeth, then hung up. By the time he knocked on Meryl's door the pain had subsided enough that she could get up and unlock it. He stood in the doorway, wisps of long gray hair hanging from one side of his scalp where his comb-over had collapsed, and stared at her stomach.

"Good Lord," he said at last. "I didn't expect to see you alive, let alone with child. How is it that you're . . . ?"

She tried to put a light spin on it. "Liquid nitrogen

baths. Nothing like a dip in the old sub-zero pool to deal with hot flashes. It's good for the skin too. Fine lines are visibly reduced."

"I meant the pregnancy," he said wryly. "We'll discuss defying God's plan at a later date. May I come in?"

Meryl stepped aside and waved him into the apartment, then tried to swivel her hips as best as she could to allow him past. It was a tight squeeze and certainly not a great moment for her self-esteem. She was envious of the slim outlines of beached whales and overstuffed couches. But, she reminded herself, at least the pain hadn't returned.

She followed Father Baytilus into the apartment and sat on the sofa across from him, thankful that she'd remembered to cover the blood with a sheet.

"Tell me," he said abruptly, "that this is the second known case of immaculate conception in recorded history."

Obviously, pleasantries and Father Baytilus had passed each other like ships in the night. "No, Father. I met someone. I doubt I'll meet him again."

He nodded. "I'll spare you the lecture on the evils of sex before marriage. Obviously, you've got bigger problems to deal with. I take it the pregnancy's been difficult? You're not exactly 'glowing.'"

Meryl gulped, then nodded bashfully. She started to tell him what had happened and then a sob escaped, and then another. She didn't know how Father Baytilus understood a word she said, but she was in his arms and her face was buried in his chest. He stroked the back of Meryl's head and told her that it was going to be all right, and things got a little better. And then the unexpected happened. The baby kicked.

She must have squeaked, because Father Baytilus tried to pull away, but she wouldn't let him go. When she'd let it all out, she released him reluctantly. He sat her down, and offered to make some tea. She would have stopped him if she'd remembered the state of the kitchen. She heard a muttered "Good Lord," but ten minutes later he'd come back with a kettle and two cups and wouldn't say a word about it.

Meryl used the time to get familiar with her baby. Because that's what it was at that moment. It wasn't a "pregnancy" anymore. It especially wasn't "a pain in the butt." It was a baby. She had kicked her mother. Meryl wasn't exactly sure why she thought the baby was a "she." Meryl knew that "if the baby rides low then it's a boy." That bit of baby trivia came straight from mother-of-three Keira Sumnabi two doors over. But Meryl certainly had no special Phoenix powers that told her the sex of the baby. "A mother knows," she told herself, and left it at that.

She wondered if the baby would be a Phoenix like her mother, or if she would take after her father. Meryl hoped for the latter, simply because she couldn't imagine immersing a baby in liquid nitrogen every evening. No, Meryl hoped her daughter was human. But that raised its own set of concerns.

"You have to take care of her," she begged Father Baytilus as they sipped their tea. "At sunset I start to burn up. I've been taking nitrogen baths to keep cool enough not to fry, but then I'm out for up to twelve hours. She'll need to be fed every three hours for the first couple of months."

His gaze strayed towards the window, then back to her stomach. He placed the teacup in its saucer, then leaned forward and clasped his hands together. "There's something you haven't considered," he said calmly.

The shadow of grief behind his eyes set off warning bells. Meryl glanced uncomprehendingly out the window. Nothing. The tenement across the street. She had to squint her eyes against the setting sun.

"No. She'll be born before then." Her hands began to rattle her teacup against the saucer so much that she had to set it down. Meryl had just been introduced to this baby—she wasn't going to lose her now. She felt the baby shift, pressing against her diaphragm, and she sat up to try and relieve the pressure.

She thought about her own survival. Sixty-one sunsets hadn't cured her of her fear of death. She had become a survivor, doing what it took to live through the night. She had enough nitrogen. But her stolen memories were betraying her. She remembered dozens of births and relived the childhood of every person whose consciousness she'd tapped to shape her own. She felt the warmth a mother feels when her baby is placed on her chest for the first time. She saw the wonder in a child's eyes when she realized the birthday cake with two candles was for *her.* She saw her child forget to call home on Mother's Day, but then try to make up for it in a lengthy phone call the next day. She saw that first real conversation about sex—the one after the official "birds and bees" business. Meryl saw her daughter's whole life, and she saw it not once, but dozens of times.

Father Baytilus' face was ash. "The Church does allow for some leeway in these kinds of situations. To spare the life of the mother."

She didn't hear him.

She'd come to a realization. She hadn't been afraid of dying. She'd been afraid of being snuffed out like a candle with not even a wick to remind the world she'd been alive. She'd been afraid of nonexistence. She'd been afraid for the very same reason there was a camera in her room with picture after picture of nameless Phoenixes. She wanted the world to remember her. And now a very small part of it would.

Death came to her as the last rays of light were swallowed by the building across the street. He stood quietly in the corner of the apartment, a hollow man lost in dark robes. Her hair lay wetly on her forehead; sweat left her body as steam. Though her hand shook like a leaf, she held it up pathetically, as if to stop him taking her for just one more hour.

Father Baytilus knelt between her legs. "I see the head," he said. A stab of intense pain corded the tendons in her neck and she screwed her eyes shut, then they flew open. "Not yet," she warned Death between grinding teeth.

"But soon," Father Baytilus said, thinking that she was talking to him. "We're nearly there. Push!"

She pushed, and as she pushed she forced the heat away from her baby. Her hair sizzled into ash and her nails blackened and charred. She pushed again, and her cheeks dried and cracked, skin like parchment flaking away. She screamed and her breathing stuttered, but she never took her eyes off her grim audience. Her time long past, Death advanced toward her.

"No. No." She shook her head, flinging a muddy slurry of sweat and ash onto the sofa. Her lips were black and flame licked at her retinas. "Not. Yet."

"One last push," said Father Baytilus, unaware of the stooping figure behind him. He reached between her legs and took a weight into his arms. "Cry," he said softly.

Silence.

Meryl twisted the material of the sofa in her hand. Father Baytilus lifted her daughter and cupped her head in the crook of his arm. The umbilical cord dissolved into ash and fell away. He brought her over to Meryl.

Her daughter's skin was angry and red from the heat, but her tiny body lay limply in his arms. Meryl choked back a sob and glared at Death through teary eyes. She stretched out her arm and brushed her daughter's cheek with the tip of her finger.

"Live."

The infant stirred, screwed up her eyes, and then wailed. The sound was distinctly human.

Meryl sighed quietly and lay back on the sofa. Her eyes focused on the ceiling, the corners of her blackened lips curled into a smile, and then she crumbled into ash. A moment later, Father Baytilus and the baby were the only two people left in the apartment.

Father Baytilus rose and said a prayer over the ashes of the Phoenix, then left the apartment, the girl in his arms. He walked up the stairs at the end of the hall and knocked on the door of apartment 304B.

A small girl with avian features opened the door, followed closely by a grandmother in a fluffy blue housecoat and hairnet. The woman's suspicious look vanished when she saw Father Baytilus. She clucked when she spied the child in his arms, her eyes lingering on the small, fingertip-shaped burn on the baby's cheek.

"Ms. Bianchi," said Father Baytilus, "may I come in?"

The Farthest Born

written by

Gary Kloster

illustrated by

MARK PAYTON

ABOUT THE AUTHOR

 Gary Kloster grew up reading any kind of speculative fiction he could find—he particularly remembers names like Jules Verne, Robert Heinlein, J. R. R. Tolkien and Stephen King. By age twelve, Gary began to write, motivated in part by discovery of a much-earlier Writers of the Future volume (he officially apologizes to the judges for his two entries then). He took a competitive writing break for a few decades, spending as much time as possible as a University of Illinois student. Later, he became a librarian at the University of Wyoming, wisely married a doctor and settled in as a stay-at-home dad.

 To help deal with Minnesota's long winters and toddlers (and in a failed attempt to avoid housework), Gary tried writing again. He credits his writing group, online critique sites like Baen's Bar, and a writing class taught by SF author Lyda Morehouse and assisted by former Writers of the Future Contest winner Kelly McCullough. In short order, Gary has managed to go from honorable mention to finalist over three recent Contest entries. Gary spends his spare time practicing martial arts, gaming and dreaming that he will one day be successful enough at writing to hire a housekeeper.

ABOUT THE ILLUSTRATOR

Mark Payton says it's taken forty-six years to learn to draw: Next year will make forty-seven. His first lessons came from his artist grandmother, who taught him how to find composition among the chaos of nature. As a missionary's child, Mark was exposed to and fell in love with Mexican art. He attended high school in Mexico City, where Mark was known as the art geek.

Back in the States, Mark attended college as an art major, but felt restless and enlisted in the Army. Things seemed good, and he thought about joining the Army's Artist Corps and making a career of it. But life had other plans: He left after two years' active duty and seven years in the Texas State Guard. Following some artistic starts and stops, he moved to Colorado Springs and made pursuit of his art career his 2007 New Years' resolution. First, he joined the Business of Arts Center in Manitou Springs. Second, he entered this Contest, which he had been aware of since the first Writers of the Future anthology came out years ago.

Mark lives with his wife, their dog and three cats. He enjoys hiking, reading, gardening and photography.

The Farthest Born

Nathan

Behind his daughter, in the darkness below the noak trees, Nathan saw the shadows shift.

"C'mon, Dad, throw it!" Lilly punched her glove and held it up, long braids bouncing as she danced from foot to foot. Nathan nodded to her, but the baseball hung motionless in his hand while he scanned the sun-dappled space beneath the trees that surrounded their picnic site. Nothing moved there now.

"Yeah, Dad, throw it hard, make it sting! Bet she'll cry."

"Shut up, Eric," Lilly growled, voice dripping with sibling contempt. Nathan didn't bother to listen to his son's taunting response or his daughter's escalation while he continued his slow search for the source of that single flicker of movement. A boy had been bitten by a fat adder last month, running through a copse of noaks not far from here. Still nothing, probably just a quirral rustling through the rust-colored undergrowth, but he made his vision slip from normal to infrared. Sun-warmed leaves glowed bright over cool shaded earth and . . . *Oh, hell.* Like a demon mask, the eyes and muzzle of the beast burned hot where it crouched low and hidden near the edge of the trees. A tavi, had to be, and it was less than thirty meters behind Lilly.

Light-years away from the clearing, adrenalin boomed through Nathan's body and sent him teetering for a second between panicked reaction and rational thought. Thought won out and Nathan tripped his com to silently cry the code, *"Help, help, Grandma, help."* Behind him, he could hear his wife still bustling around packing up the picnic leftovers and he struggled to keep his voice calm as he called to her, "May, on com."

"Grandma's here. Help is on the way. Can you tell me what's wrong?" The voice of the colony's computer was smooth and comforting in his head, but its reassurance couldn't touch Nathan now. Far London was only half a klick away, but beneath the trees death was waiting its opportunity. No one there could save his daughter.

Silently over their radio link, Nathan answered Grandma and warned his wife. *"There's a tavi out here, stalking Lilly. It's hiding underneath the noaks, May. I want you to call the kids and get them to come to you, slowly. If it moves, I'll . . . I'll try to stop it."* An ambush predator, a sprinter, and damn him for not bringing a gun no matter how close to the settlement they were, no matter that this island was supposed to have been cleared of all large predators years ago. Nathan stepped forward softly, and his world became the hot glow of the beast's eyes. He had to get between it and the kids.

"Lilly, Eric, listen. Listen!" The hard edge in his wife's voice guillotined through the kids' argument. "Start walking over to me now. Slowly."

"Mom, we're still playing," Eric whined, but Lilly started to move, eyes sharp and flicking between her parents, sensing the danger in her mother's order and her father's fixed stare. Behind her, Nathan watched the eyes sink lower as the tavi deepened its crouch, then the shadows boiled as the beast surged out to seize its chosen prey.

"Run!" bellowed Nathan, and he followed his own command, pounding forward as fast as he could as the undergrowth behind Lilly shook with the predator's passage. Blessedly, his daughter didn't turn to see what was coming for her, just dug in her feet and began to run toward her mother. Sprinting, but slow, too slow compared to the black-and-emerald-mottled monster that was charging after her, that would catch her long before she could reach her mother or her father could intercept it. Desperate, Nathan screamed at the thing, uselessly trying to break its deadly focus, then he was raising his arm and throwing, never considering for a moment in his terror what possible effect he could expect a baseball to have on three hundred kilos of fang, fur and muscle.

In desperation, sometimes there are miracles. The lumpy handmade ball, backed with all the fearful momentum he could give it, flew true. The tavi was gathering itself for one last leap forward when the little missile struck it almost dead center in the gleaming black nose that twitched above its gaping jaws. With a startled chuff of pain the animal flinched away from the stinging blow and almost tumbled, its six legs thrashing for purchase in the low meadow ferns when its momentum drove it into a slide. It came to a halt, whiskers trembling below brown-black eyes that flashed from the girl it had been chasing to the man who was charging suicidally toward it. "C'mon, you bastard! You want food, here's delivery!" Nathan shouted, and the tavi shook its head in irritation and spun lightly on its feet to meet him.

Thank God, he managed, just before the thing was on him, fangs flashing. He had one instant to throw up an arm to protect his throat, and then the beast snapped its jaws and the world became a rushing blur. The tavi whipped its head back and forth, shaking him like a chew-toy. Then it spat him away, letting him cartwheel across the ground to land in a broken heap of agony. Pain burned through torn carbonwire and then echoed in his nerves, centered in his savaged arm but flaring too in battered legs and ribs; then it hit the programmed limits and fell away, leaving him numb but clear-headed. Nathan twisted and gathered himself to regain his feet as quickly as he could, hoping desperately that the kids hadn't heard the howls of pain that had escaped him when the beast was savaging him.

Up, up, cursing the dizzying dissonance of damaged feedback loops, and then he was on his feet, limping sideways to place himself again between the tavi and his children. The beast was ignoring him for the moment, caught up in its own misery. Bastard child of a crocodile and a mongoose, it coiled like a snake as it gave a disgusted chuff and swiped at its long muzzle with its forepaws, trying to wipe the bitter taste of pseudo-flesh from its mouth. It shook its head and shot him what had to be a resentful look, then looked past him through the trees in the direction that May and the kids had run, nose quivering with the scent of more palatable prey. Nathan gave the tavi a fearsome grin and forced the battered body he rode to lurch a step toward it. "Forget 'em. I'm your dance card today, bastard, not them. So let's jig." The bravado earned him nothing but another disdainful chuff from the tavi even as it uncoiled and shot past him in pursuit of his children.

Hell, no. The damage barely slowed him now as every system slipped into overdrive, flogged on by a concentrated jolt of anger and terror. Even with that, his lunge almost missed, the thing was so damned fast, but his fingers grazed over the dark, color-shifting fur and he snatched at it with all the strength he could muster in his good arm and it was enough, just barely enough. The world spun again, and a crazed laugh hiccupped from him when he realized he had caught this ridiculous tiger quite literally by its broad tail. Not that hanging on was going to help him, though, not when this tiger could almost fold itself in half and come charging back on him, looking as frighteningly pissed as only something with eight-centimeter fangs could.

The tavi coiled around him, short claws on its stubby legs digging furrows down his thighs as it snapped its jaws down. Blackness came, hot and wet and distantly painful when the beast's teeth sheared through his face, peeling away hair and skin, blinding one eye and leaving the other half blocked by hanging tissue. Still, when the tavi jerked its head back from the sudden pop of a ruptured power feed, Nathan had some sight left. Some sight and one good arm, so he reached out and snared a stubby ear to twist as hard as he could.

The tavi didn't even chuff this time, apparently too offended by his alien flavor and the pain he'd caused it; instead it broke his hold by spinning its body around until it had one set of paws against his belly. They dug in, claws twisting and tearing, opening up his golem and spilling out the bright vivid coils of its innards like some hideous piñata. Nathan felt the pain jerk through him, too much and too fast for the block to stop it all, but he fought against it and tried to make his arm move again, tried for one last attack, but it was too late, there was too much damage. His hand fell away, useless, when the tavi dipped its head down to snap and tear with thwarted frustration at the shining coils of coolant veins and carbonwire. *Gone, they're gone, you bastard, and I hope you choke on something.* Teeth tore deeper, and with a squeal of neural feedback the connection finally shattered and Nathan's senses were wrenched back to his body as the gulf between him and his children's world slammed back into place.

Through the wide ports, the endless stars slipped behind the bright curve of Earth as the station slowly turned. The rising world's light glowed in the eyes of the crowd surrounding Nathan, parents and researchers pressing close to offer congratulations and commiserations. May finally had to rescue him, pulling him free of the throng and across the lounge to find an empty couch that faced out toward the stars.

"Settle in, love." She let go of him to flick on the privacy field, then turned in time to catch him rubbing his fingers over his arm where he had felt the tavi's teeth tear into him. "Is that still bothering you?"

"Only when I don't think about it," he muttered. The ghost pain made him feel ridiculous; his body was whole and healthy and untouched by claw and fang. Thirty long light-years separated him from the pseudo-flesh golem that the irate alien predator had torn apart, but that distance wasn't recognized by the primitive parts of his mind. Down deep in the lizard brain, the echo of that agony still throbbed, testimony of how easy it was to lose track of what was really you when over half your life was spent riding a golem on that distant world. Arali, a world he would never see with his real eyes, the world that was his children's home.

"Do you want to talk to the docs about it?" May knew something was wrong, had known since she had dismounted and rejoined him on Arali Station, the first words on her lips reassurances that the kids were fine, safe back home in Far London.

"No." His voice was harder than it should have been, and he felt bad as May fell silent. "I'm sorry. No, I'm fine. It'll fade. I'm just . . . just . . ." Nathan frowned and leaned forward, clenched his fists tight and pressed them onto the table before them. "Why does everyone act like I'm a hero? I'm not. How can I be? Today I came as close to being eaten by a tavi as I possibly ever could, and here I am getting ready to have a drink a few hours later. I'm not really there."

"You're there fourteen hours a day," she protested.

"Not in the flesh, not in the danger. If that thing had gotten hold of Lilly, she'd be dead. Torn to pieces . . . I want to be with them."

"I know. I do, too. When we adopted them, we . . . Well, how could we have known? When is parenthood ever easy? We do the best we can, like every parent before us, even if this situation is, well . . ."

"Completely insane," sighed Nathan. Through the port he stared out at the unbounded night and wished he could pick out Arali's star from the tangle of bright points that stretched across forever. Thirty light-years away, it had taken the colony ship *Hope* over a century to reach that distant star with its cargo of computers, equipment, biomechanical puppets and—most precious—the tiny frozen blastulas of a whole generation of humanity nestled still as death in its holds. Exiled children, they had been sent alone into the dark.

Easy enough to understand the logic. All the alternatives had panned out to nothing. Einstein couldn't be cheated, and the speed of light was a hard barrier far beyond the abilities of their best engines. Stasis never worked, and hibernation killed and crippled more often than it succeeded. Humans were too short-lived, too delicate, too demanding to send such distances and the dream of colonization seemed lost. Only when researchers discovered the quantum cheat that let information cross light-years instantly did the dream come back. But how sane was it, Nathan wondered, to cast your children out into that never-ending sea when you could only go with them by proxy? This evening, it didn't seem sane at all to him, but that bridge had been crossed long ago, his children conceived and packed aboard the *Hope* decades before his own birth. Questions about the logic and ethics of Earth's first interstellar colony had been swept away by its reality.

"I'd rather call our situation uniquely challenging." May gave him a small smile, and Nathan leaned into her, appreciating her attempt to break him out of the dark spiral of his thoughts. "When I left, Lilly was going over the schematics of Far London's defense grid with Grandma. And complaining about me hovering."

"That's our girl." Nathan wrapped his distantly aching arm around May's warmth and began to try to force himself to relax. "What about Eric?"

"Griping about not being allowed to go out with the team hunting the tavi. Then about not being able to go back and help collect your golem's parts." May shook her head and tapped out an order for a couple of beers on the table's screen with her toes, an ability that never failed to amaze her husband.

"Maybe we should ask if recycling would let him have the skull," Nathan said dryly, mostly to see what kind of look she would give him, and he wasn't disappointed. Then the privacy field around their table shivered and tinkled in warning as someone stepped through it.

"Nathan, Nathan, Nathan. What kind of virts have you been doing? 'I'm your dance card today, bastard, so let's jig?'" Neither the man's deep voice nor his broad smile stopped Nathan's surge of irritation at the interruption.

"He was a little busy for witty one-liners, don't you think, Jamal?" May's tiny frown marked her own irritation, but then she had never really liked the colony's publicist. Not an uncommon feeling on the station, but Jamal did bring in the money, which they always needed. The third supply ship was only a quarter complete.

"Found my golem's black box, I take it," Nathan said.

"Took a while. That weasel really didn't like you. The blanks were picking up pieces all over the clearing."

"You brought a tour group to see that?" May looked faintly disgusted.

"Of course; it was fantastic. We were one of the first groups on the scene. What a slaughter! If only the tavi had still been there, the blanks would have loved it."

"I'll bet," said Nathan. Knowing their real bodies were safe back on Earth, riding the simple white tour golems that didn't even have pain receptors, they probably would have been thrilled to be flung around by the beast. Of course their children weren't running for their lives away from the thing.

"Maybe you should work out a script for us, for the next time someone gets gutted while trying to protect their family."

"Hey, nothing personal. You did good out there. We're all proud of you." Jamal's languid wave took in the entire lounge, half full now of researchers and other parents of the farthest born, resting after another day of riding their golems across Arali. "I'll give you a call tomorrow. A heroic tale of sacrifice like this'll be great press, and our tour numbers have been slipping lately."

May frowned after the tall shadow of the publicist drifting away through the tables. "He'll probably try to make this into a melodrama, you know." She brought her attention back to Nathan and shook her head at his expression. "Enough with the fretting. You can tell him no."

"I know, I know." Nathan forced a smile. "Guess I'm just in a mood to be maudlin. Something about the gutting, maybe."

"Fine. Just get it out of your system by tomorrow. Lilly is freaked out enough, and she has a hair trigger for emotional states, even if you'll be riding a blank."

"Don't remind me." Nathan sighed, then pressed his lips to her forehead. "Eric at least wouldn't notice."

"Eric has the empathy of a noak." May pulled back a little from his embrace to give Nathan a crooked half smile. "Whatever else, I'm glad you weren't really gutted."

"Why, thank you."

She came back close for another kiss, pressing her lips to his until finally pulling back just enough to whisper, "Otherwise, who'd go get the beers?"

White, slick synthetic fingers slipped on the catches of the gun case, dumb and insensitive, and Nathan cursed under his breath. "I'll do it," offered Eric, nine-year-old eager to get his hands on a weapon forbidden to him.

"That's okay, I got it." Nathan lifted the needle rifle out of its case, barely able to feel the hard steel and soft plastic with the cheap sensors built into the tour golem he was stuck with until his new custom could be grown and wired. Five hours riding it, and he already hated the blank with a passion, a feeling others in the family shared.

"God, this is so stupid, Dad. Couldn't we just wait until you had your new body before we did this?" Lilly leaned against the shining white diamond glass of Far London's wall, dark braids swinging in front of her face as she stared, sulking, down at the red-green ferns that covered the ground. At least she was no longer watching the distant forest edge with that tight look of fear on her face thinly buried, fear undiluted by the presence of a gate barely fifty feet away and the low buzz of one of Grandma's drones drifting overhead.

"It'll be two weeks before it's ready." She hadn't wanted to come out from the shelter of the settlement's walls even this little bit. Two days, and that damned sneaky chameleon-furred predator was still out there on the island somewhere, easily eluding the vivisection-hungry exobiologists in their scout golems. The hunt had the parents on edge and the kids thrilled—all but Lilly, who huddled in front of the screen in her room and talked to her net friends on Earth. She wanted to trade her world of sharp-toothed monsters for one of bands and high schools and fan boys who thought it was fun to chat up the pretty girl who lived beyond the stars. Fifteen and stranded in the penultimate hick town, she was trapped in a "Little House on the Prairie" life when she longed for the lights and crowds of a planet that had cast her out before she was born. The tavi's attack had sharpened her jealousy and her fear, and Nathan felt his heart go out to her, aching for her, at least until she spoke again.

"This friggin sucks."

"Watch your language." Nathan checked the safety and snapped in the ammo brick while Eric laughed in the background at his sister. *Amazing how quickly deep sympathy can snap over into annoyance,* he thought, *another alchemical miracle whipped up with ease through the wonder of adolescence.*

"I didn't really say—"

"Enough. What are the rules?" Nathan snapped.

Lilly sighed and rolled her eyes, staring off into the distance with a look of bewildered amazement at this patriarchal tediousness. Nathan tapped his dull fingers on the gun, annoyed that he couldn't properly glower at her with this blank golem's idiot face.

"The rules?" he repeated.

"It's always loaded. It's always live. It's always dangerous. Never point it at anything I don't want to kill."

"And?"

"When I hold the weapon, I hold the responsibility for the life of everyone around me." To the side, Eric mouthed the ritual words along with his sister, eyes bright.

"Good." The words were good, at least, if not the aggrieved tone, but it would do for now. "Semiauto, thirty-meter target. Go." Whatever her attitude at the moment, Nathan was pleased to watch his daughter turn to the range with the gun barrel held carefully up. While she scanned the field to make sure it was clear, he nodded to Eric to sound the warning horn. Its echoes faded and Lilly dropped the gun into position, fingers tapping the controls as she settled into her stance, then fired. There was a thin yawp from the rifle followed by the cracks of the iron needles splitting the air and the target jerked once, twice, three times.

Nathan upped the magnification on his vision as high as it would go and peered out across the field. "Too far left." More yawps and cracks, and Nathan checked again. "You're all over. C'mon, Lilly, you can do a lot better than this."

"I'm trying, okay? Maybe I'm not as good as I was."

"You are; you're just nervous."

"Of course I'm nervous, with you breathing down my neck in that stupid thing." Lilly snapped the safety back on and raised the gun to glare back at her father. "Why am I even doing this? If we ever meet one of those things again you or Mom will have the gun. Me and the twerp will be running for our lives. Again."

512

"Don't count on it." Nathan had seen the naked fear flash across his daughter's eyes at her memory of that nightmarish run back to the settlement, racing for safety as she listened to the tavi tearing apart her father behind her, her fear telling her that she was too slow, that she was next. He hated what he was saying, but his daughter was too old for anything but the truth. "Don't expect us to save you. Expect to save yourself. We won't, we can't, always be with you. That's why you grow up." He could see himself reflected in her eyes, a white, smooth-faced automaton with glass-empty optics and it made him want to rage to be so distant. He checked the feeling, held it in, and raised a finger to point out over the range. "Move to ten meters. You ever see another tavi, it'll be at least that close and coming fast." Lilly stared at him, beautiful dark eyes wide in a face drained of color, then she turned and dropped the gun into position.

Lilly

There were lights of every color and their rainbow brilliance washed across the crowd, making a thousand-thousand faces glow in the never-dark city night. They were strangers, all of them, and they swept by Lilly like a river, a deluge of unfamiliar humanity. Watching them surge past, her heart almost stopped. *I don't know their names. Not one of them,* and that knowledge was terrifying, dizzying, joyous, *and they don't know mine.* Lost in the shining city lights, lost in the crowd, she tipped back her head and shouted her laughter at a sky free from stars.

"Lilly, hey, wake up." With a lurch, Lilly yanked herself up straight, almost knocking her portable screen from her lap. In the chair beside her, little Saul smiled apologetically and nodded toward the classroom's main screen. "The prof was going to notice the snoring sometime," he whispered.

"Or the drool marks on the table," Tuyen added from the other side of Saul. Lilly glared at the girl and the two silently laughing boys that flanked her. Then she pointedly looked away, wiping surreptitiously at her chin as she did.

On the wide screen that filled most of the front wall of their classroom their teacher broke off his lecture and looked up from the notes scattered across his desktop. "Was there a question?" When he got nothing but blank looks back from his five pupils, he nodded and continued on. "So between advances in nanotechnological engineering and biosynthesis, true bioengineering could begin and for the first time complex quasi-organic machines such as the golems used by your parents could be grown from a few seed structures and raw materials. This of course led to . . ."

Lilly let the words wash past, unheard as she glowered down at her screen. With quick strokes of her stylus a sketch took shape on it, tiny caricatures of Tuyen and the boys, Alec and Mahdi, all scattering before a giant tavi. She smiled thinly down at the drawing, then raised a hand to brush across her mouth, trying to stifle a yawn. After spending all afternoon at the range with her father, she had stayed up late with her screen and her friends from Earth, which made this morning come far too fast.

She had fought against coming to class, arguing with her mother and father about the stupidity of having to come in early for a lecture given over a screen, something she could just watch later. *You need time with your friends here,* they had told her. As if she wanted any of the other firstborn to be her friends.

The *Hope* had carried fifty artificial wombs, but the colony leaders had baked up only five children for their first generation. Five little lab rats, born to be poked and prodded and certified genuine A-grade humanity, cute and smart and healthy enough to mollify the doubting masses back on Earth. It was all a load of bullshit, and only Lilly seemed to recognize it. High Queen Tuyen ate that firstborn responsibility crap up with a shovel, sucking up to every adult that dropped in on Arali, striving to guarantee her position as colony mascot. Mahdi and Alec were just Tuyen's boy-shaped shadows, slaves to her will as they battled each other for her favor, each desperate, Lilly was sure, to claim the prize of humanity's first interstellar handjob. Saul, well, little Saul had been lost long ago to the nerd demons of technology. So Lilly got to be the rebel, the outcast, the bitter Loki in this teenage pantheon, all because she was the only one willing to see how lame they really were, playing the brave explorers while the adults back on Earth pulled their strings.

Central Commons was like Earth, Lilly thought—clean, gleaming, controlled. When she stepped out of the building's doors, trailing behind the other firstborn, she was surrounded by Arali. Hot sun and golden dust and scraggly groundferns, rough adobe buildings noisy with children hemmed round by the settlement's white wall, it seemed more summer camp than colony. A camp she would never get to leave. Lilly sneezed at the dust, slapped at one of the persistent redflies that for some reason seemed irresistibly drawn to her café-au-lait complexion, and stalked along behind the others to the gymnasium. Class over, they were dismissed to go work out. After that she'd be punted off to lunch at home before she spent the afternoon in the nursery with Dad. Another fine day in paradise, babysitting.

In the gym they were joined by the seconds, twenty chattering thirteen-year-olds. Lilly frostily ignored them, especially the boys who stared at her while she changed into her leotard. Beside her, one of the second girls sniffed, clearly annoyed at the unwanted attention Lilly was getting. "I hate gym class. Why do we have to do this anyway?" the girl complained as she pulled on her own leo.

Lilly threw her clothes into her cubby and arched one eyebrow at the younger girl. "You don't know?"

"Know what?" asked the second, a little nervously. Lilly had gained a satisfyingly menacing reputation among the younger kids, without having to do anything but be older and more cynical.

"Why they need us to stay in shape? Especially the girls?" Lilly twisted her braids back, fastening them together behind her. "Look, they're only using twenty of the easy-bakes at a time, right? Twenty little brats born every year when it could be fifty. They're afraid that the wombs will break before they can defrost all the thousands of kids they shipped out here. They need to make sure they've got a backup system in place, right?" Lilly reached out and slapped her hand lightly across the wide-eyed girl's belly. "Better hope those fake wombs last awhile. Otherwise we could all be spending the next fifty years popping out babies for our brave new world."

"That's not true!" the girl squealed.

"No, it's not." Tuyen snapped, glaring over at them. "Why are you lying to the kids, Lilly? Does it give you some sick thrill, trying to freak them out?"

"Am I lying?" Lilly said, meeting the other firstborn girl's eyes. "How many new wombs have they built since we got here? Besides ours?" She saw the doubt flicker in the other girl's eyes and felt a vicious little twist of satisfaction. "They can't build them here yet. If the ones they have now break before they can . . ." She shrugged and gave Tuyen a smile of pitying contempt.

"What's going on?" Lilly groaned silently to herself and lost the smile when she heard the voice. Of course her Mom was coaching today. She gave Tuyen the eye, trying to will the other girl to silence.

"Lilly's causing trouble," Tuyen growled.

Brat. "Unfortunate side effect of thinking," Lilly muttered, staring coldly down at the other girl.

"Like two cats in a bag," her mother muttered. "Enough of this, let's get ready to sweat some—" May's voice cut off, and from the corner of her eye Lilly saw her mother freeze, then begin to slowly tip forward. With startled yelps, both Lilly and Tuyen skipped back as May fell face first onto the wide noak-wood boards between them.

"Oh, damn. My mom crashed," Lilly said, staring down at the unmoving body that lay now at her feet.

"Language, Lilly," corrected Tuyen. Lilly traded glares with her for a moment again, then knelt down beside her mother's golem. Saul was suddenly there with her, bending close to examine May's blank, empty eyes.

"Grandma, Coach May's golem has had some sort of malfunction. Can you send a tech over to the gym please?" Saul's voice, usually nervous and shy, was clear and businesslike when confronted with a technical matter and Lilly stood, glad to let him take over. She hated seeing her mother like this, inanimate, corpse-like. "Grandma?"

"Yes, Saul, I hear you. Please wait a moment." The boy looked up, puzzled, at the screen where Grandma's voice had come from. Lilly understood his confusion. Grandma never made a kid wait. A minute passed, eerily silent in the gym except for the hum of birds outside and the distant wailing of an infant. "I'm sorry. I'm here now."

"Grandma, May's golem crashed."

"I know, Saul. There appears to be some sort of error in the communication system. I'm afraid all of the golems have shut down. I've been unable to speak to Colony Operations about the situation."

"Wait, all of them?" Tuyen gasped.

Calm as always, the computer's voice drifted down over the silent children. "Could the firstborn please report to Ops in Central Commons? It appears that we are currently isolated from Earth for an indefinite period, and under these circumstances you are to take charge of the situation. I have operational orders prepared for such a circumstance ready for you there."

We can't always be with you. His words to her only yesterday, on the range. "Dad . . . God, you jinxed us," Lilly breathed to herself. Then she looked up and saw the stunned, scared faces of the kids. "Well, stop standing there like a bunch of dorks. Go round up all the brats and get them to the Commons so we can keep track of them." She waved her hands at the seconds, who blinked and then began to head toward the doors. "Stay in pairs at least, and make sure you check with Grandma to see you get everyone," she yelled after them. Then she turned to give Tuyen a grin, knife sharp and humorless. "Well, well, Queen Bee. Guess it's your birthday. You finally get to be in charge. Shall we?" Lilly nodded toward the exit, cynically unsurprised at the other firstborn girl's shocked silence. *Too bad that won't last,* she thought to herself as they headed out toward Ops.

That's it?" Tuyen glowered at Saul, who shrugged nervously.

"It's all they can get through right now, I guess. They have the message on repeat, and I had to stitch it together from over two hours of samples. The damage Arali Station's transmitter took from the shuttle crash must be major. Thankfully the transmitter's tangles weren't destroyed. We would have lost contact permanently then."

"That could happen?" Alec asked, his voice faint.

"Sure. But those are well protected; the whole station would be destroyed before they were lost, and if they're telling us zero casualties then it couldn't have been that bad."

"If they're telling the truth," muttered Lilly. She looked up from her bowl of oatmeal to see Tuyen's angry frown. "Oh, sorry, too Eeyore for you, Pooh Bear?"

"Whatever. Okay, hours at least, maybe two days?" Tuyen settled back in her chair and nodded. "We can do that. We can do two days easy. We'll split the older kids up into shifts, keep watch over the little ones here and make sure to keep our two strays contained. No problem." She looked up, eyes flashing, at Lilly's snort. "What?"

"You almost had a riot over lunch. Two days of oatmeal surprise, and it's going to be full-scale *Lord of the Flies* out there." Lilly pushed away her mostly untouched bowl of lunch and stared out the wide windows of Ops. Commons assembly room was crowded with kids, huddled in laughing groups or darting around like startled fish. Across the chaos, she could see the nursery where Mahdi was currently stuck with the thirds, mired in milk and howls and dirty diapers. Four hours without adults, and most of the kids could be persuaded that it was an adventure, an Arali Never-Never Land. Tonight, though: that's when she expected the fear would set in and the tears would pour out. In the center of the window in front of her, one of the running kids stopped long enough to pull a hideous face at her through the glass. She flipped her brother off and sighed. "We're in trouble here."

"Fine. Great. We're all going to die. Happy?" Tuyen shook her head, glowering at Lilly. "Do you have a plan, or are you just going to sit there and crap on everything we do?"

"Who needs a plan? Just follow the instructions the Earthlings left for you and hope they get that transmitter fixed fast. I just don't want to hear you say that this is going to be easy. It's not. If you think it is, you're going to fall apart the minute it starts getting hard, and I might not be around to save your bacon."

"What? Where are you going?" asked Alec.

"Out." Fear twisted in Lilly's gut, the same fear that she had felt there ever since she knew she was going to have to leave Far London's shelter again. But she wasn't going to show it in front of Tuyen. "Or do you really think our strays are going to be okay out there?"

"Neelam and Ramani are in their crawler. They might get scared, but they'll be fine." Alec looked to Tuyen, but now she was staring out the window as she twisted her fingers through the long fall of her pony-tail. The boy stumbled on anyway. "Grandma said we should stay in the settlement."

"Grandma is a computer, Alec. She couldn't think her way out of a paper bag." Lilly smiled a little apology to Saul, who only shrugged. He knew best of any of them the limitations of their advisor. "I'm not leaving a six- and a four-year-old alone in a crawler outside, not when their only company is their parents' bodies and a twelve-year-old reading them fairy tales over the com. If Grandma can't bring the crawler in, somebody has to go get them."

"Maybe," said Tuyen, not looking at her. She knew it had to be done too, and it frightened her. Three days of having the tavi running loose had finally scared Neelam and Ramani's parents into abandoning their geology expedition, made them turn their crawler back from the camp on the other side of the island to return their kids to the sure safety of Far London's walls. They had only been four klicks out, trundling along the shores of the Little Muddy toward home, when the transmission failed and the adults' golems had gone limp and useless. The crawler had rumbled aimlessly on for a few meters before its safeties kicked in and stopped it, but that had been enough to send it belly deep into a mud hole, trapping it and the kids beyond the walls. So far they had been able to use the com to keep the little ones calm and inside the relative safety of the transport, but Lilly didn't see that lasting long, and she doubted Tuyen did either, whatever she said.

"But why you?" Tuyen asked.

"What, you'd miss me?" Lilly saw the other firstborn girl's eyes turn dark with pain and angry confusion at her words and felt those same feelings scratch at her. They had been best friends, once, before Tuyen had become obsessed with seizing the boys' clumsy attention, before Lilly's restless chafing against their world, before the arguments and bitter silences. "That tavi has already scared the crap out of me once. You know I'll be careful out there."

"Maybe you would. Ride a crawler out, herd them in and straight back?" Lilly kept herself from rolling her eyes and simply nodded. "Okay. You should take somebody with you, though."

"I'll grab Eric."

"Your spazzy brother?" snorted Alec. "He's useless. I can go."

Tuyen's eyes narrowed dangerously at the thought of Alec alone with Lilly, and Lilly shuddered. *As if.* "You can stay here and babysit. The little spaz is useless at that, but I can make him listen to me."

"She's right," Tuyen snapped at Alec. Then, more quietly, "When are you going?"

"Well, since I've finished your exquisite lunch, I might as well go now." Lilly pushed herself up, burying a lurch of fear under movement. "I'll just go grab my brother." *It's a big island, what are the odds . . .* "And my gun."

The Little Muddy was wide and curdled brown, so slow moving that the mats of water weeds drifting in it seemed as fixed as islands. On its banks, Lilly and Eric's crawler slowly lurched over one last hummock and stopped ten prudent meters away from the black ooze in which the other crawler was mired. Eric peered out the front port at the motionless machine and whistled. "Wow. Is it going to sink into that?"

"No, it's just mud, not quicksand. The kids might get stuck, though." Lilly frowned at the view outside. The day was sunny and bright, the noak trees and wool bushes still and drooping under the hot afternoon sun. The only signs of life were two roosting water birds and the clouds of insects that swarmed above the water. It seemed safe, but Lilly had lost all her trust in an idyllic Arali. "Grandma, what do you see?"

Above the transports a drone drifted, sensors trained down at them. Lilly wondered if Tuyen was watching this. Probably. She doubted the other girl would change one diaper no matter how long the adults were gone. "I don't see any large animals in the area, Lilly." *Yeah. Neither did I until that thing was trying to kill me.* There was a click beside her, a flood of light and wet-rot smelling air, and she spun in time to see Eric swinging the hatch open wide.

"What the hell are you doing? Stay in here until I say!"

"Tell them that," Eric said. He tipped his head toward the other crawler and Lilly swore. Neelam stood framed in the open hatch of his crawler, staring down at the black mud as Ramani tried to push her way past him to get out. Lilly pulled her brother back from the opening and leaned out of it, facing the kids.

"Hey, you two!" They both stopped, then raised little hands to wave at her. "Not another step! We'll come and get you, okay? Okay?" Under her glare they finally nodded. "Stupid kids," she growled anxiously, staring around at the still river, the silent trees, the rutted, empty mud flats. "Okay."

She ducked back into the crawler and popped open the emergency supplies cupboard. Out of it she pulled three webbed vests and handed them to her brother. "Put one on. And keep an eye on those two."

"Sure," he said, snapping the straps around his body as he looked out the hatch. "What're these for?"

"When I tell you, and only when I tell you," she emphasized as she reached up to open the overhead emergency hatch, "I want you to climb out and go to the winch up front. Clip its hook to the ring on your vest. Then wade across to the kids and climb in their crawler and get those vests on them. Then clip them to you."

"So you can pull us out if we get stuck!" he said. Lilly nodded, glad he was thinking that much, before he added, "That'd be awesome!"

"You're not helping, okay?" Lilly plucked her rifle from its rack, checked the safety, then carefully pushed it out the hatch and onto the top of the crawler. "Don't go until I say," she warned, then pulled herself up next to her gun.

Outside, it was hot. Humid. Still. Lilly stood on top of the crawler and felt the sweat bloom on her skin, heard the hum of the birds and the droning song of a redfly as it zeroed in on her. So close to her, the kids called out questions, asking what she was doing, when could they get out, and she ignored them. Nothing. Nothing. "Grandma, scan, please."

"I don't see any large animals in the area, Lilly."

"Okay," she whispered. Diagnostics on the rifle, and everything was green, the weapon loaded, ready. "Okay," she whispered again, and her thumb slid off the safety and she raised the weapon up and hit her stance. Fear coiled in her, a terrible fear that had nothing to do with what might happen to her but was wound tight instead around the lives of the children in her care, but she breathed deep and tried to let it go. Forcing herself to focus on nothing, so that she could see everything, she said it one more time, loud and strong in the turgid air. "Okay!"

"Finally! You guys just wait there for me!" Lilly heard the thump from below, then the metallic rattle as Eric fought with the winch until he finally remembered to trip the release and could bring the cable out. In her stance, Lilly breathed the agonized frustration out and waited. Her brother trotted away from her, plowing straight into the mud and sinking in immediately to his knees. "Not too bad! But I lost a shoe! Mom's gonna be pissed." His high, cheerful voice carried over mud and water and Lilly breathed out fear and anger until he was pulling himself up into the other crawler, happily tickling the kids as he greeted them.

Forever passed while he wrestled their vests on. Sweat ran through Lilly's braids, slid past her eyes, slicked her hands. The light weight of the needle rifle pulled at her. Redflies crawled over her, little feather tickles and sharp nips. Lilly breathed, held her stance and watched until Eric dropped back into the mud and helped the little ones down. The sun gleamed bright on the brown river and the water birds shifted and fell silent as the children moved oh-so-slowly through the muck while one of the patches of water weeds shifted and slid toward the shore. Smooth as the sweat that glided down her arms, she swung the rifle barrel toward it.

As if split by lightning, the dark green mat burst apart, brown water spraying up through the twisted weed stems as the beast surged out. Trailing gleaming streams of water and weeds like pennants, she saw it come, a dark mottled nightmare with bright shining eyes fixed on the children who were standing frozen between its approach and Lilly's protection. Over the barrel of her gun, Lilly watched three nights' worth of nightmares spread its jaws wide as the tavi shot toward its prey. In her head, in the space between terror and determination, thoughts flashed: *Too close, too close . . . Tuyen, you bitch . . . I hate this damn place . . .* and finally as the beast lunged forward and her finger tightened down, she heard her father's voice: *Expect to save yourself.* In her hands, the rifle quivered and its high-pitched yawp split the air.

They were waiting for them outside of Far London's gates.

The crawler had barely stopped before Eric popped the hatch and was out, whooping as he ran to wrap his arms around his mother. Lilly watched as May scooped him up, laughing and crying and looking him over as he started to babble out the story. Beside them, the smooth white face of her father's blank turned toward the crawler, watching.

"C'mon, you two." Lilly gently pushed the little ones out and watched as they climbed down and were collected by family friends. Then she stepped out herself and walked slowly toward her parents.

"Oh, Lilly." Her mother's face was calm under her tears, but Lilly heard the twisted strands of emotion buried in her voice.

"It's okay. Everything went fine, right?" Lilly felt the burn of her own tears in her eyes, and fought the almost overwhelming urge to throw herself into her mother's arms and howl out the shaking horror of what almost was.

"Come look!" Eric wriggled free from May's tight grip so he could grab his mother's arm and tug her toward the crawler. "I made her bring it back. We had to use the winch." May let him pull her forward, but her eyes stayed on her daughter and ignored the poor broken thing that Eric had tied to the front of the crawler.

"They worked fast, back on the station. Not fast enough, though." The white blank tilted its head at Lilly and she looked away from it, hating hearing her father's voice spilling from that faceless head.

"I guess we should have waited a little longer. You guys could have handled it then." Again the moment flashed through her mind, the beast so close, the twitch of the rifle in her hands, the long dark arc of blood that had flown from the tavi's head as it suddenly pitched forward into the mud a bare meter from her brother. The gun's iron needle must have parted Eric's hair as it passed to catch the thing between its gleaming eyes.

"You did what you needed to do. And everything went fine." Lilly looked up, broken out of the memory's dread by the fierce pride she heard in her father's voice. She saw her face, drawn and wide eyed in the blank's empty optics, but she heard her father's words. "You held the responsibility for the life of everyone around you. And you didn't fail."

She had her arms around him then, ignoring the stupid stick-bug feeling of his narrow limbs as he hugged her back tight, and her tears were flowing now. "I was so scared out there, so scared they were all going to die and I wasn't going to be able to do anything to stop it. . . ."

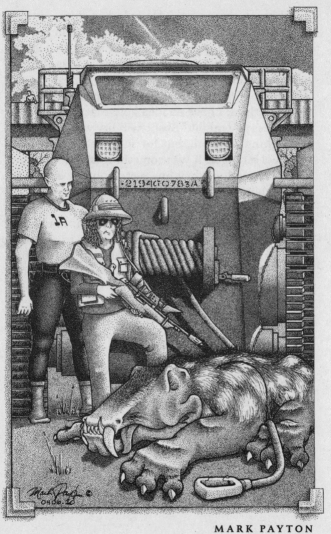

MARK PAYTON

"Lilly, oh, brave girl." He held her close, letting her cry until the storm passed, until she could breathe again and could hear her mother behind them shushing Eric as he asked what was wrong with her; he was the one that was almost eaten. When her breathing finally evened again, he spoke softly. "I think I have an idea how that felt."

"I guess you might." Responsibility was a strange, scary thing to share, but for some reason it made Lilly feel stronger. It was something older.

"Are you done bawling yet, Lilly? 'Cause we should show this thing to Dad and then get it inside. It's already starting to stink."

"That's my boy," whispered Nathan, and Lilly smiled, stepping back out of his arms to turn to face her mother and brother. Nathan stared with her at the body of the tavi, muddy, bedraggled and seeming so much smaller as it lay limp across the crawler's hood. "Did you have plans for that?"

"Plans? For that?" Lilly stared disgusted at the corpse. "No. Just let the bios carve it up." Then she frowned. "Actually, no. This damn place owes me something. I should at least get a rug out of this."

The smooth white head tilted, staring at her silently until finally a low, deep chuckle wound out of it, then boomed upwards into a laugh. Lilly slowly grinned, then suddenly she was laughing too, great belly laughs faintly tinged with hysteria and relief. Laughing together, they moved to join the rest of the family, together again under the darkening skies and the first faint stars of night.

The Year in the Contests

Writers and Illustrators of the Future celebrate twenty-five years with this silver anniversary edition. Inspired by these words written by Mr. Hubbard in the inaugural volume, *"A culture is as rich and as capable of surviving as it has imaginative artists. The artist is looked upon to start things. The artist injects the spirit of life into a culture. And through his creative endeavors, the writer works continually to give tomorrow a new form."*

And each successive year since the Contests' inception has served as testament to the attainment of this objective. For an overview of the first twenty-five years, go to www.writersofthefuture.com.

Over 600 aspiring writers and illustrators—professionally published for the first time through the Contests—have seen their works eagerly awaited in each new edition of *L. Ron Hubbard Presents Writers of the Future,* with many becoming today's most respected talent.

But, at this time, I would particularly like to acknowledge our Contests' judges—past and present—as it has been their continued support and dedication that has helped to make these the premiere Contests of their kind in the world.

WRITERS OF THE FUTURE CONTEST JUDGES

Kevin J. Anderson	Larry Niven
Doug Beason	Andre Norton
Gregory Benford	Frederik Pohl
Ben Bova	Jerry Pournelle
Algis Budrys	Tim Powers
Ramsey Campbell	Robert Sawyer
Orson Scott Card	Charles Sheffield
Hal Clement	Robert Silverberg
Stephen Goldin	Theodore Sturgeon
Brian Hebert	John Varley
Frank Herbert	K. D. Wentworth
Nina Kiriki Hoffman	Sean Williams
Eric Kotani	Jack Williamson
Anne McCaffrey	Gene Wolfe
Rebecca Moesta	Dave Wolverton
C. L. Moore	Roger Zelazny

ILLUSTRATORS OF THE FUTURE CONTEST JUDGES

Edd Cartier	Paul Lehr
Vincent Di Fate	Ron Lindahn
Diane Dillon	Val Lakey Lindahn
Leo Dillon	Stephan Martiniere
Bob Eggleton	Judith Miller
Will Eisner	Moebius
Frank Frazetta	Cliff Nielsen
Frank Kelly Freas	Sergey V. Poyarkov
Laura Brodian Freas	Alex Schomburg
Stephen Hickman	H. R. Van Dongen
Shun Kijima	William R. Warren Jr.
Jack Kirby	Stephen Youll

For the year 2008, the L. Ron Hubbard Writers of the Future Contest winners are:

For the year 2008, the L. Ron Hubbard Illustrators of the Future Contest winners are:

First Quarter

> Oleksandra Barysheva
> Tobias A. Fruge
> A. R. Stone

Second Quarter

> Aaron Anderson
> Mark Payton
> Joshua J. Stewart

Third Quarter

> Ryan Behrens
> Douglas Bosley
> Evan Jensen

Fourth Quarter

> Luke Eidenschink
> Brianne Hills
> Jamie Luhn

Our heartiest congratulations to all the winners! May we see much more of their work in the future.

NEW WRITERS!

L. Ron Hubbard's

Writers of the Future Contest

Opportunity for new and amateur writers of new
short stories or novelettes of science fiction or fantasy.
No entry fee is required.
Entrants retain all publication rights.

ALL AWARDS ARE ADJUDICATED BY PROFESSIONAL WRITERS ONLY

Prizes every three months: $1,000, $750, $500
Annual Grand Prize: $5,000 additional!

Don't delay! Send your entry to:

> L. Ron Hubbard's
> Writers of the Future Contest
> PO Box 1630
> Los Angeles, CA 90078

Web site: www.writersofthefuture.com
E-mail: contests@authorservicesinc.com
No submissions accepted via e-mail

WRITERS' CONTEST RULES

1. No entry fee is required, and all rights in the story remain the property of the author. All types of science fiction, fantasy and dark fantasy are welcome.

2. By submitting to the Contest, the entrant agrees to abide by all Contest rules.

3. All entries must be original works, in English. Plagiarism, which includes the use of third-party poetry, song lyrics, characters or another person's universe, without written permission, will result in disqualification. Excessive violence or sex, determined by the judges, will result in disqualification. Entries may not have been previously published in professional media.

4. To be eligible, entries must be works of prose, up to 17,000 words in length. We regret we cannot consider poetry, or works intended for children.

5. The Contest is open only to those who have not professionally published a novel or short novel, or more than one novelette, or more than three short stories, in any medium. Professional publication is deemed to be payment, and at least 5,000 copies, or 5,000 hits.

6. Entries must be typewritten or a computer printout in black ink on white paper, double spaced, with numbered pages. All other formats will be disqualified. Each entry must have a cover page with the title of the work, the author's name, address, telephone number, e-mail address and an approximate word count. Every subsequent page must carry the title and a page number, but the author's name must be deleted to facilitate fair judging.

7. Manuscripts will be returned after judging only if the author has provided return postage on a self-addressed envelope. If the author does not wish return of the manuscript, a business-size self-addressed, stamped envelope (or valid e-mail address) must be included with the entry in order to receive judging results.

8. We accept only entries for which no delivery signature is required by us to receive them.

9. There shall be three cash prizes in each quarter: a First Prize of $1,000, a Second Prize of $750, and a Third Prize of $500, in US dollars. In addition, at the end of the year the four First Place winners will have their entries rejudged, and a Grand Prize winner shall be determined and receive an additional $5,000. All winners will also receive trophies or certificates.

10. The Contest has four quarters, beginning on October 1, January 1, April 1 and July 1. The year will end on September 30. To be eligible for judging in its quarter, an entry must be postmarked no later than midnight on the last day of the quarter. Late entries will be included in the following quarter and the Contest Administration will so notify the entrant.

11. Each entrant may submit only one manuscript per quarter. Winners are ineligible to make further entries in the Contest.

12. All entries for each quarter are final. No revisions are accepted.

13. Entries will be judged by professional authors. The decisions of the judges are entirely their own, and are final.

14. Winners in each quarter will be individually notified of the results by mail.

15. This Contest is void where prohibited by law.

ILLUSTRATORS' CONTEST RULES

1. The Contest is open to entrants from all nations. (However, entrants should provide themselves with some means for written communication in English.) All themes of science fiction and fantasy illustrations are welcome: every entry is judged on its own merits only. No entry fee is required and all rights in the entry remain the property of the artist.

2. By submitting to the Contest, the entrant agrees to abide by all Contest rules.

3. The Contest is open to new and amateur artists who have not been professionally published and paid for more than three black-and-white story illustrations, or more than one process-color painting, in media distributed broadly to the general public. The ultimate eligibility criteria, however, is defined with the word "amateur"—in other words, the artist has not been paid for his artwork. If you are not sure of your eligibility, please write a letter to the Contest Administration with details regarding your publication history. Include a self-addressed and stamped envelope for the reply. You may also send your questions to the Contest Administration via e-mail.

4. Each entrant may submit only one set of illustrations in each Contest quarter. The entry must be original to the entrant and previously unpublished. Plagiarism, infringement of the rights of others, or other violations of the Contest rules will result in disqualification. Winners in previous quarters are not eligible to make further entries.

5. The entry shall consist of three illustrations done by the entrant in a color or black-and-white medium created from the artist's imagination. Use of gray scale in illustrations and mixed

media, computer generated art, the use of photography in the illustrations, are accepted. Each illustration must represent a subject different from the other two.

6. ENTRIES SHOULD NOT BE THE ORIGINAL DRAWINGS, but should be color or black-and-white reproductions of the originals of a quality satisfactory to the entrant. Entries must be submitted unfolded and flat, in an envelope no larger than 9 inches by 12 inches.

7. All entries must be accompanied by a self-addressed return envelope of the appropriate size, with the correct US postage affixed. (Non-US entrants should enclose international postage reply coupons.) If the entrant does not want the reproductions returned, the entry should be clearly marked DISPOSABLE COPIES: DO NOT RETURN. A business-size self-addressed envelope with correct postage (or valid e-mail address) should be included so that the judging results may be returned to the entrant.

We only accept an entry for which no delivery signature is required by us to receive the entry.

8. To facilitate anonymous judging, each of the three photocopies must be accompanied by a removable cover sheet bearing the artist's name, address, telephone number, e-mail address, and an identifying title for that work. The reproduction of the work should carry the same identifying title on the front of the illustration and the artist's signature should be deleted. The Contest Administration will remove and file the cover sheets, and forward only the anonymous entry to the judges.

9. There will be three co-winners in each quarter. Each winner will receive an outright cash grant of US $500 and a trophy. Winners will also receive eligibility to compete for the annual Grand Prize of an additional cash grant of $5,000 together with the annual Grand Prize trophy.

10. For the annual Grand Prize Contest, the quarterly winners will be furnished with a specification sheet and a winning story from the Writers of the Future Contest to illustrate. In order to retain eligibility for the Grand Prize, each winner shall send to the Contest address his/her illustration of the assigned story within thirty (30) days of receipt of the story assignment.

The yearly Grand Prize winner shall be determined by the judges on the following basis only:

Each Grand Prize judge's personal opinion on the extent to which it makes the judge want to read the story it illustrates.

The Grand Prize winner shall be announced at the L. Ron Hubbard Awards Event held in the following year.

11. The Contest has four quarters, beginning on October 1, January 1, April 1 and July 1. The year will end on September 30. To be eligible for judging in its quarter, an entry must be postmarked no later than midnight on the last day of the quarter. Late entries will be included in the following quarter and the Contest Administration will so notify the entrant.

12. Entries will be judged by professional artists only. Each quarterly judging and the Grand Prize judging may have different panels of judges. The decisions of the judges are entirely their own and are final.

13. Winners in each quarter will be individually notified of the results by mail.

14. This Contest is void where prohibited by law.